W9-BVN-994

Hunger's Season

Hunger's Season

a novel by
Paul H. Wilson

A Blue Atlas Press Book

ISBN: I-4392-6068-0
ISBN–I3: 9781439260685

Library of Congress Control Number: 2009910325

Published by Blue Atlas Press, New York

Cover Photograph © Paul H. Wilson

This is a work of fiction. With the exception of certain historical events and personages referred to in the text, all characters in this book are fictitious, and any resemblance to real persons, living or dead, is entirely coincidental.

Inscription

"You who live, what have you made of your luck?
Do you regret the time when I struggled?
Have you cultivated for the common harvest?
Have you enriched the town I lived in?"

-- from "Epitaph," by Robert Desnos
(translated by Kenneth Rexroth)

Hunger's Season

Contents

I.
Circus

He wakes to the sound of scuffling on the floor like rats fighting in the muck. Then the serpentine rustle of something long and encumbered sliding away. The truck stinks of old horse sweat and excrement. The rope twangs, snaps taut. The chair spins around in the dark and begins to move. It reaches the covered ramp and bumps over the warped pine boards pitching and swaying, throwing him against the cutdown bellyband that circles his chest and binds him to the wooden chair back. Duckboards loose on the joists rattle and drum under the wheels while daylight shooting through the rents in the canvas top stagger round him like a storm. The rubes gasp and draw back as he rolls out onto the open stage, a colossus in a handcart, naked to the waist with skin black as basalt in the morning sun. He sits ramrod straight with a head like a stone, shaved bare and crisscrossed with old scars. He looks like a giant of old that has been caged and starved, you could tell his bones from where you stood.

Stenno jams a maple chock into the winch and turns, grinning like a thief. But the onlookers aren't cheering and clapping as expected. Instead, they stand in silence gaping at the giant in the wheelchair, as though unable to make up their minds whether to laugh or throw stones. Stenno hunches his shoulders and minces over to bend his head close to the giant's ear and whisper out of the side of his mouth, "Bloomers, eh, Bonesy?" Walleyed and foul of breath, the pitchman snorts at the loop of seasonal mucus that's seeped onto his upper lip and nods toward the meager crowd of poor dirt farmers out front, as he adds, "We're gonna have to work your bloody black arse off to earn our grits today, Boy-o!" Then rising to face the audience, Stenno launches into his long con, his brogue as phony as the geniality in his manner. "LAY-DEEZ AAAND GENTLEMEN, YOUR ATTENTION, PLEASE! I NOW PREE-ZENT TO YOU, ALL THE WAY FROM DARKEST AFRICA -- THAT STRANGE AND MYS-TERIOUS CONTINENT OF AN-CIENT WONDERS, OF IVORY CROCODILES AND EBONY KINGS, OF PYGMIES, PYRAMIDS AND PREEE-POSTEROUS MARVELS BEYOND YOUR WILDEST DREAMS -- THE LAST LIVING DESCENDANT OF THE LEGENDARY SONS OF ANAK -- WHO WERE DRIVEN OUT OF THE LAND OF CANAAN BY THE ISRAELITES FIVE THOUSAND YEARS AGO -- LA-DIES AND GENTLEMEN, RO-BOT BONES! ROBOT BONES, LADIES AND GENTLEMEN! THIS BE-NIGHTED WRECK YOU SEE BEFORE YOU, A LIV-ING BLACK FOSSIL AND PARADOXICAL PILLAR OF STRENGTH, PARALYZED IN THREE LIMBS AND TOTALLY LACKING IN HUMAN FEELING -- as you will soon see for yourselves! -- WAS STRUCK BY A LIGHTNING BOLT ONE DAY WHILE OUT HUNT-ING LIONS IN HIS NATIVE SAVANNAHS...!"

As the pitchman continues, a boy goes round with an upturned cap taking up the first collection.

Stenno, meanwhile, works his way behind the wheelchair and then, speaking aloud for the sake of the audience but addressing The Robot, he says, "Smile a good morning to the folks, Robot!" and thrusts two stubby fingers into the hinges of The Robot's jaw.

The Robot's mouth springs open in a death's head grimace, and the audience finally laughs.

Pleased, Stenno steps to the back of the stage and returns pushing a block and tackle with iron weights stacked on a low, wheeled platform. As the audience presses closer, he calls for a volunteer willing to bet his own five dollars against Stenno's ten that he can lift more weight than the cripple in the wheelchair.

After some hesitation and haggling among themselves, a half-dozen men in the crowd pool their resources and send up one of their own, a strapping young farmer bursting out of his overalls, and the show begins. Under Stenno's direction, the volunteer lifts a few of the twenty-five pound iron slabs himself to prove their weight, then loads the first two onto the block and tackle. Stenno then has him pull down on the rope to raise the weights, and when he's done it, Stenno takes hold of the Robot's "good" arm, puts the end of the rope into his fist and then stands behind the wheelchair, holding it steady, and gives the order for him to lower his arm. The Robot does as he's told, and lifts the weights. The sequence is repeated, with the volunteer loading an additional fifty pounds each time. After a while, the farmer, grinning sheepishly, finds himself dangling from the rope with his feet off the ground, while The Robot goes on to raise the weights and keep them suspended in the air with his one good arm as the pitchman counts to ten. The crowd applauds and the boy goes around with the hat again.

Some of the onlookers are briefly distracted when they see urine streaming through the hole cut in the seat of the Robot's wheelchair and into the wooden bucket slung beneath it. But sending up new volunteers, they go for another round and then another, until several in the audience, put off by the escalating price of the show, decide they've had enough. Screwing their faces into twisted smiles, they shrug their shoulders and wander off, as if to say it's all a trick, that all pitchmen are liars and that sure as the lint in their own empty pockets, there's nothing new under the sun to surprise a fervent Bible reader. Fed up with fake astonishments, cranky and put out of work by drought and foreclosure, lacking the gas or grit to clear out and go west, north, or straight to hell, the lot lice saunter over the tent ground among the jugglers and acrobats with sly, sidelong glances at the jerry-built wooden platforms, the long billowing skirt of the Bearded Lady, the wind-flapped tents and the mechanic lounging by the circus trucks lighting a cigarette, and you can tell they're eyeing that match in his hand and the iridescent pool of leaking oil growing at his feet and hoping for a fire.

A mist is rising like steam out of the woods around the field and the Robot can hear the barking of the first rounds from the shooting gallery down past clown alley. With a shriek of rusty gears, the ferris wheel stutters into motion, and a ragtag band of colored musicians strikes up *Turkey In The Straw*. But the drummer can't keep time, the piano is out of tune and the saxophone and clarinet are worse. Then a new boy he first saw performing a trick the day before, juggling a half-dozen illuminated light bulbs, puts a trumpet to his mouth and blows a couple of tentative bars. In the next moment, he's soaring over the unholy din like a lark at odds with a gang of crows....

"...AND NOW, LADIES AND GENTS, FOR THE EX-TRA SPECIAL FEATURE OF OUR SHOW -- Uh,

4

some of you more sens-itive ladies may want to hide your eyes for this part...!"

Robot Bones draws the fresh, manure-sweet air deep into his lungs and closes his eyes....

✭ ✭ ✭

The man stands quiet as a ghost, holding up the canvas drop and staring into the truck for so long that the crickets started chirping again. It's past one in the morning. The crowd has long since gone home and the circus is bedded down for the night. The Robot can hear the frogs croaking from a pond nearby and it has been some time since he's heard the last car pass on the road above the camp. They are somewhere outside Gin City, where 160 crosses 71.

"What they do to you, man?" The stranger speaks just above a whisper. "Why you let them treat you like this." When Robot doesn't answer, the man hesitates, uncertain, and leans forward, peering into the dark recesses of the truck bay. A sudden growl makes him crouch and look over his shoulder. But it's only the lion, old and toothless, gnawing on the bars of its cage next door. The man eases himself onto the lip of the truck and hitches up a corner of the canvas to let in more light. As he pauses in the moonlight with his head tilted to one side, waiting to let his eyes adjust to the shadows, he seems younger, tall and lean but only a boy, after all, eighteen, nineteen at most.

"Hey," the boy says. "Man, what's going on? Shit, aint nobody fooled by that 'Ro-bot' bullshit, I know you human!" He speaks in a bluff manner, advancing warily. "What you doing here, man? Why aint you out there slammin' -- Shit, what the fuck you doin' here? Come on, why you don't say, nothing? Jesus, what they do to you?"

Puzzled by the continuing silence, the boy begins pacing back and forth, slipping occasionally on the muck underfoot. Two small beady eyes glint in the dark at the back of the truck bay, watching them.

"Man, you can't just hide out in here like this," he blurts out then, "I know -- I seen you --!" He cuts himself off, as though wanting to say more but not sure how to go about it. Then he stoops impulsively before the wheelchair and tries again. "Dig, my name's Lot. Well, actually Lotrelle, Lotrelle Dundee, but just make it Lot, okay? that was me you heard blowing trumpet in that raggedy-ass band out there today. I'm just copping a few coins on the way to Chicago, you know? I aint planning to be here but a couple days, and then...." He gestures with his hand, as if to say, later, I'm gone, then pauses a moment and tilts his head. "Dig, man, what you say I take you with me when I go? I'm serious! I aint shitting you! Drop you off in some real town with a hospital for crip -- ah, for, you know, the kind of shit whatever you got wrong with you. They'll fix you back up in no time and next thing you know, you'll be back in business...! What you say, Mr. Bones? C'mon, now, man, I mean, do you wanna go, or not? Shit, what you want to stay here for? Place smells like a shithouse! And I know that fuckin' Jew bastard, Stenno, aint paying you nothing! He aint even paying me but a dog-hair more than nothing and callin' it a living wage! Listen," he continues, bending close and reaching out to grasp the Robot by the shoulder, "I got a lil Forty-Seven Chevy, she don't look too tough, but she can run like a rabbit -- Eh, whoa!" He lurches back, dodging the Robot's arm as it shoots out wildly. "Take it easy, man, aint no need to get all riled up! Aint nobody want to force you to do nothin' you don't wanna do! Shit, you want to stay in this shithole, stay! It don't make me no nevermind." He turns on his heel as though to leave, then turns back and begins to pace again. After a moment, he says, "Fuck it, I got my own self to look out for, what I want with you? You aint nothing to me. Shit, I'm free as a bird. I got me a cool hundred dollars in my grouch bag, stashed right out there in the car, and thirty more in my pocket. And I can always pick up a gig to tide me over...." He pauses again, then says, "Well, I mean, shit, mothafucka, why you don't say something! Yell, curse, anything!"

The rat has scrambled down into a corner and crouches there, now, with only one eye showing, while the boy stands glaring at the giant in the dark, unable to understand the erratic flailing of the Robot's arm. The Robot's stomach begins to churn, and out of his bowels comes a sound like a string of firecrackers exploding in the truck bay. The boy starts and looks around, then rocks back on his heels, gagging. He moves quickly to the back of the truck to stand with his head outside the canvas, breathing heavily and muttering to himself, "Oh, Lord Jesus, what I'm looking to get myself into now?"

☆ ☆ ☆

"...I joined a band one time with a cat played piano and organ. We used to practice in the storage room over his daddy's funeral parlor...."

They're in the Chevy speeding east through the predawn darkness. The front wheels are out of alignment and the steering linkage rattles like a rusty cultivator. Robot Bones, looking straight ahead through the windshield, feels as if they're falling headlong down the flickering hollow of their own headlights.

"We were spoze to play weddings and clubs and school dances and shit like that," the boy continues. "None of us was but twelve or thirteen at the time, but we could blow. But, see, then after the first couple dances, we started doing funerals. We did a funeral one week, and the next week we did another one and the next week we did two more. Man, that cat knew more dead people than Solomon had songs. Got so, people I knew would cross the street when they saw me coming. I had to give that shit up...!"

The boy's removed the passenger seat and tied the wheelchair to the floor bolts using the same rope Stenno had used to haul Bones out onto the circus stage. The boy has also given him one of his own shirts, tearing off the sleeves to fit him into it, and his shoulders protrude through the open armholes. But now they're both soaked, having driven through a thunderstorm during the night with the convertible top open, because it wouldn't close over the Robot's tall head in the wheelchair. The radio has picked up *Red, Hot and Blue* on WHBQ out of Memphis, with the disk jockey, Dewey Phillips, pitching commercials between records, talking about REM Cough Medicine, Carnation Milk, Miles Nevine, and reeling off the names of the dozens of listeners who've called in with requests, all without seeming to take a breath. They hear Roscoe Gordon's *Jack, Have You Ever Been Booted?*, Bill Harley's *Let Your Tears Fall, Baby* and most of the Dixie Hummingbirds' hit, *Trouble In The Way*, before the station fades into static and the radio conks out. As dawn breaks, flint bluffs and yellow pine woods give way to thickets of lavender sage and rolling farmland, with rows of high cotton and soybeans stretching away on either side. A couple of pine shacks, a barn, a silo, a big plantation house, they flit by like solitary shadows against the pale helmet of the sky. They slow into an intersection where a laborer is out early working a mule to pull an oak stump out of the ground. The man raises a hand in greeting as the car turns north. Gin City and the circus are a hundred and forty miles behind them.

The boy's leaning back against the car door driving with one hand and with a cigarette dangling from his lips, as though he thinks he's the image of super-coolness behind his dark blue shades and processed hair. But Bones catches him stealing glances at him out of the corner of his eye. The Robot begins sucking audibly at the air and after awhile the boy understands. He plucks the cigarette from his own mouth and holds it out to the Robot. But he watches the Robot's arm shoot out ineffectually several times, before he realizes what the matter is, and finally puts the cigarette to the Robot's lips himself. Bones draws deeply on the butt, aspirating the windblown ash, coughs and draws again, as the boy turns away.

The music comes back on abruptly with Muddy Waters singing *She Moves Me (And I Don't See How It's Done!)*, and the boy hums along through a couple of choruses, until the radio goes dead again.

"When I was growing up back in Dividend," the boy says, "I used to listen to a deejay from up in Chicago, name of Daddy-O Daylie. Played all the great jazz cats, you know? Eldridge, Ellington, Basie, Bud Powell, Bird, Dizzy, Freddy Webster. But he'd be laying down bop talk all the time, you know, using all them hipisms. Cat had a righteous rap. I used to glue my ear to the grill whenever I could get him on the box. Then I'd go woodshed, you know, try and hit all their licks. Specially Dizzy, Bird and Webster." He laughs, "Shit, aint nobody in this world got chops like Dizzy. He be way up here, way down there and everyplace in between seem-like all at the same time! Badabada-babeep-bopboodoobadoobee-doobliap-bam! Playing false-fingers and all that shit -- choking the trumpet, you know, like playing A-flat by pushing one valve," he held up his right hand as he spoke and wiggled a finger, "and everybody else gotta push two. But you take Webster, now, he's something else. Freddy got the *tone!* And he don't play all the notes, see, he leave some of 'em out. He touch a note, then let the chord kinda echo in your mind, while he go on to the minor seventh, then back to the diminished. Like Miles do now, 'cept Webster been doing it for *days*. I learnt a lot from those cats.... Hey, man, You awright?" he says then, changing the subject. "I mean, you don't never change your expression or nothing, it's kinda hard for a person to know how you feel. You awright? You want me to -- Fuck!"

Without warning, a tractor pulls out onto the road dead ahead. The boy brakes, hits the horn and spins the wheel. The farmer, perched up on the John Deere, stops the tractor and stares down at them sullenly, as the car skids sideways around him. Once clear of the tractor, the boy scowls and cusses into the rearview mirror until the farmer has passed out of sight behind them, leaving the odors of manure and kerosene lingering in the air.

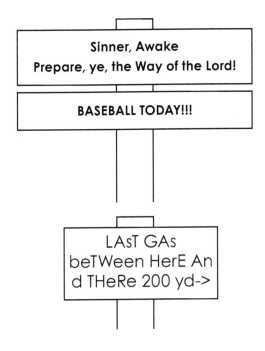

They've reached a crossroads when the engine begins to cough and sputter, although the gas gauge still points to "1/4." The boy slows to a stop and looks around. The only sign of a gas station points off to the right, but the boy doesn't seem to want to go that way. He hesitates, curses, then turns the wheel, following the direction of the gas sign. It's closer to two miles than the two hundred yards indicated by the sign before they come upon a couple of gas pumps on a concrete island in front of a roadside grocery. At the far end of the station a grounded powerline is overgrown with morning-glory. Lot switches off the engine and coasts up to the pumps. A teenager in a greasy baseball hat and overalls sits on a bench out in front of the store. They wait awhile, but when the boy doesn't budge, Lot taps the horn. The boy looks up from whatever he's been tinkering with in his lap and gapes at them but doesn't stir.

Lot sucks his teeth, "Nigguhs!" he mutters, and hoisting himself out over the car door, heads for the pump. A tall white man wearing wire-rimmed spectacles comes out of the store, and Lot hesitates. "Morning, sir," he says, respectfully, removing his sunglasses. "Mind if we get some gas, please?"

The man scrutinizes them from where he stands at the screen door. Finally he says, "Can't you read, boy?"

Glancing back at the pump, and below the meter window, Lot sees the sign he'd missed the first time. Managing to shift smoothly into an exaggerated accent without a trace of irony, Lot says, "Er-uh, does there be a *colored* pump round heah, boss, we'd admire tuh use it."

"Look like you be blind as well!" the man says and gestures with his arm, "Go around!

The second pump, standing next to the first, faces in the opposite direction, towards the store. Lot gets back into the car and turns the key. But as he shifts into reverse the engine dies. He opens the throttle, pumps the accelerator and tries again, but the gas line is dry.

"Bull shit!" he mutters under his breath and climbs back out of the car and walks around the pumps. But as he reaches for the hose on the "Colored" pump, the man gives a yell.

"Hey! What you doing, boy! You trying to be smart? Don't try to play smart with me, y'hear! I told you to move that car around, now you do it!"

Lot returns to the car, slaps the stick into neutral, and cursing under his breath, goes up front to put his shoulder against the grill. But the car starts back only to roll forward again. The front wheels are sunk in a pothole. The man leans back on the screen door watching, as Lot tries unsuccessfully to roll the car out of the hole. The ground is littered with cigarette butts and crushed soda caps. There's very little traffic on the road, and in the distance the pavement seems to shimmer and shift course through the heat waves. After a while, Lot straightens up to wipe the sweat from his forehead and calls out, "Mind if I ax your boy, there, for some help, boss?"

The man purses his lips as if considering that, and as they wait in the long silence, Bones becomes aware of a sound like someone tapping out the seconds on a metal pipe. He glances up to see a Phillips 66 sign on the pole above the pumps. It's lost its top mooring and hangs loosely upside down, tapping against the pole.

"Hey!" the storekeeper yells suddenly, turning away, "I didn't say for you to move!"

The station boy, who's risen from the bench, halts where he stands and speaks over his shoulder, "I finished with the carburetor, boss. I just gwine to put it back."

"Why don'tcha put a halter on that big buck you got in the car," the man says then, turning back to Lot, "and have him pull it out."

The Robot watches the station boy shuffle off toward the back of the lot, where a two-toned prewar DeSoto in mint condition is parked with its hood up. Beyond it, a rusty cannibalized Ford pickup stands on wooden milk crates beside a corrugated iron toolshed.

"...Crippled!" the man is saying. "He don't look crippled to me! He look like a goddamn black bulldozer to me!" And as Lot bends to put his weight against the car again, the man mutters to himself, loudly enough for them to hear, "...Blind, ignorant and hard a hearing too! Hey yall!" he calls out now, turning to speak through the screen door, "Come on out here, looka this! We got a big nigguh too lazy to roll a lil nigguh outta ditch!"

In a moment, there are three of them standing out before the screen door chuckling and joking among themselves, while Lot strains with his feet slipping on the oil-slicked ground and the car rocks and rolls back on him.

"That big nigguh look like he got hisself his own slave!" the older man says.

"Big and ugly, too," the woman says. "Musta scaped outta the horra show!"

"Horra show!" The two men give a hoot.

"Look like he oughta be in a cage," the woman says. "Yeah, he do, too!"

But Lot is murmuring in the Robot's ear, "I don't know if that strongman act you do is real or not, but, man, if you got it in you, I need some help!" He's uncoiled the loose end of the rope tying the wheelchair to the car and looped it around the vertical iron crash-pole that stands anchored in the cement island to protect the gas pumps. Now he draws the Robot's right arm back until it's stretched out behind him. "You understand what I'm telling you, man?" Lot says, pressing the end of the rope into his fist. "We gotta get outta here!"

"Hey! What you doing, there!" the storekeeper hollers.

Lot, ignoring him, puts his shoulder to the front grill once more. "Pull!" he calls, keeping his voice down, "C'mon, Bones, man, pull!"

The voice seems to be coming to him from a great distance as though addressed to someone else. But the Robot feels the tension of the rope in his fist and responds automatically, swinging his arm forward. The crash-pole gives a loud metallic groan, bends under the strain, and the car raises its nose and starts to move. Once out of the hole it accelerates until the rope pays out and the crash-pole bends around the other way, jerking the car to a stop and nearly pitching Bones out of the wheelchair. For a moment, Lot just stands there gaping at him. But the storekeeper has started yelling. Lot runs up to put his own weight against the door post and start the car moving forward again. He steers it around the concrete island then puts his foot on the brake, bringing it to rest beside the "Colored" sign on the second pump.

"BY GOD --! WHAT THE HELL YOU THINK YOU'RE DOIN! WHAT IN THE GOD DAMN HELL --!"

"Terrible sorry, boss...!"

The storekeeper is striding toward them with the woman and the other man in tow, "YOU SONUVABITCHES! YOU GOAN PAY ME FOR THAT POLE, Y'HEAR! BY GOD, YOU WILL...!"

Lot reaches into his pocket and pulls out his Philadelphia roll, a twenty wrapped around a wad of singles to impress the girls, but the men demand to know where he got all that money and accuse him of stealing it. The older man makes a grab for it and in the next moment, they have the boy crowded up against the car wrestling for it. But to the Robot, it's all old news and stupid and his mind begins to wander. The woman, meanwhile, steps up to get a closer look at him in the wheelchair, sniffing at him like a dog. She herself smells of fatback and ham and fried chicken and over-cooked beets and stale beer, and he becomes aware of the fact that he's hungry, has been hungry for awhile, for as long as he can remember. He feels his mouth begin to drool and he rolls his eyes away --

-- And all at once, sees, in his mind's eye, a woman with yellow hair floating on the sunglazed shell of the highway and leaning close before him. Her eyes are cast down and she holds her hands behind her back shaking her head, no. Behind her, a crowd urges her on. She finally raises her head and, taking hold of a hat pin, with her eyes shut, pushes the pin into his arm. When she opens her eyes again, she cries out, "Oh, my! He don't say nothin'!" She is staring, amazed, at the hat pin sticking out of his arm. "He don't even holler!" "Course not, deary," the Robot hears Stenno's voice say, behind her, "He don't feel a thing." She bends her head to examine the wound more closely, as the pitchman says, "LA-DEEZ AND GENTLEMEN, GATHER CLOSER, PLEASE, CLOSER! WHAT YOU ARE ABOUT TO SEE IS FULL OF WONDER AND MYSTERY...!" The woman seems to notice there's only a trace of blood where the pin entered the Robot's arm, and he watches her studying the beads of perspiration welling up on his scalp and running down his face. She follows one with her eyes as it makes its way down his neck and over his bare chest and pools at his waistband. Her own eyes are blue and lively. He sees her clearly, though it must've been days ago. Drawing her lips back, hesitant, she taps the protruding head of the hat pin with her finger. She's fair, maybe thirty, with dirty-blond hair worn in bangs over her forehead. She's pulled the rest into a bun at the nape of her neck, where the lighter strands glimmer in the sun. One front tooth has grown a little over the other, giving her mouth a slight pucker. "Why don't he holler?" she mutters to herself, just loudly enough for him to hear. "Even if he don't talk, he oughta holler." Amidst the heat and surrounding odors of sweat and circus animals, he catches the scent of her lilac perfume and sesame powder and inhales audibly in spite of himself. She gives him a sharp look, but he keeps his eyes focused straight ahead, unblinking, though the whites are bloodshot and brimming over. Stenno hands her a spring tine, and the crowd OOUU's and AAAH's at the sight of the curved steel needle which is over a foot long and taken from a tedding machine. The woman, staring at the

15

needle in her hand, doesn't seem to notice the pitchman's paunch pressing up against her hip as he bends over behind her to push her arm forward, guiding the point of the tine. But as the tine pierces the Robot's thigh, his arm shoots out wildly, and the woman jumps back in alarm, only to rush forward again to slap him across the face. She strikes the Robot again and again, while the crowd roars and the pitchman tries to pull her away, and a shower of coins falls over them like a wedding veil --

-- Voices yelling beside him draw the Robot out of his reverie, and he looks around to see the old man on the ground and the shopwoman running back toward the store screaming for the police. The tall man calls after her to bring his gun and then he gets down on all fours with the older man and the two men vie with one another in snatching up the scattered bills that have fallen out of Lot's hand. Suddenly, there's an explosion and pieces of automotive debris begin raining down around the DeSoto at the back of the lot. The men jump up stuffing Lot's money into their pockets and run toward the DeSoto, where a pillar of flaming smoke is boiling out of the engine well. They are hollering for the woman to call the fire station and the police and to bring them a case of soda gas to smother the fire.

Lot, meanwhile, takes advantage of their distraction to reach for the gas hose, but the station boy is already there, and while the men dance and yell around the burning DeSoto trying to beat back the flames with a car blanket and a rubber floor mat, the boy is pumping gas into the Chevy. But the woman comes back out of the store just as the pump bell dings.

"Floyd! What you think you're doin'! Get away from that car!"

The station boy freezes, with the gasoline overflowing out of the car and onto the ground.

"Hey, man, you better split!" Lot says, vaulting into the driver's seat.

The woman puts down the case of soda-gas, and as Lot keys the ignition and pumps the accelerator, she stands up again holding a hogleg .38 pistol in both hands and swinging the long barrel toward them. "Floyd, you hear me! Come on over here and get this fizz!"

The station boy, dropping the gas hose, disappears behind the pumps, and the woman's first shot goes wild. The engine finally catches and the Chevy jumps forward as the woman fires again. The bullet ricochets off the gas pumps, and there's a loud WHOOMPH! as the spilled gas ignites and they are engulfed in a wall of flames. The woman's next shot pings off their rear fender as the Chevy reaches the roadway spinning its wheels and speeds out of range behind the screen of morning-glory.

The car shimmies and shakes as though it's about to fly to pieces and the needle on the gas gauge swings wildly from E to F and back, as Lot pushes the car passed seventy down the middle of the empty straightaway. A siren rises in the distance behind them, and Lot begins to rub his fingers sensually over the dashboard and recite pornographic phrases in low seductive tones, squirming sexually in his seat, using body-english to coax the Chevy to greater speed. Approaching a blind turn in the road, they hear the klaxon of a fire truck only a moment before the truck itself comes roaring head-on toward them over the median. Lot swerves out of the way then races on, struggling to keep the Chevy under control as it pounds along the broken pavement on the shoulder, with the overhanging bushes whipping at the Robot's face. When they've passed the truck, Lot coaxes the car back onto the cement and takes the first turn-off, onto a narrow unmarked road that crosses a culvert. The road climbs steeply before turning into packed dirt and dropping away to zigzag through a swamp. In a moment, they find themselves at a dead-end facing the closed wooden gate of a hog farm. Lot hesitates, looking for another way out, but finding none, swings the car around and heads back the way they'd come. At the top of the hill they hear the police siren approaching from the highway, and the boy starts to mumble and chant, speaking in tongues now, and floors the gas. The Chevy bursts out of the side road just as the state trooper's car comes barreling in. The cop hollers and yanks his arm inside his own window as the Chevy's rear end sideswipes him. The cruiser spins out and slams sideways into the bushes with a rear wheel hanging over the drainage ditch, as the Chevy speeds away with the boy's foot pressed to the floor and his eyes fixed on the road ahead.

They race on for several miles with Lot glancing up anxiously into the rearview mirror, before he finally relaxes his grip on the wheel. "Fuck," he says, then, speaking aloud to himself, "now you know this aint the direction I planned to be goin'!" He lights a cigarette, takes a puff and glances over at Bones. "Here, man, damn, smoke yown." Holding the wheel steady with his knee, he lights a fresh one and pushes it between the Robot's teeth. "She-e-it," he drawls then, settling back against the door, "You something else, man, you know? You flipped that ole buckra over like you was swatting a fly. I mean, how come you can still do all that shit, lift weights and pull cars outta ditches and all, and yet can't even wipe yown ass --! Excuse me, I'm sorry, man, I don't mean no disrespect, but I mean, that's just crazy, you know? That's a real fuckin' puzzle! Shit, you know that reminds me of one time when we was on the road with Louis -- did I tell you my daddy used to train with Louis? Yeah, he was Joe's sparring partner for awhile before Joe got famous, back in 'Thirty-Three, 'Thirty-Four, when he won his first fight against Jack Kracken in Chicago. He was one bad mothafucka, my daddy...!" He pauses and tilts his head to look at Bones along his eyes. But the Robot sits staring straight ahead and only his right arm is moving, floating in the slipstream with his fingers gesturing in the air....

"You ever been to Memphis?" the boy says after awhile, then makes a wry face and answers his own question, "No, huh? Well, maybe you heard of a cat name of Phineas Newborne, Jr.? No again, huh? Well, Junior's a musician. Like me. Only he blow piano. He's tough, too. Him and me go way back. I sat in on a gig with him one time in Savanna when he was touring with the Basie band. In fact, it was kinda funny how it happened. I was with Moe Brandywine at the time, playing another gig in town the night before? And some of Basie's boys dropped by and sat in with us, cause Moe toured with Basie in the 'Forties. So then, the next afternoon, we all got together, you know, scrounged up a jug and some chicks and made it out to a field out by the edge of town to play some baseball. Well, so now, I'm behind the plate, catching, see. Jimmy Rushing's pitching, Harry 'Sweets' Edison's covering second base, and I think Freddy Greene was playing first. Anyway, here come Phineas to the plate. Jimmy throws him two strikes, womp! womp! one after another. Junior just fanning the air, man -- cause he wear bifocal shades, calling himself cool, you know, and can't see shit. But next pitch, POW! Phineas lined the ball right back at the mound. Ole Mister Five-by-Five was sure glad he wasn't no taller that day, cause the ball missed his head by a short hair, then it took a funny hop and caught Sweets right in the crotch! That nigguh went down for the count! And Junior, man, he didn't even run! He still standing there with the bat in his hand scratching his head, cause the cat aint seen the ball yet! Man, that was some funny shit. But meanwhile, Sweets did a number on me, too. He'd seen me staring at him, you know, kinda watching every move he made, cause to me he was like a living legend, man.

And so, before the game, when I'd seen him take his trumpet out the case and put it between two blocks of ice we'd brung with us to keep the beer cold, I axed him why he did that. And Sweets gave me one of those wise old looks and said if I wanted to experience some fantastic playing I should try it. So, I figured, shit, this is Harry 'Sweets' Edison, and if it's good for him it sure can't hurt me, so I did. And after the game, I go and check out my horn, dig? So, I pick it up off the ice to blow a scale -- and man, the mothafucker's cold as a witch's tit! The valves are stiff, my teeth is starting to chatter and next thing I know, my lips are froze to the freakin' mouthpiece! And the other cats stand there watchin' me trying to get my mouth unstuck from the horn, and they all know the joke, and they're fallin' out! Man, I was so ma-a-ad...!" He laughs and waves a hand in the air, as though bidding his callow youth goodbye. "Anyway, later that night at the club, I got my own back. Cause Basie let me sit in for Sweets! -- who still wasn't feeling so well by then. And when we get into *Corner Pocket*, Basie points to me to take a solo! Well, now, I'm steppin', Jim! -- What? Wait, now, lemme tellya!"

Bones is hissing, trying to get his attention, but the boy's on a roll.

"-- I'm scared, see," the boy continues, too carried away with his own story to look around, "but I tell myself, fuck it, and I go, I do my four bars. And Basie, he just nods and tells me to do four more! And I do four more! And now, Basie's smiling and he says go again! But right then, the fuckin' cops come bustin' in the goddamn door and -- Say what? I don't know, maybe they was running whiskey in the back room, or something -- Anyway, Basie don't miss a beat, he just tells us play louder, like nothing's happening. But meanwhile, I'm seeing nickel bags pap! pap! pap! dropping all over the bandstand! -- Huh? Hmn, yeah...! Man, a whole lotta shit gone under *mucho* bridges since then. Fact, Junior got his skinny ass drafted. But I hear he out the army now. And must be he's back in Memphis, cause Junior love Mem -- Hey, man, what you doing to my car!"

Bones, panting and hissing over the last several minutes while the motor-mouth was running on, has been shooting his hand back and forth crazily in the air in a fruitless effort to rid himself of the cigarette butt, which has burned down to his teeth. Finally, as he bangs his fist on the passenger door, Lot snatches the butt from his mouth and tosses it away.

"Damn, Rico -- I mean, Ro...!" the boy doesn't finish. Instead, he spits on his own fingers and reaches over to rub the cooling saliva on the Robot's lips. He leans back against the door then, and in a sober tone, says, "I don't know bout you, man, but I'm gittin' *hon*-gry!"

The sun is high, fierce and white. The boy is driving in silence, purposely avoiding main arteries and anything approaching a town, not wanting to draw the attention of the curious or the law. He's trying to find his way back north but he doesn't know the territory, and heat waves ripple the air, warping the countryside like a carnival mirror and making portions of solid road and farmland shimmer and spill into phantom bayous, confusing their sense of direction. The car's worn shocks make it jolt and joggle like a wooden wagon over the pitted roads and Bones, upright in the wheelchair, can feel it hammering at his spine. He can almost hear the old piece of shrapnel that had severed his vocal chords singing in his neck. Shadows crowd up and rush by. He blinks and rotates his eyes, trying to stay awake, to push back the ghosts and the voices buried deep in memory that are rising up now out of the wind and the rattle of the steering linkage, as they race down one dogleg road after another only to lose and find and lose their way again, driving now through the swamp and swale of bottom lands.

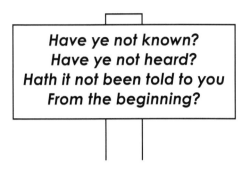

Have ye not known?
Have ye not heard?
Hath it not been told to you
From the beginning?

They cross the river at Stalking-Horse and pick up 61 north, past Redmanville and DeLaye. The land on this side is flat and bright as a copper skillet, with a lone church steeple or silo in the distance the only sign of a settlement. For awhile, they make good progress, passing signs for Boyer, Sudfetter, Pentecost, Doddsville, Saracen, Two Ton and Penny, none of them more than a country store at a crossroads, or sometimes just the crossroad itself running straight as a plowed furrow through fields of cotton or peas stretching away to the horizon. Then they come upon a series of construction detours and suddenly they are headed east again, dodging the roadapples and banging in the ruts over a stretch of washboard winding through the flats of Mockingbird County. The boy's turned sullen, but the radio is on again and they hear a second-string group singing *Yellow Rose of Texas*, before the news comes on. Germany has been admitted to NATO, Eisenhower has collapsed with a heart attack in Denver, the first artificial diamond has been created, and Albert Einstein, Jimmie Dean and Charlie "Bird" Parker are dead.

At Sharon Creek they find a congregation gathered on the riverbank, where a double row of men and women in full-length white robes stand solemn as black angels singing *Precious Lord*. They're guiding a line of reluctant youngsters down to where church elders stand waist-deep in the water to receive them. The elders bend the young ones backward until their heads go under and they come up gagging. Bones sees the muddy water speckled with dead fish and cow pies and reeking of acidic runoff from the chemical factory visible beyond the fields, and the sight recalls the taste of almonds to his mouth....

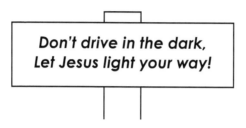

**Don't drive in the dark,
Let Jesus light your way!**

Entering LeVane County, they pass through a series of small towns where the hand-wrought pine shacks and fences are all the same weather-worn Confederate gray and an opaque film of stagnant moisture overlays the mud where the soft shoulder of the road meets the line of fences and building steps. It is a line oddly straight along streets where the telegraph poles, fence tops, building corners, windows and roofs are so generally out of square that they seem to have sprouted there out of cracked seeds sown by the wind. Negroes in their Sunday clothes stand about talking quietly together in the shade of the cottonwood and pecan trees, while the whites peer out from under their own porch eaves to stare somberly at the car as they drive by. But black or white, there don't seem to be any young people. And the stores, plastered with signs offering Coke, Nehi and Bull Durham, Florsheim shoes and Levis at discount, Chill Tonic for fever and malaria, Carter's Little Liver Pills, Tums, Vicks Vaporub, Liquozone for asthma and ulcers, Lydia Pinkham's Vegetable Compound "for those difficult days" and sundry other remedies, are all boarded up. When the last town is well behind them, Lot, who's driven for the past hour without saying a word, his eyes narrowly fixed on the road ahead, abruptly pulls over by a roadside stand where there is a sign for lemonade. The vendor lies dozing in the shade of a tree with his bare feet pressed against a block of ice on the ground. At the sound of the horn he rouses himself and ambles over to help them. He's an old man with tobacco-stained teeth and a growth the size of a golf ball rising out of the woolly nape of his neck. Lot doesn't respond to his friendly overtures and the old man looks them over warily as he pours out their lemonade. When he is paid, he gives them a broad, mischievous grin and as they drive off, the Robot hears him call out, mysteriously, "Yall watch out for the sleepin' dawg!" But the lemonade is good and cools his throat -- as well as his shirt front, where much of it spills as the boy, driving one-handed, holds it up for him to drink.

They come upon a work gang lining track along the Illinois Central right-of-way, and the last thing the Robot remembers before dozing off is the boy flooring the gas for no apparent reason and the silver shimmer of sunlight rising on a wave of hammers....

"What the hell you doing in there! Get up! Get outta there!"

Startled awake, Bones finds himself alone in the front of the car, parked along a deserted road in the woods. The voice comes from behind him. There's the sound of a struggle, then the voice yelling. "Goddammit, nigguh, git your black ass outta my car! Come on! Out!"

"Oh, sut!" another voice says, "Ow! Hey, okay, mistuh! Ow!" He hears the sounds of someone scrambling over the door behind him and feet landing heavily on the ground.

"What the fuck you think you're doin'?" he recognizes the voice, now, as Lot speaks again, "You thought you'd be going along with me? With us? F'git that! I got no time to be fooling with fools like you. You wanna go somewhere, get your ass out on the road and fuckin' walk! Shit, this aint no freedom train!"

Bones can see him now, the other one, as he backs away from Lot. It's the boy from the filling station, Floyd. He's holding his greasy baseball cap with both hands and twisting it nervously around on his head. He's taller than Lot and heavier, but clearly younger. He stands in his oil-stained overalls and hand-me-down army boots, gawky and stooped with dejection and not saying anything.

"What the hell you trying to do," Lot goes on, "get us all lynched? Where your head at, man? Are you crazy, blowing up the place like that? And what you come on to me for, anyway. Huh? Who axed you for help! All I axed you for was gas! Aint nobody ax you to blow up the fuckin' gas station! Shit!" He shakes his head and glances over at Bones, "Mothafucka's crazy!"

While Lot rails at him, Floyd is eyeing the Robot and sidling over toward him, and his adolescent voice cracks as he says, "Who that man?"

"Say what?"

Floyd leans forward to peer at Bones intently, "How he get so messed up? Was he in a accident or something?"

"Get away from there!" Lot says, stepping forward.

"He don't look like he hardly alive!" The boy reaches out to touch Bones gingerly on the shoulder, before retreating, "What's the matter with him?"

"That aint none of your business!" Lot says, heading back toward the driver's side of the car. But as he brushes passed Floyd, the boy reaches into his pocket and takes a step toward Bones again.

"What I tell you!" Lot wheels around with a switchblade in his hand. "Back up! Take your hand out your pocket! I done had enough of you!"

"Whoa, mister! I didn't mean nothin'!" Floyd says, backing away. "I just wanted to --"

Lot feints with the knife and the boy, dodging away, trips over his own feet and sprawls on the ground, scattering a deck of cards that has fallen out of his pocket.

The Robot, unable to turn his head, squints sidelong at the cards.

"Swear fo' God, mistah, I didn't mean no harm! I just thought I mighta knowed him!"

"Boy, if you know what's good for you, you won't budge from there till we're outta sight!"

"I just thought --!"

"And you won't say another fuckin' word, neither!"

The boy makes a show of clamping his lips closed with his teeth, whether in fear or mockery, Bones isn't sure, and silently nods his head. Lot spins on his heel and climbs back into the car. But as the motor kicks over, the boy, raising himself up on his elbows, has already begun muttering under his breath, and when they pull away he calls out, "I just thought I mighta knowed him, is all! Why yall can't take me with you...?"

As the car drives on, Bones stares through the windshield at the road rushing toward him like a dark skein unraveling in the light and sees an old man, dwarfed behind a huge mahogany desk, pouring out generous shots of good Jack Daniels neat, while a high, coffered ceiling fills with smoke....

They've turned onto a fork that appeared to circle back to the highway, but they come upon another car, a big blue and white Mercury Monterey, parked crosswise in the road. Lot slams on the brakes and leans out to curse the driver, then spots the star of a deputy sheriff blazoned on the door. Setting his face into a grim mask, he carefully places his hands on top of the wheel in plain view. The cop, meanwhile, sits calmly in the cruiser studying them through his own window, taking in the condition of the Chevy, the license plate, and the large, dark figure of the Robot in the wheelchair. In his own good time, he climbs out of the cruiser, a tall man with a face that looks haggard and old beyond his years. His pistol rides on his left hip and he favors one leg as he walks toward them. Without a word, he extends a hand for their license and registration. Lot passes them over. While he's examining the papers, the deputy absently taps the bottom of his shirt pocket, popping a cigarette out of the pack he carries there. But he's used his other arm, and the Robot stares furtively at the curve of a steel claw where the man's right hand should be, as the deputy goes about putting the cigarette between his lips and drawing a lighter from his pants pocket. The cop is taking his time about their papers, and as they wait, Bones, laboring to breathe in the damp airless pocket of the woods, shifts his eyes to the souvenir dangling from a chain on the police car's rearview mirror, and feels his breath pass through him like a fever. Then the deputy hands back the papers and speaks for the first time.

"You boys looking for the fair?"

2.
Rue River

"...Had a dream last night, an I aint lyin',
Had a ... an I aint ly...
Saw an angel, an he was cr...!"

"'The gambling of the wicked is an abomination to the Lawd -- but the contribution of the upright is His delight!' So saith the Good Book, brothers. Who'll gimme six-to-one on the One-Eye dog. Six-to-one on One-Eye...."

A light-skinned Negro dressed in a clerical collar stands behind a counter made of fruit boxes chanting his pitch like a sermon to the men milling about the racetrack, where the dogs are being groomed and exercised in front of their cages. The man has a festering ulcer on his nose, but those crowding up to place their bets are eyeing the clutch of bills folded like bow ties around his fingers that he waves hypnotically before them.

"Okay, okay! One at a time, brothers! I see yall are anxious to make your contributions this evenin'! Yessuh, five dollahs on Shoofly at two-to-one, thank you brother!" Giving the bettor a paper chit, he bands the money together and tosses it into a cardboard box on the counter before him. "'He that is greedy of gain troubleth his own house,'" the bookmaker goes on, "'but he that putteth his faith in the hands of his Redeemer shall prosper in his soul!' Awright, now, Ratmouth Suzie is seven-to-two! I said seven-to-two on Ratmouth Suzie...."

Bones and the boy have stopped in a large field at the edge of a bogue rimmed with cottonwood, swamp oak and chokecherry trees, where the various activities of the annual LeVane County Negro Farmers' Field Day Picnic are spread out over a couple of acres around them. Earlier, a banjo player was sitting on an orange crate under a tree singing a strange blues, but he's gone off somewhere. The afternoon sun is bright and hot, shining through a chain of mare's-tails moving rapidly across the sky. Beyond the racetrack, across the way, the surface of the water shimmers like tarnished silver. A spur of the I-C Railroad runs below a bluff on the far side of the bogue, and on this side a cowpath leads down to a bare mud shelf flanked by cattails and reeds where a couple of men stand with poles out, fishing for catfish and bass. The Robot is in his wheelchair, with the boy, sitting on a grass hummock beside him, studying the bookmaker through narrowed eyes and blowing quietly into the mouthpiece of his trumpet. Dzzz-dzzz Dzzz Dzz-dzz-dzz! he goes, tonguing the brass cup as though, even without the horn itself, which lies in its tattered slipcase beside him, something impels him to play against the rhythms of the bookmaker's speech. It occurs to Bones that until now he hasn't really looked at the boy, looked at his face. And even now, he finds it difficult for some reason to make him out, maybe because the kid has a way of holding his head turned a little to one side. He tries to give the feeling of youthful assurance, Bones thinks, but even when at rest, like now, something within him seems constantly in motion. Dzzz Dzzz-dzz Dzzz...!

"Every tune that ole whistle blow is true! Go on by!"

Startled by the new voice that comes like a whisper in their ears, the boy, who'd been scooping suds from a bucket of warm, soapy water he'd conjured up, pauses and turns to see who's spoken.

"Wheels on the track say, 'TAKE-a-chance! TAKE-a-chance! TAKE-a-chance!' Huh. Cast your eye on them pipes."

An old man stands a little distance off with his face hidden in the shadow of a faded gray fedora. He strokes the belly of a jackrabbit cradled in his arms. The rabbit is trying to kick free, but the old man holds it firmly against his chest. With his last words, he'd nodded toward a patch of slender Indian pipes growing along the edge of the water. They seem to be shuddering in the still wind.

"See how they tilt over like that and start to waverin'?" He speaks in a low soothing voice, as though crooning to the rabbit, "They bobbing they heads like they wanna boogie-woogie. That be the train make'm do that way. That ole train make'm be a-longing to go! Now, if you wasn't wearing them city-walkers, you could feel it in yo' feets like they do, and like I does." He wriggles his bare toes on the ground and smiles, showing a set of startlingly white false teeth that appear to be loose in his mouth, for you can hear them clicking along as he speaks.

They can hear the train whistle now, too, but across the water the tracks are still empty.

"You can't see'er yet," the old man says, "but that ole Yaller Dawg be coming out from around that bend over yonder any minute. Course, you can also tell by the time o'day, cause she run reg'lar. But sometimes the fog come up over the bogue, and you won't see'er at all. Won't know she's there, cept for that whistle and the sound of them bogies drummin' on the rails." The jackrabbit has stopped kicking and lays back now in his arms twitching its whiskers and blinking drowsily as he scratches its throat. "But it'd be like from a long ways off then, you know? Be like missing her. Like you never did have no kinda chance to catch'er. But, like today? When it be clear like this? Seem like she be your train! Like she be coming here just for you! Like them side-rods gonna reach right out and grab you up and shoot you to Chicago! Say, 'Dontcha worry, honey, that ole sheriff aint gonna ketch ya, I'm a-coming back to gitcha! When you hear my whistle blowin', you be here, an we'll be goin'!' HOO-boy!"

He's broken the rabbit's neck with a deft twist of his wrist, and now he glances up at them with a look of surprise, as though aware of them for the first time. Turning abruptly, he draws a strip of rawhide from his pocket and begins to lash the dead rabbit onto a towbar extending from the back of a jeep parked nearby. He speaks again over his shoulder as he works, wetting the carcass down with a foul-smelling mixture he scoops out of a bucket. "You sit back there in the house," he says, his soft, reedy voice carrying easily over the distance between them, "and it be like being in jail. You hear that whistle blowing off in the distance, and it just seem like a dream...." With the agility of a much younger man, he's climbed into the jeep and drives it slowly passed them now with the hind legs of the carcass dangling off the towbar so that it looks almost as if the animal were still alive and loping along behind him. "Like a dream," the old man says, again, his voice floating back to them as he heads out onto the track, "like all them dreams you dreamed as a child that're gone, gone...!"

After a moment, the boy turns around again and gives the Robot a long curious look. The Robot is still strapped into the wheelchair with the soapy lather gone dry and turning to powder on his cheeks. He glares back at the boy through bloodshot eyes.

"Don't you be looking at me like that, man," the boy says, coming toward him with the straight razor swinging open in his hand. "You just gonna have to trust me."

> "...Said, 'Angel, Devil's hound dawgs 's trackin my soul!'
> Said, 'Angel, the D... trackin my s...!'
> Angel said, 'Boy, he's with you, wherever you g...!'"

The banjo player is back, picking out his cranky tune in stop time and letting the instrument sing the words he doesn't. He glances up and his lower eyelids seem to pouch out in a lurid grin as he watches the boy pushing the Robot along toward him in the wheelchair. The old man's skin is dry and brittle as aged tobacco, but his voice is deep and lusty. Other musicians have arrived and are setting up their instruments behind him.

Meanwhile, the Robot finds himself struggling to ignore a thought pressing at the back of his mind that was probably set off by the drive across country and the festive scene around them and maybe by the music, too, and the pungent odors of hot food that now draw their attention to a group of women further along, who are stoking campfires and loading wooden picnic tables with platters of fried fish, hop-n-john, barbecued chicken and ribs.

Lot pushes on to investigate, and a couple of the women turn and smile as they approach. He steps from behind the wheelchair and goes forward with a grin and a dimple that's suddenly materialized in his chin, squaring his broad shoulders and stretching his tall, athletic frame to its full height, young, strong and full of himself, the Robot thinks, and foolish, as he once was....

But as Lot greets the women, his eye drifts toward a lone girl in a yellow apron coming toward them carrying a basket of strawberries and picking her way through the blue September weed like a mare in a melon field. She rests the basket on the picnic table and turns to face him with one hand on her hip.

"Don't I know you?" she says.

Lot, who's slipped his trumpet out of its sleeve, toys with the valves and gives her a shy smile. Then, glancing over at the band, he says, "Baby, you know someplace here I can cool my horn?"

> "...Angel said, 'Boy, he's with you wherever you go,
> 'Yeah, he's...wherever...,
> 'Devil walks in yo' shadow, just like me,
> 'Only he's what you do, an I'm what you s...!'"

The two of them have wondered off, and the Robot is left with the older women, who are grinding up meat and vegetables and spoon-feeding him like one of their babies. Then a big woman with bold eyes and hips like a sugar mule who reminds him a little of Hazel Scott bends to put the spoon into his mouth -- And all at once, the shadows are back, crowding up again behind his eyes and he has the sensation he's falling backward. He realizes what's happening to him and begins mentally cursing Lot, blaming him for not stopping to think what demons he'd set loose trying to "liberate" somebody like him. For the Robot knows that once it begins he won't be able to stop it. His eyes are drawn reluctantly to the woman's shawl and to her long green skirt spiraling in the breeze, and then it happens...

-- He'd caught the evening train out of Baltimore, pissed off because he'd just had another fight with his manager. On top of that, the yardmen had awakened him three times during the night to move to different coaches, as they shifted the boundaries of the colored section each time the train got shunted onto spurs, changed engines or dropped cars. Each change had been worse than the last, he and the other Negroes having had to crowd into fewer and fewer carriages that had no electricity, no working toilet, broken windows and seats, and were filthy, besides. By the end, they'd been herded into a single coach, attached right behind the coal car. With screaming babies and all, they'd had to climb in over the benches because the floorboards were rotted out, and had to ride through the rest of the night crammed together like cattle for slaughter, hanging on to the stanchions and window frames to keep from falling through the gaps, with their ears deafened by the rattling trucks, their eyes burning from smoke and cinders and the only light coming from the afterglow of the engine fire and the sparks flying up out of the darkness racing below them like the forge of hell. Six-thirty next morning, as the train pulled into Atlanta, he remembered the newsboys shouting along the platform that Hitler had invaded Poland.

But his mind had been filled with thoughts of home by the time the Southern And Pacific local crossed over into Alabama. And then a cheer had gone up as he'd stepped off at the Dardan station.

A dozen homeboys had turned out to welcome him back. His kid brother, Jax, standing there on the platform four inches taller and thirty pounds heavier, with a big grin on his face, had put the word out that he was coming. Having the best part of Sunday ahead of him, he'd leaned back against the concrete pillar of the loading dock to joke and shoot the shit, when all at once, they were startled by a blinding flash of light and a sound like a pistol shot.

"Rico Jones! I be damned! Hiya, Rico!" A whiteboy stepped forward grinning at him through the smoke of the shattered flashbulb and waving the film clip from a big Speed Graphic. "Whaddya say, boy? Long time no see. I'm gonna make you famous!"

The other men had quietly drifted away, as the smoke blew off leaving a harsh odor of burnt phosphor. He just stared at the whiteboy, then picked up his suitcase and, prodding Jax to go on ahead, started for the car. He remembered hearing a train whistle blow in the distance and recognized the familiar sound of the southbound express as it descended the grade from Piedmont.

"Hey, Rico! Hey, boys, wait up!" The whiteboy called, trotting after them. "Lemme get one of you and your little brother together."

"Nah," he said, "he dont like pictures."

"C'mon, now Rico!" the whiteboy persisted. "Help me out, here. I'm tryin' to get my first feature in the paper. I'm a reporter on the Lima Star, now!"

He didn't stop, but it was coming back to him who the whiteboy was.

"Look-a-here!" the boy said, "I'll make it worth your while!"

He waited until Jax got into the car, then turned, and saw the whiteboy holding up two crumpled five dollar bills, as the flash went off again. He closed the passenger door, protecting his kid brother from his own curiosity, and gave the other a long hard look. "What you up to, boy! What you want!"

"Sir!" the boy said. "I'm a full-growed white man, now. You call me 'sir!'"

He stepped toward him, his voice hoarse with anger, "What you want our picture for, John Lee!"

John Lee backed cautiously away from him. "I done told ya, to put in the paper!"

He took another step toward him, "Don't bullshit me, boy! What you tryin' to pull! You git on outta here!"

"Sir!' You call me 'sir!'" John Lee said, then stumbled and fell, nearly dropping his camera, as a gust of wind snatched the money from his hand. "Shit! I'ma fix you, nigguh!" he said, pointing his finger at him and shooting him with his thumb, "I'ma fix you good!" Then he scrambled up and ran after the bills spiraling past the loading dock.

Rico Jones returned to the car and got in behind the wheel.

"What he say, Rico? What he want our picture for?"

Preoccupied, he stared through the windshield without answering. He could see John Lee running toward the tracks chasing his money, the two bills swooping and fluttering just out of his reach.

"Hey, man, we in trouble or something?"

He suddenly turned and glared at his kid brother in mock anger, changing the subject, "Hey, nigguh, what the fuck you do to my car!" He reached over and caught his brother in a head-lock. They wrestled playfully for a minute, then he pulled free and started the car. It was the same Nineteen Thirty-Two Packard sedan he, Rico, had bought secondhand and customized himself the year before he'd left home. Back then, he'd cut away the roof behind the front seat, removed the back seat and laid wood planks lengthwise along the floor into the trunk. The shocks had been re-enforced to carry extra weight, and he'd used it for hauling timber and roofing. While he'd been away, Jax had wired in an Emerson radio, carpeted the dash with Baltimore Elite Giants pennants, and installed a sun visor over the windshield. The car was a lot cleaner now, too, and smelled of wax and neat's foot oil. He kept the Packard in second over the rutted gravel and cinders. The wind had piled up dead weeds along the inner curve of the loading dock and he was glad to get it behind him. It reminded him too strongly of when he'd had no choice but to be there hauling packing crates and bails off trucks, stacking them in the bay, and loading them onto boxcars. Even for him, it had been back-breaking work, and still he'd had to hire himself out for odd jobs to keep food in their mouths. Loading those boxcars one after another, from before sunup to past sundown, had made those freight trains seem to go on forever, longer from engine to caboose than any distance he, himself, would've expected to travel if he'd lived to be a hundred. But in the three years since he'd left, all that had changed....

Jax had taken an old baseball out of the hollow of the door handle on the passenger side and was tossing it from hand to hand. With a light tap, he sent it rolling along the gutter between the windshield and the sloping dashboard to Jones's side, and Jones tapped it back as he spun the wheel, climbing up the embankment onto the paved two-lane. Good to be home, though, he said to himself.

The inbound express whistled again, as he shifted up the line, but the station and its network of tracks were hidden from view by huckleberry and juniper, growing thick along the power lines on the shoulder. That little peckerwood, John Lee, had been just another rock-throwing kid when he'd left, he was thinking. And the boy's daddy, Clement Bledsoe, had been a hard man. Died from a heart attack the previous spring, the boys'd told him, while drunk and beating his wife. Bledsoe had been supervisor of the depot, bossing the lineup. Anybody wanting to work there had had to call him Mister Boss. Now, just what was that sly John Lee up to, taking their picture, he wondered. Reporter! he said to himself. Bullshit! They both knew the Star wasn't about to put no nigger's picture in the paper! Just what was that little motherfucker trying to pull?-- "What's the matter, boy," he said aloud, "cat got your tongue?"

Jax was trying to tell him something, but seemed to be having trouble getting it out. "It's Momma," he stammered, finally, "I mean, nothing serious, you know, but I mean, like lately...!"

But his words were drowned out by the train roaring under the embankment with its steam breaks hissing and its wheels shrieking against the tracks. As he recalled, the express had never used to stop there, but it wasn't his business anymore. He asked Jax to repeat what he'd said, and as the boy spoke again, he, himself, was thinking that this baby brother was the only one left at the house. Their sister had married and gone north. Well, now that he finally had some money in his pocket, he said to himself, he'd make sure his momma got all the care she needed. He stepped on the gas and smiled to himself at the small cloud of dust that blew across the road behind him in the rearview mirror, fine and white as snow.

But the sun had barely come up over the trees the next morning, when Sheriff McKeller came beating on their door. The old man handcuffed him and took him down to the jailhouse without any explanation -- except that he kept muttering, "Dont know what happened to you, boy. Thought you was one of the good ones, fore you left here!"

Over the next two weeks, whitefolks came round almost every night banging on the bars of his cell window and screaming at him, "Murderer! Gonna lynch your black ass!" and throwing rocks and bottles into the cell. McKeller would go out and disperse them. But his new deputy, a big ex-football player with eyes like chipped lime, would threaten to let the crowd in to lynch him and make nasty remarks about his family and threaten him with all kinds of shit, trying to make him confess to a robbery and murder he didn't know anything about. He didn't even know who it was had been *killed. But he wasn't going to confess to anything he hadn't done and he told the cop that right out. Deputy told him he didn't like the way he talked back and would jab him in the ribs or the kidneys or the back of his head with a baseball bat. But he didn't back off and he didn't mince words, he'd been out in the world and he wasn't going to take that shit anymore. Finally, one evening when McKeller was out the deputy went too far. Started talking about his momma and his sister, which the ofay didn't even know, and went to hit him one time too often with the bat. They were in the small jailhouse office with both his hands handcuffed to a heavy metal table they had there, but he jumped up and swung that damn table round and slammed the cop into the wall. The cop slumped to the floor, still breathing but knocked out. He knew he had no choice then but to make a run for it, because they'd send him to the pen for sure. He dragged the table across the floor and wedged it in the iron gate separating the office from the cell block and with his foot on the table, levered his arms against the bars of the gate until the chain between the handcuffs burst. But it had taken a couple of minutes, and as he turned to head for the door, he saw the bat swinging toward him....*

He didn't come to until five o'clock the next morning, when McKeller and the deputy came into the cell, woke him up and took him out to the patrol car. They had put him in bilboes. He found he couldn't walk on his own, couldn't see out of one eye and he felt as though he'd been run over by a truck. They didn't say a word, and as they drove him along the deserted back streets, he thought they were delivering him to a lynch mob. But they turned down his own street and he saw through the window that somebody'd firebombed his house. Part of the front and one side wall had been blown out, leaving the roof sagging and the charred framework exposed. His mother was sitting out front in her rocker on what was left of the porch wrapped in the green and white flowered bed quilt he'd brought home for her, with Jax standing beside her. The two of them just stared silently at him as the car drove passed, as though they'd been waiting out there, told to expect him. His mother waved as they passed out of sight. They finally pulled up at the train station and McKeller got out and flagged down the eastbound express. The cops carried him onto the train, removed the bilboes and went back down the steps without a word, leaving him hunched over on the floor. As the train started to move the deputy turned and said, "You take a pretty picture, boy. I'ma keep it on my wall...!"

"...ANCHORMAN!"

Somebody behind him is tapping on his shoulder and somebody else pulling on his shirttail. He can't turn and can't see. Disoriented, not sure whether the voices he hears are real or imagined, he thinks he might be dreaming. But they are tugging at him from both sides. He feels someone climbing on the back of the chair and then slipping an arm under his chin choking him. The women are gone. He's down by the paddock not knowing how he'd got there, with nobody but the horses milling around on the other side of the rails. He reaches out for the one who had him by the throat, but his arm swings round uncontrollably. The chair begins to rock back and forth on its wheels, and at the corners of his limited field of vision, a flurry of small brown hands tap and tug and pull at him like wrens at a worm nest. He catches hold of the one hanging on his neck, but it's only a child. Dragged off the back of the chair, she comes tottering around to look up at him, frightened, no more than seven or eight. She has a ribbon plaited in her hair. He lets her go, and she gives him a gap-toothed smile. But then others swarm into view, bigger and mostly boys, pushing cards in his face.

"Hey, you the Anchorman?"

"You Rico Jones, mister?"

"You him for real?"

"Autograph my card?"

"Mine's, too, mister?"

"Do mine's!"

"I axed first!"

The chair swivels and rocks precariously as they vie for his attention. One, grabbing at him, tears his shirt. He swings his arm around, trying to fend them off, but they're quick, dodging away and scooting in again. In the middle of the mix-up, he hears a voice warning the others off.

"Hey, wait, yall!"

"Look how he movin'!"

"He look like a duppy!"

They shrink back, now, gaping at him.

One loose-jointed boy, in frayed Levis too short for him, stretches out a hand and waves it in his face.

"What's the matter with him?"

"I don't know. Something!"

"Phew! He stink!"

"He aint no ballplayer!"

"He can't even hardly move!"

"You ever seen a duppy before?"

The boy in the Levis takes out a clasp knife and bending down begins cutting a piece out of the Robot's frayed, dirt-stiff khaki pants, careless of the sharp point of the knife gouging into the leg beneath.

"What you doing, man?"

"I dunno bout yall, but I'm gettin'me a sivvenir!"

In the next moment, they're all at him again, cutting and tearing at his clothes. The chair swings round and goes over with a crash. His head smacks the ground, the slop bucket upends and he's awash in his own shit and urine, with the kids yelling, the frightened horses rearing and charging around in the paddock and his own legs in the air with the shreds of his pants streaming like pennants.

"Bones! Goddammit! Bones, man, you awright? Get off! Get outta here! Goddammit, beat it, I said! Bones!"

Kids leap, tumble, are tossed away. And then it's Lot, bending over him, cursing and in a rage.

"Bones, you awright?"

He blinks, and his right arm jerks spasmodically.

"God damn! Goddammit! God damn sonuvabitch!" As Lot pulls the chair upright and looks him over, a small hand steals into Jones's lap. Lot grabs it. "Boy, I'm gonna kill you! Didn't I tell you to get outta here!" But in the act of tossing the boy off, he sees the card in his hand and snatches it away. "What's this? What you trying to steal?"

"Nothin'! I aint steal nothin'! That's mine! I dropped it."

"What the shit you mean, yours!" Lot holds it up and examines it, a Black Top baseball card framed with a television screen and containing a full-color picture of the Anchorman, Rico Jones, star outfielder and homerun king of the Kansas City Monarchs, standing at the plate with a bat in his hand. Lot stares at the photo, glances at the Robot in the wheelchair, then whirls on the kid. "Where you get this!" he demands. When the boy doesn't answer, Lot twists his arm behind his back, "I say, where you --!"

"Oww! I bought it! I bought it, that's all. I bought it with my own money. Ow! That's the truth, swear fo' Gawd! Lemme go!"

"Where you buy it from."

"From that other boy, said he come with you."

"What boy. You lying, I didn't come with no boy."

"Ow! I aint lying, mister. Ax them. Ax the resta them. They all got'em same as I did. He sold'em to us. He got a whole bunch of'em. He told us Rico Jones was here, and we could get autographs. Is that really him, mister? Is that Rico Jones? Is he a duppy?"

"Git out my face!" Lot shoves him away.

"Je-sus Lawd Christ, what they do to that man?" Jones recognizes the voice of the woman who'd been feeding him earlier, the one who reminded him of Hazel Scott, and he sees her green dress billowing up behind Lot. "Child, don't you know no better than to go off and leave this man out here by himself!" she says, railing at Lot as she stoops to loosen the bellyband tying the Robot to the chair, allowing him to breathe more easily. Rising, she presses his head against her bosom. "If I get my hands on them little fools, I'ma beat the black off'em! And just look at you!" she adds, giving Lot a once-over.

Jones sees then that Lot, himself, is bleeding from fresh knife wounds about his head, arms and chest. "I believe you aint much better then them chillen! What you been doin', fightin' over a crap game, while this man's out here, burnin' up in the hot sun? Umh!" Whirling round without waiting for an answer, she calls some of the men to come and help.

As they wheel him into the tack room, one of the men, stooping over to take a good look, says, "He look familiar to me. He ever worked the levy over to Cairo?"

But the woman keeps up a constant stream of chatter, lulling Bones with soft noises, cussing the kids and fussing at Lot and the other men who stand around trying to help, ordering them about like errant children. She tells them to spread a horse blanket on the ground, to fetch soap and water and to go and find some fresh clothes. They lift Jones out of the chair, lay him on the blanket and strip off what's left of his own clothes. As they set about sponging him down with saddle soap and bucket-water, he lies there, sprawled on the ground at their feet, naked, helpless, shamed....

...He opens his eyes again to find himself back in the car. The sun has set and there's a picture-book moon hanging big and low in the sky. Some of the men down by the track are packing up the animals and others are moving off toward the campfires across the field, where the strains of a fife and drum band can be heard, now, the music haunting in the distance, with the fifes playing in strange, fractional intervals over the driving polyrhythms of the bass and snare drums.

Lot, meanwhile, is beside him and driving slowly over the rough ground heading back toward the road, muttering angrily to himself and peering around through the gathering dusk as though looking for someone. "...Peel his theivin' ass like a onion...! Mothafucka hitch a ride in my car and steal my money right from under my seat! If he think I'm gonna let him get away with that, he got another think coming...! Fuckin' grease monkey nearly even got me killed, cheating them nigguhs at dice and then telling'em I put him up to it! Shit, he done his last trick fo'sho, if I get my hands on him...!" When they reach the granite boulder marking the exit to the park, he stops the car and takes another look around.

Meanwhile, Rico Jones, sitting next to him, is feeling strangely calm. And clean. Smelling of saddlesoap and lily of the valley. He can still hear the voice of the woman in the green dress reverberating like an organ pipe in his inner ear.

Lot slips the clutch and the car turns past the boulder and starts back up the incline toward the high road. A breeze carries the odor of wisteria and damp river reeds.

At the top of the incline, Lot stops the car again and tilts his head, listening. He looks both ways, then drives slowly along the deserted road, where the only sounds are the chirp and rustle of birds settling down for the night. Then, there's another sound, a voice, low and plaintive. Lot inches the car forward until they pull abreast of a clump of sycamore, and stops again. The voice seems to be coming from just behind the trees.

"...One hard-luck, nigguh! Umph! ...Always messin' up! Shit! Every time... opportunity...dumb-ass mothafucka spoil it! Umph! ...Coulda rid all the way to Memphis. Memphis! Shit! 'Steada settin' out here in the fuckin' bushes -- Umph!-- 'thout a dime! No wheels, no scratch, no nuthin'! ...Your mama musta borned you under a ugly star! Don't -- Umph!-

- never have nothin' but hard luck, hard luck, all your life!
-- Oh sut!"

Lot has let the car roll quietly forward until they see him, Floyd, the gas station boy, alone and talking to himself, squatting with his pants around his ankles, taking a dump in the hollow of a tree. But as Lot pulls up the emergency brake, Floyd hears it and jumps to his feet. He's already running as Lot puts his leg out over the door, but trips on the pants hobbling his ankles and falls headlong. He scrambles up and takes off again, hopping from leg to leg, trying to pull up his pants as he goes, with Lot racing after him skirting the tangle of thornbushes at the edge of the road, until Floyd ducks through a gap in the bushes and Lot disappears after him. A moment later, Lot comes running back to the car, jumps in and makes a U-turn, barreling back down the graveled incline and skidding out onto the grass, where they see Floyd racing bare-assed over the field, apparently having lost his pants somewhere in the bushes. A group of men who've lingered at the track recognize him and make a grab for him, but Floyd dodges away, leaps the fence and strikes out across the track. Lot, driving right up to the fence, grabs a coach whip from one of the men and vaults the fence after him, lashing the younger boy across the back and the legs as he runs. When Floyd stumbles Lot tackles him and they go rolling among the rushes at the water's edge. But Floyd is soon up again and takes a header into the water, with Lot diving in after him.

When, after a moment, neither boy surfaces, the men nearby trot over towards where they were last seen. Others, hearing the commotion, begin drifting down from the campfires. Among them is a gaunt yet striking young woman carrying a little girl in her arms with two more hanging on to her skirts. An older woman marches heavily a few paces behind them. She has a face like scorched earth.

A voice cries out, and Jones sees Lot climbing out of the water dragging something after him. But the men standing over there shy back, wanting no part of it. Finally, a few go up to help and they pull the thing out of the water. It's a body, much larger than Floyd, who must have gotten away. Covering their noses with their shirttails and kerchiefs, the men stoop to examine it. One man turns away to vomit into the reeds. Two others go off toward the tack room behind the paddock and return a moment later with horse blankets and a set of leather traces. They roll the body into the blankets and carry it back, two lines of men moving awkwardly, trying to keep their distance from the bloated burden swinging in the traces between them with its arms reaching out to either side.

3.
The Deputy

Chief Deputy DelRay Hope was having his own problems with the heat. The steel ball joint in his hip had expanded, making him limp more noticeably than usual and at the same time uncomfortable sitting still to drive, and he'd been doing a lot of driving lately. And his phantom hand itched like hell. He could live with the limp but the itching was driving him up a wall. He hadn't been conscious of scraping the steel claw back and forth along the edge of the slab until he'd noticed the preacher glancing around curiously. Made aware of it now, a sound as of someone honing a blade against a stone, he gritted his teeth and put the offending arm behind his back, waiting for the woman to get done. But she wouldn't even raise her eyes to look at the body. For the last several minutes Lorna Rhoder had been just standing there staring at the concrete floor and shivering like a feral animal poised for flight. He thought he could understand how she must be feeling, seeing her husband lying dead on that slab beaten and bloated almost beyond recognition. But the trail was getting cold and he had a lot of ground to cover. The preacher had already given his statement. DelRay looked at him, a stocky, brown-skinned man named Sampson with eyes made large and a little too bold by the horn-rimmed glasses he wore. It hadn't escaped the deputy's notice that Sampson's manner seemed particularly tender as he put his arm around Lorna's shoulder and murmured in her ear, quietly urging her forward. Not that DelRay could blame him. She was a pretty attractive woman. Dark-skinned though she was and distracted by grief, with her hair uncharacteristically disheveled and her skirt twisted about her hips, you couldn't deny Lorna Rhoder had a certain elegance about her. The thought crossed his mind that Sampson, himself a widower with three small children, might be a little ambivalent about the death of Benjamin Rhoder.

A few minutes later, after the widow had finally given her statement of identification, he was walking toward the blue and white Mercury parked in the hospital driveway when the preacher called him back.

"Excuse me, officer, but is there any news?"

"What about?"

The man had used a respectful tone, but he had an air about him that rubbed the deputy the wrong way. Sampson was relatively new to the county and was gaining a local reputation for his fiery sermons. But the question in DelRay's mind was whether he was turning out to be an agitator, as well.

The preacher hesitated, "Well, Ben Rhoder was a deacon of the church, he wasn't the sort to go looking for trouble. Have you found out anything at all about who might've... done this?"

"We're looking into it." Privately, DelRay was thinking that unfortunate as it was, this had been a break, after all.

Rhoder had been missing for eight days -- and the Hill boy for two, so far, he reminded himself, though he still hoped the boy would prove to be only scared and hiding out in the woods somewhere. Whereas most of the Negroes who'd gone missing in LeVane over the years had not been found -- unless you counted the bones that occasionally turned up after a flood....

They were distracted by a sonic boom that momentarily dulled their ears and rattled the hospital windows. DelRay looked up to see the formation of new "Delta Daggers" zoom overhead on their regular morning test flight out of the High-ville Air Force Base. They were Convair F-102As, the fastest, most technologically advanced jet fighters in the world, he noted with a certain pride. They could climb to 53,000 feet, exceed 900 m.p.h., and had a range of over 1,100 miles. Within seconds, they were only bright specs disappearing into the distance, leaving vapor trails like cotton candy expanding across the sky. When he lowered his eyes again, the preacher had retraced his steps to his own car, in which the Rhoder woman sat waiting. DelRay rested his elbows on the open door of the cruiser and watched them drive off in the dusty secondhand Studebaker. Bumper stickers affixed to either side of the license plate read, "His Mercy is Everlasting" and "Sing unto Him a New Song!" Preoccupied, he tapped a fresh smoke from the open pack of Luckies in his shirt pocket and remained standing there a moment, holding the unlit cigarette in the prosthesis that had replaced his own right hand, and staring at it moodily. By dint of constant practice, he'd learned to do quite a few tricks with that claw. He could open a beer can without a church key, stop a line drive to the mound and even scratch his ass, now, without gouging an extra hole in it. But there were things that still bothered him. Driving back and forth across the county earlier, he remembered thinking the road signs had flashed passed like unpaid debts, Cut Off, Circle Center, Sweet Hog, Revenant.... But it'd also occurred to him that his own observation had sounded secondhand, like something out of the detective stories he'd been reading lately -- something he was a little ashamed of, because even as a kid he'd read more serious stuff. The back of the Merc was still littered with thumbworn old copies of Aviation, Sports Illustrated, American Rifleman -- and if truth be told, old Lash LaRue and Captain Marvel comics and girlie magazines, too, that he and Bee-Line had used to swap and spend whole afternoons together absorbed in when.... Out of the corner of his eye, he thought he saw someone watching him. Glancing around, he saw it was a doe, standing still as a statue in the bushes across the road. "...Her stillness can fool ya," he heard Bee-Line's voice whispering in his inner ear, "Sight up along that muscle behind her shoulder, but don't squeeze off till you feel you're bout to pee in her heart...." Him and Bee-Line had been born on the same day and had grown up in each other's houses, they'd fought for favor with each other's mamas and their daddies had taken a belt to either one of them more times than he could remember. But Bee-Line had proven the better man when it came to bagging game. They'd joined up for Korea together, too, him and Bee-Line, butt-fuck buddies, going off to kill Commies like they'd used to go fishing or hunting.... Well, he was a grown man, now, he reflected ironically, and a grown man was supposed to have his mind set on other things, on the hog at hand, as his pop used to say, and plans for the future. He wasn't supposed to be maundering on about the past, about friends and opportunities lost.... But in his old room back at the house, the notches were still there, carved into the windowsill for each of the girls he'd had in those days. Between himself, Dody, Al Junior and Bee-Line, he'd been the first one able to boast of having had at least one piece of ass in every town in the county. But that was less impressive than it might sound. LeVane was the third biggest county in the state by area, but it was mostly woods, water and plantations, the cotton fields stretching away seemingly endlessly, row after row, with the towns small, few and far between. Other than a few more TV antennas, it still looked pretty much the same. Except, the girls he'd known were mostly married and making babies, now....

"...Hi-i, DelRay!"

"Welcome back, stranger!"

He could hear their voices ringing clearly in his ears, as though they were standing right there beside him now. Two fresh graduates of Dividend High, in bobby socks and white buckskin shoes, stepping out of the shade of the marquee over the Royale, on Farraday, as he'd got out of the car. Making believe he hadn't recognized them, he'd tipped his hat and moved smartly toward the small red brick jailhouse next door to the theater, where the sheriff had his office. But the yellow-haired girl had crossed neatly in front of him, blocking his path and batting her eyes flirtatiously.

"Aren't you going to say hello?" she'd said, coming up close to feign a hug and run her orange ice pop along the back of his neck.

"Uh! Hello, Nancy! 'Lo, Sara Beth."

But as he'd ducked away, Nancy had slipped off his hat and then held it coquettishly behind her back, as she'd said, "You look real cute with your hair cut!"

"You coming to the Cotton Pickers' Ball, DelRay?" Sara Beth had chimed in, speaking between licks on the other half of the ice pop she'd been sharing with Nancy.

"Well, I don't think..."

"Farrah Lise was voted Queen of the Ball!" Sara Beth had continued, referring to her older sister. But it was hardly news, people all over town had somehow deemed it necessary to tell him the same thing.

"Uh-huh, I heard."

"She's been wondering when you were gonna stop by and congratulate her."

"Well, I've been kinda busy --"

"She hasn't decided on her escort, yet. A lot of boys been asking her, but she just can't seem to make up her mind. You know what I mean?"

He'd cleared his throat emphatically, as though to put an end to the conversation, but all he could think to say was, "Yeah, well, tell her I said hi."

"She still wears your ring."

"Whenever anybody asks her about it, she says she just never gets around to taking it off."

"That's what she says, anyway!"

"It makes the other fellas real jealous! You know what I mean?"

"I'll tell you what I think," Nancy'd said then. "Cross your heart and promise not to tell?" And as though prompting him to do the same, she'd drawn a finger slowly down and across her chest, giving him ample time to admire the pink tips of her new bra poking through the weave of a tight cotton sweater. He recalled that the last time he'd seen her, only four years before, she'd been half as tall and skinny as a rail. He'd finally managed to put a stern tone in his voice as he'd said, "Sorry, girls, the sheriff's waiting. Best you give me back my hat and run along, now!"

Making a wry face, Nancy had handed him back his Stetson and whirled away with an umbrella-step.

"Come see us, DelRay!" Sara Beth had said, speaking over her shoulder with a toss of her dark hair, in a gesture that had reminded him painfully of her older sister, as the two girls had sauntered off, with their matching blue and white ballerina skirts swinging saucily above their knees....

...And the boys had gone their own ways, too, he thought. Crazy Dody had moved to Shenoba County to practice law, Al Junior was now running his old man's hardware store up in Dancing. And Bee-Line was dead.

For much of the preceding nineteen months, it'd seemed like he, too, had died -- or died and come back as somebody else. But things could have been worse, he said to himself wryly. He'd only lost his right hand, after all, and he was a southpaw. He'd just pitched a shutout that weekend against the Shenoba Choctaws in his first start since he'd rejoined the county team. Skip a detail or two, he continued bitterly, and you might even consider him some kind of hero, they'd given him a medal, hadn't they? Ah, hell, maybe he would ask Farrah Lise to the ball. So what if he couldn't dance anymore, everybody said she still had a feeling for him. Driving around later, after meeting the girls, he'd found himself humming an old Bill Anderson tune and looking forward to stretching out that evening in a cool bath with a bucket of ice and a sixpack to watch Whitey Ford whip his whammy on Stan the Man. Until the car had hit a bump in the road and the familiar blinding pain had shot through his hip making him groan aloud in spite of himself, thinking, Yeah, boy, just you go on playing the fool in the woods, while the truth runs you down --!

-- What was it...? His mind had just made a leap to something that had struck him the previous morning. He'd woken up feeling almost human again, after the game, and had found a clean shirt and pinned on that chief deputy's badge, thinking, hell, maybe one day he'd even learn to be around other people again without feeling like a freak. And later, when he'd driven into town through the traffic circle around the Confederate monument, after an absence of almost four years, Main Street had looked so cozy it'd seemed unreal. From the low audible rattle of the old Philco air conditioner over the door of McCoomb's barbershop, where the good Judge Ed McCoomb, retired from the bench, kept his hand in presiding as the town's barber, all the way down to Laurel, the old whitewashed buildings behind the line of white oak and maple trees on either side, tinged red-gold in the sun, had looked somehow smaller and newly made. It had looked like a little candy town he'd only had to bite into to feel better. But when he'd driven up to the courthouse and seen the TV crews camped all over the lawn and reporters milling about, his mood had changed. He'd found the sheriff inside, bent over a reading table in the circuit clerk's office, with the clerk, Calley Donaghue, standing beside him, his bushy eyebrows now turned gray and twitching nervously behind his bifocals.

"What's up?" he'd said, when neither man had returned his greeting.

Cally had glanced up then, but had merely pushed his spectacles higher on his nose, without saying anything. Finally, Clooder had turned and studied him a moment, before saying, "You find those two belong to that burnt-out Chevy?"

"Not yet. But they can't have got far...." Curious, meanwhile, about what'd had the two men so engrossed, he'd glanced over the sheriff's shoulder, expecting to see something to do with last-minute preparations for the pretrial hearing of the Hill case that was to begin in a few minutes. The case had drawn the attention of the national news services because the boy was from up north and had only come down to visit for the summer, when he'd gone missing. But what he'd seen, instead, was just one of the old, well-thumbed, large green volumes of the county business records lying open on the table. Puzzled, he'd added, "Anyway, I don't suppose we'll get much out of those boys, they were only passing through."

"That's how most trouble gets here," the sheriff had said, turning back to his examination of the ledger, as though dismissing him.

It wasn't until he, DelRay, had taken a second look at the binder, that he'd realized some fifty or more pages had been neatly cut out, and Clooder was running his fingertips thoughtfully along the severed edges. "What's up?" he'd asked, again.

"I'd like to see those two in the jailhouse," Clooder had said then, over his shoulder, "before any more fires get started round here."

"Oh, well, personally, I don't believe --"

"What." Clooder, cutting him off, had stood up and turned on him impatiently.

He'd felt himself flush and bite his tongue to avoid answering in anger. He'd had to remind himself that he owed the man. "Bee," he'd said, finally, "I just don't think those boys had anything to do with it. Fact, I think one of them may actually be a local --"

"We'll find out what they had to do with it when we get ahold of them. By the way, what do you know about a nigro name of Robeson, or Robertson, something like that, new round here."

But he hadn't known the name.

"Long-ass nigguh in loud clothes, hangs around the Channel Cat."

"What about him?"

"Look into it, will ya?"

"Sure, Bee. What --?"

"I wanna know where he come from and how soon he's goin back there. May be just one more troublemaker than we need round here."

"Awright."

"Oh, and that little undertaker, Crouch," the sheriff had added, speaking confidentially as he'd walked him to the door, "if his name come up, don't you bother about that, just let me know, awright? You go on, now, to the jailhouse and bring those two boys back for the hearing." Then, as he'd turned to go, the sheriff had reached over and touched his arm. "Listen Del," he'd said then, in a softer tone, "later, after this little shindig is over," and he'd waved his hand dismissively in the direction of the reporters, who were then crowding into the courtroom down the hall, "I want you to meet me round by the office this evening. I want to take you along with me to a little get-together out to Thackery's place.

"Oh, now, hold on, Bee --"

"I know, I know," the sheriff had said, offering him a stick of Spearmint, which he'd declined, watching the sheriff put it into his own mouth as he'd continued, "but you know this is election time, and what I'm trying to teach you, son, police work's a business, just like any other business. I just want to introduce you to some of these political big shots blowin' their horns round here now. They might be some help to you, later on...."

There he goes again, DelRay had thought to himself, trying to treat him like the son he, Clooder, had never had. But he wondered, now, why that should have bothered him. Clooder and his daddy had been good friends. The two men had met in the Navy, serving together on the York-town, though Clooder, who was originally from Alabama, was younger. They had both earned the Navy Cross at Mid-way -- Clooder for helping to rescue a squadron of airmen trapped below decks when the damaged ship had been sink-ing. His father, who'd been trapped along with those airmen, had been grateful to Clooder for saving his life, and when he'd returned home to take up his old job as sheriff, he'd brought the younger man back with him and made him his chief deputy. They'd had some differences toward the end, but Clooder had always looked out for the family. It had been Branford Clooder, after all, who'd driven all the way out to the V.A. Hospital in Birmingham that spring and had burst unannounced through the doors of the rehabilitation ward to find him, DelRay, lying there digging himself into a hole of self-pity. Waving away his objections, the sheriff had clapped his own old chief deputy's star into his hand and had gruffly ordered him to "get what's left of your rear end back to Dividend on the double, because some fools down in Washington just raised the rock off a nest of rattlesnakes and trouble's brewing awready...!" DelRay had to admit to himself that Clooder'd been a pretty good sheriff, overall, and a natural born politician. He'd been sheriff ever since his father died, and had been uncontested in the last two elections. But something had changed. Maybe it was just him, or maybe it was the war. Or maybe it was lying there all that time in the V.A. hospital, afterward, with nothing else to do but think about the fact that if he'd made sure that Commie soldier had been really dead before giving the all-clear, he'd still be in one piece and Bee-Line would be alive.

When he'd decided to take the chief deputy's job, he'd bought Bee-Line's old Merc from the family on purpose to use as his patrol car, intending to keep it just like Bee-Line'd had it, with the rusty fishhooks in the floor, the old magazines, the cigarette burns in the upholstery -- even that nasty "souvenir" from back in the 'Thirties hanging on the rearview mirror that Bee-Line's daddy had given Bee-Line when he was kid -- everything that spoke of what he, himself, had always ignored or taken for granted, so he'd have it all right there before him, to remember....

A sudden shift in the breeze caught him unawares. It carried a fragrance that was like fresh bread baking. But he knew it wasn't bread, it was coming from the cotton gin two miles away. This was what he'd missed the most, he said to himself. Every year at this time, from late August through November, the smell of ginning cotton pervaded the surrounding countryside and left its trace of sweetness on the breath. This was what he'd really been missing, this feint, pervasive odor that his grandma used to say could make a prim mouth water and old men horny. This, and the way the late summer colors glowed in the long, slow light of the evenings, when the shadows seemed to reach to the far horizon....

The doe was gone, had probably slipped off into the woods behind the hospital. Maybe he was just tired, he told himself, and short on sleep. He'd been on the go steadily since he'd been awakened in the middle of the night by a call from the sheriff to drive out to the Rue to follow up that anonymous tip that Rhoder's body had been found. He'd already spent the previous afternoon combing the woods around there for traces of the missing Hill boy, after having driven out to the Brennan place to question the two suspects who worked there, Borden and Minton. Initially, they'd both come up with alibis, claiming they'd been with Brennan, working right there on the plantation that day. But their stories hadn't matched, and Brennan proved to be out of town at the time. Eventually, they'd both admitted to having driven the Hill boy out to Rue River the night before, although stubbornly maintaining they'd only given the boy a whipping and let him go, "only meaning to scare him," they'd said, "and teach him a lesson." The whole business made him sick to his stomach. Not to mention that he had his own grievance with that particular body of water. When he'd gone back to investigate the report about Rhoder, the only thing he'd been able to be sure of, by the light of his flash out in the dark field, was that it wasn't the Hill boy. The decay had been too far advanced and the body swollen up to half again the size of a full-grown man. Meanwhile, the two Negroes who'd discovered the body had been long gone. He'd been heading back to Dividend, when he'd crossed paths with the fire engines and had turned and followed them out to Ida Temple's whorehouse in the colored section. The house had already collapsed in flames by the time they'd got there, but the '47 Chevy the two Negroes had been driving when he'd stopped them earlier in the park, was sitting right out front, smoldering in the yard. And the outrageous Ida Temple, herself, was picking through the debris with a flashlight trying to save her lost valuables and cussin' left, right and center. He had to laugh, remembering how she'd acted as though it'd been his fault the damn car'd ended up on her property and she'd expected him to haul it away personally. Searching the ruins, he'd found the remains of a wheelchair, along with torch butts and empty buckets strewn about the grounds and the whole place reeking of gasoline. But the two Negroes had vanished. There'd been nothing in the Chevy but a few rusty tools and a trumpet locked in the trunk.

By then it had turned light, and he'd barely had time to shower and shave, before heading back to meet the preacher and Rhoder's widow at the morgue. Still, he wondered, in passing, why Lotrelle Dundee had come back. It had given him a start when he'd recognized the boy. He'd known the boy's daddy years ago, and he'd never really believed what they'd said about him. The investigation had pointed to him, but as far as he, DelRay, was concerned, that had been inconclusive -- with the boat lost. And yet, seeing the boy again had brought back all the old unanswered questions. At the time, he'd figured it was more than likely Lotrelle would have been too young to have known anything about all that, though, and after scrutinizing the older man in the wheelchair, who'd been with Lotrelle in the car, and deciding he wasn't from around there, he'd let them go. But fate seemed to want to put them back into his hands. Although he still didn't know

-- and this was something that bothered him, too, the fact that he'd never really made an effort on his own to find out -- just what it was he'd hoped to learn after all these years, he was beginning to feel it was something that, like it or not, couldn't be avoided. And all the driving around in circles was giving him a bad feeling. At one point, earlier in the day, he'd even thought for a moment he'd been hallucinating when he'd seen tiny shells exploding on the hood of the car. It was the rain. The sun had been bright and the shower only a thin veil between himself and the view to the north where, in his mind's eye, the flat fields of LeVane had given way to the low rolling hills of Korea, carpeted in brown winter grass and woven in barbed wire, with fortified ditches and enemy bunkers crisscrossing the terraced rice paddies that faded away into patches of dusky red and purple mist spooned out in the distance -- Until he'd heard Bee-Line's voice shouting in his ear and seen that "dead" soldier's arm swinging up again with the grenade like a black chrysanthemum opening in the air between them....

He bared his teeth at the memory. He'd had that nightmare a thousand times in the hospital and it still came back to him at odd moments, dreaming or wide awake. Lately, he'd been trying to make himself believe he'd just been drawn this way, like a character out of a comic book, half-steel and half-man, with a metal plate in his head, his jaw wired together with pins and his insides riddled with Kryptonite. He glanced down at the star, with it's paint barely dry, on the Merc's door, and put the cigarette between his teeth. Whatever it's gonna be, he told himself, he was going to follow those boys wherever they led him. Clooder's suspicions notwithstanding, he didn't think the two Negroes had come on purpose to make trouble. But he also knew that most any time a white man had to go looking for a black man, trouble followed like an ugly dog.

He managed to get one good spark from the Marine Corps Zippo, before the flint gave out.

Hunger's Season

4.
The Night At Ida's

Ida Temple paused with her hands in the air and scowled through the smoke of her cigarette into the silver-chased mirror. Goddamn headache, all this mess! she said to herself. Sonuvabitch come back two times sorry and four times guilty! And I fucked him anyway! Like a fever. All up my ass. Serve me right, I should of shit all over him! Stead, the feelings all shoved up, now, shut up again, like bile in the back of my throat. "Bitchin' ho!" she said aloud, spitting into a tissue and tossing it into the wastebasket, "I still got her taste on him in my mouth!"

Over her Carla of Hollywood peignoir, the red and white silk bandana looked ridiculous on her head. "Box plaid, for Godsake! Like I'm some kinda Aunt Jamima!" She snatched it off and threw it to the floor, but it seemed the rhinestone brocade on the open bosom of her nightgown winked at her in the glass.

"Hmn, that new preacher, Harold Sampson, dig my cakes, though, don'tcha, boy. Uh-huh, that bulldog just too shy to bite. But that's awright, honey, you take your time," she added, taking a deep breath herself and glancing around with some satisfaction at the mementos of jewelry, knickknacks and stuffed animals crowding the table tops, shelves and counterpane on the bed. "They all come round to Ida after awhile, preachers and all."

She meant to apply a cold cream rinse to remove her makeup, but in reaching for the jar she accidentally knocked over one of a matching pair of Venetian swans she'd brought back herself from her last trip to Italy. She caught it as it fell, but the neck broke in her hand, and she began cursing again -- at her own carelessness, when normally she was never careless! -- and at the memory of "that horse-faced sonuvabitch" who occupied her thoughts. And just where in the hell he at with that child this time of night! she wondered, glancing over at the empty crib standing against the drapes in the bay window. She should never've let him take it down to the hospital, the child's mother, poor woman, might've had a fit and done something to that baby! Shit, she said to herself, I hate it when I get this bad feeling!

"Whatcha gonna call'im?" she said aloud, ironically quoting the girl, Shawnette's, question into the mirror, and answered, silently, Nother barefoot nigger, what he be, no matter what anybody call him! With a bastard like he got for a father, he aint got much chance to be nothing else! Aint no wonder the mother ended up in the 'sane asylum. Willmore must be full of womens driven out they minds by crazy niggers. Nerve of him bringing that child to me in the first place! I aint got enough to deal with, now, I'm supposed to start running a orphanage! Back of my hand's still burning from when I slapped him upside his head...!

She shivered, as though at the touch of premonition, and glanced at the vanity tray, where a tangle of costume jewelry overflowed a large tooled leather box. Against the glimmer of genuine crystal perfume bottles, ornate silver-backed combs and hair brushes and 18-carat gold ornaments she had paid for and brought back from Europe herself, the faux pearls, glass "rubies" and semiprecious stones in the jewelry box, pasted into rings, bracelets and earrings with their silver and gold paint yellowed and peeling, looked even cheaper, if possible, than they really were.

Junk! Years wasted! she said to herself, too caught up in her bitter ruminations to notice the front doorbell ringing downstairs. Cheap, ugly shit I don't want, don't need, and sure as hell wouldn't keep, except to remind myself not to make a fool of myself for no nigger ever again! Men aint got no kind of idea what a woman want! They just drop the shit off as they pass through! And don't ask where they get it! She gave a snort of dry laughter, thinking, bastard's clothes even uglier than his presents! With a name like Virgil Robinson Pope, III, you'd at least expect him not to be so freakin' tacky! If that is his name. He lie so much, he probably don't even know what his real name is hisownself, no more! Talkin' bout having money to burn back East and being descended from the only landed freedmen in North Carolina! Shit, he don't sound like he come from North Carolina to me, he sound like plain LeVane County colored to me! Truth is, he aint got nothing but nerve, what he has! He got arrogance and wile and bad temper and sly ways and smooth words and meanness and double-dealing and ears like a mule and a heavy hand and a stroke like a jackhammer --!

Someone was knocking on the door, two and two.

-- Don't need no goddamn man around, anyhow, soiling my curtains, putting his feet up on my couch, rubbing hisself up against my cambrics --!

Knocking at the door again.

-- A shuck and sham, playing with his polka-dot tie between my legs, his big bald ugly cock standing up there, standing up and seem like never going limp and tired like no ordinary man, but like a devil born with brass balls and a railroad spike always afire and ready to scorch and ride --!

"Miss Ida?" Knocking louder again.

"Go way, don't bother me, Shawnette, I'm in no mood!"

"Got comp'ny, Miss Ida."

She grabbed an atomizer and fired it at the closed door. The heavy crystal cracked the door panel and bounced across the thick Persian carpet, coming to rest tauntingly upright and intact, against one scrolled maple leg of the chaise longue Robinson favored when he came.

"Miss Ida! You awright?"

"Shit! Child, what you know bout 'awright'? Tell the mothafuckas, whoever they are, to go fuck themselves tonight, I won't charge'em nothin'!"

"He said to tell you Dundee --"

"I don't give a shit if they was sent by Pope Pius!"

But Shawnette went away only to come back upstairs twice more to tell her that the fellow had a cripple in an open car shivering out there in the chill and they refused to leave.

By this time, the doorbell was making her madder anyway. Shawnette nearly jumped out of her high-heeled sateen mules when the bedroom door swung back against the wall with a crash and Ida Temple stood glaring down at her with smoke flaring from her nostrils.

"Cripple! You break up my night rest to come talking bout a cripple, now! At one o'clock on a Monday morning! Child, what on earth is wrong with you! What you think I'm running here, the Saint James Infirm'ry? Tsk, git out the way!"

The girl stepped aside, and Ida swept passed her to march down the lily-and-lavender-wallpapered hall through a bevy of startled girls. She paused at the head of the stairs with one hand on the newel and glanced back along the confusion of baby-blue, chartreuse, pink, black, red and violet negligees, and fixed her eye on one tall, slim girl the color of burnt butter who stood apart, naked as the day she was born.

"Marvella! How many times I done told you to cover your butt in this house! I buy you clothes good as mine," she said, grabbing at the puffed sleeve of another hapless girl within reach and waving the moiré silk as an example in Marvella's face. "If you nekked when you work, that's tween you and the john. Elsewise, I don't care if you sleepin' or shittin', you put something on, y'hear! This aint no jelly jamboree! This a respectable house!"

"Yes, Miss Ida."

"Don't lemme have to tell you again!"

"Yes, Miss Ida."

"Don't you 'Yes-Miss-Ida' me! You go do it!"

"Yes'm!"

Been meaning to get rid of that one for awhile, Ida thought to herself, proceeding down the stairs. Robbie been having his eye on her ever since I took her in. The only reason she'd kept the girl around this long -- besides the fact that the girl brought in a lot of customers -- was because she could keep an eye on the two of them while she had Marvella and Robinson together under the same roof. Marvella'd been behaving herself, but if she put her out, that man would be on her quick as a snake on a bird. She'd only have to go and cut'em both. I know what I'm gonna do now, though, she muttered to herself, crossing the foyer toward the front door. That other one, Gloria, done give me a good idea today. Aint nothing like a little jealousy to help keep the troops in line!

"We closed!" she snapped, as she opened the front door. "You understand 'Closed?' Now git your black ass offa my porch!" She slammed the door in the young man's face and turned away. But he rang again. Snatching the heavy turquoise vase full of flowers off the pier table, she turned back to the door. Without wasting words, this time, she simply opened the door and swung the vase at his head.

But the young man was fast, and to give him credit, she noted grudgingly, he had some style. He'd ducked and managed to slip the vase out of her hand in one neat motion as he spun around. "Whoa," he said, then, "hold up, ma'am!" and stood there drenched and presenting her with her own vase, right side up, long-stemmed yellow roses and all. "Just lemme explain --"

But Ida wasn't fooling. She stepped in with a straight left to his jaw that sent him sprawling against the porch rail, where he lost his balance and went over backwards into the flower bushes. As she turned to go back inside, a flash of lightning made her pause and look out again. There, at the end of the footpath, sitting up high in an old convertible, was a figure enthroned and glittering in the forked light like an image of the Devil in black granite. She went up to the railing to get a better look. But the figure was just a shadow now, in the dark, out at the edge of the porch light.

"Damn!" muttered the young one she'd punched, as he climbed out of the bushes, "Evil ole witch!"

She heard the tinkle of broken glass as she started down the steps. "Best you not break that vase, boy," she told him over her shoulder. "You aweady owe me for messin' up my petunias!"

Following the flagstone footpath down toward the car, she went up close and peered at the man in the wheelchair, taking in the livid, runic welts on his scalp where patches of grizzled hair, like encroaching moss, had begun to grow again. She couldn't guess his age, his gnarled head seemed ancient. He was only skin and bone, but his bones were big as hammers and even in the dark his skin had sheen. Without moving his head, his eyes swiveled round to probe at her.

"You bringing me a death," she said. "Aint you."

✳ ✳ ✳

An hour later, she sat in her parlor staring in grim silence at the man in the wheelchair and twisting the rings round and round on her fingers. She'd laughed in the young one's face when he'd told her he'd been drawn into a fight against his will with some men shooting craps at the fair, but when he'd started talking about finding the body, she'd hustled them into the house, for fear someone would overhear. She'd acted against her own better judgment, and she was already having second thoughts. She'd known that the church deacon had been missing for over a week, and from the boy's description, guessed that it had been his body they'd found. If they'd known what was good for them, she thought, they'd have kept on driving, straight out of the county. Though she also knew it was true, what the young one said the other men had told him out at the bogue, that Negroes from other parts who were found on the LeVane roads at night were likely to be arrested just on "suspicion," if they weren't caught first by some roving band of mean-spirited whites. It had been a bad summer around there and most anybody might be taken for an outside agitator. She had no business sticking her neck out, either, she thought, cause it wasn't any safer in a whorehouse than anyplace else in town. The troublemakers in Dividend didn't like her anyhow for being so successful -- not to mention for having the occasional white client sneaking round, like the judge and that high and mighty Mr. Thackery. It wouldn't surprise her if somebody came beating on her door in a minute looking for these two. Yet, when the boy had finished telling his story, he'd stood there staring at her and shifting from one foot to the other, shivering and looking so pathetic.... She'd forbidden him to sit in any of her chairs because his clothes were still wet and dirty from the bogue, but she'd finally gotten up and led him to the bathroom to wash up, bandage his wounds and change into some clean clothes. Then, he'd had the nerve to turn around and ask her whether she thought her girls could try and do something for the cripple before the two of them left next morning, maybe the girls might make the poor man feel a little better about himself one last time, he'd said, before he put him in the hospital! That had only made her mad again, and she'd cut him with a look and walked away without a word.

Now, she was sitting there brooding and trying, unsuccessfully, to comfort herself with her beloved copies of nudes by Delacroix, Renoir, Bonnard, Denis and Vuillard, with their reflections glowing in the full-length mirrors that covered the doors and lined the walls around them. Most of what the boy had told her was probably true, she thought, though far as the cripple was concerned she didn't know anything about baseball and couldn't have cared less. God knows, she said to herself, it didn't take any luck to find a body in the waters around here! So many Negroes had "disappeared" in LeVane County over the last few years that colored folk were shy of fishing. She was sorry about the deacon, but at the same time, she had to admit she was somewhat relieved. Ben Rhoder and his schoolteacher wife had been bringing trouble on all of them by going around asking people to sign those school integration petitions. But now, she was going to have to make up some excuse to tell the sheriff when he found out, as he almost certainly would, that these two had been there. She shook her head, thinking, again, that she should never have let them in.

She looked up now, as the boy returned from the bathroom. He was a lot better-looking cleaned up, she thought, tall and broad-shouldered, with clear, wide-set eyes and a mischievous dimple in his chin. There was something about him that looked familiar now, too -- though, for the moment, she couldn't decide whether or not that was in his favor. And yet, when she finally spoke, the sharpness in her own voice surprised her.

"You heard me, what you come here for!"

The boy, taken aback, gaped at her. "I just...like I said, I just wanted a place to --"

"Yeah, you-all just want someplace to hang out, huh? I should let this one have some lovin' on charity, and what about you? I suppose all *you* want to do is *sleep*?"

He hesitated, then nodded, "Yes ma'am, just a few hours. I aint got much money, but here, you can have whatever I got." He pulled the few dollars out of his pocket and held it out to her. "We going to Memphis in the morning."

She turned to look at the other one, glaring back at her from the wheelchair. She didn't like that one. Not because of the anger in his eyes. All the Negroes coming to her these days had anger in their eyes. But this one was worse. His whole presence seemed forbidding. He was huge and craggy, like something from before the Flood. With all his scars and the wasted look of undernourishment and abuse, just sitting there in the wheelchair, crippled and unable to talk, he dwarfed everything else in the room. His image, reflected in the mirrors, crowded her thoughts, his mood pressed in upon her, his blackness made all her colors pale.

She suddenly rose from the piano bench and flung the front door open, not even sure, herself, why, except maybe intending to order them out of the house again. But the lightning was still there. She stood watching its crooked white fingers raking the horizon, knowing -- and not-knowing -- what it might mean.

She turned out the porch light, closed and latched the door, and went to the bottom of the stairs to call the girls.

But they were already there, waiting expectantly on the landing.

"Marvella, Gloria, Mama-Girl...and Shawnette. Come on down here, lend a hand. The rest of you go on back to bed."

The girls exchanged glances, but did as they were told. With the help of the four girls, they got the older man out of the wheelchair and carried him upstairs into Marvella's room. The girls gave the boy lingering don't-go-away looks, but he only smiled and went back downstairs. Ida dismissed Shawnette, and took the other girls aside.

"Don't know what he can do," she said. "But the man need some good news. See that he get it."

The girls went back into the room and closed the door. Ida stopped at the head of the stairs and looked down into the parlor, where the embroidered period chairs and tables she'd special-ordered from Galeries La Fayette in Paris stood cozily arranged.

"Git yo' feets offa my furniture!"

The boy looked up, startled, and lowered his leg from the arm of the recamier sofa where he'd sprawled out to relax.

Sonuvabitch, Ida thought to herself, I gotta bite my own tongue to keep from screaming. It was only ten years ago when they'd run some of the Negroes out of this part of town for getting too uppity! All they'd been trying to do was get the county to give them a couple dollars to buy books for the kids in the Negro public school. But when they got turned down, they started coaching folks to register to vote, so they could petition again after the elections. That was Fontana got that started. Fontana had a reputation, they'd warned her about him. But he was a good-looking widower trying to bring up his boys all by himself. He was lonely, he'd told her. And she could tell he was intelligent, he'd saved his money and had bought that little piece of land he'd been working for Thackery, and he'd been sober whenever he'd come around, so she'd let him come. Fontana Dundee had been the first one she'd let into her own bedroom from the day she'd moved into this house -- which had been only fair, since he had given her a little help with the down payment -- Jesus God! she muttered aloud, and looked down again at the young man asleep on her sofa, suddenly realizing who he must be. He was Fontana's boy, the one used to come around blowing that tin horn all the time, like to drive her crazy. Now it was all coming back to her. In the end, she'd had to bar Fontana from coming round the house. There was folks said they didn't believe he'd done any killing, but she couldn't afford to take the risk, she'd had to protect the reputation of her house. And then, early one morning they'd found him crashed into that tree with his clothes reeking of whiskey and the car littered with empty bottles. The sheriff'd called it suicide, but she knew better. They'd all warned Fontana about that voter registration business. The car'd even been set afire, but the rain had put it out. County Welfare sent the boys-them off to the orphanage....

And now, this one come back. But what would he be coming back here for? she wondered, narrowing her eyes. There wasn't nothing here for him. And she'd be willing to bet the police is after him, too. Things been nice and quiet since Fontana died. People had other things on their mind, including the war. By the middle of Fifty-One, there'd been hardly any healthy black boys left, they'd all run off to join the army and go to Korea. Not that you could blame them. Soldiering paid a right smart more than any other work they could get around there, and they didn't have patience to chop cotton for thirty cents a day anymore, like their daddies. Meanwhile, she'd had more choice of ripe young women than she'd known what to do with. With all of the men gone, the women had wanted to leave, too, and turning tricks was the fastest way to earn bus fare. Just fortunately for her, the white boys over to Highville

Air Force Academy took a taste for poontang, and she'd had three houses going by the time they'd signed the peace. Pretty good years, all in all. When the war was over, she'd figured the black boys would come back and pick up the slack. But they hadn't. Most of those that hadn't got themselves killed overseas had chosen to discharge straight out to Chicago or Detroit or New York. Lord Almighty, she said to herself, she'd thought all the bad time was behind her, and now, here this one come bringing trouble back to her door again...!

Well, she was just going to have to make up her mind. Business had been so bad, lately, she'd been giving some serious thought to packing up and going north herself. She had a cousin in Kansas City would help get her started. Because if she stayed, she was going to have to refinance her mortgage, and she knew sly old Tom Crouch was going to try and gouge her. On the other hand, she also knew Crouch wouldn't want that dicty wife of his, with her pinched nose and her straightened hair piled up on her head like scrap iron, to know about his little side-trips here to see Mama-Girl. But, stop right there, she said to herself. That's another thing been bothering her, lately. What was the two of them doing out there in the car? She'd happened to look out the window one morning, earlier in the week, and had seen Crouch's shiny black Cadillac sitting across the street. It wasn't his usual day, which was what had made her curious to look again. Then, she'd seen Robinson sitting in the car next to him, and that had really got her going, because those two dogs weren't likely to run together. She wouldn't have imagined them even knowing one another. They hadn't stayed there long, they'd just sat in the car talking a minute, then driven off. She'd meant to ask Robbie about it when he'd come in this morning, but then she'd found out about him fooling around behind her back, and had got off on that and forgotten about Crouch-them. And come to think of it, she reminded herself, where the hell was

Robbie with that baby child of his this time of night, anyway? She didn't think the sanatorium would let the mother keep it overnight. And he best not have took it over to that other old ugly bitch he been fooling with, she said to herself, cause if he do, I'll know! That nigger been acting mighty strange, lately. I'm gonna have to straighten him out quick. I got enough on my mind! Why the fucking peckerwoods gotta start they shit all over again now! she said to herself. Hassling innocent folks just minding their own business. Then they go and kidnap that poor child, Morris Hill, from out his uncle's house, right down the street, here. A child! And God help him, cause aint nobody seen him since. And now, Ben Rhoder. Jesus, Mary and Joseph! Why can't they just leave us alone! Wish to God somebody'd go and beat-up on them for a change! Shoot them and cut them up and burn their houses down, see how they like it!

The creak of the floorboard startled her. She whirled around to see a girl in a pair of chocolate pajamas trying to slip back into Marvella's room.

"Shawnette!"

The girl came out on the landing rolling her eyes.

Ida nodded her head toward the young Dundee boy below, fast asleep with his arm flung over his eyes and his leg up on the arm of the sofa again.

"Put him in the spare room downstairs and give him a blanket."

Shawnette peeked over the banister, but on hearing Lot snore, she gave a pout of disappointment. "Is that all?"

"That's all he's payin' for!"

Back in her own room, Ida started to check on the baby out of habit, then stopped and stared at the empty crib a moment, before turning out the lamp. She still had that bad feeling she couldn't account for. She lay awake for some time listening to the feint strains of music coming from the radio down the hall. And she thought she was still awake, when she began to dream of...

...Being a child at home again, sitting in her daddy's lap out in the front yard. She was crying because somebody had scattered peanut hulls in the yard and she thought it was going to bring them bad luck. But her daddy strummed the banjo and, giving her a nuzzle, began to sing her a song.

> *"The birdy say, 'Chit, chit, chit,'*
> *The cow go, 'Moo, moo, moo,'*
> *The donkey say, 'Honkit, honkit, honkit,'*
> *And the farmer boy look at the lil pretty girl,*
> *With her eye so brown and her hair so curl,*
> *And he say, 'Lil girl, I love you, yes, I do-o-o!'"*

She put her arms around his neck and pulled herself up to put her lips close to his ear, and whispered, "I love you, too, daddy. And you know what? When I'm growed up..." and she made him one of their secret promises. But a woman stood at the sink in the kitchen looking out at them through the window. The expression in her eyes was hidden in shadow. It should've been her mother, but it wasn't her mother, it was herself suddenly grown up. And she could see, through the unhinged wooden gate out front, a donkey standing there, reaching down over its breastband to chew on the cornflowers. While the man in the yard strummed the banjo and rocked the little girl gently on his knee, she could hear the wheels of the cart behind the donkey creaking.

> *"This old wood house keep out the wind,*
> *The grain is straight, the beams is strong.*
> *This old wood house been up so long*
> *The oldest singer with the oldest song*
> *Tell how the cotton, afore the 'gin,*
> *Growed all around the windows, in*
> *The shade and in the sun..."*

Make up a happy end for the child, she said, in her mind, she'll be knowing soon enough where you gone. I can see The Man's fist on the rein. He don't waste horses on blackfolks. And that donkey's ears throw a long shadow, like a knife and fork across the dooryard....

...While, in his own dream, Lot was deep down swimming in waters thick as blood and tasting of cinders. He had no pole or line, he was fishing with his bare hands. The current was strong, faces he knew and didn't know, his mother, his brothers, strangers, flowed past like bubbles along the muddy bottom. Everything clung to him, reeds, eels, crawfish, old clothes and bad habits, all entangled, dragging him down. He'd done this before, has been doing it over and over again. Suddenly, as he was on the verge of knowing who he'd been searching for, a hand touched his face --!

"Ahh!"

He woke up swinging his fists. He didn't know where he was for a moment, the parlor, with its overstuffed chairs, mirrors and fancy lamps confused him. And the girl in the negligee, sitting across from him rubbing her wrist, must, he thought, be a hallucination, something left over from the dream.

But then, she spoke, "You awright, honey?"

"Uh! Yeah. Yeah, I'm awright. Did you --?"

"I just touched your face," she said, speaking at the same time. "I didn't mean no harm."

He waved it away, "No, that's okay. Sorry, if I --"

"That's awright." She smiled, a pretty smile, "it's nothing."

They sat looking at each other a moment, as though uncertain what to say next. Lot thought she couldn't be much over seventeen. At one point, she started to speak, then glanced up at the second floor landing, and thought better of it. He turned to follow her glance, but no one was there. Ida and the other girls had gone to their rooms.

"What's your --?"

"I'm Shawnette --!"

They'd spoken again at the same time, and laughed.

"I'm Shawnette," she said again, fiddling with the hem of a blanket she had folded under her arm. "What's your name?"

"Lot."

She nodded, but seemed puzzled.

"You're a pretty girl, Shawnette."

She smiled, again, showing a full set of good teeth, "You aint half-bad, yourself." She looked at the bandages on his face and arm. "You were in a fight, huh? You sure you're awright?"

"I'm fine." He gazed at her a moment with a flattering hunger, then said, "That blanket for --?"

"You want me?" she blurted out at the same time, then threw her hand up before her face, but he didn't know whether it was because she'd embarrassed herself by what she'd said or because she had interrupted him again.

He laughed and looked at her mischievously, then shrugged his shoulders, "Empty pockets, baby."

"Shoosh!" She put a forefinger to her lips, and with another glance up at the landing, leaned forward with a childlike earnestness, as though unaware of the womanly cleavage filling the scoop neck of her gown, and whispered, "You wanna open a charge account?"

-- Hundreds had come down out of the stands to whoop and holler and waltz Rico Jones, the Anchorman, around on their shoulders. But his own attention was fixed on a woman with a crown of black hair sitting quietly by herself above the dugout staring back at him out of luminous brown eyes. So, she's come back, he thought, come back, after all --!

"...She say he can hear, but I don't think he can do nothin'!"

"Shut up, fool!"

"Damn, Mama-Girl, don't you know no better'n to talk in front of the man like that?"

Jones is lying on the bed naked and being poked and prodded like a mud doll or a hoodoo fetish cast by ignorant witches. They've lowered the lamp until the light barely glows through its hand-painted shade, and now they stand there staring at him as though he's something they'd dug up from the earth that's brought a chill into the room. Finally, the big one, humming off-key to the Frankie Lyman tune on the radio, pushes off and starts toward him, her loose, heavy breasts swinging like hanged heads under her slip. The short one they call Gloria, almost as black as himself in her see-through brassiere and panties, comes next, showing him her teeth and slitting her eyes, which glitter violet in the lamplight. Cooing at him, as though he's a child, or a beast to be tamed, the two start to undress him, the big one unbuttoning his shirt, the small dark one opening his trousers and undoing the boot laces.

-- He'd stepped up to the plate with the bases loaded and two out in the bottom of the twelfth. The Monarchs were losing four to two and he was supposed to be their big gun. Except that he'd been in a slump for three weeks and popped up and grounded out his last three times up. But by then, he'd realized that the opposing pitcher had been using frozen baseballs. Pitchers in the Negro leagues were still known to do that sometimes, freeze the balls overnight to deaden them when facing heavy-hitting opposition. But it was a trick he knew that particular pitcher, John Wright, would never have stooped to in the old days, when he'd first known him as a young and promising right-hander. Wright still had a mean knuckler and a serious fastball and he'd pitched no-hitters back-to-back his last two games. He bore down with a fastball to open, and Jones watched the ball, looking no bigger than a pea, sizzle and skip over the plate like a mad hornet, crossing the inside corner at his knees. Strike one. Wright, letting slip a smile, leaned over to get the sign for the next pitch. Seven years earlier, Wright had been the second Negro hired into white baseball, when he'd been signed by the Dodgers organization along with

Jackie Robinson. But it hadn't lasted. Meanwhile, Jones, preoccupied with the thought that for all he knew, that might be his own last time at bat, found himself gaping at a knuckler crossing the plate for strike two. Harris, out in right field, moved in shallow and began scratching his armpit and wiggling his hips, giving Jones the monkey sign. Harris had "accidentally" spiked Jones's teammate, Frank Barnes, sliding into second base two innings earlier. As Jones chewed this over, Wright wound up for the third pitch. In 'Forty-Seven, after only one season, Wright had quit white baseball, unwilling, he'd said, to put up with the ostracism and abuse. Jones watched the ball jitterbug toward him on the next pitch, coming in high and wide, and he stepped over -- "... Integration, my ass!" Wright had told him, when he'd seen the pitcher again, back in the Negro leagues in 'Forty-Eight. "I don't want to be integrated with them! Fuck the mothafuckas! They aint nothing but animals! They talk about the Communists and the iron curtain, but they've had a curtain of shame stretched across this U-S-of-A for four hundred years! But they better look out, man, cause that curtain's coming down! Oh, yeah! We gonna tear that sucker down, and when we do, aint nobody gonna sleep good, because what they don't realize, anything kept in a cage is only biding its time...!" -- The ball took off with a solid knock on a high line drive to right field. Harris, caught off-guard, started racing back for it. Minutes later, when Jones crossed home plate behind the other three runners, Ernie Banks grabbed his hand and ran him around the bases again to celebrate. It wasn't until they'd stepped across the plate the second time, that they'd realized Harris was hurt. He was stretched out on the grass below where the ball had sailed into the stands, having run himself head first into the right field wall --

The tall, tawny one was first out of her clothes, but she's been standing to one side as though waiting for something. Now, as the other girls remove Jones's boots and they fall to the floor one after the other with the hollow ring of discharged artillery casings, she reaches up, her long, lithe silhouette arched against the dull glow of the lamp, and begins running her fingers through her light brown hair until she has it crackling with static electricity.

"...Sent for you yesterday," sings a familiar voice on the radio...But today is way too late...! Jones is thinking. And yet he can't control the memories that barge in now confusing the present with disconnected moments from the past...

-- Lester was up on the bandstand blowing choruses, holding his horn out like it was too hot to handle, and spinning his sly, lingering phrases out in that over-and-beyond-the-beat way he had, while Jimmy Rushing, clean and cool, sat at the table with Jones swirling the drink in his hand and trying to cut Lester, scatting back at him from across the room. -- The boy'd lied. Jimmy was too dignified to set foot on a ballfield after he'd put on all that weight. -- Frank Barnes, Ernie Banks and himself, they were all there, at the Sunset Club on Twelfth and Highland, celebrating because all three had been called up to the majors for the following season. Frank was going to the Cardinals, Ernie to the Cubs, and he, Jones, to the Braves. Piney Brown, bringing them another round of drinks on the house, cracked a joke about Jones having already been initiated by having spent a night in the Milwaukee jailhouse. He'd gone up to visit with the Braves the previous weekend and had got arrested for unwittingly taking a Saturday night stroll on the wrong side of town. But at least it wasn't going to be like the previous year, he thought to himself, when the Braves, still in Boston then, had withdrawn their offer to Elston Howard because they'd been afraid Howard was going to be drafted. This time, the papers were full of the peace talks in Panmunjom. The war would be over any day, they said, now. And besides, he, Jones, had already collected his medals at Normandy, the last time around --

"...Mmmm, yumm! Am I giving you pleasure, baby? What you like, huh? You wanna taste some pussy? Move over, Mama-Girl."

The fat one, who's been lying on top of him and smothering him with her huge breasts reeking of cheap jasmine cologne and licorice taffy, heaves off him, while the small dark one slithers up to squat above his head and rake her coals over his face, her taste like soured wine.

-- But three weeks after the celebration in the Sunset Club, a cop had shown up at Muehleback Park in the middle of a night game against the New

York Cubans. The noise from the night-light generator in left field had been so loud that Tom Baird, the team's owner, had to send Frank Barnes down the line to call him in. Downtown, the Kansas City police chief told Jones he was wanted in Milwaukee for robbing a gas station and shooting the attendant. The gas station had happened to be a few blocks from where he'd been arrested up there. According to the police report, the robbery had occurred hours after he'd already been in jail, but that didn't seem to make any difference to the police. He fit the wounded attendant's description of the robber, the cop told him, "a big black nigger." "On the other hand," the police chief added, "Milwaukee aint done me no favors, lately. And you aint been no trouble round here, in fact, the young colored boys seem to look up to you. I seen you play some pretty-fair ball out there, with them Monarchs. So, mebbe we can work out a little something here...." The cop gave him a choice. Jones could go back to face trial in Milwaukee, where, in the chief's words, "they been known to hang a nigguh for less'en a lil robbery." Or, if Jones felt he wanted to make a voluntary contribution to the Kansas City Police Community Chest, it just might be possible for him to reenlist in the army and be out of town by the end of the week, before the understaffed local police force could catch up with him --

The whores, not getting any response from him, have started to come on to one another. Two lay beside him on the bed primping and petting and kissing each other, and rolling their eyes at him in the dim cartoon-red-and-blue lamp light, while the tall one stands over him tossing her head, her long electric hair shooting sparks like tracer bullets into the shadows.

-- When the train had pulled into Baltimore, after the sheriff and his deputy, who'd beaten him, had put him aboard in Darden, he'd been unconscious. Tom Wilson, the Baltimore Elite Giants' owner, had met him at the station and taken him straight to the hospital. His skull had been fractured and he'd had several bones broken. Jax, his kid brother, had telephoned long distance, Wilson told him, and Wilson had called a lawyer he knew of in Washington. But it wasn't until he'd finally gotten out of hospital and had gone to see the lawyer himself that he found out what had actually happened

back in Alabama. Fleece, the lawyer, told him the whiteboy, John Lee, had apparently been down at the train station trying to earn extra money by snapping pictures of any strange Negroes who came through town and turning them over to the sheriff, in hopes of collecting a reward if any of them turned out to be fugitives. It was John Lee that he'd been accused of murdering. But the lawyer said he, Fleece, had managed to call in some favors and get a statement from the engineer of the S&P express to the effect that John Lee had been alone when he'd run out onto the tracks and he'd simply ignored or not heard the train whistle. The boy's death had clearly been an accident. With the railroad engineer's statement in hand, Fleece had then called long distance to Sheriff McKeller, in Dardan, and acting as though he, Fleece, had been just another good ole boy who'd known the sheriff half his life, he'd said to him, "That you, Sheriff? This is ole Mort Fleece, doing some lawyering down here in Washington. Been out your way a few times. Understand you picked up a nigra fella last week, something to do with poor ole Clem Bledsoe's boy, got hisself killed by a train there. Well, the thing about it is, that nigra fella's aunt works for me, don'tcha see...." The lawyer waved his hand in the air, a gesture implying that Jones could probably fill in the rest of the details himself, and leaned back in his chair to blow a smoke ring at the ceiling. His full name, according to his card, was Colonel Mortimer Mount Zion Fleece, Esquire. He was originally from Tuskegee, he said, and over the years he'd made a bit of a name for himself in the federal circuit. Dwarfed by the huge distressed mahogany desk upon which he rested his feet, the sly old councilor gave Jones a long, appraising look, then reached down and pulled a bottle of whiskey out of a drawer and gestured toward the box of Havanas on his desk. He'd always been keen on baseball, himself, he said. At one time, he'd even had hopes of playing shortstop professionally, but his father wouldn't hear of it. "I'd wanted to be like you," he said, "and like Joe Louis and Jackie Robinson, you guys are the new heroes of the race." Fleece went on to speak of his own early experiences as a young lawyer making his way, and told him how he'd come by his title. He'd never been in the military service, but from the time he'd gotten his law degree and set up practice, the whites back in Tuskegee had taken to calling him "Colonel," because they just hadn't been able to bring themselves to call a Negro "Mister." He'd retained the title, he said, because a black man needed a sense of irony to prosper in this world. They sat together for some time, sipping generous shots of good Jack Daniels, neat, and talking of one thing and another, while the sun went down over the bay outside the windows and the high, coffered ceiling filled with smoke, until their conversation came back to where they'd started, the problem that had brought them together and that in all their talking they'd only circled, like a sacrificial stone, leaving them silent and staring into the darkness, grim as reapers --

One of the women is drawing her fingernails back and forth across his chest, and whispering close in his ear, "Hey. Man. Big. Strong. Black. Man. I know you're there!" It's the tall, tawny one, Marvella, whispering in his ear, "You don't gotta say a mumblin' word. Big. Strong. Black. Man. I'm gonna find your love hand...!

-- The Monarchs had thrown a big party for him after the game, and presented him with a fourteen-carat gold baseball inscribed, "To Da Mostest, Rico 'The Anchorman' Jones, B.M.F." Some of the musicians he'd met during the season had shown up, too, including Jimmy, Basie, Lester in his porkpie, and Jo Jones, whom he'd met earlier, back in Birmingham, where they'd had friends in common. It was Jo who'd surprised him by bringing Venus. He and Venus hadn't seen each other in over a year, not since she'd walked out on him the last time. But after the first awkward moment, when they'd stood facing each other without speaking, and feeling like strangers who'd been in love in some other lifetime, he took her in his arms and knew he wasn't going to let her go again until the Army tore him away and shipped him off to Korea --

...Marvella has moved in close, misconstruing the violence in his eyes, and with her head bent low over him, she's drawing the length of her hair up and down along his body. She seems to think that he only wants to raise hell, to get the blood to catch fire and his useless, outsized limbs to swell up with their old force and let the good times roll. To stand up. Fight back. Be the Black Warrior promised. Her hair-ends sputter over his chest like a strafing...

-- *He wants to stay there, with Venus, now, in his mind, but his mind won't do his bidding, as though there's something it doesn't want him to remember. And suddenly, he's in Seoul, where he'd spent his last night of liberty walking the streets at the edge of the city. He remembers a small park, up on a hill, full of trees decorated with colored paper, gifts to the Korean tree spirits. The city had been ravaged, changing hands four times in the war, and yet, a few of the old Choson Dynasty palaces still stood, strange to him but beautiful in their way, colored saffron by the girdle of lights remaining and the moon that illuminated the white granite mountains like a coliseum around them.... When he'd reported back to Company B, on the main line of resistance, the lieutenant announced an attack on Hill 773 for the following morning. Again, he thought. Hill 773 was the eastern snub-end of a line of ridges called "Bloody Ridge," where the network of enemy trenches along the ridgeline looked like a cotton field plowed by a mule with the staggers. Individual hills of the ridge had been captured, lost and recaptured a dozen times during the stalemate over the preceding year. Hundreds of Chinese were known to be hunkered down up there, protected by small artillery and mortars. Attacking from the valley below the hill, you were likely to be in their laps before you knew it. The slopes, partially covered with ming trees and dry scrub, were seeded with mines and the enemy bunkers camouflaged behind a double-apron of barbed wire...*

> *"Coal black Cora, she's full grown,*
> *She's full grown,*
> *She's full grown,*
> *Jumps on a weenie like a nigguh on a pone,*
> *And licks it clean like an ice cream cone...!"*

The dogface manning the BAR in the forward listening post was singing to himself again. Jones recognized him in the gathering dusk by the sound of his voice and the corny patch on his jacket that, like a special invitation to a Commie bullet, said, "American by birth, Southern by the Grace of God." He was a white Marine corporal from the Delta, who'd gotten separated from his own regiment two weeks earlier, when the Chinese had made a sur-

prise night attack on the Marines' position while he and his buddy had been out scouting a diversionary force. He'd been sitting next to his dead buddy in a ditch, delirious and half-starved, singing the same stupid song, when Jones had found him. His buddy had swallowed the muzzle of his own M-1 rather than be captured by the Chinese. Now, the kid was fighting with the Third Infantry until they could transfer him back to his own outfit. But it was Jones's hard luck to have had the boy assigned to his platoon, for he turned out to be an arrogant son of a bitch, who'd assumed that a white Marine corporal was just naturally superior to a colored Army Technical Sergeant. His only saving grace, to Jones's mind, was a sizzling spitball. When they'd been behind the lines one afternoon, the Marine had struck out five guys in a row, and had got 2-and-0 on Jones, himself, before he'd slammed the boy's next pitch right back past his ear -- unfortunately, lining it straight through an open tent flap into the officers' mess.

"Shut up," Jones whispered, slipping into the foxhole beside the Marine. "You wasn't put out here to be a dicky-bird for the Chinks, Ace!"

The Marine glanced around, then made a show of blowing an imaginary fleck of dust off the barrel of the Browning before he replied, "Evenin', Sarge."

They stood the first watch together, staring out over No Man's Land, while Red River Valley and Till I Waltz Again With You blared weirdly at them from loudspeakers up on the ridge. The music, sung by Chinese vocalists and played on Chinese instruments, was supposed to be demoralizing. The Americans laughed at it, but it wasn't without effect. Later, "fireflies" droned overhead dropping illuminating flares for friendly artillery that began to pound the hill in preparation for the next morning's attack --

...Marvella's tracing his eyes, the bridge of his nose, his cheek with a fingertip. Jones sees the faint line of mustache hair on her upper lip spread into a smile. Long and sinewy, with small breasts, angular hips and eyes like bloodstones, she straddles him, leans over and tries to read what is hidden behind the mask that is his face. Then with a strange instinct, she reaches down and takes hold of his good fist...

-- *When he opened his eyes, the muffled sounds of friendly artillery could still be heard through the sandbagged walls of the bunker. It was damp and chilly, despite the Yukon stove smoking in the corner. Outside, it was raining. All he could see in the pale light were the rice paddies, terraced above the stream in the valley, and the first line of trees. The rest was fog. 0400, July 26th, 1953. Stalin had died in February. The generals sitting around the table in Panmunjom had decided that the armistice would go into effect the next day. But the soldiers out on the MLR didn't know that. And an hour later, his platoon was up to its knees in yellow mud climbing toward the first knoll, when he was suddenly knocked on his ass by shrapnel from a Chinese mortar. His flak jacket had protected him, the shoulder wound only superficial. But he'd lost his helmet and the spool of wire he'd been carrying for the sound-powered telephone. He saw it rolling down the hill and started down after it, only to see it blown away by another shell. Turning back to resume the charge, he saw one of his own men killed and another wounded trying to work their way to a saddle below the last knoll, fifty feet from the enemy trenches. Fog lay over the crest of the knoll, but he could see the muzzle flashes of the enemy small-arms fire bursting out of it. Their own artillery support was dying away. They probably couldn't distinguish between the enemy line and the advancing battalion anymore in the fog --*

...Marvella has raised his good arm, opened his fist, and rested it on her shoulder. "Yeah!" she whispers, and a fool's light comes into her eyes, as he begins to squeeze...

-- *He'd just loaded his last clip into his M-1, and was crouched down screwing the pegs into a pair of concussion grenades, when the white Marine corporal ran up with a flame thrower yelling curses at the Chinks. A stray bullet had pierced the pressure tank making it useless, but the kid, not aware of that, or of the gas hissing out of the tank on his back in the uproar of the fire fight, was standing up there like a John Wayne cartoon, ignoring the crossfire and preoccupied with taking the flame thrower apart trying to fix it. Just beyond the kid Jones saw one of the many native graves that studded the surrounding hills, a mound of earth three feet high with its top gouged out by an artillery shell that had left the corpse, buried Korean fashion in a sitting position, with its head exposed. The grave was drawing fire from both sides in the fog, and Jones, having fired his last rounds, yelled at the boy to get down. As the words left his lips, the Chinese countercharged, leaping out of the fog bank above them firing burp guns and screaming like demons. But the Marine just stood there yelling --*

"...Help me!" Marvella's crying out to the others, frightened, now, and only wanting to escape, but buckling under the grip of his hand. "Oh, shit! Help me!"

The other two rush forward and, misunderstanding, thinking she wants them to help put him inside her, they take hold of him, a part of him he'd thought dead, atrophied, and push it up into her...

-- Yelling like a fool, trying to wrestle free of the flame thrower harness, and not seeing the Chinese coming down on top of them. Jones, reacting on impulse, dove headlong, tackling the kid at the knees, and they both went rolling toward the shelter of the grave. But the ground began to shift and heave as though the dead man in it were coming violently back to life, and the next instant they were blown into the air, with Jones, convulsed, dazed and sickened at the sight of the headless Marine floating passed him, realizing too late the grave had been mined --

...Now, seized and shuddering in the aftermath of sex, and still clinging to the woman crouched above him, he's unaware of the others screaming in the hallway and the wall of flames rushing in the window.

5.
Fire

"Son of a bitch!"

The hurled rock struck the water with an obscene sound and sank into the rust and rot at the bottom.

"My car, my trumpet...!"

Lot picked up another rock and threw it, and another.

"God damn mothafuckin son of a BITCH!"

He went twenty paces to find another one large and heavy enough to suit him and heaved it after the others, with the absurd thought flashing through his mind that if he kept it up, he might eventually breach the levee and drown the county. But the water rolled back in an impotent loop over his shoes.

"This can't be real!" he went on, muttering to himself in a rage. "This got to be a dream! Man, this...! I aint no cotton-pickin fool, I'm Lotrelle Dundee! Aint no fuckin way this could be happening to me...!"

...He'd awakened in the middle of the night gasping for air. He'd had that dream again, of his father's hands reaching up to drag him underwater, and it occurred to him then that he'd been having that dream on and off for years, and now he'd actually found a body. There couldn't be any connection, he said to himself, he wasn't psychic, and besides, in the dream it had always been his father, but this guy he'd pulled out of the water hadn't looked like anybody he'd ever known -- not that it would've been so easy to tell, the body being as disfigured as it was. But the coincidence gave him the willies. He'd shuddered involuntarily and wiped the perspiration from his forehead, then he'd sat listening to the deep regular breathing of the girl sleeping beside him, trying to calm himself. But he'd started coughing again, then he'd smelled smoke and had thought maybe he was still dreaming. He'd barely been able to make out the outline of the four-poster by the dim starlight from the window. Reaching over to turn on the table lamp, he'd hesitated, hearing sounds outside, like the muffled clatter of a bucket, and someone moving along the exterior wall. He'd slipped out of bed and gone to the window. But it had looked out on a narrow garden thickly planted with fan palms and philodendrons, screening off the house from the neighbors and he hadn't seen anybody out there. Then he'd heard footsteps running off, and a moment later, a car starting up and driving away. Meanwhile, the smell of smoke had been getting stronger. He'd felt his way along the wall, found a light switch, and turned it on, then he'd seen the smoke seeping under the bedroom door...

"Hey! Hey, baby, wake up!"

The girl moaned and turned her head without waking. He had to go over and pull the sheet off and shake her shoulder.

"Girl, get up! Come on, wake up, the house is afire!" He didn't remember her name, just then, but as he looked at her, lying face down, naked and peaceful in the bed, it occurred to him he really had to do something about his way of living because he'd just been missing too much lately. He shook her again and finally got her to open her eyes.

"What? Oh, hi."

"Jump, sister, we got a fire in the house!" He grabbed his clothes and began to dress as he spoke.

"What? A what!"

"Fire, you heard me! Come on, I gotta get Rico outta here!"

But on opening the bedroom door, the smoke in the parlor was so thick he choked. He shut the door and went back to get the blanket and put it over his head. But the girl, who'd finally gotten up, was simply standing against the wall, rigid with fear. He went over and shook her, urging her to get moving, but she just started to scream. He had to slap her to get her out of it, and drawing the blanket around the both of them, he dragged her out of the room. He could feel the heat now, and the parlor, previously dark, glimmered with an eerie light as flames from somewhere at the back seemed to blow along the mirrored walls like a crimson wind.

Groping their way across the room, they knocked over a lamp and he stumbled against a chair. Then the girl impulsively broke from his grasp and ran off.

"Hey! Hey, Shawnette!" Her name came back to him as he hollered after her, "Shawnette! Goddammit, come back here! Help me find the stairs!"

But she paid him no heed. "My clothes!" she hollered, already lost to sight in the thickening smoke, "Help! Fire! My clothes!"

He started running toward the sound of her voice, but banged into a table, then turning, took a few steps one way, then another, then started hollering, himself, to rouse the others, meanwhile growing more alarmed as he realized he'd lost his sense of direction. The parlor was a maze of furniture and mirrors and everywhere he turned, he seemed to be running into his own reflection. Hearing footsteps on the landing, he turned again, found the newel of the stairs and pitched headlong over Rico's empty wheelchair. The lights were finally switched on above him, and he could hear voices crying out and footsteps running along the upstairs hall. The smoke grew thinner as he climbed the stairs, and he glimpsed two of the girls who'd been with Rico before, the big fat one and the small dark one, racing toward the far end of the hall. At the same time, other doors were flung open and the landing was soon filled with women screaming and running back and forth in confusion.

He remembered that Rico had been taken into the near room at the head of the stairs, and he kicked the door open. Inside, the smoke was thicker and the window wreathed in flames. Rico was on the bed and the tall yellow girl, apparently unconscious, was kneeling hunched over him with her wild mane of hair covering his face like a pall. The fire was creeping along the baseboard toward them. With his own eyes burning from the smoke, Lot got down on all fours and scrambled toward them. He was able to rouse the girl and then turned his attention to Rico. The man's eyes opened, but he was wheezing and having trouble breathing. Lot took him by the arm and pulled him across his shoulders and hollered to the girl to grab Jones's clothes. Together, they carried him out into the hall.

"MARVELLA! GIRL, WHAT IN HELL YALL DOIN WITH THAT CRIPPLE! F'GIT'IM, HE'S HALF-DEAD ANYWAY!"

Ida Temple had taken up a position of command out on the landing, having first apparently thrown on as many precious garments as possible in the effort to save them all from destruction. She stood there like a monstrous effigy, ballooned in layers of satin, lace and taffeta dresses and nightgowns, two fur coats and a tower of hats and veils that rose precariously from her head with the feathers of birds of paradise trailing in the smoke. She held a small strongbox tucked snugly under one arm, and a dozen necklaces swung, clattering, from her neck as she gestured imperiously to right and left attempting to impose order on the chaos around her. "YOU, TAKE THIS PICTURE! GLORIA, GRAB THE CHAISE LOUNGE! MAMMA-GIRL, GET THE LINENS OUT THE HALL CLOSET! EMMA JEAN, GIRL, YOU GO BACK IN THAT ROOM AND GRAB SOME CLOTHES, I GOT NO INTENTION OF BUYIN YOU ANY MORE...!"

But most of the girls were running for the doors carrying whatever they'd thought to salvage. Others, too panicked to think for themselves, dashed back and forth at her commands, trying to save the furnishings.

"MARVELLA!" Ida bellowed again, as Lot and the tall girl struggled with Jones at the first turn on the stairs, "GODDAMMIT, Y'HEAH ME? GO GET MY SOFA! GET MY SOFA OUT TO THE YARD! GIT MY SOFA! HURRY...!"

Another girl ran down the stairs passed them clutching to her naked breast a pair of new satin shoes and a bundle of letters tied with a ribbon. But Lot gratefully saw that Marvella paid no heed to the surrounding confusion. At the bottom of the stairs a draft had momentarily cleared a tunnel through the smoke, and he could see the front door was open and two of the windows had been knocked out. But the heat of the fire was more intense than before, and he felt it searing his face and hands as he struggled to get Jones into the wheelchair. Marvella, having grabbed a blanket from upstairs to cover herself, used a part of it to cover Jones's head, as they started to wheel him toward the door.

"GODDAMMIT, MARVELLA! YOU HEAR WHAT I SAY! F'GIT THE NIGGUHS! F'GIT'EM! GO HELP EMMA JEAN WITH THE TABLE AND THE SOFA...!"

He and Marvella had managed to drag Jones as far as the piano, when the front wall of the house erupted in flames. A supporting beam collapsed and the crystal chandelier crashed down, creating a fiery barrier across the foyer and blocking their path to the door. Marvella tugged at his arm and pointed back under the stairs. He swung the wheelchair around and followed her back through the clutter of furniture and the tumult of frightened women toward a small door under the stairwell, as the side walls began to bulge and crack.

They got down the two steps under the stairwell and opened the small wooden door toward the back of the house, but the wheelchair wouldn't fit through the door frame. Lot had to lift Jones onto his back again and follow Marvella through the narrow passageway into the kitchen. Once there, they found they couldn't open the back door. Apparently unused for some time, it was paint-sealed and the bolt was rusted in place. He lowered Jones to the floor, where Marvella propped him up against her, while he attempted to break the door down. It was low and narrow, but made of stout, solid pine and resisted his efforts to ram his shoulder through it. Some of the other girls, meanwhile, had followed them into the kitchen and were trying to claw their way passed him. One of them picked up a wooden kitchen stool and began knocking it to pieces in a useless effort to break through the door. Lot managed to push the women aside and kicked the door until the hinges and lock strikes loosened, the screws popped and the door finally fell out of the door frame. As the other girls scrambled over them to get outside, Marvella helped him to lift Jones up over his shoulders again. But it was a mistake, the doorway was too narrow, and as he crouched and twisted back and forth trying to squeeze through, he heard a crash behind him and felt a rush of heat. Stuck in the doorway and unable to turn, he called over his shoulder, but Marvella didn't answer. He swung an arm back to feel for whatever it was that was holding them, but felt only the searing heat. Trying again to force his way through, he felt Rico slipping from him and realized it was Rico who was caught. By that time he could hear Ida behind him in the kitchen, yelling over the noise of the fire and cursing at him for blocking the way. Then all at once, they were free and he and Rico burst through the doorway and went rolling out into the backyard among the lamps, linens and bric-a-brac that the women had tossed out of the upstairs windows. But the next moment, he heard the small dark one, Gloria, yelling at him to come back and help Marvella. He ran back and found Marvella lying unconscious under a fallen section of the ceiling. He and Gloria struggled together for minutes, it seemed, slapping out flames that kept starting in their own clothes and hair, before they were able to get Marvella free of the wreckage and could carry her outside, where they laid her on the grass next to Rico. She was severely burned about the face and upper body, and didn't seem to be breathing. They took turns giving her artificial respiration, blowing into her mouth, slapping her face and hollering at her, trying everything to bring her around, but she didn't respond. Her head was badly bruised and one arm was broken. It was a nasty compound fracture, with the split ulna jutting out of the skin below the elbow. A sound behind him made him turn, to see Rico, with his eyes still open, apparently choking. Lot rolled him over, face down, and Jones began to cough and spit up a sooty phlegm. He was clenching his one good hand spasmodically on the grass, and Lot saw that it was badly burned. The skin was peeling and oozing blood. He glanced back at Marvella, where Gloria remained, bent over and crying, and saw clear fingermarks, deep and purple around Marvella's wrist, and guessed that Rico must have been holding on to her when she'd got caught under the fallen ceiling and in trying to pull her free, had accidentally broken her arm.

Lot got up and ran zigzagging through the flame-tossed shadows of the bushes along the side of the house toward the car, parked in front. Gloria, he was thinking, must know where the nearest colored hospital or doctor was, where they could get help. But as he turned the corner of the house, he saw the porch roof collapse and the Chevy already in flames. He tried picking his way toward the car through the burning timbers, but the heat drove him back and he found himself standing there helpless and yelling with rage.

When he returned to the back yard, the neighbors, roused by then and milling about carrying ineffectual buckets of water, were murmuring among themselves that the sheriff was looking for two Negroes in connection with a man killed out at the bogue. As soon as they saw him, they turned to stare at him suspiciously. Then Ida pointed a finger at him and started yelling and cussing him and Jones, both, as though the fire had been their fault. He tried to tell her Marvella and Jones needed a doctor, but she wouldn't listen.

"GIT OUT!" she said. "I SHOULDA KNOWN BETTER THAN TO TAKE IN STRANGE NIGGUHS! I SHOULDA KNOWN BETTER! I KNEW YALL WAS TROUBLE THE MINUTE I SET EYES ON YA! GO ON! GO ON! TAKE THAT BLACK CRIPPLE AND GIT YOUR ASS OUTTA MY SIGHT...!"

Dumbfounded, he'd hoisted Jones onto his back and stumbled off, wondering how the woman could've been so cold. He couldn't believe she hadn't remembered him, even after all those years. He'd walked off in a daze, carrying Jones down alleyways, through vacant lots and across cotton fields in the early morning dark, avoiding open roads and traveling with only a vague notion of where he was going until, exhausted, he'd finally come upon the railroad tracks, here, by the levee, where he'd set Jones down and put his own hopes on a northbound train.

What's he going to do now, he wondered. Where could he hide? Come full day, somebody was bound to spot them out there. But for Jesussake, he thought, what was he doing back here in the first place? From the time he'd run away, he'd vowed never to set foot in that county again! He'd tried to forget he'd ever been born there. It had nothing but bad memories for him, his hands frostbitten in the winter and pierced by thorns in the summer from picking cotton, year in and year out. He knew he didn't have any family left there. His little brother, Robbie, had gotten sick and died of pneumonia the year after they'd all been sent to the orphanage. And it'd been hardly a month after that when his older brother, Newton, had gotten caught for the second time in the girls' dormitory and they'd decided he was too old for the orphanage and had sent him away to some reform school. Now, after seeing how Ida Temple had carried on, he knew he didn't have any friends left in LeVane, either. Even that pretty girl he'd met at the picnic. When her father'd seen them together and found out who he was, the man had told him to his face he didn't want any of Fontana Dundee's people associating with his daughter, and he'd just grabbed the girl and dragged her off. Well, fuck him, anyway, Lot said to himself, aint nobody want to be associating with him, either! But damn, after all this time you wouldn't think people'd hardly remember Fontana Dundee, much less still get so worked up about him! What had his father ever done to them? He may never have amounted to much, but he'd never hurt anybody but himself. They'd tried to say his daddy was a murderer, but he didn't believe that. He wouldn't ever believe it! His daddy'd only killed himself, the poor sonuvabitch, driving into a tree one night coming home drunk. Fontana Dundee never drowned nobody! He remembered Newton telling him that he, Newton, knew what had happened out at the bogue that day because he'd been there. But Newton wouldn't tell him what he'd seen. Newton'd said he, Lot, was too young to handle it and he wanted to "protect" him. But from what? Sides, he said to himself, Newton lied so much a person never could know when he'd be telling the truth. He'd never seen Newton again, and never did find out what really had happened. Shit, he said to himself, being as I'm already back here, if things were different I might even try to clear daddy's name. But as it is, if I don't look sharp I'm likely to land my own ass in jail!

Served him right for going against his own better instincts, he said to himself. He shouldn't have joined up with that last sorry-ass band like he had, going all over West Hell to play in rinky-dink nocount joints. He should've headed north like he'd planned and hooked up with some real musicians. Sure, he'd needed the bread, but that wasn't no excuse! By the time they'd hit that big social in Texarkana, he'd had it. The dance hall had been packed, and halfway through the gig the band leader, a piano player who'd fancied himself another Nat King Cole, had taken a request and segued into Ebb Tide. But by then, he hadn't given a shit, himself, and maybe he'd had a little too much to drink, too, and was feeling pretty loose. So when the piano player'd hit that inverted fourth and signaled for him to come in with his solo, it'd triggered an idea he'd been toying with in his mind since hearing the Negro fife and drum band in Como shortly before, like the one at the picnic yesterday. He'd used to hear them often as a kid growing up here. And so, on impulse, he'd gone into an improv using scales, instead of chords, dipping into some old church modes. It sounded weird at first, even to him. But next thing he knew, there was blues up in there and a new kind of rhythm and a new feeling of freedom. All kinds of funky shit started happening, and it was almost as if he could feel the doors opening all over his mind. Suddenly, he wasn't boxed in anymore by harmonic expectations and he didn't have to worry about how it was supposed to end, he felt like he could go on forever and never run out of ideas! But meanwhile, all the hicks on the dance floor had froze and the piano player'd turned to look at him with his eyes bugged out and his konk stood up on end. But he didn't care, he'd never heard nobody else play jazz like that -- except maybe Mingus, a little. He'd felt he'd hit on something new and he knew he was cooking and so he went on and took another chorus...! But then, halfway into it, some motherfucker twice his size climbed up on the bandstand and slapped the trumpet out his mouth and sent him flying into the back wall. Next thing he knew, he was running for his life down some dark alley with half the niggers in the neighborhood chasing his ass. He hadn't had but about sixty-some dollars left to his name by the time he'd stumbled on the circus. Still, it'd been fantastic. Even thinking about it now gave him a kick...except....

He shifted uneasily and glanced over his shoulder, thinking, except it hadn't been him. It'd been the alto player who'd gotten chased and beat up, a cat named Connette Oleman. And what Oleman had been playing that night had been even weirder than church modes. But it could've been him, Lot, too, because he'd thought of it. He had! he insisted to himself. He'd thought of just letting loose and playing what he'd heard in his own head, instead of that lame juke jive they were supposed to play. But something'd held him back. It most always did when he played in public. But if it had been me, he said to himself, I'd've swung that alto and broke some heads before they took me down! But Oleman hadn't done that. Oleman had just wrapped his arms around the horn and taken his lumps like he was gonna protect that cheap plastic alto no matter what. The niggers ended up taking it away from him anyway and breaking it up on a fence. By the time he, Lot, and the rest of the band had caught up with them and chased the mothafuckas off, Oleman was on the ground all bloody and mumbling, "My horn! Mothafuckas took my horn, man! Where's my horn!" He, Lot, had picked up the pieces and given them to him, and Oleman had sat there cradling that busted horn in his lap and crying over it like it'd been a baby. The band leader had cussed Oleman out before about playing like that, though Oleman could play straight when he wanted to. And after that night, the other cats in the band would kid Oleman behind his back like they thought he was a little crazy in the head. But deep down, they all knew Oleman had heart. They'd all respected him after that. And he, Lot, had begun to think on that -- not that he wanted to imitate Oleman, because Oleman's style wasn't his style, and he didn't want to imitate anybody, he wanted to sound like himself. But Oleman had taught him something, that heart came from the deep conviction that you really knew what the fuck you wanted to say. So, he, Lot, had begun to study himself, in a way, analyzing his own musical habits and impulses and what it was, exactly, that drew him to certain rhythms and improvisational styles. Because, to be honest, all his licks sounded to his own ears like so many tricks. He was borrowing brilliance, like in that side-show trick he does of juggling illuminated light bulbs -- keeping their eyes on the lights, so they don't notice the wires. What he wanted was to go deeper, to get down under everything he'd picked up from everybody else, to where the flint struck fire....

He shook his head irritably, realizing he'd allowed himself to be distracted from more important things by getting involved with Jones, bullshitting himself into trying to play the hero, thinking he could actually rescue the man. He, Lot, wasn't no hero. He owned he might fantasize a little, now and then, but truth was he wasn't even interested in being a hero, he just wanted to make music. Heroes were big, tough guys like Rico Jones -- only it turned out that might not buy you much in the end, either. That old whore, Ida Temple, cold as she was, had been right, in a way, he said to himself. Jones had been as good as half-dead when he'd found him. He'd just felt sorry for the man. What the hell had happened to Jones? he wondered. When he was a kid, Rico Jones had been right up there with Joe Louis and Jackie Robinson and Dizzy. At the time, everybody knew that Rico Jones had been one of the first Negro soldiers to be awarded the Silver Star for bravery. And when he'd returned to baseball, after the war in Europe, he'd played for the Birmingham Black Barons for a couple years, then joined the Kansas City Monarchs and had the best season of his career. He'd batted four-twenty-seven, beating Roger Hornsby's record of four-twenty-four, and he'd hit seventy-seven homers, topping Josh Gibson's seventy-five! He remembered seeing Jones play, once, in an exhibition game between the Negro American League All Stars and the Brooklyn Dodgers. It was in October of 'Fifty, down in Jacksonville. He remembered that the All Stars were leading two-to-one, with the Dodgers up and two out, in the bottom of the eleventh, when Robinson singled off Satchel Paige and then stole second. Then Duke Snider got up and hit a line drive to center field that looked like it would drive in the tying run for sure. Jones was too deep over in left center, but he went after it. It looked like he had no chance, but he dove for the ball, tumbled ass-over-apples and came up with that sucker on one bounce and pegged it all the way to home plate -- while still on his knees! Josh Gibson gave a yell as he caught it and slapped Robinson out, and Robinson flipped. Robinson couldn't believe it, he just knew that ball was still out in center field somewhere...! But then, shortly after that, Jones had disappeared. Word had it he was supposed to go up to the white majors the following season, but instead, he'd simply dropped out of sight. Nobody knew what had happened to him. And to see him now, Lot thought to himself, strapped in that wheelchair with ignorant motherfuckers sticking needles into him and tying him up in the back of a truck like he was some circus animal...! Jones had changed so much since he, Lot, had seen him play that he'd probably never have recognized him, if he hadn't been staring at him because of the way they'd been treating him at the circus. Still, if he hadn't taken it upon himself to try and save Jones, none of this shit would've happened! He didn't even know why the police were after them. They hadn't done anything. It wasn't like they'd come there looking to find nobody's body! He shuddered involuntarily, recalling the clammy feel of it and the sickening smell. He had to get his ass out of there, he said to himself. But even as he thought this, he found himself gazing back along the tracks in the direction of the spur that he knew branched off toward the cotton gin and ran passed the farm where he'd been born. He wondered whether he could even manage to lift Jones up onto a moving train when it finally did come through. Might even be better to leave him right where he was. Jones was safe there, he said to himself, the police wouldn't do anything to him once they realized he was crippled and couldn't have done anything. And anyway, he'd done all he could for the cat. It'd cost him everything, too, his money, his car, his practically brand new Selma trumpet that he'd just hardly got through paying for --!

"Motherfucker!" he said aloud, struck by a thought, and turned to call over his shoulder, "Hey, Rico. Man, you know what day this is? It's my birthday, man! I'm eighteen fuckin years old! Aint that a bitch?" But Jones lay silent and motionless in the hollow of the levee with his feet pointing to the stars.

By now, the first birds had begun to chitter and fret in the fields across the right-of-way, where the ripe cotton gleamed in the half-light. Over the river, the moon was high and white as a nail.

102

6.
Sampson

"'...Blessed are they that mourn, for they shall be comforted....'" The Reverend Harold Sampson paused and stood with his head bent, thinking he'd never known so many to come together at one time in that little church. The congregation filled the pews, spilled over onto wooden folding chairs in the aisle and stood fidgeting at the back, where three full rows of men's hats hung on the ten-penny nails driven into the wall. They'd come, yes, but he could feel the fear among them, and the anger, and with that a clear sense that whoever presumed to stand before them now to pray or to preach had better have a firm grip on the horrors these people faced every day of their lives, he'd better be ready and able to seize upon that fear and anger and turn it to advantage, to match their heat or be gone. He was painfully aware, besides, that there were more than a few members of the congregation who considered him a newcomer and still unproven, although he'd been pastor there for over two years. And he knew his message that morning would bring them no peace. But the Lord worked in mysterious ways, he reminded himself, and as He, in His wisdom, had found a way to stir these people up this morning, so he, their pastor, had been preparing for this moment for a long time. When he spoke again, his voice was firm and carried easily to the back of the church. "The Lawd giveth, and the Lawd taketh away."

"Taketh away!" the congregation echoed. "Oh, yes!

"Blessed be the Name of the Lawd."

"Hmn."

"Amen."

"He divideth the sea with His power..." Sampson continued, "and by His understanding He smiteth through the proud."

"He smiteth, yes!"

"Uhm-hmn."

"Man that is born of woman is of few days, and full of trouble."

"Full of trouble!"

"Lawd, yes!"

"He cometh forth like a flower, and is cut down."

"Cut down!"

"And when he is cut down -- like Brother Benjamin, here -- what can we do?"

"What can we do?"

But it wasn't a rhetorical question, it was a question the reverend intended to answer that morning, come what may. For he was well aware of the sacrifices that would have to be made, by himself and by others, like the bereaved family sitting in the pew there before him. His eyes rested on Lorna Rhoder, Benjamin's widow, sitting nearest the casket with her three daughters at her side, the youngest dozing in her grandmother's lap. In the rows behind them were some faces Sampson didn't know, and several lapsed church members he hadn't seen inside the building in months. Jonah Johnson, for one.

Jonah, an honest tenant farmer and longtime friend of the deceased, with whom he'd been known to quarrel lately, had been publicly humiliated by the sheriff, who'd accosted him on the street one afternoon, while the Johnson family stood by, to suggest that he, Jonah, had had something to do with Benjamin's disappearance. And there were others, crowded shoulder to shoulder in the pews, now, who'd refused to walk on the same side of the street with one another for years. But Sampson only hoped he would prove, now, to have the strength and wit to shape the fear and rage that had finally brought them together, that had been so long a-building, into a positive force for change, before it wasted itself, as it most often did, in divisive or self-destructive ways, and relapsed into the usual paralyzing apathy. At the back, there was also one white face present, which the reverend recognized as Phillip Kurf, a reporter from the national news service down in Jackson. And just across the aisle, was the stout, smug and impeccable Thomas Crouch in his mortuary pinstripes.

"...We prayed," Sampson was saying aloud.

"Prayed, oh, yes!"

"...We've read our Bible, hmn..."

"Read the Bible!"

"...And time after time, we've buried our dead, huh."

"Oh, Lawd!"

"For fifteen GENERATIONS," the reverend continued, letting his voice rise, "we have lived in Pharaoh's land...AND TRIED to do right, huh!"

"Sho did!"

"It's true."

"AND FOR FIFTEEN GENERATIONS, they have worked us to our knees, huh..."

"To our knees!"

"...WHIPPED us, when we stumbled..."

"Yes!"

"...AND WHEN WE STOOD UP, they cut us down!"

"Tell the truth!"

"Tell it!"

"We been 'buked and scorned, SO LONG, oh Lawd..."

"So long!"

"...Whence cometh deliverance?"

"When, Lawd?"

Sampson, recently widowed himself, with three small boys of his own, paused and let his eye linger for a moment on Lorna Rhoder. She sat with her back trim and straight in a tailored black dress and matching hat, looking as though she'd worn smart clothes all her life. One would never have guessed, he mused, that these were probably the first new store-bought clothes she'd had in years. As he raised a glass of water to his lips, Lorna turned her head to stare through her veil at the coffin in the aisle beside her.

"In our own hearts," Sampson went on, "selfishness and false pride divide us..."

"Yes!"

"Lawd, it's true!"

"...And a house divided must fall."

"Must fall!"

"But a house united is strong."

"Uhm-hmn!"

"AND A PEOPLE THAT OVERCOMES selfishness and false pride, CANNOT BE oppressed, huh!"

"Awright!"

"WHEN THE JEWS UNDERSTOOD UNITY, THEY WALKED AWAY OUT OF THE BONDAGE OF PHARAOH!"

"Ah!"

"Yes, they did."

"EVEN ROME had to fall one day!"

"Even Rome had to fall one day!" some voices echoed.

"FOR TOO LONG, we have allowed the oppressor to divide us from one another, huh..."

"Divide us."

"...TO SET US AGAINST ONE ANOTHER, hmn... TO SAY TO ONE ANOTHER, 'I am BETTER than you, I take CARE of myself, if YOU get into trouble, that's YOUR problem! Must be you DESERVE trouble! ME, I'M TOO GOOD FOR TROUBLE!' haa --"

"Hah, too good for trouble!"

"I know that man!"

The pastor removed his glasses, "-- But then, one day, trouble comes knocking on our own door..."

"Trouble come, fo sho."

"...And then, we cry, 'NO-O-O-BODY KNOWS DE TROUBLE AH SEEN!'"

"True, that's true!"

"'...LAWD, WHAT I DONE TO DESERVE THIS TROUBLE?' huh..."

"'What I done.'"

"'...I been a GOOD Christian,' hmn..."

"'Yes!'"

"'...I go to church EVERY Sunday,' haa..."

"'Yes, indeed!'"

"'...I mind my own business,' uhm-hmn..."

"Uh-huh."

"'...I invite only the right, the light and the near-white to my home, Lawd' uhm-mah..."

"Aint that somethin!"

"'...I DON'T NEVER HAVE NOTHIN TO DO WITH NOCOUNT NIGGUHS,' uhm-mah..."

"Call the number!"

"'...LAWD, WHY YOU BRING THIS TROUBLE TO MY DOOR?'"

"'To my door!'"

"'SURELY, LO-A-W-AD, THERE MUST BE SOME MISTAKE!' huh! 'THIS THE SORTA THING SUP-POSED TO BE FOR THAT OLE BUSTER JONES-THEM DOWN THE STREET!' huh! 'SURELY, LAWD, THIS TROUBLE DONE COME TO THE WRONG ADDRESS!' haaa!"

"'Wrong address,' hah!"

"Ho, my!"

"Some mistake! Hah!"

"Ho, Lawd, aint folks something!"

The reverend, already soaked with perspiration, paused to remove his horn-rimmed glassed and wipe his face with his handkerchief. The air was thick and hot in the church. Several women had taken out woven straw fans to try and cool themselves and their young ones. Many had inserted handkerchiefs into their neck bands. The youngest of the Rhoder girls, just four years old, began to play cat's cradle with a piece of string in her hands, until the grandmother, Basheeba, without speaking a word, firmly covered the girl's two small hands with one of her own and folded them on her lap. Basheeba, who was Lorna's mother, wrapped in an old brown shawl and grim and grey as a boulder from the field, sat staring unblinking at the reverend with the birthmark that crossed the upper part of her face livid as a grudge.

"FALSE PRI-I-IDE, BROTHERS AND SISTERS! FALSE PRIDE AND SELFISHNESS bring us down, uhm-hmn!"

"Bring us down!"

"WE TOO 'GOOD'...FOR OUR OWN GOOD, uhm-mah!"

"Too good!"

"Tell the truth!"

"WHEN, my brothers and sisters, when...shall we come to understanding?"

"Lawd, when?"

"Awright!"

"Uhm-hmn."

The reverend opened his mouth to continue, but hesitated, as his eye was caught by a sudden movement at the back of the church. There, visible through the crowd standing on either side of the closed door, stood a table holding a guest register and a contribution box. On the floor below the table, his small brown and white spotted dog, Buttercups, had come alert, pointing her ears and going to sniff at the door. Sampson took another sip of water and waited, his attention fixed on the little feist.

But he also noted that the white reporter, Kurf, seemed to have nodded off. Sampson regarded the man out of the corner of his eye, slumped over and breathing heavily out of a large, prominent nose suffused with capillary sprouts, his eyes shut. For people like Kurf, the reverend reflected, unconsciously working the muscles in his own heavy jaw, the murder of a local Negro was of as little moment as the passing of a summer day. To the reporter, although he was a Southerner himself, the big news was elsewhere. Now that the body of the child, Morris Hill, whose funeral he, Sampson, had presided over only the day before, had been found and shipped back up North to the poor child's mother, the "news" had moved to the courthouse, where the two white men who'd admitted to kidnapping the boy were to be tried for his murder. Kurf, Sampson felt, was simply killing time, waiting for that trial to begin. The reverend anticipated that the news services would have a field day with it. Trucks from several television stations were already parked on the courthouse green with their crews busily setting up cameras to broadcast it right into people's homes. Sampson wasn't sure how he felt about that, himself. He believed that the world surely needed to see what was going on down there. And there was the faint hope that the exposure might embarrass the white judge and jury into an honest effort at justice. On the other hand, televising the trial to the nation would show up the worst side of the South and make them all, black and white, vulnerable to censure or ridicule. Worse, it was bound to increase the tensions and violence already sparked by the recent Supreme Court decisions on school integration. And there was no question that, whatever good might come out of it, it would be the local Negroes who would be made to pay the price. All that not withstanding, Sampson still gave Kurf credit for at least showing up that morning. There were no colored journalists present. There was only Clyde Beevis, the lawyer and field representative from the NAACP office in Jackson, who stood near the door, where the reverend now saw that the dog had gone back to lie down under the contribution box.

As he considered his next words, Sampson thought to himself, I know that here among you, too, my brothers and sisters, there are slanderers and Judases, and I think I know who you are. If I can't convert you this morning, I'm just going to have to take my chances. But he also knew that he couldn't expect to reach his congregation by appealing to their logic and reason. If he tried he'd lose them. They'd turn their backs and walk out on him, as they'd done to the pastor who'd preceded him, because they well knew that their oppression defied logic, and reason was cold comfort against the resources of those who oppressed them. For a Negro to live in the South and try to be reasonable was to contradict himself and court disaster. The previous pastor, a good simple man from back East, had been shunned by the congregation, but the whites, who'd taken him seriously, had run him out of town. Sampson knew he'd have to "shout and squall" to get his message over, to stamp and holler and use all the old-time tricks to encourage his flock, to get them up on their hind legs and shake off the habit of fatalism and lethargy. He normally disliked that old shouting style, but he understood that it provided a structure and momentum the people here knew and trusted, and he knew it was the only way he could get them to follow him.

Drawing himself up, he said, "Brother Benjamin Rhoder lies here, before us, in a closed casket. Closed, because his face was too brutally beaten, and his body too decomposed for us TO BEAR to look upon him! Lawd!

"Jesus, have mercy!"

"Save us, Lawd!"

"THE DEACON OF OUR OWN CHURCH! Murdered. WHY?"

There was a beat of silence, before one small voice was heard to utter, "We know why!"

Sampson pulled his head in, making his bulldog jowls roll, and continued in a husky whisper that reached the ears of everyone in the church, "Brothers and sisters, it's time we done something about this!"

"Time!"

"Yes, it is!"

"Time, Lawd!"

"Some of us, here, this morning, been saying, 'We waiting for a sign, huh."

"Um-hmn."

"OUR LORD, JESUS CHRIST," Sampson roared, suddenly, pointing to the large wooden crucifix on the wall behind him, "BEEN HUNG UP ON THE CROSS NEARLY TWO THOUSAND YEARS, NOW -- but here, in LeVane County, we still waitin' for a sign, huh!"

"Blessed Lawd!"

"Awright!"

"WELL, NOW, THE SUPREME COURT OF THE UNITED STATES OF AMERICA DONE GIVE US ANOTHER SIGN -- " he pointed over the heads of the congregation toward the northeast, "AND STILL, we waitin', uhm-mah!"

"'With all deliberate speed!'" voices in the crowd recited, echoing the May ruling.

"A sign, yes!"

"But our senior senator said this state should defy the Supreme Court, and close down the public schools!"

"He did!"

"I heard'm."

"And now, Judge Tom Brady of the White Citizen's Council warned, that 'BLOODSHED AND REVOLUTION WOULD FOLLOW IN THE WAKE OF ANY ATTEMPT TO ENFORCE' desegregation!"

"Oh, Lord!"

"'Bloodshed,'" he repeated, nodding somberly, "'and Revolution.' Well, brothers and sisters, we aint done nothin yet about the Supreme Court Decisions. But mysterious fires been burnin around here already. AND YOU SEE, BEFORE YOU, HERE, WHOSE BLOOD THEY PLANNIN' TO SHED!"

"Lordamercy!"

"And yet, I say to you, now, IT'S TIME FOR A CHANGE!"

"A change, Lawd!"

"It's time, yes!"

"I'm ready!"

"ONLY YESTERDAY MORNING, WE WERE HERE TO PRAY FOR THE SOUL OF A CHILD, Uhm-mah..." he struck the pulpit with his fist.

"Yes, Jesus!"

"...A CHILD, accused of whistling at a white woman..." He threw up his hands and cast his eyes about the room as if seeking reason in such madness.

"Save us, Lawd!"

"Tell it! Tell it!"

"...A CHILD, found dead in the Rue River! A CHILD! TORN FROM HIS LIFE LIKE A FLOWER CUT OFF AT THE ROOT BEFORE IT EVER BLOOMED, uhm-mah -- IS THAT A SIGN, haa!"

"Tell it! Tell it! Tell it!"

"A sign, yes!"

"Oh Lawd!"

"AND JUST LAST SATURDAY, WE WERE HERE BURYING CLARENCE JOHNSON! PULLED OUT OF THE TOD RIVER WITH A ROPE AROUND HIS NECK! MY GAWD! IS THAT A SIGN?"

Several people had begun to stamp their feet and move excitedly in their chairs.

"A sign, Lawd!"

"Too many, Lawd!"

"MY BROTHERS AND SISTERS," he pounded the pulpit again for emphasis as he continued, "WE DONE HAD ENOUGH SIGNS! WE DON'T WANT NO MORE SIGNS!"

"No, Lawd!"

"Enough, Lawd!"

"THEY DONE KILLED THREE NEGROES IN THE LAST TWO WEEKS -- AND WE AINT EVEN DONE NOTHIN YET, huh! I TELL YOU, THIS IS A SIGN THAT THE MAN'S SCARED WE GONNA DO SOMETHING, hmn!"

"Scared, yeah!"

"Tell the truth!"

"I SAY, THE MAN'S SCA-A-A-RED WE GONNA DO SOMETHING!"

"Hell, best he be scared!"

A few voices among the women began to hum and sing in a low tone, forming a sort of counterpoint to the preacher's theme, and their voices gradually rose in volume, with more and more of the congregation joining in, as he continued.

"I want to be ready,

"I want to be ready,

"I want to be ready,

"To walk in Jerusalem just like John...!"

The white reporter had opened his eyes and he looked around, taking in the excitement building in the church. The Widow Rhoder's veil had slipped away, exposing her slender face as she looked up at Sampson, and he felt a rush of heat at the back of his broad neck, where the flesh overwhelmed his round white collar. Ruwana, Lorna's eldest daughter, glanced curiously from her mother to the preacher and back, then dropped her eyes, as Lorna readjusted the veil over her face and self-consciously tucked her hair beneath her new hat. Lorna Rhoder hadn't the money to buy herself the black dress she'd needed to mourn for her husband, and she would not have accepted a loan from him or a gift of money, Sampson knew, and so, he'd had to use the subterfuge of repaying her for a loan that he'd told her Benjamin had previously made to the church. But he couldn't deny the fact that, in spite of the occasion, the sight of the young widow he'd always admired looking so fine in those new clothes made his heart race.

He drew his lips back, showing his teeth, as he continued, "I SAY THE MAN'S SCARED, haah! AND IF HE'S SCARED NOW...JUST WAIT!"

"Awright!"

"Oh, boy!"

"CAUSE WE GETTIN READY TO MOVE, now, haah!"

"Move, yes!"

"Now, yes!"

"Awright!"

"Here we go! Here we go!"

"...I aint been to heaven, but I been told,

"To walk in Jerusalem just like John!

"That the streets are pearl and the gates are gold!"

"To walk in Jerusalem just like John...!"

"DON'T LET'EM TURN YOU AROUND!"

"No, Lawd!"

"No, we won't!"

"THE NEGRO HAS A RIGHT TO VOTE, huh!"

"That's right!"

"THE CONSTITUTION SAYS SO!"

"Yes it does!"

"Yes!"

"DON'T LET'EM TURN YOU AROUND!"

"Oh, no!"

"'BLESSED ARE THEY WHICH DO HUNGER AND THIRST AFTER RIGHTEOUSNESS,' hunnh, 'FOR THEY SHALL BE FILLED!'"

"Praise God!"

"NOW...now...brothers and sisters..." Sampson raised his hands for quiet, "Now...I'll be comin' round to all of your homes to get your names on the petition, and to coach any one of you that wishes it, to pass the voter registration test."

He paused, and let his gaze touch several individuals, before he said, "Along about now, Deacon Rhoder would be passing the collection basket amongst you. In his memory, I'm askin' any of you got a little extra change, to put it in the box back there. It will be distributed to those who need it for the poll tax. And Finally, I'm looking for volunteers -- No, no! Don't put up your hand now. When I come to your house, you tell me if you want to do this. We know what this is all about. Some of you got families and--"

The sound of a car door closing outside had made him pause. The dog sat up under the table growling. Heads turned toward the door.

Sampson wiped his brow with his handkerchief, replaced his glasses, and began to recite, "'The Lawd is thy keeper, the Lawd is thy shade upon the right hand. The sun shall not smite thee by day, nor the moon by night. THE LORD SHALL PRESERVE THEE FROM ALL EVIL.'"

"Preserve us from evil."

"Jesus save us!"

"'HE SHALL PRESERVE THY SOUL.'"

"Preserve our soul."

Now they could hear static from a car radio and low voices outside. The people began to shift about nervously in their places.

Sampson cleared his throat and stood up to his full height, radiating as much confidence as he could muster under the circumstances, as he continued, "'THE LORD SHALL PRESERVE THY GOING OUT AND THY COMING IN FROM THIS TIME FORTH, AND EVEN FOR EVERMORE!' Let us pray. 'The Lord is my shepherd; I shall not want. He maketh me to lie down in green pastures....'"

The voices of those present rose to join with him. "'...He restoreth my soul; He leadeth me in the paths of righteousness....'"

The church door opened and Sheriff Branford Clooder stood in the doorway, his slate gray eyes raking over the congregation. He seemed to be taking special note of the unfamiliar faces present, Clyde Beevis, in particular, who stood nearby, and another man with marcelled hair and large ears who sat next to Crouch. The white journalist gave Clooder a nod, but the sheriff ignored him as he stepped inside, his ruddy features composed in a bland mask. A half-dozen deputies came in after him and spread out along the back of the church to stand with their hats on and their arms folded or their thumbs hooked leisurely in their gun belts, eyeing the crowd.

The parishioners who had been standing at the back crowded toward the side walls to keep their distance from the law officers. The tension was palpable in the crowd, but they continued the recitation without faltering.

"'...Surely goodness and mercy shall follow me all the days of my life, and I will dwell in the house of the Lord for ever.' Amen."

The scuffling of the deputies' boots rang loud in the silence at the end.

Sampson dropped his eyes to the open Bible before him on the pulpit, then said, "Lord, we welcome those who have come to join with us to pay their respects to the deceased and his bereaved family. And we join in prayer with them that Brother Rhoder may rest in peace, and that peace will come into the hearts of all men, by the Christian example of our Lord in Heaven. A-men."

"A-men!"

"A-men!"

The young woman seated at the piano began to play and to sing in a light sweet soprano, and the congregation joined in with her. Crouch and the pall bearers, led by the dead man's brother, came forward, and the pastor led them back down the aisle and out the door, as the congregation sang.

"Closer, my God, to Thee..."

Clooder and his deputies watched with veiled eyes as the people filed by, several dropping coins or small bills into the contribution box as they followed the coffin out of the church. The deputies filed out after them, and the sheriff, last to leave, picked up the guest register on his own way out.

Outside, the morning was quiet. There was no traffic on the street. Apart from the police cruisers, there were half a dozen old cars parked around the church lot that belonged to

117

the congregation. They were all freshly washed and waxed for the occasion, but with their dents, cracked windows and broken mirrors, they looked much the worse for their proximity to the brand new Cadillac hearse pulled up in the driveway. And yet all of the vehicles bore a common ring of mud encrusted around their lower edges, like a high water mark.

As Sampson assisted the pall bearers in loading the casket into the hearse, he kept a sharp eye on the police. He'd forewarned the driver of the hearse to be prepared to race over to the train station to call the NAACP office for help, in case of emergency. But the sheriff and his deputies came quietly out of the church and stood by their cruisers, with the younger men ogling Lorna Rhoder as Crouch ushered her passed them toward the car where the other relatives waited.

"Reverend Sampson?"

He turned at the touch on his elbow, "Ah, Mr. Beevis, thank you for coming."

The gaunt graying man gave him a wan smile and glanced briefly toward the police cars as they shook hands, then turned back to study the pastor's collar abstractedly before he spoke, "You know you're taking a chance."

"We're all taking a chance just being here, now."

"Yes, but...you realize that package of voter registration petitions they found scattered near Rhoder's body didn't have the NAACP name on it, just a post office box for return. And it was only addressed to the church. Someone must have known --"

"I understand," the reverend said, glancing curiously over Beevis's shoulder toward the tall man with marcelled hair who stood speaking with Crouch in the shade of a tree. He'd been told the man's name was Robinson. They hadn't spoken, and Sampson had seen him only once before, coming out of the courthouse in town. But Robinson had been wearing a similar ill-matched suit of clothes, then, too, he recalled, with the same sardonic expression.

"...I certainly don't want to discourage you, of course..." Beevis was saying.

At that moment, Robinson glanced up briefly, his eyes glittering in the rotating lights of the police cars, and Sampson looked away, to see Kurf strolling toward Lorna's car.

"...And we know you've got youngsters of your own to think of," Beavis continued. "So, if you wanted to reconsider, we'd certainly understand...Reverend Sampson?"

Sampson turned back to the man before him, seeing all the fatigue and strain he, himself, felt but was striving to hide, apparent in the stoop of the lawyer's shoulders. "Thank you for your concern, Mr. Beevis. But I'm fully prepared to help any way I can."

Beevis nodded. "I have more material for you, then, and some information."

"Good, yes. Would it be convenient for you to stop over at my house after the cemetery?"

"Of course."

Sampson turned and strode quickly toward Lorna's car, where Kurf stood leaning on the open door with one foot up on the running board, apparently attempting to get a quotation from her.

"No, that's not true!" he heard her saying, as he approached. "My husband would never have...you're just -- I mean, just because...!"

"Is that 'Yes,' or 'no,' Lorna," Kurf said. "Was Ben in the habit of passing bad checks, or are you saying that Mr. Brennan, his employer, is a liar?"

"Begging your pardon, sir!" Sampson called out, interrupting. "I believe Mrs. Rhoder is too distraught to be interviewed today. But permit me to assure you, that Benjamin Rhoder was a devout Christian, a dedicated father to his children, and the trusted deacon of our church, who was brutally murdered -- murdered, sir! -- while on his way to this church on a simple errand from the post office."

Kurf raised his head at the pastor's words and turned to stare him down.

But Sampson held his gaze, adding, "If you need further information concerning the investigation of his murder, sir, may I suggest you make your inquiries of the sheriff. Good day, sir."

The reporter gave him a shrewd look, then walked away.

Sampson bent his head to speak to Lorna, but she'd already closed the car door and turned to hide her face against her mother's shoulder.

"Oh, Sampson!"

He looked up again, to see the reporter standing, now, beside the sheriff and addressing him from across the lawn. Kurf was lighting a cigarette, affecting a casual air as he spoke, but his voice was purposely raised at that distance so that all of those standing before the church could hear the exchange.

"Just one other thing," Kurf continued. "If I'm not mistaken, you went to a meeting with Governor White and the legislative committee on education a few weeks ago. The purpose of the meeting was to discuss a proposal for voluntary segregation in the public schools -- in defiance of the Supreme Court ruling. Is that correct, Reverend?"

Sampson took a step toward him, then answered clearly, "I was one of thirty Negro community leaders throughout the state invited to that meeting, yes, sir."

"And, what was the outcome of that meeting?"

"The proposal was unambiguously rejected by the Negro representatives, sir."

"'Unambiguously...?'" Kurf hesitated for effect. "But, I understood that at least one of the coloreds present did, in fact, vote to endorse the plan. That's right, isn't it?"

The deputies were listening attentively, obviously amused, but Clooder stood with his back turned, speaking into his car radio. From where he stood, Sampson could just make out the telltale bulge in the sheriff's pressed white suit jacket that indicated the pistol holstered there, in the small of his back.

To Kurf he said, "You have your sources, sir."

"I'm asking you whether the information is correct," Kurf insisted.

"It's possible, but I don't see --"

"'Possible?' Either it's true, or it isn't. You were there, weren't you?"

"Just what are you getting at --!" Sampson said, impatiently. But immediately, he saw the deputies stiffen and he could feel the tension rise among the Negroes, who stood about with their eyes averted, fidgeting with coat buttons, car keys and imaginary lint. He was angry enough, nevertheless, to finish his thought and put the sarcastic white reporter in his place, but when he saw the smile creep into Kurf's eyes, he admonished himself to keep the safety of his congregation foremost. "-- sir," he added, finally, and felt the tension around him ease.

"I want to know," Kurf said, glancing around to gauge the effect of the conversation on the waiting congregation, "exactly which Negro -- uhm -- leader it was, who cowardly buckled under and voted for the Governor's proposal."

The reverend didn't answer.

"Who was it, Sampson? Was it you?"

Sampson let his own gaze wander away to the church that occupied the corner lot where they stood. The First Baptist Church of Holy Christ The Savior. The name almost seemed to carry more weight than the small old wooden building could bear. And yet the unassuming structure, mounted on concrete blocks, had withstood three different attempts to burn it down over the years. The heat of the morning sun had already formed bubbles in the freshly whitewashed clapboard siding and along the edges of the newly laid tar paper where the roof shingles had not yet been replaced. But the church remained a sanctuary and a venerable sight there, situated between its two majestic white oak trees. And it was his church, now. There was a hand-painted sign nailed above the roof that said:

OUR GOD IS ALIVE,
We spoke to Him this morning.
WE'RE SORRY ABOUT YOURS!

When he spoke again, the reverend's voice was calm. "Please excuse me, sir. I believe that you should be able to get whatever information you require about that matter from the Governor's office. But now we have a church member to bury." He forced himself to wait until the white reporter, flashing a smug grin, finally lowered his eyes to step on his discarded cigarette butt, before he turned and walked back to the hearse.

"Fine sermon, Reverend."

Sampson looked around at the dry comment murmured in his ear, to see Thomas Crouch standing beside him. He gave the undertaker a long cold stare.

But Crouch, affecting a wry superiority, merely pursed his lips, "Are we ready?"

"Quite."

As the driver eased the hearse into the street and turned north, Sampson glanced around apprehensively at the police. But the sheriff merely gestured for his deputies to return to their cruisers as the congregation dispersed. Sampson sat back in the air-conditioned car with a sigh of relief. Not yet noon, and the temperature had already risen above one hundred for the fifth straight day, and there was still no breeze. The humid air was thick as dreams to move through.

He was still brooding over the untimely death of Benjamin Rhoder, his own church deacon whom he was now going to bury. But as the hearse drew passed the last shade trees at the end of the street and the sunlight burst upon him, he looked up and felt as though he'd been pitched headlong into the landscape of a mirage, for he suddenly found himself riding on the belly of a great white cloud that stretched away on every side as far as he could see. In fact, the road crossed a vast bright plain of ripe cotton plants that grew right up to the walls of the town and he could see in the distance crop-dusters wheeling and shimmering in the air like dragonflies. He shook his head and smiled to himself to think that, after all this time, the Delta could still astonish him. He'd been born in the heart of the Piney Woods, down in Jefferson Davis County, amid a host of favorite trails, hollows and hunting grounds that he'd grown up to see disappear before his eyes. Longleaf, slash and loblolly pines, live and red oak, hickory, cypress, and ash had all fallen victim to timber-cutting over a period of barely fifty years. And he had done his own share of the damage. But at the time, it had seemed a good life, offering an ambitious Negro an opportunity to work his way up to relative independence, advancing from laborer to cutter, and then to producer, as his father had done, and had taught him and his brothers to do. But, in fact, independence had been an illusion, and the end result was not much different from sharecropping. Because the way it worked, the producer had to take out a loan from an established white dealer in order to buy wood and hire the cutters and the labor to haul it to the rail yard. Then, the producer would have to over-extend his credit to secure enough stock for a good market, only to have to sell out to the dealer at a loss when the market crashed. And there was no chance for a colored producer to ever become a dealer, because no railroad or lumber company would contract with a Negro. But in the end it hadn't mattered, because they'd all been blind to the fact that they'd been tearing down the very structure that had supported them. By "high-grading," cutting all the good timber and leaving only the poor stock, they'd depleted the woods and left dealers, producers, cutters and laborers, alike, all without a living. His father had died in debt, even as the woods had passed away. At the time, it had all seemed to happen so gradually that it wasn't until they'd suddenly awakened one morning to see daylight pouring through what had once been dark woods, that they'd realized what had befallen them.

After his father's death, his older brothers had gone north, and he, pressed by his mother to fulfill his father's dying wish, had gone into the ministry. Upon graduation from Morris College, in South Carolina, where he'd met and married Serena, rest her soul, the Baptist Synod had posted him to various churches in Georgia and the Carolinas over the years, before sending him back here and assigning him to the parish in Dividend. He'd thought, then, that he was going home, to a part of the South he knew. But when he'd arrived, he'd found himself bewildered, at first, by a way of life so different from what he had known in the Piney Woods. Here, the almost irrepressibly fertile land gave one the illusion of a perennial plain of peace and plenty. In reality, the plenty was in the hands of a few and the rest knew little of peace until the grave. But who was he, to attempt to dispel the illusion? Was he scared? Yes! he said to himself, answering his own question. Scared shitless, in fact -- 'scuse me, Jesus! But it was true. Healthy and regular all his life, he'd been on Ex-Lax, now, since the shooting of Reverend Lee, and hadn't had a movement at all since they'd found Benjamin on Sunday. But, did he want to reconsider? No. He loved his children, and he wanted to believe he was a good father. He provided for them as best he could. And he'd like, now, to find another good mother for them. But he couldn't lie down with that. He had the will to stand up and be a man, to be respected as a man. His own father'd brought him up that way, and he wanted to set that example for his own boys. He'd loved Serena, and had made himself be patient during her long illness and the boys' infancy. But when she'd passed, he'd made arrangements with her people in Sumter to take the boys if anything happened to him. And ever since they'd shot Lee, he'd drilled the boys on taking precautions. Don't play outdoors after dark. Jump into the bathtub if you hear gunfire around the house. He made them lie on the floor to watch television. He'd even rearranged the furniture to make sure nobody sat or slept in the direct line of a window. Lord, it was like living in a battle zone. And it was only the beginning. Was he scared. God damn right! Would he reconsider? No. He'd made up his mind. And there, in church this morning, he'd taken his stand. He wasn't turning back. Was he at least optimistic? That was a harder question. He'd always believed his people would eventually win their rights. Eventually. But he had no illusions about how soon or how easy it was going to be. Things had been wrong too long to expect they could be set right overnight. People don't change that easy. And they sure don't like to be told to change. There was going to be a lot of hardship. The hard-liners were going to resist every inch of the way. There'd be threats and worse. People were going to lose their jobs, have their credit pulled, their relief cut off, their mortgages foreclosed. And there'd be more violence. But was he discouraged? No. It was harder to explain that to himself. Except, when you've wanted what you believe is your natural right hard enough, and waited long enough, and been tested harshly enough, there comes the moment when you feel your time is due, it's just time to act. It wasn't even about courage, courage really had nothing to do with it.

But the fight was going to be especially tough here, because everything else here seemed so easy. In a hard country, you got used to struggle. In the hills or thick woods, every family seemed isolated from the others, and grew up independent. The problem there was to get them to work together. But in a place like this, where you could just about pull the cotton up like a weed out of the cracks in the sidewalks, it was much more difficult to get started. The tendency was to look out on this broad flat lowland pushing up riches row upon row out to the horizon, and just bend over and pluck some, and let the philosophers and Washington bureaucrats sort out the rest in their own good time. Yes, there were the oppressive heat, humidity, fever and snakes. But in the end, one was overwhelmed by the place. The sputtering hedgehoppers, tractors, mechanical pickers and other efforts at modernization had had little impact. Like the swarming of the inevitable mosquitoes, they were all dwarfed by the ancient vastness of the place. True, they'd built a new atomic generator at the electric plant up there in Augury, one of the first of its kind in the country, the same kind they'd put in the Sea Wolf submarine. They were very proud of it, here, except that so far they hadn't been able to get it to work. All it seemed to do so far was kill the fish. And true, the crop-dusters that rove back and forth through the air trailed ribbons of insecticide the length and breadth of the growing season. DDT suffused the soil, made breathing hazardous, and doomed anyone living here more than a season to have his sweat begin to smell of it. But at night, the stars seemed closer here than anywhere else. Here, you could see to where the sun began and where it ended, to the ends of the earth, it seemed, in every direction. It made you want to suppose that anything not already apparent on this great plain couldn't matter, must, in fact, be the business of some other world. In the evening, the sun came right down to the ground, painting every stalk and stipple in a breathtaking chiaroscuro and interweaving shadows like a subtle web in which every man's shadow was bound up with the shadow of another.

But here, too, was his riddle: how to draw strength out of this tainted sweetness, a land seemingly running in milk and honey? How did one raise up even one man, if it meant having to raise them all? It was the confoundingest place he'd ever known and it troubled his sleep. And yet, as an early riser, he'd developed the habit of driving out in the predawn dark to Augury, at the headwaters of the Rue where the Tod and the Phlegashaw flowed together, and leaving his car by the I-C tracks, would climb up on the levee to say his morning prayers. And there, he would watch the sun rise up like a rooster spinning itself to life one flaming feather at a time, until its fierce bright wings dulled the stars and pushed back the curtain of darkness to reveal the acres of everlasting cotton rich and raw as a wedding bed....

"Aint that a bitch!"

Sampson was startled out of his reverie by the sound of the undertaker's voice. He turned to look at the man. Thomas Crouch was leaning against the opposite car window apparently agitated about some item in *The Dividend Times*, which he held open before him.

"This is history bein' made, here, and these hardnosed bastards got to put their two cents in! Lawd, tsk!" Crouch stamped his foot in annoyance -- apparently he'd been talking for awhile, though Sampson, preoccupied, hadn't been listening -- and went on, "It say, here, Jerry Dean's spoze to pitch -- that's Dizzy Dean's son. He play for De-troit now. And Goose Curry's gonna put Ollie Brantly, from the White Sox, to go up against him. You know, Curry usedta manage the Memphis Red Sox, fore he retired and started that baseball school for black boys here, in town...."

Sampson nodded politely, but mentally withdrew again to consider his plans for the voter registration drive, letting Crouch's voice reach him as though from a distance.

"...Now, the *Times* says the White Citizens Council been dropping leaflets from airplanes, saying 'Are You Proud Of Dividend?' and threatening to boycott the white merchants -- the *white* merchants, now! -- and to stage a sit-down strike right there on the Sportsman's Stadium diamond if the Chamber of Commerce don't cancel the game! Tsk, now, tell me, please!" He looked up at the pastor, "You follow baseball?"

"Er, not really...."

"Don't matter," Crouch went on abruptly, more animated, as usual, by his own opinions than anyone else's. "Point is, every time they make a step forward, they take two back! Folks tryin' to make some headway here, and somebody all-ways come along and rock the boat! You know, back in Burmin'ham, the po-lice wouldn't even let white players into the stadium on the same day with black players! And here, they actually got the Negro Big League All-Stars scheduled to play a exhibition next Sunday against the white Southern League All-Stars -- it's the first time in the Delta that a Negro team'd play a white team! And here, the Citizens Council-them tryin' to stop it! Tsk! It makes me wanna --! I was really lookin' forward to seein' the whites get they ass whipped, too --" he grinned, "not that that's so hard to do! The Negroes got some real good players. Casey Jones's a heavy hitter, and George Handy and Marshall Bridges. Shoot, makes me thinka the old days." He turned and said, "You know the Burmin'ham Black Barons, right?" and continued without pausing for a reply, "Uh! Once upon a time, they were a great team. Specially when Rico Jones was playin' for'em. They used to call Jones "The Anchorman!" What a athlete! Jones was the greatest homerun hitter in all baseball -- I'm talkin' black or white -- and that includes even the great Josh

Gibson! It was something to watch Jones in action. Come to think, I don't know whatever happened to him.... Anyway, I used to have a season box at the stadium for all the Barons' games. I knew all those boys. Burmin'ham's my home, you know...."

Sampson shook his head, not, as it might appear, in sympathy with Crouch, but in exasperation. The man could talk the Devil to distraction, he thought. And whatever the conversation, he would bring it round to citing chapter and verse in the catalog of his own virtues. But that probably explained his success in selling all those dubious burial insurance policies. He had most of the Negroes in the county putting change in his pocket.

Taking advantage of Crouch's self-absorption, the reverend rolled his window down a discrete half-inch to put his nose into the wind, trading a moment of heat for the oppressive smell in the air-conditioned car. The undertaker was in the habit of anointing himself heavily with various scents in the attempt to mask the persistent odor of embalming chemicals that seeped from his pores, but the resulting combination only made matters worse.

"...The Monarchs don't even play in Kansas City no more," Crouch was saying. "Was a time, after I moved to the Delta, I used to arrange my business trips to coincide with their schedule, when my boys-them was young, you know, I used to take'em. Of course, they all away at college, now...."

In a moment, Sampson thought to himself, gritting his teeth against the anticipated onslaught, he's going to remind me what areas of business his boys were preparing for, and detail how he'd scrimped and saved to put something aside for their schooling, and enlarge upon how he'd nevertheless managed to advance himself to the unique position of not only owning the biggest funeral parlor in the county, but of running the only Negro bank in the Delta. But what Crouch would never admit to was how he'd come by such privilege. Crouch liked to claim that it was the result of his own enterprise. But the reverend knew it would take more than ordinary enterprise for a Negro to be so successful -- much more to ever aspire to owning a bank -- in LeVane County. It was common knowledge that Crouch had somehow managed to ingratiate himself with the sheriff, but the nature of the arrangement had remained a matter of speculation.

"...Reminds me," the undertaker was saying, "I been meaning to look up Welch again, too. That nigguh -- oh, sorry, Reverend -- anyway, he still owe me money. He manage the Barons, you know. But he up in Cleveland this week with the Globetrotters. Me and him used to run together out in Shreveport, when he was managing the Acme Giants. Now, he a big mucky-muck, managing the Barons, and the Harlem Globetrotters, too. Yeah, Winfield Welch. Huh, we got enough stories on each other to keep both of us honest!"

He paused, at last, and turned to gaze out the window, perhaps, Sampson thought, reminiscing about his old hell-raising days.

The powerful car, doing at least seventy, seemed to be barely moving on the level straight-away, as it skirted the endless rows of cotton crossing one plantation after another, where teams of Negroes were bent over working in the fields with their duck cloth sacks dragging behind them as they crept along. A fragment of their song momentarily touched the pastor's ear, before being torn off in the wind.

"This integration thing work kinda funny, don't it."

"Sorry?"

"I mean, now, the irony is the black ball players are in the majors, and the Negro leagues that gave them all their start is disintegrating."

"Oh. Well, I guess the Negro leagues served their purpose. Blacks had to get into the majors to prove --"

"Yes, yes, I know!" Crouch said, cutting him off as though he were a dull student. "Don't get me wrong, it's very satisfying to see 'em playin' -- and most times out-playin' -- the whites in the majors. But all the same, something's gone out of it. I mean, the thing is, they was, all of 'em, our black boys. You'd watch them play with pride and passion. It was something of our own. But, of course, like you say, it wasn't enough, and we wasn't satisfied. Now, we satisfied, but the pride and passion is gone. I mean, that special intensity. Now, the game belongs to everybody, it's not our own thing anymore -- "

A horn blared, and the driver eased over to let a big two-toned Oldsmobile driven by a white couple pass. The woman tossed a dirty tissue out the window which blew back against the windshield of the hearse and caught, fluttering, in the wiper blade.

"GET DAT SHIT OFFA MY WINDA! GET IT OFF! GET IT OFF, GODDAMMIT!" Crouch had jumped forward in his seat to yell with sudden coarseness at his driver, and then sat back recomposing himself and muttering, "'Scuse me, Reverend." But his eyes looked wild.

The driver was already manipulating the window wash and wipers, but the tissue moved back and forth leaving a smear of mucous on the windshield before blowing off.

The undertaker stamped his foot, "Fuckin' white trash!"

Sampson stared glumly at the receding car. It had a tattered bumper sticker which read,

"...Most Lied-About State In the Union."

The air suddenly cracked like thunder, startling them. Crouch ostentatiously pulled up his sleeve to check the time on his expensive Elgin watch, the solid gold case and bracelet on his hairy walnut wrist like sin grinning in a dark wood. Sampson leaned over to look up and see a chevron of jet fighters speeding overhead like a fistful of thunderbolts, their silver wings aglitter and vapor trails expanding across the sky.

Crouch sighed, pursuing his own train of thought. "Man, they really starting up again. Only, why they'd want to burn down Ida Temple's place beats me. It's ridiculous, claiming the woman been harboring outside agitators! Ida always been respectable and ran that old whorehouse like a proper business. And everybody know some of them same peckerwoods burned it down been doin' business there, too, humpin' poontang on the sly. Seem like they gone completely crazy, now. And you know," he added, following a connection in his own mind, "Rhoder left those children without a dime."

The reverend shifted in his seat, roused by his own interest in the new subject, "Well, I suppose they'll repossess his mechanical picker," he ventured. "But Benjamin was always... well...frugal. I thought he had some savings --"

"Withdrew every cent. Closed the account."

"But, I thought --"

"I counseled him against it. I even offered to extend him a little credit, I figgered it was the least I could do. The man been banking with me for over ten years. But, he insisted."

"Why?"

Crouch threw up his hands, as though to say, What you gonna do with ignorant niggers?

"But then, what happened to the money?"

"Musta been stole. He took the money out the same day they killed him. Most likely, that's why they killed him. The cracker he'd been workin for -- whassis name, Brennan -- Brennan claimed Rhoder had stole money from him, that's why he fired him and deposited his security check. Course we know that's prob'ly a lotta bullcrap. But the point is, Rhoder had given him the usual security check -- you know how they do, it's a promissory note, that's all, sometimes it's just a little hand note the tenants write for the seed, fertilizer, family food and what-all they gonna need to live on and farm with each season, what they call 'the furnishin,' that they give to the plantation owner till the crop come in and they pay'im back end of the year. Aint nobody expected to try'n cash that, it aint never worth nothin', just a good-faith note.

"Anyway, once Brennan made the deposit, Rhoder was in trouble. He didn't have enough to cover it. And Brennan, knowin' that, o'course, was gonna prosecute him for writing a bad check. Rhoder would've gone straight to jail. I suggested he put his money in a friend's account, so what he did have left wouldn't be confiscated, and he'd at least have somethin' to live on, while he arranged credit to cover Brennan's claim. But either way, we had to bounce his installment check on the mechanical picker. And o'course, he had other checks outstanding. Whatever, he decided to take the money out. I know he had his heart set on trying to make a go of the business with that picker, and my guess is, he was on his way to make good on the bounced check with a cash payment for the picker, when they got him."

"But, the NAACP leaflets...?"

He shrugged, dismissing the subject.

Sampson grew thoughtful. Moments later, he looked out to see a familiar stand of willow and chinaberry trees growing high up on an Indian mound in the distance, and realized they were approaching the cemetery. It was one of thousands of such mounds scattered throughout the state that were built long ago by an unknown people for unknown reasons. Negroes had been buried there for the last hundred years, and fragments of clothing, crockery and other signs found in the network of caves and tunnels dug into the mound indicated it had probably once served as a hiding place for fugitive slaves on their way north. It was strange, given the richness of the soil, but for some reason the trees up there had never borne more than a handful of leaves. And though he knew it was only an effect of the light and the angle from which one viewed them, here on the road below, he noticed again how the bones of the trees had seemed to grow into the shape of a large sphinx couchant on the crest of the hill.

But in the back of his mind, he was still mulling over the previous conversation, and he said, "Didn't he have an insurance policy?"

"Who, Rhoder?" Crouch shook his head, "Cashed it in -- to pay for the picker."

"I see." But something about it still troubled Sampson.

As the car slowed and turned onto a dirt road heading into the cemetery, Sampson caught a glimpse of a police car trailing them at a distance. "Well, Tom," he said, turning back with a gesture that took in the hearse, coffin and gravesite, "I must say, it's generous of you to extend credit to the widow for all this."

Crouch waved it off with a self-deprecating smile.

The Mount Eden Cemetery of the Afro-American Sons And Daughters of Sinai had spilled over its original boundaries, and several graves had been dug outside the old wooden gates on the slope of the mound. The driveway skirted an unpainted pineboard house that stood on a weedy plot in the shadow of the cemetery. A small wiry old man in faded denims and a straw hat was out there, now, wading through a meager clutch of guinea fowl as he measured off the distance in long strides between the most recently dug grave, still open and awaiting the remains of Benjamin Rhoder, and his own sagging front porch. He carried a 12-gauge shotgun with a huge, thirty-eight-inch barrel slung in the crook of his arm. He looked up as the hearse approached, and paused to stand and curse them at length for being niggers and worse, as they drove past. You always found the old coot out there during a burial. They called him Old Paully. Old Paully'd be measuring his yard, or cursing the funeral cortege from his porch, and he'd usually wind up threatening the grave diggers with that ancient weapon of his or chasing them off with his dogs. He, Sampson, had tried to talk to the man on a couple of occasions, but the fellow would rave on without listening, and he'd finally given up on him. The old boy was irascible, but seemed harmless.

Meanwhile, his mind was still on Lorna Rhoder, sitting in the car behind him. He couldn't see her from where he sat, but he imagined her, heartbroken but trying to be brave for the children's sake, and for all her suffering, still looking young and vibrant and, despite her widow's weeds, beautiful enough to tempt any man.... He turned suddenly to glare at Crouch and muttered, "You sly sonuvabitch!"

But the undertaker was gazing out at the countryside, absorbed in his own thoughts, and mused, aloud, "You'd think in a place as wide open as this, you could see trouble coming a long way off. But you never know."

7.

Rhoder

The six of spades snapped out onto the table, leaving the six of diamonds showing in the window.

"Split! Split!"

"Split, my ass!"

"Aint datta bitch!"

"Fuckda fuckuh! Fuckit!" A man threw up his hands and stomped away from the table.

"Bettemup, bettemup!"

The boxman slid the second and third of four wooden markers down along the counting wire of the six card on the overhead casekeeper. The game was red dog, a local variation of faro, and a round of yelling and crying went up in the back room of the Channel Cat as the boxman raked in the chips, all bets going to the house.

Benjamin Rhoder watched his own bet scooped off the painted six, and shook his head. Shaking his head was a mistake, it immediately began to swim, and the arms of the layout started to ripple around the center card like a mojo spell to the thump and howl of *Mule Train*. Somebody kept playing the Frankie Laine record over and over on the jukebox back in the bar, like to drive him crazy. The cussing and signifying started again as the men slapped down new bets for the next turn. Rhoder stacked four red chips on the upper edge of the deuce, in the bottom row, tipping the stack over toward the queen above, without realizing it was the fourth time he'd played the queen in the last two deals. Hands whipped back and forth stacking white, red, blue and yellow chips on, between, or tipped-over-between the three rows of cards on the painted layout. The cards were all spades, king to eight in the top row, ace to six in the bottom, and seven alone in the middle. White chips were two bits each, red chips a dollar, blue five bucks, yellow twenty-five. The only one playing yellow was Eddie "Steamboat" Washington, sitting catty-corner on Rhoder's right, dressed to kill on his off-night in a tan silk suit, dark brown silk shirt and yellow, red and brown necktie with the fat Windsor knot pulled loose under the wide-roll "Mister B" collar. Rhoder would've given anything to see the flamboyant Negro from Detroit walk into Dividend dressed up like that. The police down here often-as-not hassled a black man for wearing even a white shirt in town. He chuckled to himself, imagining Washington turned inside-out and locked up so fast he wouldn't know south from Sunday.

The three of hearts was dealt out of the shoe, with the ten clubs showing in the window.

"Ten up, three down!"

Washington grinned and reached for his winnings. Men laughed, cried and disputed fate. The boxman slid the trey and ten counters down along their wires and raked in the chips. Rhoder felt a tap on his shoulder and looked up to see Jonah Johnson standing beside him.

"I'ma shift on down the line," the sharecropper said, his long narrow features twisted in a wry frown as he watched his white chips whisked away. "This ole red dog too mean for me tonight, I'ma try my hand at the bones. Catchya later on, Ben." He turned and made his way toward the crap tables.

"Yeah, okay, Jonah."

"Bettemup, bettemup!"

Rhoder peered through swollen eyes into the crowd looking for Thomas Crouch. He didn't see Crouch, but he saw Jim Bidder, the owner and manager of the club, standing in the gangway between the gambling saloon and the bar. Bidder caught his eye and nodded toward the closed office door, indicating Crouch was still in the meeting.

"Hey, man, when you goin up against Steamboat again?"

"Hey yeah, Rhoder, I give ya couple pointers how to take him out."

"Fuck yo' ass!" he snapped over his shoulder at the two bigmouths breathing cheap whiskey down his neck. "Get fuckin' lost!" But talking hurt his jaw and made his head ache again, and the faces around the table started bloating up, quartered in blue and orange under the kerosene lamps that swung like metal bandits from the ceiling wires.

"Cases onna jack! Cases onna jack!"

Rhoder gave the dealer a baleful look and pushed two chips out onto the queen, thinking to himself that the pigeon-chested nigger'd been settin' over there cool as cotton in his cheap green suit dealing him bad cards all night. Crouch better fuckin' hurry up. He felt like a damn fool hanging around here, losing money by the fistful. The fight the previous night must've fucked up his brains, as well as his eyes, he thought to himself. He'd been coming to the Channel Cat off and on since it opened, stopping off after work for a quick beer. But he'd never drunk busthead, and he'd never gambled more than fifty cents at the slots. Now, he's on his third whiskey, down forty-two dollars at red dog, and the reek of corn liquor and stale beer was making him sick. The heat, too. He was soaking in his shirt-sleeves, the slowly revolving wooden ceiling fans nearly useless in the crowded saloon. He felt the hot foul breath coming down on his neck to make another dumb remark, and spun around on his stool swinging a fist like a sledgehammer over his shoulder. The man behind him blew air like a ruptured tire. Rhoder turned back to the table, ignoring the uproar and crash of glass behind him, to press an arm against the stunning pain in his own broken rib and watch the queen of hearts drop out of the shoe, leaving the ace of spades grinning at him in the window.

"Ace up, queen loses!"

He closed his eyes and cursed Crouch under his breath for keeping him waiting. He'd come on purpose to see him the previous night. He wasn't asking nobody for no favors, he said to himself. He was gonna make Crouch a good offer. The man had plenty of land planted in cotton that he had other people working, and he was always complaining about "the escalating cost of manual labor." Rhoder just wanted an extension of credit to cover his checks till he could pay it back at the end of the season. He was offering to pick Crouch's cotton in the meanwhile, give him a good rate for the mechanical picker, and work off the interest and most of the debt. He been doing business at the bank long enough for the man to know he could trust him, he said to himself. He just didn't want to go to the bank office in broad daylight and put his business in the street. Wasn't like he was some nocount drifter. He been living right there in LeVane County all his natural life, had a family and was doing all right, till Brennan suddenly turned on him. Motherfucking peckerwood was crazy! But he'd known that from the beginning, which was why he'd never wanted to have anything to do with Brennan. Except that seven years before, when Lorna'd got pregnant with their second child, work had became slow all over and he'd got laid off from his previous job. So when he'd found out Brennan was hiring, he'd put his reservations aside. But every day, from the first day on, he'd studied Brennan out of the corner of his eye, wondering whether Brennan knew he'd seen what Brennan and the other one had done, out at Rue River years earlier. It had taken its toll on him, living with that knowledge and working for the man day after day. But he'd stuck it out for seven years, picking cotton by hand, and later operating the mechanical picker Brennan had bought, before he'd got his own picker. But there were plenty of acres out there in the Delta, and he'd thought it would've been all right. Even though he knew Brennan wouldn't want the competition, he, Rhoder, would have been willing to make some arrangement, even contract his picker in another county. Wasn't like there wasn't enough work for both of them. Sides which Brennan got plenty money coming in, he said to himself, he's a crop-duster, too, and a surveyor, he make plenty money on the side flying that plane all round the place. But the ignorant chickenshit piece of whitetrash up and got nasty. He jump behind the screen when I took out my razor, cause he knowed I'd cut him down right on his own fucking doorstep, talking about "tradin' lil poontang fo' lil credit!" When he said that, I throwed all caution to the winds, fuck it! White man don't got no special rights to play the dozens with the mother of my children! That was the other reason he'd come down last night. He'd been so mad he'd driven off the road twice, and the roads out there didn't have any turns. He'd needed a drink. He hadn't wanted to go home like that and maybe take it out on Lorna and the girls. As it was, he'd crept in after they were asleep and snuck out again early in the morning, before they'd woken up and seen the mess he drew.

Going over it in his mind now, he remembered he'd put up the picker when it had turned dark and driven out to the Cat to find it noisier than usual. The Channel Cat was an old

River Valley packet boat that had been hauled out of the water when the Tod had been dammed and rerouted as part of the federal flood control project after the war. The boat had been abandoned in a clump of cottonwoods behind the new levee, and Jim Bidder had bought it for scrap, refurbished it and opened it as a private club. He'd done well, too, and the Cat had become the main watering hole for Negroes in the county. The whites had several "country clubs" of their own, all private establishments for members only. LeVane was a dry county and gambling was illegal, but nobody bothered you if you called yourself a private club and took care of the sheriff. Jim Bidder owned the club, but had no title to it. It lay propped up on a corner of an abandoned plantation that the Afro-American Savings Bank had foreclosed. Bidder paid rent to the bank, a tithe to the sheriff, and presided at the sufferance of both. So, when Bidder had begged off signing the school integration petition, he, Rhoder, had understood and hadn't pushed it, especially as Bidder, who was older, and who'd worked on Brennan's place for years before taking over the club, had gotten him, Rhoder, the job there. They'd known each other a long time.

That night, he'd been able to hear niggers yelling over the racket of the Delco plant before he'd even come within sight of the place. He'd found the last tight space remaining in the parking area behind the club, and pulled in next to a new lemon yellow Hudson Hornet convertible, sleek as a pistol. On climbing out of his own beat-up old Ford coupe he'd stood for a moment running his fingers sensually along the door of the Hudson and feasting his eyes on the red leather upholstery. "Yeahhh," he remembered sighing to himself, "that Virgil Robinson sho know how to live!"

The joint had already been crowded when he'd entered, with the men all worked up and paying little attention, for a change, to the handful of women among them. But the cause of the commotion had become immediately apparent. He'd forgotten there was supposed to be a fighter coming through. The man was standing up on a chair at the back of the bar, stripped to the waist like a side of beef and sneering down at the crowd of men around him, who were screaming and falling all over themselves, excited at the prospect of seeing their own blood shed. Rhoder, edging over to the bar, ordered a whiskey, surprising Bidder, who'd drawn him a beer when he'd seen him come in. Meanwhile, Robinson, the owner of that sleek, yellow Hudson parked outside, a tall horse-faced man wearing a Panama hat, who ran the gambling concession, was making the pitch.

"...Just three rounds, boys!" he was saying, his big deep voice carrying easily over the hubbub in the bar. "The Steamboat's tough, but he's only human. One hundred dollars...!"

"Hey, Crawdad, whyn't you do it!"

"Fuck you, man, what I look like, a fuckin' punchin' bag?"

"You tough, man, you tough! Go for it...!"

"When ya gonna come see me, sugar? Don't tell me your wife treatin' ya that good...!"

"Hey, Jimbo, you see that triple-play Gilliam made today? That's my homeboy, man, he from Nashville! Hey, what you say, Ben, you seen the game today...?"

But Rhoder didn't respond. He was following the twists and turns of his own thoughts, spinning them out and reeling them in again, feeling them tug and dive like live fish in the eddies of conversation around him.

"--Nonna us even know the woman -- I mean, we do know whose wife she is, but she aint never said a 'boo' for good mornin'. This afternoon, me'n Jethro and Jonah Johnson standin' out by the post office, and she turn to us, say, 'What yall doin' here? What you talkin' bout? Move along! Yall got no business blockin' the walk!' Aint that a bitch?"

"So what, nigguhs aint spoze to talk, now? They got a new rule, now? Shit, you shoulda ast what the fuck she was doin' there!"

"Well, see, that's the other thing. She was on line with a buncha white mens applyin' for the executioner job up at the prison...!"

"...Just a kingsnake, you know. But the goddamn mule took afright and jumped for Judas. Harrow caught in the barn door and she split the singletree. Boss come tellin' me hit's my fault, he goan take it outta my account...!"

"...Sheeet, woman so ugly, I offered her a dollar just to stand out in my cornfield -- No, not you, darlin'...!"

"...One hundred dollars, gentlemen! One hundred! A full summer's wages for nine minutes' work...!"

That Robinson's a natural-born speaker, Rhoder said to himself. Voice like a choir of black angels. Anything he say, it set you thinking.

"Hey, Robbie! I go in for ten, man!" A stocky young boy pushed forward through the crowd to press his money into Robinson's hand.

Bidder, his thick bush of grizzled hair standing around his head like a mane, slid a tumbler of white lightning down the bar toward Rhoder with a conspiratorial wink at the crowd's expense -- or maybe at Rhoder's -- and went on jawing, drawing and punching the register, both hands flying and never missing a beat. Rhoder downed the watered booze, washing it back with the beer, grimaced at the nasty aftertaste, and ordered another. Meanwhile, four or five men were pushing money into Robinson's hand, the others egging them on.

"...Every time you look around, here lately, preacher, teacher, planter, banker, they all sneakin' off to secret club meetings. And I wanna know what them ofays is up to, cause when whitefolks start havin' secret meetings, you know it don't mean us no good...!"

"Tsk, vote my ass! Who I'ma vote for? Jim Bidder, here, plannin' to run for sheriff...?"

"No kinda way, man! Charles gonna wipe out Hurricane Jackson, I put money on that!"

"Go on, man! Ezzard Charles finished, man!"

"...One hundred dollars, gents! Buy yourself couple acres, get your lady friend a new dress, stock up on bootleg, tell the bossman go fuck himself...!"

Eddie "Steamboat" Washington, the one flexing his muscles up there on the barstool, had been a promising heavyweight when Joe Louis retired in '49. But he'd lost to Joe Walcott. And after Charles beat Walcott to take the title, Louis came out of retirement and KO'd Washington in an exhibition fight. The next year, Washington got himself put into the hospital by a young white fighter named Marciano. Now, he was a roadshow booze-hound with a drooping gut, taking on hillbillies and amateurs for ten bucks a head. Even in the pros, he'd been known as a dirty fighter, penalized for belly-blows and rabbit-punches. But he had arms like hams hanging off powerful sloped shoulders, and had put a few fighters into the hospital himself.

Damn fools! Rhoder thought to himself, watching the others promoting themselves for a thrashing. But after downing the second boilermaker, he began to think about that hundred dollars.

"I don't know where Bidder get this panther piss at, man," a short fat man said to his neighbor, eyeing the emptied tumbler in his hand before setting it down, "but I thowed stuff outta my oil pan taste better'n this shit!"

"Say what?" Bidder surprised the man by suddenly appearing before him across the bar.

The man thought quickly, "I said, when you gonna have another piana player, man? We could use some live music in this place."

Bidder grunted, "If you know one don't drink more'n he earn, send'm round."

"Hey, what you know, Ben."

Rhoder turned toward the tall lanky man in the peeked cap who'd spoken to him. "Hey, awright, Stitches. Man, I thought you was in the jailhouse."

Stitches laughed and indicated the others he was with, "That's what I was just tellin' these nigguhs, here. Every year, it's the same damn thing! I'm the best fuckin' crew chief the man ever had working for him -- no, no, it's true! That's why he do it! Wait, now, lemme tell you how it go. First week in March, soon as the ground thaw, he go my bail, see, lets me outta jail, and puts me back to work in that earth-moving company he owns. I rents the tools, hires the trucks and labor, and so on, right? So, he give me the work loan to cover all that. Then, I take the gang out to do the job, might be diggin' a trench and layin' pipe, or haulin' rock for construction, whatever. Come time the job's finished, I done paid off everybody else. Now, I go and ax the man for my pay. He tell me, he don't owe me, I owe him! Yeah! He say, I'm in debt to him for the work loan. I say, 'I thought you was deductin' that outta my share!' He say, the interest on my bail done et that up! You see what I'm saying! So, now, I done worked all season, and all I got to show is debts! And aint no use trying to argue, cause he the high sheriff. So, what I'm goan do? I gots to feed my family. So, then, I do whatever I got to do. Next thing, Clooder's sitting up in his car out there in my front yard, again, cause I done got in trouble with the law, and my ass is back in jail -- till next season!" Stitches closed his eyes, shook his head and his cheeks started to fill up and grow round. They got bigger and bigger until he began to look like Dizzy Gillespie or somebody fixing to blow down a house. The others, who'd turned back to their own conversations, stopped and one by one, turned to look at him again.

Then Stitches stamped his foot and jackknifed, bellowing with laughter.

Rhoder, meanwhile, heard somebody calling out his name. He turned and saw the crowd around Steamboat Washington looking in his direction and Robinson had turned to catch his eye. He realized they were going to try and talk him into going into the ring. Rhoder was husky himself, shorter than Washington, but broad and heavier in the shoulder. He'd scrapped plenty around the Delta, but only because he didn't take crap off anybody. But he didn't have any delusions about taking on a pro. Still, he knew he could take a punch....

Just then, Crouch came in. Well-dressed as always in a dark business suit, he smiled benignly, waved and shook hands with the men who greeted him. Behind the bar, Bidder reached into the icebox for a frosted highball glass, already sugared and packed with powdered ice, and carried it to the bulkhead, where a four-foot-one-inch blue and silver catfish was mounted under the mirror. He stood so that his back was turned to the bar, blocking his motions from the view of the customers, but Rhoder knew that he was releasing a hidden catch below the fish mount, which was fixed to the bulkhead by a spring-loaded hinge and behind which was hidden a safe where he kept individual bottles of his bonded liquor. He poured a generous double-shot of bourbon into the glass and put the bottle back into the safe. Slipping a sprig of fresh mint down the side of the glass, he put the julep on the bar with a wave of his hand, as though to say, On the house. Crouch took the drink and turned away, never having given a thought to paying for it.

Rhoder raised his hand to catch the banker's eye, and started toward him. But Crouch, apparently not seeing him, turned away and moved off through the crowd. Rhoder called after him, but Crouch, laughing and joking with the others, passed on through the gangway toward the saloon in back.

Rhoder stood there staring after him, wondering whether Crouch had just not seen him, or had purposely cut him. Maybe, he thought, Crouch had just figured that he wanted to beg for credit, or a loan or something, and hadn't wanted to turn him down to his face. Nah, he thought then, why would Crouch want to do me like that, I been banking with the man for years. Must be I'm still ticked off about Brennan, and it's the whiskey talking. He felt a touch on his arm and swung around so fast that four men jumped back along the bar.

"Whoa-up, Ben!"

"Easy, now, man, just wanna ax you if you wanna take a go at Steamboat, here."

"We stake you, man."

"The four a us'll put up the bread to see you do it."

"Okay, Ben?"

He frowned menacingly at each one in turn, then said to the first, "You didn't sign the integration petition the preacher sent round."

"What? Well, uh...."

"You didn't, either."

"Uh-rum, no, but, uh...."

"Neither did you!"

"Well, ya see, I --"

"You goan sign it?"

"Yeah, Ben, yeah!"

"You?"

"Sho! You got it witcha?"

"Don't be cute! I'll bring it round to you tomorrow, personal!"

"Okay! Sho!"

"I'ma bring the voter registration form, too. You goan sign'em both!"

"Okay, Ben!"

"Yeah, Ben, we'll sign'em!"

"That okay, now, Ben? We'll all sign'em tomorrow."

"Swear fo' God, Ben."

But one of them had slipped away. Rhoder turned to holler after him, and then saw that the other men at the bar had fallen silent and were looking vacantly off into space. But it was Jim Bidder's expression, as he stood staring down at his own hands frozen on the bar, that made Rhoder ease up.

"Yeah," he said. "Okay."

The men who'd approached him started to turn away. But one, looking down at the money they'd collected that he still held in his hand, tried one last time. "Um, what about, um, Steamboat, man? I-mean-I-mean, you wanna take'm on?"

"Up to you, Ben, howsomever you wanna play it."

"Yeah, how bout it?"

He looked from one to the other, feeling the whiskey still hot in his stomach, then turned and saw Washington, grinning down at him from the stool.

Washington sneered at the first man who climbed into the ring, hit him one time, and had him carried out before he'd ever got his guard up. Then he toyed with the second one, a husky eighteen-year-old, for most of one round before nailing his knees to the floor with an uppercut just in time to have him counted out at the bell.

They'd folded away the gaming tables and strung hemp ropes around an eighteen foot square in the middle of the saloon. Wooden chairs were set up on all four sides and high stools in the back row. The air was thick with smoke and whiskey fumes, the place packed to the walls, nearly two hundred, easy, shouting, whistling and making side bets. Most of the side bets had to do with how many seconds of the first round the rube was expected to last.

149

There were three more before Rhoder, then Washington gave his arms a rest, and simply ducked, slipped and side-stepped while the last man wore himself out punching air. In the middle of the second round, Washington hit him with two quick left jabs, a right below the belt and a left cross, which sent the fool over the ropes into the first row seats.

When Rhoder stepped into the ring, his pals whistled and howled, and the betting got heavy. Some thought he could hold out for three rounds, but the odds against were thirteen-to-two. Rhoder, with three boilermakers under his belt, was feeling high and able. The eight-ounce mitts felt like mere work gloves on his large hands. He decided, since Washington must be at least a little fagged after putting away five guys, he might as well make his play before he got his own ass hauled out. When Robinson swung the brass cow bell to start the first round, he rushed forward and threw a flurry of punches while Washington was still fixing his grin, scoring two glancing blows to the shoulder and the side of the head. The punches were harmless, but Washington, surprised, got mad and careless, and came back with a couple of haymakers. Rhoder ducked inside and countered with an uppercut to the jaw, before the Steamboat got serious and let loose a barrage of punches that drove him backwards three or more times around the ring before the bell rang, ending the round.

The crowd was roaring. Rhoder stumbled away along the ropes, while Washington stood in the middle of the ring snarling and cursing at him. Bidder, refereeing, had to coax and crowd the Steamboat back to his handler. When Rhoder reached his own corner, three pairs of hands were swinging sponges at his head. But dazed, drunk and mad at the world, he shrugged them off and told the niggers to leave him the fuck alone, he wasn't no fuckin' golden-glover, just get on with it.

When the bell announced the second round, Washington was all over him again before Rhoder'd fairly got off his stool. He doubled over with his arms wrapped round his head and took twenty or more punches, before he risked opening himself. He didn't know much about footwork, and figured there was no place to run anyway. He just planted his feet, and blocked, slipped and clinched best he could. Washington delivered so many combinations Rhoder felt like he'd fallen into a thresher. Every time he threw a punch, he got hit by six. Finally, a rabbit punch knocked him flat on his face.

He knew the round must be over, he'd been hit too many times for it not to be over. But Bidder, bent over him, counted and coaxed, and there was no bell.

"ONE! TWO!" Then a whisper, "Come on, Ben!" Counting, "THREE! FOUR!" Whisper, "You kin do it, Ben!" FIVE! SIX!"

"Where da bell?", he mumbled.

"Get up, man! SEVEN! C'mon, Rhoder!"

"Goddammit wha' happen ta da fuckin' bell!"

"EIGHT! Getcha lazy ass offa the floor! NINE!"

He gave up on the bell and climbed to his feet. He thought the Channel Cat was back in the water and felt the deck heaving under him. He felt broken open in so many places he didn't know what to hold on to. He turned to ask Bidder to put him ashore, and got a mouthful of fist. It must've bent him over sideways, because he was spun around by a glancing right hook that would've taken his head off if he'd caught it full force. He tried to raise his hands to protect himself, but he'd taken so many punches to the biceps that his arms were numb and he couldn't be sure of where he was putting them. The crowd hollered continuously, the roar blending with the pounding of blows to his head. Bending over made him feel sicker, so he just stood up and took the punches. He couldn't block anymore, so he stopped trying, and just started swinging wildly at a moving shadow that hit him at will. Next thing he knew, Bidder had his arms around him and was pushing him back to his corner. The bell must've rung, but he hadn't heard it.

"Attaboy, Ben! You wearin'm out, man! Hang in there!"

His mouth wasn't working anymore, so he didn't bother to argue. Bidder was gone by then, anyway. Now, he was being drowned in sponges and cheered to his funeral. The women were screaming and throwing their clothes into the ring, blouses, stockings, brassieres, but he was too tired to care. His one repeating thought was, soon as I can get my ass offa this stool, I'm goin' home! Then, he caught sight of Crouch, apparently having a hot argument with Robinson. He couldn't hear what they were saying because of the noise of the crowd around them, but the sight of Robinson gesturing there suddenly seemed to jog something in his memory. But he'd taken too many punches by then to follow it up, and he became distracted by the shadow of the ceiling fan spinning on the dome of the banker's large bald head. To his blurred eyes, it looked like a water spider seeking a footing, its two stalked eye-globes seeming brighter and more real to him than the lights they reflected, and for some reason unclear to himself, the vision set him off. Forgetting for the moment whose head it might be, and overcome by sudden anger and an irrepressible urge to crush that spider, he surged to his feet. But Robinson had turned his back on Crouch and rung the third round bell, and as Rhoder ducked to go under the ropes after that imaginary spider, Washington, having come out fast and let loose with a haymaker that swung passed where Rhoder's head had been, lost his own balance and fell against him. In reaction, Rhoder spun around with an uppercut to Washington's sternum that had all his strength in it, catching the pro by surprise and sending him stumbling backwards. And Rhoder, now seeing the spider before him in his mind's eye, followed up with a left and a right to the head that dropped Washington to one knee. Rhoder wasn't boxing, he was raging. He hit the downed man four or five more times, before Bidder could back him into a neutral corner.

Washington was on his feet again before Bidder started the count, and he came forward with such purpose and science as to give a glimpse of what he must have been like in his prime. Instead of going for the big KO, he began to take Rhoder apart an organ at a time, pulverizing his liver, solar plexus, heart, eyes, mouth. Rhoder, blinded by his own blood, gagging on a tangle of swollen tongue and broken teeth, stood rocking in the center of the ring, surrounded by the stamping howling crowd, barely able to breathe with his diaphragm paralyzed, his head batted back and forth like a paddleball, but his arms still swinging, wild and dangerous. He didn't fall down, and Washington maneuvered him against the ropes, purposely keeping him on his feet, keeping the target viable, butchering meat.

When the bell had finally rung to end the third round, and Rhoder had earned his hundred, Washington stepped back and stood studying the older man soberly, as Jim Bidder and Jonah Johnson led Rhoder out of the ring....

...But all that had happened the night before. Meanwhile, Rhoder reflected, here he was, tonight, still losing money at red dog and wondering how much longer Crouch was going to keep him waiting.

"Nine up, deuce down!"

"Sonuva--!"

"You believe that? You believe that? I got the goddamn eight and ten!"

The boxman moved the counters on the casekeeper, and cleared the layout. "Le's go, gennamens, le's go, bettemup, bettem up!"

Rhoder gingerly massaged his temples and tried to focus on the gaming table. Then he saw the dealer look up, and following his glance, caught Virgil Robinson standing in the shadows before the office door, with his Panama haloed in the rainbow cast by his, Rhoder's, own watering eyes. Crouch was inside by the desk with his back turned. Robinson made a motion as though brushing something from his forehead, then turned and went back into the office closing the door. Rhoder turned back and saw the dealer with his hand resting on top of the shoe rubbing his index finger on the corner of the box and staring at him with eyes like reechy pecans.

It was near the end of the deal. Three of the four queen markers had been moved to the frame end.

"Cases on the bitch!" he called, stacking five chips on the painted queen. "Fuck it. Cases on the bitch!"

The dealer waited until all the bets were placed, then snapped out the next turn.

"Queen wins, five down!"

"Shit, you believe this! You believe this!" another man shouted. "That's the second time! I got the goddamn king and five!"

"Bout fuckin' time!" Rhoder said, but hesitated a moment before pulling in his chips. It was the first time he'd won in a while. He eyed the house and player cards on the table, checked the casekeeper, and then stacked five chips in front of the dealer behind the five card, betting that the next winning card would be odd. When he looked up, the pigeon-chested little man had his eyes closed and was sucking a long black tooth protruding like a broach between his lips.

"Bettemup, bettemup!"

A four was dealt out of the shoe, leaving a seven in the window.

"Seven up, four down!"

"Cases on the trey!" Rhoder took his winnings and placed two bets, one for the odd card again, and one for the last three in the card box.

"Trey wins, eight loses!"

"New deal! New Deal!"

Rhoder pulled in his winnings. The dealer removed the last four cards that had remained trapped in the shoe pocket, and spread them out on the table. The house won all bets placed on those cards.

"Goddamn!" said Hoggitt, and snapped the straps on his bib overalls in frustration. He'd placed bets on three of the four cards. "I got a fuckin' curse on me, sho as shit!"

The dealer gathered up the cards and shuffled the deck. The boxman reset the casekeeper and cleared the layout. The players stood, stretched, went for fresh drinks, some giving up their places to new players. Rhoder remained in his seat staring moodily at the small fortune in chips now heaped, as though by magic, before him, and recalling how he'd returned to the Cat earlier in the evening determined to speak to Crouch. He had a proposal to make, and wanted to get an answer one way or the other. Still hurting from the fight the night before, he'd downed two quick boilermakers and then taken up his position at the front of the bar, intending to buttonhole the banker as soon as he'd shown his face in the door. But Crouch had got there before him....

"Hey, Ben, how's it going!"

Surprised, he started stammering, in a rush to get the words out, "Oh, uh-uh, Mr. Crouch, I--!"

"Bidder, what you standin' there for, man?" Crouch said, interrupting him to address the barkeeper, "You see the man's glass is empty, give'm another! This here's a goddamn hero, Bidder! His money's no good tonight! Everything Ben Rhoder want tonight is on the house! Fact, let's have a round for everybody!"

Rhoder, embarrassed, glanced over his shoulder and caught Bidder's eye. They both knew that when Crouch said "on the house," he meant on Bidder. Crouch didn't pay for anything.

"Hey, yall," Crouch continued, "a drink to Ben Rhoder, the man that grounded the Steamboat! Awright, Big Ben, here's to ya!"

He kept that up for a while, talking fast and glad-handing everybody, keeping the crowd clustered around them and yapping about the fight, so that Rhoder couldn't get a word in. Finally, when the others took a pause, Rhoder opened his mouth again, but the banker spoke first.

"Say, Ben, listen, there's something come up you oughta know about. Come on over here, a minute, I want to talk to ya --"

"Yeah, well, I wanna talk to you, too! You--"

"Good! Of course, of course!" Crouch said, guiding him by the elbow toward a vacant spot by the front door. "But this can't wait, Ben, listen. There's a opportunity that's just come knockin' on your door. It's going to make you a man a property, Ben. Independent. Now, I aint given to exaggeration, but I'm telling you, this going to turn your life around, you hear?"

"Oh...what do you mean? I wanted to --"

"But you gonna have to act fast on this, Ben. You gonna have to grab the eagle as she flies, you understand what I'm trying to tell you? You can't hesitate on this, you gonna have to be decisive! Decisive, you see?"

"What you talking about, Mr. Crouch? Decisive bout wha --"

But Crouch was looking at his watch, "Now, I'm only gonna be able to go over this with you once, Ben. One time, just once -- I'm not trying to put you under no pressure, now. I know you got things on your mind. I know about Brennan and the picker, and so on. But you been a good client with the bank, Ben, a long-standing good client, and truth to tell, a lot more, you been a friend. And there aint no reason on earth you shouldn't have a chance to get yours back when things get a little tough on ya -- Now, wait, no need to thank me, yet. Sides, I'm only doing what any conscientious businessman would do in my place. I throw something your way, sooner or later, it come back to me. What goes around comes around, aint that right?"

"Well, I mean, what is it? What're you talking about, Mr. Crouch?"

Crouch studied him in silence a moment, as though trying to anticipate the effect of what he was about to say.

"So, go on, what is it?"

"You interested?"

"Sure! -- Well, I mean, I suppose so...! But there's something I wanted to.... Well, I mean, go on, what's the opportunity?"

"Are you ready for a change, Ben? Are you?"

"C'mon, Mr. Crouch, what you mean, am I ready?"

Crouch nodded to himself, then turned away, "Well, I tried to help you...."

"Hey, wait a minute!" Rhoder went after him, "Hey, Mr. Crouch -- Hey, awright. Awright! Okay!"

Crouch turned and came back to clutch his arm, smiling. "You a strong man, Ben Rhoder, strong in body, strong in mind. You gonna do awright, now. Wait for me." He turned and started away again.

"Hey! I -- Mr. Crouch, what...?"

The banker turned again to give him a confident wink, "We gonna get on this right away, Ben, soon's I get outta this here meeting. Can't wait till tomorrow. Don't go 'way. Have a coupla drinks -- not too many! -- or play some cards, somethin'. Just be a while."

"But I...don't gamble...."

Crouch trotted back to him, his hand in his pocket, "That's why I trust you, Ben. You aint like the rest a these no-count nigguhs, drink and gamble their life away. But, I think your luck about to change. Here, take this. On the house," he winked again, thrusting a crumpled bill into his hand. "You go in the saloon, there, sit through a few turns of faro. You play faro, and don't worry, you'll be richer by-n-bye!"

Rhoder glanced down, astonished at the fifty dollar bill in his palm. When he looked up again, Crouch had slipped away through the crowd....

"Seven wins, queen loses."

"Traps! New Deal!"

"Sombitch, my fuckin' cards in that fuckin' trap, too!"

"Lawd, whatta night!"

Steamboat Washington, brooding over a chewed toothpick as the boxman raked away his remaining chips, got up and stalked away from the table.

"Ey, Rhoder, bluebird musta shat on you this week, man!" Hoggitt cackled and nodded his head meaningfully toward Steamboat's receding back.

"Aint over till it's over, Hoggitt," Rhoder said, chuckling, as he pulled in his chips.

"Bettemup, gennamens, bettemup, bettemup!"

But his luck did seem to be changing. He leaned back and stretched, gaping at the hundreds of dollars worth of chips stacked before him. Maybe there was something to this gambling shit afterall, he thought to himself. Couple more deals like this, and he might not even need Crouch! -- speaking of which, where --

"Man lookin' for you, Ben."

He turned at the sound of Bidder's voice in his ear, and saw Crouch beckoning to him from the open door of the office. "Hey, Jim," he said, catching Bidder's sleeve, "cash these in for me, will ya?"

"Sho thing."

Rhoder got up and slid a folded ten across the table to the dealer, then turned and headed toward the office. The dealer took his time lighting a cigarette before pocketing the tip, as the smoke curled over the lamps.

Ten minutes later, after counting out the fifty dollars Crouch had loaned him, Rhoder shifted uncomfortably in his seat to look out the porthole of the office, but the night mist was opaque against the glass. He glanced down at the clutter on the large oak desk before him, which included bags of coins, bundles of folding money tied with string, an overflowing ashtray and a well-thumbed copy of the *Chicago Defender* lying open to the sports page. Nearly hidden under the paper was a big green ledger, on the spine of which he was able to make out *...LeVane County: Property Deeds and Taxes For the Ye....* He shifted again, trying to ease the cramping in his legs. He was sitting in a child's schoolhouse chair, with one knee pressing on the underside of the writing arm and the other jammed against the molding of the desk, which nearly filled the tiny office off the saloon. He could feel the vibrations of the Delco generator, running below-deck under the office, coming up through the soles of his shoes. It resonated right through him, aggravating the soreness in his rib cage and throbbing in his head. The noise from the juke and the gambling crowd beyond the partition didn't help, either. And yet, he was feeling pretty good, all in all, some four hundred and sixty dollars richer, between the fight the previous night and his winnings at faro. Even so, he wanted to think this thing through some more.

Playing for time, he said, "Who else know about it?"

"Nevermind about that," Crouch said. "What's important is, are you willing to get to him before somebody else does."

"But I mean-I-mean, that's up by Mount Eden way, right? Aint that Fontana's land?"

"Fontana? Fontana? What Fontana got to do with the price of tea in China?"

"Well, I mean, didn't he --?"

"Fontana Dundee been dead for ten years, Ben, what you talking about? What's --?"

"Well, yeah, but I mean-I-mean, I remember, when he died.... What about the boys-them?"

"What boys?"

He looked away, still feeling uneasy, then said, "Who own it now?"

"Ben, you asking all the wrong questions! Point is, the man got a note in his hand, right now, saying another man's promising to take it."

"So then, so then, how I'ma get it, if he awready --"

"Tsk!" Crouch stubbed out his cigar impatiently. "Man, money shout, a promise just a whisper! You gotta bring him cash. Not a letter of intent, not a bank check. Cash!"

Rhoder squirmed around in the little chair to get his knee out from under the writing arm, then gave in to impulse, and tried to voice all his concerns at once, "So then...so, okay... so if that's the case why the bank don't gimme the mortgage right now why I gotta take out all my savings and destitute myself for the down-payment what I'm gonna take and pay the loan for the picker spoze --"

"C'mon, Ben! You know how these institutions work. Bank can't give you a mortgage without..." he put up a hand and counted the items off on his fingers, "proof of intent to sell, full description and appraisal of the property, evaluation of the applicant's credit rating...! Time we get through with all of that, the other man going to snatch that property from out ya hand! You gotta get the owner to commit the property to you!"

Rhoder sighed, and gazed up longingly through the haze of heat and cigar smoke at the wooden ceiling fan, dusty and dead-still over his head. "That fan don't work?"

Crouch stared at him with silent intensity from the height of the captain's chair behind the desk.

"How much time I got to decide?"

"Up to you. You can celebrate tomorrow, or, you can cry about it at leisure."

"And you say the property going to gimme income right off?"

"First of the month. You know how these Negro preachers are. They dip a hand into the contribution box once in awhile, humph, but they know where their bread's buttered. The Lord hold the key to Salvation," he said, then leaned forward with one elbow on the desk, his fingers joined together as though holding a precious stone, "but the *landlord* hold the key to supper! Throw the preacher out of his church, and he's nekked as a lamb in a wolf run. Look, Ben, you gonna have two churches, here, like I told you. One on good town property, and one pinning down the corner of a good-size piece of plantation. Plus the four residentials. Any time the rent don't suit you, you can turn'em all out and plant cotton. You need cash later on, you can always turn around and sell at a profit. An-y-thing you do, here, you gonna make money, Ben!"

But Rhoder hesitated. He felt there was something else he needed to resolve, but he didn't know what it was. Casting about for the right question, he said, "How I know the man -- I mean, the one got it now -- I mean, why he don't wanna keep it, hisself, then?"

"The question you should be asking, is how come I'm giving you the opportunity, and not grabbing it my own self! The owner..." he waved a hand, dismissing the person, "the man's a outsider. He come into the property, but he don't know the Delta, and don't have any idea what the place is worth. And he don't wanna hang around collecting rent. To him it's just an opportunity to turn over a quick dollar and go. Now, I want to be honest with you, Ben. You know I'm a business man. I don't mind doing a friend a good turn, but I aint likely to throw away good money to do it." He smiled, tapping his finger on the five ten dollar bills Rhoder had just returned, "Like you see, here, I invest in people. But the fact is," he nodded his head in a gesture of modesty, "I done so well this year, with one thing and another, I'm gonna have a fit come tax time. If I grab this, now, I'll end up losing money this year. Yes! Humph. But still, the way it works out, it's gonna pay me to do you a favor. The bank'll get a percentage of the mortgage loan -- that's only business as usual -- and don't worry, I guarantee you the mortgage, right here, right now, with a lil extra over the appraisal, so's you can cover what-all other expenses you got for your loan on the picker, your own house rent, bills, 'cetra. That's just 'tween you, me and the gatepost, now. Leave the details to me. And come next year, when you get ready to start making improvements on your property, why, you'll come round to the Afro-American Savings And Loan Association for your financing. It's whatcha might call a circle of prosperity framed by friendship." He reached into his breast pocket and offered Rhoder a fresh cigar. "You do have friends here, Ben, I suppose you know that."

Rhoder's lip twitched into an involuntary smile, and he shook his head, declining the cigar.

Crouch raised his eyebrows, as though mildly surprised, and unwrapped the cigar for himself. He moistened it, inserting the ends alternately into his mouth, then walked the flame of a solid gold lighter up and down its length, turning the cigar in his fingers. After a moment, when Rhoder hadn't spoken, he said, casually, "Everything awright at home?"

Rhoder looked up sharply, "Whatcha mean."

"You, Lorna and the kids-them, yall gettin' along awright?"

"We gettin' along fine! Why?"

"Just askin'."

"We gettin' along fine! Just fine! Whatcha mean, you got some reason to think we aint?"

"No need to get riled, Ben. I didn't mean nothin'. We just two friends talkin', that's all."

Rhoder looked away again, unconsciously grinding his teeth.

The banker clipped the end of the cigar with a gold-plated tool and lit it, rolling it carefully to get the ash going evenly all around. "So, what'll it be, Mr. Rhoder? Does we see ya at the bank tomorrow? or doesn't we?"

Rhoder, preoccupied, started at the sound of the other man's voice. He turned to see the banker standing with his open hand extended across the desk and a big smile on his face behind a cloud of cigar smoke. He hesitated a moment, then took the hand in his own.

Crouch shook it warmly. "Congratulations, Ben Rhoder, you a new man today!"

Rhoder climbed awkwardly out of the small chair, and turned to open the door.

"Oh, by the way. What was it you wanted to talk to me about?"

"Uh?"

Crouch gestured with his hand, "Before. You said you wanted to talk to me bout something."

"Oh. I...uh, 'snothin'"

"See ya tomorrow, then."

"Yeah. Yeah. Tomorrow."

✷ ✷ ✷

The dogs had started up as soon as Rhoder had turned in off the road, early the next morning. Preoccupied, he drove slowly along the packed dirt track, barely fifteen feet wide, that ran straight as a furrow through a field of cotton plants high as the car windows. Back when he was a boy, the finer grade of cotton used to grow to well over the head of his father, who'd stood over six feet tall, before age and rheumatism had got to him. But that tall cotton had been harder to pick, hadn't yielded as much as the short-stemmed coarser variety, and had taken longer to mature, allowing the boll weevil more time to destroy it. Over the years, the government research station at Stoneville had developed the crossbred plant that was grown throughout the Delta now. It was easier to reach and had a high yield of fine long staple. But it was still vulnerable to weevils, and it still had burrs. The four older Johnson kids were already out with their sacks working in the next field over. They looked up and waved at him as the car passed. The cotton had already been pulled from the bolls in the rows adjacent to the driveway, leaving a woody thicket on either side, where the razor-sharp burrs, dotted with blood from the hands of the pickers, remained among leaves still green, glossy with dew and beginning to steam in the sun. He gave thanks to God for the mechanical picker, for he felt it was going to free him and other Negroes in the Delta from this backbreaking labor and put real money in their pockets. But that thought brought him back to the problem that had kept him tossing and turning all night. He'd decided when he'd gotten up that morning to get his mind off it by coming out to go hunting with Jonah, who'd always been willing to take the risk and get a jump on the season.

He flipped the visor down as he drove the last two hundred yards toward the house and squinted against the sun, which was spearing at his eyes from behind the eaves of the cabin. A thin pancake of smoke drifted above the kitchen chimney. The sky was clear now, but he thought it might blow up later, maybe rain. Where the road ended a four-year-old girl in a freshly ironed blue and white striped dress sat on the porch steps of a dogtrot cabin dandling her baby sister on her knee. The cotton grew right up against the bare pine boards of the cabin leaving only a narrow footpath between the toolshed and the porch. He turned the car around in the swept dirt clearing before the toolshed, pointing it back out toward the road, and killed the motor. As he climbed out some chickens fled cackling from beneath his feet.

"Mornin', Desiree," he said, leaning against the car. "Where's your papa?"

The girl didn't answer, but her smile faded. A strip of cotton cloth bound around her arm held a lump of red clay soaked in vinegar. He could smell the vinegar from where he stood. The bandage had come loose, exposing a fresh cut on her elbow. The infant began to cry and the dogs in the kennel out back, who'd fallen silent meanwhile, began to whimper. The girl got up and climbed the stairs carrying the baby awkwardly before her with its feet dangling against her shins. She kept her head turned to look back at Rhoder over her shoulder until the front door closed behind her.

Jonah didn't appear. But his National guitar lay with its neck broken against the wall in the breezeway and a fresh rosette of number-9-sized holes was visible spread over the top of the door and the lintel. Rhoder went up and leaned over a sagging crack in the porch railing to rap on the doorjamb. There were sounds inside and then Essie, Jonah's woman, came and stood at the kitchen door without opening it, a familiar but indistinct shape behind the screen.

165

"Where Jonah," he said, when she didn't speak.

"He aint here!"

He guessed she was nursing the youngest in her arms there, in the shadows. "Where he at."

"He aint here!"

"I done heard. Where he--"

"Out, dammit! Gone to hell, for all I know! And don't you be hangin' there bustin' down my railin'! Yall bust dis'n bust dat, won't fix nothin'! All yall knows how ta do is bust-up 'n' shoot-up 'n' fuck-up! Go on! I done told ya he aint here!"

She'd slammed the wooden door behind the screen. But he hadn't heard the floorboards creak, and as he climbed back into the car and drove off, he knew she was still standing there, listening for him to leave or for who knows what.

He caught up with Jonah a short while later, finding him hunting along what he knew was Jonah's favorite stream. Jonah greeted him with a nod, and turned his attention back to his dogs.

"Attaboy, pup. Good dog, good pup, you learning. Done beat out Buster. Good puppy."

The black and white setter had caught the scent and gone on point forty yards ahead before a patch of purple loosestrife and mock-orange. The clouds had thickened and the dark canopy of tupelo, sycamore and sweet gum cast a pall over the marsh. Jonah continued to murmur praise, and the setter began to wag its tail, as the men approached cautiously along the edge of the stream.

"Hush, nigguh, you distractin'm."

"You tellin' me how to train my own dog, now?"

"Gotta be told, if you don't know," Rhoder said, as Buster, the older dog, trotted up and took a stand a length behind the setter, honoring the first dog's point.

"Well, now, looka here!" Jonah said. "Where you come off at bein' so smart? Somebody appoint you Dog Expert? I been trainin' dogs all my life, you going to tell me how to do it, now? What you know about it. You hear me tellin' you how to run your business? Some folks gittin' too high-n-mighty round here," he added, turning back to the dog. "Good dog, good pup!"

But the setter, still wagging its tail, began to whine and back off.

"Fuck! See that, now? You the one distracting him!" Jonah said, and spoke to the dog again, "Hold steady, fool!"

Buster held steady-to-wing-and-shoot, but the young setter turned away with a whining growl and put its nose in the grass, as though to seek a new trail.

"Huh, something out there done put him off," Rhoder said. "Mebbe something he smell in the water."

"Mebbe my fuckin' ass! You the one fuckin' put'm off!"

Jonah stalked off after the dogs through a thickening tangle of alder and arrowwood, impatiently slapping branches out of his way and inadvertently flushing a covey of rail. At sight of the birds, he dropped to one knee and swung the muzzle-heavy 20-gauge Browning over. But careless in the moment, he allowed the barrels to strike a limb that whipped back in his face. He cursed aloud and slipped sideways, with the gun swinging back to discharge against his shoulder, just as Rhoder snapped off a shot coming up behind him.

Next thing Jonah knew, he was on his back, looking up through leaves spattered with blood. He didn't know whose blood it was. He was dazed, and his head was ringing from the gun blasts. He couldn't figure out whether he'd been knocked unconscious or not. He raised himself on his elbows and looked around. The sun was still inclined at about seven o'clock. He couldn't have been out more than a few minutes, if that. His gun was there in the grass beside him. And just behind his head was the upturned sole of Rhoder's shoe. He got to his feet and looked down at him. Rhoder was lying on one side, his face turned away, blood seeping from under his head onto the ground. His Winchester had been thrown to one side and leaned teetering in the bushes. Jonah hesitated, then tapped the sole of Rhoder's foot with his toe, but Rhoder didn't stir. Jonah looked around, confused and frightened, then picked up his own gun and began to edge away.

He'd gone about twenty yards, when he stopped. "What the hell's the matter with me!" he said, and turned and ran back. "Ben? Ben?"

The setter had trotted up to sniff at Rhoder, and was licking his face as Jonah came up.

"Shit!" Rhoder said, coming to and shoving the dog aside.

"Ben! You awright?"

"Shit...yeah...think so."

Jonah stooped to help him sit up. Rhoder was bleeding slightly from his neck and ear, but the wounds were superficial, a couple of number-9 lead pellets having grided the flesh as they passed.

"Can you move awright?"

Rhoder shrugged his shoulder, turned his head, lifted his arm. "Huh, it's better then it was. It was still stiff this mornin'."

"F'a minute, there, you scared the shit outta me!"

"Scared the shit outta you! You most killt the shit outta me!"

Jonah laughed, "Well, mebbe the bull shit, anyway."

They bound the wound with a torn-off piece of Rhoder's shirt, and Jonah helped him up. Rhoder went to pick up the Winchester, and Jonah turned to look out on the stream to see whether any birds had fallen. But dogwood and poison sumac growing thick along the bank obscured the waters. He turned back toward Buster, still on point beyond the thicket, and gave a short trilled whistle.

Buster bounded off into the stream, and the setter followed.

The men stood silent for a time looking off into the woods as contrary breezes gossiped through the foliage. A hawk drifted through the trees on the opposite bank. They watched it swoop down to rake the water then rise with empty claws and glide off like a shadow.

"Got somethin' on ya mind."

Rhoder didn't answer. He broke the Winchester and replaced the spent shell, shut the breech again and looked away toward where they could hear the dogs splashing in the water downstream beyond an ambush of rotting logs and white dodder.

Jonah turned, speaking over his shoulder, "Essie mention we had a lil diff'rence last night?"

"After a fashion."

Rhoder watched the man make his way stiffly toward firmer ground. Stooped and sinewy from a lifetime of sharecropping, Jonah trudged through the vine-choked bog as though climbing a steep slope. Coming out behind him, Rhoder overheard him talking angrily to himself.

"...All fuckin' day, from kin ta cain't, breakin' your hump all god damn summer, and fo' what! Chopmeat twenty-five-cent a pound, cotton seven. And then the planter, he take half a that. One year, ball weevil. Next year, river flood. This year, finally get you a good crop -- and the man at the gin, he say he aint takin' no mo' cotton, it aint worth shit, world is fulla cotton! But yet-still, he takin' it from the white folks, and from some other nigguhs, too! And, if that aint enough, planter get a sudden bug up his ass, say I aint pickin' fast enough, if I don't look out he goan fire me off the place! I'm the fastest hand-picker in the county, and he say I aint pickin' fast enough! Shit! How a person spoze ta live! Woman ack like it's all my fault. Nelly howlin' out there in the kennel tryin' to give birth to two dead puppies. Dog put food on her table every winter. Ask'er to come help me with her, woman tell me me'n the dog both can go ta hell! Lump a black blood come outta that dog big and hard as that!" he held up a scarred fist. She don't understand if I don't shoot rail today, she'n the kids-them goan eat shirttail tomorrow. Shit really git my goat!"

Rhoder reached out and put his hand on the other man's shoulder. "Jonah, listen, you done right to sign that school petition, man. People can't go on takin' that shit all they life, it aint healthy. Come a time a man gotta stand up for himself."

Jonah nodded and turned away, letting Rhoder's hand slide off his shoulder. "Heah, boy! Give it here, Buster!"

The mongrel shorthair came up and stood at his knee, but kept its jaws clamped. Jonah had to lean his gun against a tree and prize the dead bird out of the dog's mouth. He handed it to Rhoder to look at, a Virginia rail with a long red bill, cinnamon wings and barred black-and-white belly. Its breastbone had been crushed.

"Dog got a hard mouth," Jonah said. "He'll run a rabbit a month, clear across the county. But he's a mothafucka with birds. This'n, here, now, flush more birds than he find," he added, turning to the eighteen-month-old setter that stood ten yards off, nuzzling the other dead bird in the grass. "He aint but half-trained, yet, but he got possibilities. He quick to pick up a trail. "Attaboy, pup, bring that lil chickenbill here! C'mon, now, dammit, bring it on here!"

The setter barked playfully at Jonah, picked up the mottled-brown sora from where he'd dropped it, came three steps closer, dropped it again, and stood wagging his tail.

"Dammit, fool, bring it to me!"

"What's his name?"

"Aint got round to givin'm a name yet. But 'Fool' just might be it. Let's go, he'll figger it out 'ventually."

They moved on, following the shorthair, who'd picked up another scent.

"Nelly, now, she a born bird hunter," Jonah continued. "She practically trained her own self. She the best ole hound. But she got another kinda problem. Every year, just when the season open, like now? she go to having her period, and I lose three weeks without her. Gotta go out with Buster, or take one a the younguns."

"Thought you was gonna see Basheeba bout that."

"That's what I'm saying! I did! Soon as she finished her last one, I did. But that woman...!" he glanced quickly at Rhoder and bit his tongue, then said, "Basheeba gimme something to put off the period, see. A 'coction a red-beet root, chinkafoil, raspberry, willow bark, toad tongue, chicken tooth, bat balls, you know how she do. Anyway, said to boil it in milk and give it to the dog every day starting a month before her time. Okay, but then, she say she want five dollars for that. 'Five dollars!' I said. 'Fo' what? I don't even know if this mess'll work!' I offers her two dollars, and another dollar later, if it work. Figgered that was reasonable. Lawdamussy! Woman jump up and start to puttin' a curse on me for trying to cheat her! Man, I gave her the last five dollars to my name just to git outta there walkin'! But I knows from that she don't mean me no good. Sho-nuff, here it go: steada gittin' her period, dog givin' birth to two dead puppies! I don't mean no disrespect, Ben, I mean, she your mother-in-law, and all. But that's one mean ole hoodoo woman, for true. Now, Lorna a nice fine woman, but, personally, speakin' for my ownself, now, I'd think twice fo' marryin' into a family like that --"

Rhoder stopped and whirled to face him, "What the fuck Lorna got to do with it!"

"What? Lorna? I didn't --"

"Why the fuck everybody talkin' bout Lorna--!"

"Simmer down, man, I was talkin' bout the ole woman, now, didn't say nothin' gainst Lorna--"

"--Lorna aint none a yall's fuckin' business --!"

"Awright! You right! I didn't even mention her name."

"--Lorna got nothin' to do with yall --!"

"'S what I'm sayin'! Calm, brother, calm!"

"-- All yall oughta mind yown fuckin' business!"

"I just -- look, we just discussin' a lil dog, here, and -- Whoap!"

Gesturing for silence, Jonah nodded his head, indicating where Buster had gone on point again up ahead. They checked their guns and followed without speaking. They'd taken only a few steps, when the other dog dashed past them, dropping the sora along the way, and charging up to burst in ahead of Buster's point.

Jonah whistled to stop him, but it was too late. A fall of woodcock burst into the air and scattered out of range beyond the trees. Buster, snarling, wheeled and lit into the younger dog, chasing him into the brambles and snapping at his flanks. Jonah cursed and whistled again, but the dogs ignored him.

Rhoder heard the plaintive "Peent! Peent! Peent!" of the fleeing woodcocks echoing back through the swale, and felt a strangeness in the air. "Just as well," he said. "Sheriff catch us with woodcock this far outta season, we in trouble."

"Don't know bout that," Jonah said, whistling again when the dogs hadn't responded. "Hunger aint got but one season. That's a year-round trouble. Then again," he added, in another tone, "mebbe you doin' so well, here, lately, you done forgot that."

Rhoder turned to look at him. "What's that spoze to mean."

They could still hear the dogs fighting in the thicket, and Jonah whistled for them again.

"From what I hear, you fixin' to be the big man round here."

"What you talkin' bout, man? What you hear?"

"You sayin' it aint true?"

"I aint sayin' shit! You the one doin' all the sayin'! What's this 'big man' shit? Whyn't you come on out and say what you got to say!"

The other man rolled his tongue around inside his mouth, as though tasting the words, before answering. "You fixin' to take over Fontana's old property from that Robinson fella."

Rhoder, taken aback, just stared at him.

"Well aint that right?"

"...Robinson...?"

"Well, Crouch, Robinson, same diff'rence, Robinson won the fuckin' property offa Crouch in the poker game last week, but I wouldn't be surprised if they all in cahoots together. You sayin' you don't know what I'm talking about?" When Rhoder continued to stare at him in puzzled silence, the farmer grew impatient, "Tsk, c'mon, man, don't stand there looking at me like I'm talkin' Chinese! You gonna tell me you didn't know that Fontana --?"

"No -- I mean, yeah, everybody know Fontana usedta did own it, but he --"

"And everybody know Crouch stole it from him, too!"

"He -- Fontana couldn't pay the mortgage and the bank just --!"

"Bullshit! You know well as I do Fontana never missed a payment till the day he died! Crouch said he did, but aint nobody believe that because everybody knew Fontana! You, especially, you knew him good as anybody. You used to go over there and take his oldest boy fishin' -- what's his name, the ugly one they put in reform school. You f'git you used to go round with Fontana middle of the night tryin' to get all the rest of us to register? You f'git that?"

"Well, well, I mean --"

"Crouch took the man's cotton, which Fontana done awready picked and loaded up for the gin, took the land, took the house and packed his boys off to the Welfare! That's just as good as stealing, if y'ask me --!"

"...People don't --"

"-- Fontana worked like a dog on that place, too. But that always been a hard-luck place. You know, y'self, aint nobody want nothin' to do with that place since Fontana died --!"

"Tsk! Man, that was all a long time ago!"

"...So, you sayin' it's true, then."

"What?"

"That you buyin' it!"

"Where you hear that?"

"Shit!" Jonah turned away and spat, disgusted, then turned back angrily, "I heard! What fuckin' diff'rence it make, who told me! Everybody know you makin' moves round here! You done bought that mechanical picker and awready put some folks outta work. That aint no secret! Now, look like you settin' up as a planter y'ownself, gonna have the people you done put outta work turn around and have to go to work for you...!"

But Rhoder wasn't listening. He stared, unseeing, toward the thornbushes, where the dogs had disappeared, his mind racing.

"Well?"

"Well, what?"

"Well, fuck you, then! You hear me? Fuck you!"

"Hey, man, wait a minute!"

"Fuck wait!" The farmer turned on his heel and stalked off.

"Jonah, wait!"

"Wait fo' what!" Jonah shouted back over his shoulder. "We been knowin' each other since we been kids! Now, you don't wanna be straight with me? You wanna keep secrets? Well, go fuck yo'self! I don't want your fuckin' money! I make my own livin'! *Honest* livin'! I aint the one goin' round causing trouble with school integration petitions and shit and putting other folks out they livelihood! And another thing!" He paused to turn and stab the air with his forefinger, "Before you go givin' other people advice bout their business, best you look somebody aint fuckin' you in y'own!"

Rhoder watched him turn and stride off through the trees. He was still standing there when the rain came.

Straight-away, no turns. He could let go the wheel, and the car would practically take him there by itself. In just forty-five minutes, he'd be a Man of Property, he said to himself. Sonuvabitch! He'd met Crouch that afternoon just as the bank was closing, as arranged, and the banker had had all the necessary papers filled out and ready for him. He'd signed for the mortgage, withdrawn his balance and closed out the account. Crouch was to meet him later at The Channel Cat. Rhoder had stopped at the post office afterward, gotten his own mail and picked up some letters for the church, including a large heavy package in plain brown wrapping paper with no return address. Then he'd driven over to the church, which was deserted at that hour, and let himself in and just sat there in a back pew praying for guidance, as the shadows reached up the walls and the daylight bled away. Because just thinking, he couldn't make any God damn sense out of it. No more then he'd been able to when he'd sat there ten years earlier and his good intentions had got him into trouble the last time, pulling that damn boat out of the water -- after seeing Brennan and the other one sink it and then come back with the state police to drag the wrong end of the bogue for three days, calling themselves trying to look for it. Except afterward, he'd lost his nerve and hidden it, and had made the boy, Newton, swear on his mother's grave not to say anything, because he, Rhoder, had been too scared to tell anybody what they'd seen there that day while they'd been out fishing. And now, it had come back to haunt him. What the hell was he supposed to do now? Because the boat was still there where he'd hidden it, and if he does buy that old farm, people were going to be watching him. They'd be watching and telling every turn he made...!

"...Why didn't he put up cash? He got plenty."

"You know sly ole Tom Crouch," Bidder had said, "he don't carry cash, don't admit to havin' any, and don't never give none away." He'd driven over to Bidder's house, after leaving Jonah, to ask him what was going on.

"So then, why would he put up property he thought was worth something in a poker game?

"Robinson wouldn't give him no more credit. By that time, Crouch was owing him mucho dinero."

"You shitting me! Crouch spoze to be pretty slick at poker."

"Oh, yeah! Used to be, he'd take the pants offa most any nigguh in the county. But since Robinson come along, he aint been winnin' too reg'lar. In fact, he been losin' a lot. Myself, I thought he figgered he could buy the property back cheap, once Robinson found out what was on it. Robinson aint got no use for churches. Huh, he pitched a bitch when he found out. So then, he tried to sell it back to him. But, Crouch, now, he playin' another game. He say he didn't wanna buy it back."

"He didn't?"

"He didn't, no. Why?"

"What do you mean? I mean, I just thought he did."

"Well, fact is, he do. Now."

"You done lost me, man."

"Well, see, at first, he didn't. But he do, now. See, in between the time he didn't, and the time he do, Robinson did some thinking, figgered Crouch upta something. So, he kinda went round behind the scenes, and found out something, and then he came back and give whatever he found out to Crouch as a reason he should buy the property back afterall. Crouch didn't much like the reason, but he over a barrel, now, see. Got to buy it back."

"So, then...so, why didn't he?"

"Robinson raised the price on him. Huh, Crouch 'tween a rock'n a hard place, now. Now he gotta buy it -- but he can't afford it!"

"Oh."

"Uh-huhn.... So, why you so interested, lil brother?"

"Me? I aint interested!"

"Oh, uh-huhn."

"So, what was the reason?"

"What was what reason?"

"The reason Robinson found out to make Crouch wanna buy the property back."

"I don't know."

"You don't know?"

"Furthermore, I don't even wanna know!"

"But --"

"And you don't wanna know, neither! You understand what I'm sayin', Ben?"

"...? Uhhmm.... Funny, I always thought Crouch was pretty slick."

"He is! Ole Tom Crouch is real slick. But Robinson slicker. Robinson surprised him, see? That cat aint been in the

Delta long, but he a quick study. Yeah, Robinson slicker'n Dick Tracy...!"

"...So," he'd told Crouch, later at the bank after signing for the mortgage, "come to find out, this property belonged to you, before it come to Robinson. He smiled to himself when the banker looked caught off guard. "That right?"

Crouch studied him a moment. "Go on."

"Well, if it's a good property, and if it was yours fore Robinson got his hands on it, how come you don't buy it back yourself? How come you arrangin' for me to buy it?"

Crouch pursed his lips and sat back in his chair.

"And while we talkin'," Rhoder continued, "how come you expect Robinson goan sell it to me for a good price, when, what I heard, he want a lotta money for it, now?" He sat back on his side of the desk, then, and waited for the banker to explain himself.

But Crouch shook his head. "You disappoint me, Ben. I thought you was a thinking man. But you not thinking at all. You're listening to other people's foolishness, and you're not using your head. You think I'm a fool? What, you expect I'm gonna fessup to trying to make you throw your money away on worthless property, so's the bank can take your six percent for the next thirty years? You think that's how I got to be where I am today? Six percent? Look around ya, boy, you see any other Negro banks in the Delta? No! You lookin' at the only black bank president in the Delta! How'd I do it? Enterprise! You wanna know what's really going on, you gotta talk to the right people, ask the right questions! You been living here all your life, and you still aint hep to what's happening here. But you straight, Ben. You always have been. And we friends. So, I'ma give you a little help, so's you can help yourself. I'ma give you a small advantage over these other nigguhs, what don't know nothin' bout building themselves up, but always tearing one another down. I'ma give you some information. *In-for-ma-tion*, Ben, not rumor!"

He reached into a drawer and tossed a piece of paper on the desk for Rhoder to read. It was a check from the Quartermaster's Office of the United States Air Force Academy at Highville. It was drawn on a bank in Washington, DC, and was made out to "Dividend Associates, Inc." for seventeen thousand, one hundred and sixty-six dollars and sixty-six cents. Crouch, Rhoder knew, from seeing it on his monthly rent receipts, was president and treasurer of Dividend Associates. Rhoder read the amount of the check over several times, moving his lips as he read, then looked up, astonished.

"Guess you didn't hear no rumors bout that, did ya." Rhoder shook his head.

"No, course not. You think I got this far by runnin' off at the mouth, and throwing good opportunities away? Ben, just look at yourself. You own a mechanical picker. That's still a new technology here. There aint many in the Delta, and you the only black man in LeVane County that got one! -- Wait, now, hear me out! Cotton's coming in good this year. 'Spite the weevils, they averaging six hundred-and-thirty pounds a acre. Now, with your machine, you can pick over sixteen acres a day, aint that right? That's over ten thousand pounds a day! Good hand pickers do two-fifty, mebbe three hundred. You a strong man, say three hundred pounds. Well, you picked cotton by hand a lotta years fore you got that picker, and you know aint nobody giving you more than three dollars for every hundred pounds you carry in on your own back. How many years you earn nine dollars a day, working can-to-can't, six days a week? And how much you earning now? You charge two dollars a hundred pound for what your machine pick, and you picking ten thousand pound or better every day. You think you a little better off, now? You want to know how much better? I got a calculator, here, on my desk, but I spoze we could figger it out just by comparing what Jonah Johnson's woman, Essie, puttin' on the supper table, and what Lorna puttin' out for yall.

"And, while we talkin', who was it told you about that cheap used picker in the first place? You shoulda come to me about the loan, too, Ben. You got yourself in a bind, now. You do know it's Brennan's stepsister's husband own that loan company, don'tcha. Oh, yeah!" he added, seeing Rhoder's look of surprise. "It's all in the family! You mean you didn't hear about that from Jonah Johnson or Jim Bidder-them? Huhn, no, they wouldn't know about it. Bidder got some sense, but the rest of'em don't know a balk from a bear trap. And if they did know, they wouldn't tell you, cause they don't want you to be no better off than they is. Tell me," he said, hunching forward, "Jonah told you he's happy with how well you doing?" When Rhoder didn't answer, he leaned back. "No, again. I wouldn't expect so. The only one gonna tell you something for your own good is the one in a position of responsibility in the community whose looking to share a little good with his neighbor -- we don't have to mention names, here, Ben...."

The truth was, Rhoder had thought to himself, *nobody'd* told him about mechanical pickers. He and Lorna had been saving to buy a used one for years, ever since she'd read him an article about it in *The Farmer's Weekly*, which was even before Brennan had bought his. And he, Rhoder, had found the one he'd bought by himself in the papers. It had been advertised by the loan association over in Highville that had repossessed it from its previous owner. The loan rate was high, but they'd been willing to let the picker go cheap, and he hadn't wanted to put it off any longer. He'd taken the loan from them because he'd had no choice, it was a condition of sale. But he hadn't known the loan company was owned by Brennan's relations. He hadn't had any idea that Brennan could have had him tied up like that at both ends!

He was still trying to absorb, now, what Crouch had told him when he'd first walked into the bank that afternoon, that Brennan had tried to cash his security check, which of course had bounced. So, he'd thought to himself, as Crouch had yammered on, that Brennan was going to try and put him in jail for writing a bad check! He'd heard of that happening to other Negroes, but he'd never thought it could happen to him! As the full implications had sunk in, he'd realized there was only one man he knew in a position to keep him out of jail, and he'd looked at Crouch with new eyes.

"...Don't waste your time listening to rumors," Crouch was saying. "Rumor's usually wrong, and never more'n half-right. But it's the 'wrong' that can hurt you. 'Rumor,' as the Bard said, 'is a pipe so easy, that only the jealous multitude would play upon it.' Speaking of which, you also heard a rumor, some big northern corporation wanna buy land down here to raise cotton for export?"

Rhoder shook his head.

"Yeah, well, you will. But, like everything else, it's only half-right. But I'm gonna set you straight -- because I always have...."

Crouch had gone on to explain that the Air Force Academy wanted to expand their facilities to test a new series of supersonic jets, and they'd expressed interest in a large tract around Dividend, which included a sizable portion of Crouch's land. The sale would realize a considerable profit. But Crouch told him he couldn't sell it directly to the Air Force without creating a problem for himself, because the fact was, he was already supplying them with liquor "and a few other unmentionables," as he'd put it, and as these were all illicit goods in a dry state, he didn't want to call undue attention to himself. He'd said he'd been planning to bring him, Rhoder, and a few other associates into the deal when he'd brought the negotiations to a favorable point. They'd make paper transfers of the property and sell it under a different name, then share the profits equally. But when Robinson had won some of the property in poker, Crouch had realized he'd had to act fast, before Robinson found out about the Air Force deal. Rumors had already been going around about "a Northern corporation," but that had been put out purposely by the Academy, Crouch had told him, to allow itself time to negotiate a good deal in private, before committing to public bids. Robinson simply had a personal grudge against him, the banker'd said, for private reasons Rhoder didn't need to know about, and that was why Robinson had been reluctant to sell the property back to him. But the circumstances were perfect for Rhoder to take advantage of.

"I can't be doing no deals from the jailhouse!" Rhoder'd said, finally, interrupting him.

"Jailhouse? What are you talking about?"

"Brennan goan have the sheriff arrest me for that bounced check."

Crouch had pursed his lips and nodded, as though he hadn't thought of that himself. Then he'd said, "Well, I don't think you have to worry about that now. I'll speak to the sheriff, see what I can do."

Rhoder had added quickly, "Can you sell me the house, where me'n Lorna livin' at? Rent coming due on that, too."

Crouch gave him a strange look, then smiled. "Well, let's take it a step at a time. We'll see. Meantime, leave Clooder to me."

Yeah, Rhoder thought to himself now, well, he wasn't going to take too much comfort in that! "De Lawd help them which help theyselves," as the saying went. Oh, Crouch was slick, awright. Maybe he was even slicker than Robinson, after all. Maybe he'd lost that poker hand on purpose. But if so, what game was he really playing?

As the banker had predicted, Rhoder had overheard some white planters at the post office, later, speaking about a Memphis canning company looking to buy land in the county to start a big catfish farm. But if there was big money to be made, he thought to himself, why would a rich banker like Crouch bring a small-time farmer like me into the deal? Every which way he turned it, nothing seemed to be what it seemed to be.

Just suppose, he said to himself, there wasn't no big corporation deal. What could Crouch gain by having him, Rhoder, buy the land back from Robinson...? Then it suddenly occurred to him that by making him, Rhoder, close out his account, all his checks would bounce, his credit would be lost, his mortgage foreclosed...and the property would be taken over by the bank for nothing! What Crouch, for whatever reason, could not buy back from Robinson, he could take from him, Rhoder, for free, and then keep it or sell it as he damn pleased!

As he approached the crossroads, Rhoder touched the thick envelope in his pocket that contained his and Lorna's savings, together with his own winnings of the last two days, two thousand three hundred and sixty-two dollars and twelve cents. It was all the money they had in the world. Continuing straight through the crossroads would take him to meet Robinson at the Channel Cat. But he spun the wheel, turning the car onto the road leading west, to Highville. Fuck Crouch and his big deals! he said to himself. He had to feed his kids. The picker was all there was right now between them and starvation. Lorna had lost her job at the school. They'd fired her soon as he'd started going round getting signatures for the school integration petition. Since then, she'd tried to take in washing, but nobody'd hired her. Except Mrs. Thackery. And Sampson.

His hands jerked impulsively on the wheel. The truth was, he and Lorna hadn't been getting on so well lately, not since this petition stuff had got started. They'd bickered and fought, with him accusing her of flirting with Sampson, and her accusing him of jeopardizing their livelihood by going around with the petitions. He was caught in the middle, because he was sick and tired of being poor and of being told he was dumb, just because he was a Negro! He wanted his kids to have a good education and to make something of themselves, he said to himself, not like the rest of these ignorant Delta niggers. Not even like Lorna, who could be a school teacher only as long as the whitefolks said so. And though he didn't like Sampson especially, and didn't trust him around Lorna, he felt the preacher was solid on Negro rights. He trusted him there. And he owned that Sampson was the first and only one to come along in a long time in LeVane County with the guts, brains and education to lead that fight. The last one who'd tried it, five years ago, was mostly nothing but mouth, and had buckled and run at the first sign of trouble. Sampson would stick it out, he felt -- but he'd have to watch that preacher closely.

Meanwhile, Thackery was another matter. People had already started to spread rumors about Lorna and Sampson, when the Thackerys offered her work. That old bastard was a notorious womanizer, and everybody knew his wife tried to keep him supplied with black pussy on the back porch, just so's not to be embarrassed by having him seen with other white women. Well, he could settle with Sampson, man to man, if it came to that. But Thackery was another matter. He wasn't afraid of whitefolks, he'd even straighten Brennan out if he had to. But Thackery was too powerful. Thackery owned more land than anybody else, he owned the only cotton gin in the county and had politicians right up to the governor at his beck and call. The sheriff did his bidding, and the local citizens voted the way he told them to.

But, Jesus Christ, he said to himself, he missed Lorna, missed being close to her. All this other shit was making them both crazy. He didn't really believe Lorna would two-time him. It was just that, sometimes, when he saw how other men looked at her...! They hadn't really talked in a long time. They used to be able to talk -- once he'd got her away from that old witch, Basheeba -- not just fight and fuck, like Jonah-them. It occurred to him that he ought to tell Lorna how he felt. He should tell her now, he shouldn't wait, because things were going to get hot and heavy around there soon. And they were going to need more than just friction to keep them to-gether.

So, the only thing that made sense to him, now, was to make his payment on the picker, and to use the rest of their savings to live on, till he collected the money for cotton pick-ing from the planters. Which was the other reason, besides being fired by Brennan, that had made him want to go and see Crouch in the first place. Some of the planters had cancelled their work orders, too, when they'd heard he was circulating the school petitions. And he realized it would only get worse, now that he'd started with the voter registration forms. In fact, he was beginning to have second thoughts about all that. It was all right for Sampson and them, preachers could live off the church...! He shook his head, angry with himself for being tempted to quit. Shit, he thought, it was a bitch any which way you turn. Fuck it.

He floored the accelerator. With luck, he could just catch the loan company before it closed.

Preoccupied, he almost ran into the truck before he saw it. It was sitting just beyond the low-spreading branch of a white oak thick with Spanish moss. He jammed on the brakes and skidded into a crawl. It was only then, for some reason, that he remembered he'd forgotten to drop off the mail at the church. He'd drop it off on the way back, he thought, peering through the gathering dusk at the vehicle in the road before him. He recognized it as one of Brennan's trucks. It was skewed at an angle and jacked up, blocking the right lane of the two-lane road. The driver must be changing a flat on the far rear wheel, he thought.

As he pulled over, skirting a ditch to pass on the left shoulder, Brennan came around the front of the truck carrying a tire iron. Two other white men, whom he recognized as Brennan's hired hands, Minton and Borden, stood behind him. When Brennan saw him, he turned and said something over his shoulder to the others. Minton reached into the cab of the truck and pulled out a hunting rifle. Brennan smiled.

8.
Mount Eden

```
WARNING!
CONSTRUCTION IN PROGRESS
Property of South-Central
TV Corporation.
Trespassers Will Be Prosecuted.
```

For mile after mile, Jones had ridden on Lot's back through woods, swamps and cotton fields, alien territory Jones unaccountably seemed to recognize. Traveling mostly by night to avoid being seen, they'd dodged the police and any whites whose paths they'd crossed, only to see the sun come up again and again in almost the same place, until they'd realized they'd been going round and round within the same tortured circle of the rivers. They'd tried waiting in the bushes alongside county roads trying to hitch a ride, but most times fewer than a dozen cars had passed in an hour, and half of those, it seemed, had been police. They'd nearly been caught twice lingering by the railroad tracks waiting to hop a freight. But the trains never came when they were there. Sometimes they would hear the train whistles blowing in the distance, but the way the sound came through the damp woods where they'd be hiding, they couldn't judge the timing or sometimes even the direction. And the local Negroes they'd tried to flag down on the road had refused to stop. Then, Lot had decided to head for Mount Eden, the Indian mound near the farm where he'd grown up, thinking it might be a good place for them to hide until he'd worked out an escape. But when they'd got there, they'd found a nightmarish place fenced off and posted with a construction sign, where bulldozers and back-hoes stood idle in the moonlight and fresh-gouged yellow walls of earth rose fifty feet into the night sky. They'd slipped through the barbed wire fence and moved on to the far side of the mound, until they'd reached the cave beneath the cemetery, where they'd found the old hoodoo woman bent over on the floor like a beast grubbing for worms by candlelight. After the initial surprise, Lot had just laughed at her, until she'd raised her eyes and his knees had gone from under him.

"There somethin' in here you want?" she'd said. "You think you can just come in here and take what you want and go?" She'd told them her name was Basheeba, and she knew all about them. Jones can still hear her voice rolling like a stone in the stream of his thoughts....

They've been hunkered down in the cave for hours, by this time, or maybe even days, Jones can't tell, anymore, with Lot striking matches at suspicious sounds and throwing stones to scare off the rats and snakes. Having lost his trumpet, the boy's been blowing through the mouthpiece to while away the time, blowing short, curious phrases, leaving space for the echoes to drop in and then playing over against them, managing to make a strange music out of his scrap of horn. Jones, meanwhile, feels his tongue like a knot of burnt rope in his mouth. He's thirsty all the time, and nauseated when he drinks. They've had nothing to eat for days but some fruit and a rabbit the boy'd killed with a stone. But he's been unable to swallow anything since. He feels the clay wall cold and hard as a spade at his back, and between himself and the darkness enveloping him there are only the boy's intermittent chatter and the dizzying fragments of his own memory....

"...We had eight guys in the band," Lot is saying, now, "four horns and rhythm section. Did roadshows and small club dates, shit like that. I'd joined up with him in Alpharetta. Was a little amateur-hour there that I won and Moe heard me there and took a liking to me, offered to let me travel with him. I was only fifteen at the time, but I was tall for my age and Moe would make me put on one of his suits and paint a mustache on me to make me look older." He laughs, "He did! But still, I mean, we had some dates where the club owner said I was too young to go inside. Coupla times, I had to stand on a box out in the alley with my horn stuck in the window to play with'em. But Moe Brandywine was bad, man, Moe played piano like some other people breathe. He taught me structure, how to think ahead. You okay over there, man...?"

-- *Maybe somehow Venus had always known, Jones is thinking. Deep down, maybe she'd been able to see it coming. She'd only been in Baltimore a few months when he'd first met her, living with cousins, and hadn't known how long she'd stay. After awhile, they took a little house together, and he paid for everything, didn't want his Venus to work. Then the boy came, his son, good-lookin' tyke, too. She'd nicknamed him "Pretty-Baby." He thought she was gonna start doggin' him, then, to get married. But she didn't. That almost bothered him more, her always being so unpredictable --*

...The husky burr of the brass mouthpiece sizzles again in his ears. The boy's gone into a jazzy riff, with phrases that slip over the bar line, while the echoes swell and roll over one another, resonating like a church organ....

-- He'd finished the season with a .406 batting average, played in his first All-Star game and was voted Most Valuable Player. Some ofay reporter from The Daily Worker even showed up to offer tryouts for the Pittsburgh Pirates. The guys on the team all knew it was a joke, still they wanted to believe it. They felt the white teams had to let Negroes in sooner or later, they needed the talent. Him, Campanella and Sam Hughes, their second-baseman, went to Pittsburgh and trotted their stuff. Made those white boys look like minor-leaguers. Benswanger, the Pirates president, was there in person to see'em do it. Said he liked what he saw and they'd be hearing from him in a couple days. They never did hear from him, but it wasn't like any-body really expected to. As for himself, he didn't care. He felt so good when he got back, the only surprise was hearing himself actually talking Venus into going with him to find a preacher. The very next day, he got his induction notice. He took the marriage certificate down to the draft board and tried to get reclassified. But they refused his request because he'd gotten married the day after the induction notice had been mailed and they said it made the marriage "suspect." He filed an appeal, but by the time they'd notified him for the hearing, twenty-two months later, he was in Normandy, and Venus had taken the boy and gone back to Charlotte --

"...When I was little," Lot is saying, "we used to sneak up in here and tell ghost stories and scare each other shitless talking about how all them dead people gonna come jumping out the walls and carry us off. I remember we'd find old arrowheads, cigarette butts, the bones of dead animals, used condoms, all kinds of shit. Newton used to take the condoms and chase the girls, and they'd scream, cause they thought if they got touched by one they'd get pregnant and give birth to a duppy. Once, we even found a set of rusty chains look like they coulda been here since slavery time. We'd play cops and robbers and make out like all that shit was evidence...!"

-- By the time he'd got back to Darden, his mother had died. Kidney failure, heart failure, diabetes. And the house was empty. It had apparently

been empty for days. There was no sign of Jax, and nobody, neighbor nor friend, was willing to say what had happened to his kid brother. "Sorry!" they said. "Sorry!" and shook their heads and closed their doors in his face. Until finally, he'd got Cue Ball drunk in a bar one night and Cue Ball told him. Cue Ball had barely got the words out of his mouth, before he was tearing up the highway with a loaded gun in his belt looking for the mothafucka --!

"...When I got my first horn, I'd come in here by myself and play for hours, man. I be playing against the echoes, and it was great, man, it was like playing against a whole brass section. It was a nice instrument. It was my granddaddy's old horn, a old Pan-American flugelhorn. My daddy gave it to me. It was all cracked and dented, but me and Newton sealed up the cracks with tape and glue, and it sounded pretty good. Except it didn't have no pearls...."

-- At the cemetery, the rope had scrolled off the deck and snaked through Jones's fingers like something alive. More than enough to hang a man, he'd thought, as the coffin scraped and bumped its way down. "Gimme a hand, suh, please." Not really prepared for the one funeral, he'd had to sit through the double ceremony, his mother's grave still waiting there, open, until they'd finished with Jax. But his brother's coffin got stuck halfway down at a bulge in the wall of the grave. He stood there a moment hesitating, as though this were a sign telling him the ground was not yet ready to receive this one, as though the boy had too much life left, was still growing, still dreaming, too young and too alive to be cut off and crammed into this dark hole. "A hand, please!" He's laughing! he told himself, he's in that fucking box laughing! It was just a joke! He could hear the boy's hiccupping cackle echoing out of the grave as clear as day! Rascal was lower than a snake in wagontracks for playing a joke like this. "Mister! If ya please!" He reached down to rip off the cover, he was gonna have to beat some sense into that boy! "No! Push! Push!" His long arm reaching down into the grave, he gripped the edge of the cover and yanked. "Push!" The coffin tipped up, then fell like a stone, hitting the bottom with a crash. He was left with one end of a white pine plank in his fist, the nails sprouting like thorns from his fingers, and below, Jax lay

staring up at him, mouth agape, a gas bubble rising over one eye -- "Shot,"
Cue Ball had said. "By the deputy. 'Resistin' arrest --!'"

"...I'd slip in here with a lighted candle and woodshed,"
Lot was saying, "call myself running changes. After awhile,
I'd be all bloody-fingered from playing without the pads, you
know, the bare brass keys sticking up into my fingertips. And
meanwhile, Newton, man, he'd sneak in here with frogs and
toads and spiders and blow out the candle and make noises
and shit and run my ass outta here. Newton was a motherfucker.... Funny, I'd always played against these echoes like
they was just back-up. But listening to them now, sounds like
each one's doing its own thing, telling its own story -- I guess
that sounds like some weird shit to you, huh...?"

-- He'd known the cop's favorite hangouts, and tracked him to a bar and
grill in the northwest panhandle, up by Stillman Field. It was about three in
the morning when he finally caught up with him. He'd parked his own car
a little distance away and had just gone up to wait in the shadows within
a few feet of the police car, when the cop came out of the bar with a bunch
of other yahoos, drunk and carrying on. There must've been eight or ten of
them, the cop a head taller than the others. The owner was locking up behind
them and turning out the lights. As the others scattered toward their cars and
the deputy crossed the lot toward him, he thought about what Cue Ball had
told him, how the cop had stopped Jax in a speed trap and then accused him
of stealing his, Jones's, old Packard that he'd purposely left home for Jax to
use, and then, when Jax, young and foolish as he was, got impatient and
maybe a little disrespectful, the cop had pulled his gun and shot the boy as
he attempted to get back in the car. Cue Ball had said a hospital orderly he
knew had called him and he'd gone to see Jax before the end. Now, as the cop
crossed the lot toward him, Jones could see he'd been drinking, but he wasn't
drunk. As he waited for the other cars to pull out, the deputy started his own
car and began to back up, driving without lights. He saw the car drifting
away from him, already barely discernible in the darkness, and he ran after
it, as the taillights of the other cars tipped up and turned out onto the road.
But the deputy'd shifted gears, and the bumper struck him on the leg as the

police car started forward. He jumped, landing on the hood, and the deputy stopped the car and turned on the headlights but could see only his silhouette against the windshield. The cop got out the car carrying a flashlight in one hand and his gun in the other. "What the fuck you tryin' to do, boy!" the cop said. "Don't shoot, boss, it's me." "Freeze, I said! Who the fuck is 'me!' What you want!" "Me, boss, Rico. Didn't see you comin' with your lights out. Didn't mean no harm!" "Rico? Shit!" the deputy said then, recognizing him, "Now, I thought I was rid of your ass. What you doin' here?" When he didn't answer, the deputy stepped toward him cocking the pistol. "You aint gone deaf, are you, boy! I asked you a question!" "Just passin' through, boss! Mind if I get down offa here? Think I hurt myself when I run into the car." "Best you don't budge or breathe till I tellya how! Thought you was told to stay outta Dardan. You come back here lookin' for more trouble?" "No, boss, I don't want no trouble. Had some folks passed on. Come to bury'em, 'sall." "Aint no burying going on this time a night. I think you come looking for trouble." "No, boss, I --" "Get down offa my car, goddammit!" Jones eased himself to the ground, a step away from the cop, now, and as the cop snapped one cuff on him, he knocked the pistol away with his free hand and drove his fist into the cop's jaw. But as they fought there in the dark he felt his own gun slip out of his belt and heard it fall to the ground and go skittering away over the gravel. But he wasn't planning to let the cop get away alive, and he snapped the loose handcuff on the cop's wrist, chaining the two of them together as they wrestled to the ground. The cop was strong, but Jones had him by the throat slamming his head against the ground, when suddenly a shotgun went off close to his ear. He looked up, blinking into the bright eye of a flashlight to see the barkeep standing over him with the shotgun and yelling at him to stand off. The next minute, half-a-dozen guys had got hold of him. The deputy's buddies, having heard the ruckus and turned back, were holding him down and trying to beat him up. But when they found the deputy's key and took the handcuff off the cop's wrist the man didn't budge, he lay there on the ground still as death. And when a couple of the men got off him to go and try to revive the deputy, he broke away and took off into the woods, driving back to Charlotte that same night --

Telltale puffs of air tell him the boy is blowing the tube clear of spit. Then there's another sound, muffled by distance and the thick walls around them, a high, mournful, familiar sound. From the boy's silence, Jones can tell he's heard it too.

After a moment, the boy says, "Did I tell you my daddy was a ballplayer...?"

Another idle boast, Jones thinks, like the one about playing with the Basie band and the rest, stories made up mixing truth and lies, as if the boy himself doesn't know anymore where one leaves off and the other begins, almost as though he were ashamed of who he was, or didn't know who he was. Boy's a fool, Jones says to himself, to be able to blow a trumpet like he does and to be wasting his time down here knocking around juke joints and circus freaks. What's the matter with him that he don't just say, Fuck you, Jones, and make a run for that train while he's got the chance? Maybe he's got no guts. If he was my kid....

-- *He breaks off, remembering his own son, back in Charlotte. The boy must be about eleven or twelve now, he thinks, and wonders, ironically, what the boy might know about him, his father, the famous Rico Jones. But as he thinks of this, he's also trying to recall his son's name, and finds he can't. All he can remember is "Pretty Baby." The boy had been born while he was away playing on the road with the Elite Giants, and Venus had named him. Once he'd left, he'd never bothered about the boy, he'd been too busy looking out for himself. If he hadn't left the boy, abandoned him, really, if he'd stayed or if he'd taken the boy with them as Venus had wanted him to, it might all have been different, maybe they wouldn't have had that fight in the car, maybe...!*

-- He hears the train whistle again, coming closer, as though taunting him.

"Shit!" Lot says abruptly, "I wonder --! Maybe that's why Bidder took us there! Maybe that was Newton in that house in the woods, maybe he's come back, too! But then, what the fuck's he shooting at me for? Tsk, nah, shit, what am I talking about, that's crazy! But then why --! I mean, Bidder didn't say nothin'...!"

Late one night, maybe two or three o'clock in the morning, they'd found themselves hiding in the shadows of a parking lot behind a juke joint called the Channel Cat, waiting for the last customers to drive off and the lights to go out. When the owner had finally come out to lock up, the boy'd got up and gone to meet him. The man, startled, had drawn a pistol out of his pocket and called out, "Who's there! Speak up! Best nobody try and mess with me tonight, cause I aint gonna put up with no foolishness!" "It's me, Mr. Bidder, Lot Dundee!" the boy'd said. "Who you say?" "Me, Lotrelle, Fontana's boy." The man hesitated, "Boy, I sure hope you know what you doin', this gun is loaded. Step up! C'mon, step up into the light! Who you got with you?" "Just him," the boy said, moving into the light as he was told, with his hands held up and nodding over his shoulder toward Jones. "He's a friend. He won't do you no harm, he's crippled." The man stepped over to look at Jones and check the bushes around him, before lowering the gun, holding it loose and ready in his hand. "What you want, boy. What you come back here for? You know the police after you." "We didn't do nothing," the boy said, and began to tell him what had happened. But the man waved it away, "Boy, I knew your father," he said. "Aint no need for you explaining nothin' to me. Aint nothin' going on in this county lately make any sense worth explaining anyway. But what you come here to me for? I aint got no place to hide you. If I was you, I'd be looking to get gone outta here...." He couldn't risk helping them himself, he said, he had a family and a business to think of. The boy'd commenced to beg and plead and curse and argue, but the man wouldn't budge. Finally, the boy'd changed the subject and begun to ask the man questions about what he knew or remembered about Fontana and about a murder that had taken place near there long ago and whether he knew what had happened to his brother, Newton. But the man called Bidder had turned and walked away. He came back a few moments later carrying water and kitchen scraps and told them to get in the car, he'd do what he could. He drove them to a deserted place where a cinder path led off through the trees, then let them out and drove off without another word. At the end of the path they found a small wooden house in a clearing with a sleek new Hudson convertible parked in front. The house was dark and quiet except for the flickering light of a television showing in one window. The boy set him down under a tree and continued on alone, skirting the yard and keeping to the shadows. As he watched Lot approach the house, Jones thought he heard the muffled sound of a baby crying. Then, as Lot raised himself up to look in the window, they heard a shotgun go off inside the house, blowing a hole through the clapboard siding inches from the boy's legs. Lot turned and ran.

-- In a moment of silence, Jones becomes aware of something stirring in the walls, an inaudible throbbing he feels at his back like a heartbeat. But it's not his heart. He thinks it is here, in the present, something roused to life amid the quiet of the graves, but it becomes entangled with the memory of another place, and another heart beating strong and quickening against him, beating twice as fast as his.... It had been his last day with the Elite Giants, and was his last moment together with Venus before he was to leave for Fort Dix, and there in the grass -- "Rico, no!" "Yeah!" "Wait! Later, we --" "Now, baby! World aint waitin' on 'laters!'" "Oh, God! But not here!" "Right here! Right now!" "God, Rico!" "Shityes!" -- and there, in the midnight shadows of the left field wall, in the stadium full of shooting stars, the two of them, alone, were the Lord's abundance --!

"...He's probably up there somewhere right now...!" the boy is saying, his voice low, barely above a whisper, almost indistinguishable from the echoes in the darkness. "And if he is, he's probably looking down at me, here, and saying...!" He hesitates, as if listening. Although he's stopped playing, the notes seem to continue, merging with the words into a sort of unresolved argument. "Huh...!" the boy continued, "He's probably turning over in his...! Listen, uhm...I want to tell you something I never told nobody. See, my father never really heard me play. I mean, he heard me toodle around when I first got the horn, but soon as I got serious about it -- and that happened pretty quick -- I'd wait till he left the house, or I'd go out in the field, or come in the cave, here, to practice cause I didn't want the other kids to fuck around and distract me, and I didn't want my father to hear me till I...till I got good. And then he died so sudden, I didn't...I mean, they aint even had no funeral for him or nothing! And that hurt me, man, almost next as much, I mean, as him dying in the first place. Because, somehow, everything happened so fast, it was like a bad dream! It wasn't till long after that I really felt it. I'd be thinking, could we just escape from out that orphanage, man, we could fly on home and he'd be there, like always. Yet still, a part of me knew it wasn't a dream, he was really dead. And it was like I had two minds, man. I'd be thinking daddy was alive, and same time, I'd be thinking he was dead...but nothing'd be in between. It felt like, I mean, like I was walking in my sleep. Things would go by around me -- and I mean, there was some heavy shit happening in that orphanage, too! -- but nothing touched me. Then one night I had a nightmare and woke up hollering. It musta been round about three, four weeks after I got there, and it was like I suddenly got sick to my stomach, only worse than that. It was the middle of the night and I sat up in bed feeling like I wanted to scream but afraid if I opened my mouth all my insides would come bustin' out and I'd die or somethin'. I'd've woke up Newton to talk to him, but they'd put him in another building with the older boys. So, I thought the onliest way I could deal with the feeling was to blow my horn. And I reached under my bed -- and the horn wasn't there! It wasn't there! It was gone! Some mothafucka had took my horn, man! And I went crazy! I went clear outside myself. I didn't know who'd took it, I just jumped up and started dragging niggers out they beds and beatin' on'em. I snatched up whatever came to my hand in the dark, shoes, bed slats, I know I bust one guy's face open with a footlocker. I just ran from one bed to the other, from one of them cats to the other -- and they was most of'em bigger and badder then I was, but I didn't care, I just ran from one to the other and kicked and punched and scratched and tore up mothafuckas everywhich way. And then the lights went on and seemed like a hundred hands grabbed me and held me down, and I was frothing at the mouth and I remember somebody said 'I think he's got rabies!' And somewhere around there, I musta passed out. I woke up in the infirmary. They kept me in there almost a week. They wouldn't let Newton visit me, and I wouldn't eat nothin'. I almost went crazy, because I kept thinking about my father, but I couldn't see him any more! In my mind, I mean. All I could do was see him from the back, like when we was picking cotton and I was following him up the rows, or from the side and in shadow, like when he'd set out on the porch in the evening when the sun was down and his face would be hidden by the brim of his hat. But that was all! Two or three times the attendants had to tie me down cause they'd find me flipping out, banging my head against the bedpost and shit like that. I mean, I could see his long arms and the crook'd knuckle on is right hand where he'd been stepped on by a bull, and even the cracks in his size twelve boots -- I can see all that right now, clear, as I'm talking to you. But I couldn't see his face! Couldn't see it! I still can't call it to mind.... And I never did get that horn back, neither.... Shit, you know, this place still spooks me, man. I aint all that fond of graveyards in the first place, but I mean, being under one like this, that's some weird shit. Like being in a friggin' hole at the bottom of the world -- Fuck!"

He breaks off at the sound of something moving nearby to throw a stone and strike another match. Shadows leap from the yellow walls, and in the brief, flickering light, the boy seems hardly more than a shadow cast by Jones, himself. Jones watches as the boy takes the butt of his last cigarette from behind his ear and lights it, rotating it lovingly over the flame of the match. "Sorry, man," he says, with a shrug of his shoulders, putting the butt to his own lips. He tosses the match away and they are swallowed again by the darkness, with the end of the cigarette glowing like an antenna.

Then out of the silence comes a sudden explosion. The walls shudder and rocks rain down, and they hear the muffled roar and clangor of machines in the distance. Startled, the boy scoops Jones up in his arms and rushes outside, only to stand shifting from foot to foot, disoriented by the shock of daylight. The old woman, Basheeba, had told them to wait there, back in the cave, until she'd returned with help, a preacher, she'd said. But she'd been gone for some time, and they can hear the sound of the earth-moving machines clearly now from the far side of the mound. The boy starts running again, laboring under their combined weight as he heads across a field of hawthorn and poison ivy toward a clutter of dilapidated farm buildings beyond.

9.
Burnt Church

The light was low and red, like it is now, when Basheeba met the Devil at the crossroads. She hadn't gone down that road intending to meet him, but he was due. She'd been seeing signs of him everywhere. The bottom of her left foot had commenced to itch and prickle soon as she'd stepped out of the house, and the sun, going down under a blanket of purple cloud, had blazed again with a sudden brightness. Now, in the lengthening shadows, there were figures that crossed and crossed again by threes, and bloodworms driven out of the earth by the heavy afternoon showers and crushed by passing cars lay along the muddy roadside twisting in a gory web that she descended barefoot like the rungs of a slaughterhouse ladder. She moved with legs half numb and lanced with knife-edge pains, her body bent over under its own obesity, as she made her way along the shoulder of the road peering up warily at the trees that stood above the low-lying fog like a nation surprised, sprung rootless in midair. An abandoned axletree rotting in the sumac at the side of the road bristled with termites flooded out of their towers. For a brief moment, she saw a heron standing in a stream with its blue hood haloed in the mist and a small crappie twitching in its beak, and then it vanished. The air was heavy with the stench of dead things flushed up out of the loam, and jays, crows and buzzards swooped and bickered over the feast. From among these riotous shadows she felt disgorged spirits come fluttering to her hand to be dispatched, rifling away through the corridors of mist on ghastly errands. Grudges swung like totems upon the walls of the fog around her, emitting voices of the quick and the dead, which she ignored, half-heard, or confuted in a coded tongue.

"...I got to speak what's on my mind," Dulorn's voice said. *"I'm a man, Sheeba. I aint goan roll over like a dog...!"*

"Bug-ugly ofays!" she muttered, *"Ogun, Ogun, Ogun, l'ari oke...!"* and swung one big hand down and across and down again like a sword.

She'd heard Dulorn's voice, all right. But she'd long since given up arguing with Dulorn. She was thinking of her widowed daughter, Lorna Rhoder, whom she'd had to leave at the house frightened to distraction, and thinking, too, of the money she herself had loaned that might now be lost. Lorna was the only one had any brains, she was thinking to herself. The two boys-them run off and ended up in jail. Except Lorna was willful. She'd come back from the Clarksdale Normal School and married the same hardmouth nigger she'd purposely sent her off to get away from. Never shoulda had nothin' to do with the Rhoders, she said to herself, they all no account. Girl used to play the piano and sing like a bird. But she aint done nothin' but weep and gnash her teeth since she married that man. Folks used to say she was "gifted." Now she grown, they saying she's uppity. And the whitefolks just call her crazy, like they'd called Dulorn, and herself, too, because they didn't shuffle and whine like niggers supposed to do. It aint no "gift" that bring so much trouble! Brains, will-fulness and clever ways aint but a curse in a Negro, she said to herself, a treachery, deluding them into thinking that was all they needed to better themselves in this world. Sooner or later, if they lived long enough, they found out being "gifted" was a sword that drew blood at both edges. But to the young it shines like a shield....

-- Everybody on the place had to work at cotton-picking time. But when she was carrying Lorna, Dulorn had refused to let her go out when her time was on her --

The previous evening, she'd come in and found Lorna still sitting at the kitchen table asleep before the unwashed supper dishes. The rain had stopped and the heat risen up again like steam off a mule's back, and the girl was sitting there, slumped over and shivering with her eyes half-closed. Hadn't had a full night's sleep in weeks. Soon as she'd touched her, Lorna'd started up like the house was afire wanting to know where were the children. But the next moment, she'd sunk back into the chair overcome by confusion at a surge of feeling she hadn't understood. But *she'd* understood. She knew her own daughter, and had seen what Lorna had been going through, and had recognized that look of confusion that weakened the knees. She'd known it, herself, years before when Dulorn had died. But Lorna was still young and would have to learn on her own. She'd seen Lorna leaning over the tub earlier that morning, doing the Thackerys' wash, when she'd suddenly gone into a rage and then broken down in tears, and it had taken some doing before she could get Lorna to tell her what had happened -- not that she'd really needed to be told, because she had eyes to see farther than most people, but because she knew the girl would have to tell somebody to get it out of her system. And, sure enough, it was about the gin owner, Thackery, and his latest nasty remark when Lorna'd gone to pick up the wash the evening before, and he'd told her again how he'd "look after" her and the children, "now that her big nigger had run off!" From the first, Lorna had tried to keep everything to herself, but there's only so much a body could bear. That first night the girl had gone to bed angry that Benjamin hadn't come home, wondering if he'd suddenly taken up with that nocount whore, Marvella, who'd called out to him on the street more than once. At the same time, Basheeba heard her arguing aloud to herself that it wasn't like Benjamin to do that way. And the next morning, when he still hadn't come or sent word, she'd walked all the way to the sheriff's office in Dividend to report him missing. But she, knowing by then what must've happened, had not gone with her, because she'd known the sheriff wouldn't give a damn that another nigger'd gone missing, and she shut herself up in her own tarpapered shack in the woods to conjure up the help she needed to find Benjamin herself and to get retribution. And later, after supper, she'd found Lorna standing in the dirt road out in front of the house Benjamin had rented for them when the kids had come, standing and staring into the gathering darkness until the pink campion and thorn apples at the side of the road had taken fire in a flash of heat lightning, standing and waiting like a dog at the door and counting off the seconds, waiting for the thunder. Yes, Basheeba said to herself, she knew the feeling all right. It had come on herself only weeks after Dulorn had died, a feeling, nowise like a thought or a memory or even a fantasy, but a feeling like a fever. She hadn't felt anything like that maybe since the first year they'd been married. It'd come out of nowhere, and she'd told herself it was crazy to feel that way, to be thinking of such things then, but she couldn't shake it off. It'd come, again and again, in waves, churning through her, making her sweat hot and cold, leaving her distracted and dizzy for wanting it, dreaming about it with her eyes wide open, dreaming of making love, making love down on her hands and knees with Dulorn behind her, covering her, as they hadn't done for years. But the feeling had come with shame and confusion because in her heart was nothing but grief and in her mind only a red rage and all she'd wanted then was to get back what she'd lost and to tear to pieces them that'd taken it away from her, and so where this other feeling had come from she didn't know and what to do to be rid of it she didn't know. Since then she'd known new-made widows so distracted with that feeling they'd taken a pig sticker to themselves to cut out the offending parts, known some who'd given in to the hunger like beasts in the field, and some who'd died inside, their hearts turned to stone and their minds entombed. And the men know when that weakness is on a woman, too, Basheeba said to herself, they can scent it like a dog scent a bitch in heat. Like with Lorna, now, and Crouch comin' round mumblin' about insurance, and the preacher, Harold Sampson, comin' round talkin' about praying together! But then just as suddenly as the feeling comes, it goes, and you wake up one day feeling numb, feeling nothing at all, not grief, not rage, not even fear, just exhausted....

It had been that look of exhaustion she'd seen on Lorna's face when she'd gone to the house on the seventh morning after Benjamin had disappeared to tell her that was the day. She'd found the girls-them playing around a water moccasin nest out back and Lorna inside lying on the couch staring at the ceiling with eyes like ashes. Lorna hadn't even turned to look at her when she'd spoken. Not until she'd told her they had to go down to the bogue, *had* to go. Lorna looked at her then, and she knew the girl's first thought was she'd lost her mind. But when Lorna saw the look in her eyes, she understood it wasn't the Field Day Picnic she was talking about. And that afternoon, while the others had cooked barbecue and raced dogs, she and Lorna had stood on the bank and stared out at the Rue until, come sundown, that boy went in and pulled Benjamin's body out of the water....

Basheeba shifted the small bundle she carried to her other arm. The medicine was strong, but she knew the one she was bringing it to was too far gone to benefit. The man carry a curse, she said to herself, picturing the gaunt cripple, Rico Jones, in her mind. It was no surprise to her, though, that the boy, Lotrelle, had come back. She'd always known the Dundee boys would come back, known he would, or one of them would. She'd been knowing it since they took them away. Crouch leaving their daddy unburied at the house like that was no better than blaspheming. But when she'd first heard these two stumbling through the thornbushes at Mount Eden she'd wondered who it was, and how they'd found the cave. She'd gone in there to dig for Indian bones, like always, and had stood amazed to see the coffins dug up and the graveyard half demolished. And then, when she'd seen these two coming through the passageway, one riding on the other's shoulders and the two like one thing made huge by their shadows in the candlelight, her heart had leapt into her mouth. She'd thought it was Eleggua, come as his own double, Trickster and Messenger, come to catch her off-guard, to hold her to account for the ofays digging up the graveyard. She'd been calling for him since Benjamin had gone missing, but she never knew when he would appear. But when she'd thrown a pinch of salt into the flame of the candle and turned to stare him down, the specter had tumbled into pieces. Then she'd smelled the sickness in Jones and had seen the dogs lurking in the young one's eyes --

-- Mr. Purdy, the foreman, told Dulorn to send her down, but Mr. Purdy-them was scared of Dulorn, and Dulorn knew Purdy wasn't gonna do nothin' by hisself. She'd begged Dulorn to let her go. Aint no way they was gonna let'em get away with it. But Dulorn was stubborn as a mule when he set his mind to something. Stead, he offered to work double for her share.

He was big and worked like ten niggers anyway. But it didn't do no good. Purdy came back that night with the 'ssistant foreman --

She was there when Brennan came. She and Lorna had been upstairs putting the girls to bed when they'd heard the truck driving up toward the house, and for a jarring moment they'd both thought it might've been Benjamin. Lorna went down to see, thinking then it must be somebody from the church. But when she, herself, heard the truck drive right passed the side of the house and then heard the door of the cab open and close out back, she had second thoughts. She didn't hear anybody call out like you'd expect, only a heavy step on the back porch. She put out the lamp and went to look out the window, but in the pale moonlight she could barely make out the shape of the truck parked under a tree and only a wide straw field hat and a pair of overalls on the man standing below at the kitchen door. She heard Lorna ask who it was, but the man didn't answer right away. She saw him trying to peer in through the kitchen window. Lorna asked again who it was, and finally, the man spoke in a hoarse whisper, his voice indistinct so that she, at the window above him, could barely make it out.

"Lorna? That you? It's me, I got some news for ya. It's about Ben."

She didn't wait to hear the rest, she went downstairs, moving faster than she had in years, faster than even she thought she could, and ran to get Benjamin's shotgun off the mantle. As she loaded both barrels with birdshot, which was all she could put her hands on right quick, she could hear Lorna, in the kitchen, asking again who it was and what he wanted and the man's voice, coming muffled through the door, whispering something about having news and not wanting to wake the kids-them. By the time she got to the kitchen, Lorna had opened the door and stepped back in fright, and the two of them stood gaping at a thing tall as a man with a face like no human face she'd ever seen, with two gaping holes flickering in the moonlight under the hat where the eyes should have been and steel rings jutting out like stalks on either side of the nose. The man made a lunge for Lorna, but she jumped back, avoiding him, as she cranked the lever of the shotgun and yelled at him from the doorway, "Don't move another step! What you want! Get outta here, fore I blow ya to Kingdom come!"

The man hadn't seen her until then and he stopped, surprised.

"Who are you! What you want here!" she repeated, and then, when Lorna turned on the kitchen light, they saw from his hands it was a white man. The straw hat had slipped off when he'd rushed in, and she saw he was wearing a leather cap with goggles and a gas mask attached that covered the lower part of his face. She recognized the hedgehopper's pilot cap and knew, then, who it was. "What you want, whitefolks!" she said, "You got no business comin' in here, we aint done nothin'!"

"Yeah," Brennan said, finally, removing the mask and goggles to reveal his face, "I got business here, awright! Yall stole money from me!"

"What?" Lorna said. "Please, mister, what money, we didn't --"

"Shuddup!" Brennan said. "Don't yall try to play innocent with me! Yall stole my money! You and that big ugly buck a yours. Stole over a thousand dollars!" He made as if to try and grab her again.

"Hold it!" Basheeba, said. "Git out! We don't owe you nothin'! Git out! Git out, or I swear 'fore God, whitefolks, I'll shoot ya dead where ya stand!"

"I want what you owe me, y'hear!" Brennan said. "I aint leavin' here without it. And I'm gonna get it," he added, reaching again for Lorna, "one way or the other!"

She fired, missing him on purpose, the shot splintering the doorframe at his back, but it was enough to scare him.

He turned and yelled at her, "You crazy jarhead bitch! You tried to kill me!"

"Git out!" she said again, cocking the hammer on the other barrel. "Git out and don't come back!"

"Fuckin' bitches!" he said, backing out the door and down the porch steps. "I'ma get the sheriff out here to throw your black asses in jail!" "Y'OWE ME MONEY!"

She'd kept the gun trained on him as he'd made his way back to his truck, and she'd followed him down the driveway with the barrels pointed through the truck window at his head and had stood out in the road watching him until he'd driven out of sight, daring him, in her mind, to turn around, and fearing that one day he might....

-- Purdy and the other man had just pushed open the door and walked in and pulled Dulorn outta the bed beside her and tried to whip him. But he beat'em up and chased them off. Next day, Mr. Bowman, himself, come. "Dulorn, you got to let Sheeba go to work. Everybody works at cotton-picking time, you know that." Dulorn say, "Sheeba in her time. She not workin', suh, I's sorry." Mr. Bowman say, "Everybody works! No exceptions!" Dulorn say, "Miss Alethea don't work." Bowman say, "Miss Alethea is my wife! And sides, she's not feelin' well." Dulorn say, "Sheeba be my wife, and she not too sprightly herself, just now." Just what he said, "She not too sprightly just now." Her belly was big and heavy with Lorna, and she stood hiding behind the door not knowing whether to laugh or cry, she was so scared. "Not too sprightly!" Aint that something! Man had a mouth like a 'lectric switch --

She'd known the Rhoders from the time Benjamin was a child, she knew he didn't drink, but he was always sullen and he'd grown up meaner and more pig-headed than the rest. Married Lorna with hardly a cent of his own. Nigger go and buy a expensive old secondhand cotton-picking machine that don't even work good, she said to herself. Be up all night half the week just to make it run the next day. All that money throwed away for what. Fool don't even have it long enough to pay her back, fore he get Lorna fired and hisself killt over this school integration bullshit. Man get aholt of a idea, couldn't nobody talk'm out of it. What you get for takin' a preacher too serious! Sampson and him, both turned foolish for a idea. But, leastways, they both men, she admitted to herself. Hard-headed, but they stand up. None of'em take shit from nobody. But Jesus Christ, why the women in her family always gotta go with such kinda mens? You can't keep'em, they born to strike fire and die young. The man's body don't even be cold, fore the loan company come and repo the machine!

Whitefolks all the same. They done got so greedy they don't even play by the old rules no more. Now, they working day-hands, steada hiring a family for the season like they used to. The old way leastways kept the colored families together, and the whitefolks and the Negroes, too, for better or worse, was common-bound to the land. But now, everybody's a stranger. Now, they don't want to know you. After picking-time they don't care no more if they never lay eyes on you again. It done got so now, blackfolks aint no better. Every one get his own pay and go his own way. But things is coming to a head, now. They all got their eye on that trial at the court-house. Whole nation got it on the TV. They all gonna be seeing for themselves what's going on down here. Jesus, they can't even let the dead lie in peace, she said, thinking again of the construction out at Mount Eden, they gotta go dig'em up and transport'em like they aint nothing but hogs.

"Mothafuckas want to play," she muttered aloud, her mind unconsciously going back to Dulorn, "but they aint play that shit with me no more! Sheeba fixed they asses good! Fixed'em with alum and lye and cooter-blood and wild mallow and grave-dust. Huh, Sheeba done mess'em up a right smart!"

-- Dulorn had crossed the line. He knew it. He took to staying out all night with his shotgun. He be propped up in the hawthorn bushes by the path to the cabin, where he could see them coming. But they didn't come. At dawn, Dulorn went out to the field, working like always -- except he was carrying his gun, now -- working till dark, and coming home to eat and going out again to watch all night, not knowing when they were going to come. They had let a week go by. Then, in the middle of the night, she woke up to hear him yell her name, just once --

...All her savings! Lorna had begged and pleaded, till she'd given in. And Benjamin, calling himself independent, didn't stop to ask where it had come from when Lorna gave it to him. What she supposed to take, now, to bury herself with? Never did trust no burial insurance, not with sly niggers like Tom Crouch slipping round trying to sell it all the time. Like when they killed Fontana, another one who tried to stand up for himself. Crouch claimed the policy lapsed! Them poor Dundee boys had nothing to bury their father with. Crouch just send the body back. The morning the Welfare woman come to take the boys off to the orphanage, there be Fontana's body, lying on the gallery step without even a box! Chillen come out the front door to see their daddy naked and stiff as a board lying under a cotton sack. Crouch! Phugh! She spat in the road. Man smell like skunk pudding in July. And his icty-dicty wife, walking round with her nose stuck up St. Peter's ass and her hair ironed out stiff enough to chop cotton. She wouldn't trust Crouch-them to dress a dog's body without picking it for fleas.

"Don't trust nobody!" she muttered to herself, aloud, thinking, pickaninnies just off the titty sneakin' round after dark, now, with a stolen twenty-five cent or a dollar asking for a love potion, or a poison, or where can they get a gun! Then they come back wanting to get they fortunes told. They can't see they all bound up together like spokes on a wheel, running fierce at one end and fool at the other.

-- She'd run outside looking for Dulorn, but didn't see anybody and didn't hear anything. She'd called out to him. Next thing, a couple of white men ran up and grabbed her and threw her down on her stomach. She felt the baby kick like it was gonna come right out her backbone. They tied her hands behind her back, put a pistol to her head and then made her get up and walk through the black woods till they came to were she could hear the others talking and laughing, and then she saw them all standing around a fire under a sourgum tree. They'd put a noose around Dulorn's neck, tied his hands behind him and had him heist up on his toes on a wooden Coca Cola crate. His back was turned, but they'd stripped him naked and she could see him bleeding all over his back from where the lash had cut him. He never said a word. She looked around at the white men. They all had handkerchiefs tied around their faces, but she recognized them, she recognized some of them all right! They pushed her into the light, and the ones standing around Dulorn saw her and laughed out loud. One pulled out a long switchblade and ducked down, and they pushed her forward so she could see how they cut him. Dulorn twitched on the crate and almost fell off, almost hanged himself. But if he cried out, she didn't hear it. She saw the blood spouting from the gash between Dulorn's legs, and the man stood back with the switch and holding up Dulorn's nature in his hand. They jumped around like that, laughing and poking Dulorn's manhood in her face, then threw her to the ground and started kicking her, with Dulorn staring at her out of eyes like burning coals. The rest of them pulled out knives and started cutting off his ears and his fingers and even his toes for souvenirs. Then, one of them said he heard somebody coming. They threw Dulorn's manhood into the fire that was burning there in the crate he stood on, and they ran off. She jumped up and ran under Dulorn to hold him up on her back, and tipped over the crate and tried to pull his manhood out of the fire with her teeth because her hands were still tied. But when she bent close the fire blinded her and then her dress caught fire. Dulorn swung himself from the hip and knocked her down, hoping to put out the fire on her dress and let her save herself and the baby. But she ran back under him and held him there while the box, knocked beyond her reach, kept on burning. She stayed there all night, fighting against the cramps that had started in her womb, until sunrise when Dulorn had long since stopped moving and had *begun to grow cold on her back and she knew that she'd lost him. And that was when the baby came, sliding between her legs into the cinders. She'd stood there, stooped between them, raving till they'd found her --*

She took a gourd rattle out of her pocket and began to swing it like an ax, chanting, *"L'ari oke, l'ari oke, oke, oke, Shango l'adoo! L'ari oke, l'ari oke,* Loki, Mercury, Moloch or Judas!" She was conjuring Eleggua, calling him up by any of the names he might be using, and she began to mince in a chicken-walk with her head bobbing, *"Ago, ago, ago, ago! Iburago, moyuba, Elegba Eshulona...!"*

A limpkin called in its haunting voice, and she saw its long speckled brown wings sliding, headless, through the mist. She paused, then, aware she'd entered Eleggua's precincts. A nightshade grew out of the exposed roots of a fallen log, the stamen sac of its only flower bright yellow in the circle of blue petals. The log lay in a bed of lavender phlox by the side of the road. Holes drilled into it by woodpeckers and worms looked like bullet holes. Its limbs were broken off, roots riven and twisted. A sprig of witch hazel curved down to brush it lightly with spidery yellow fingers. And she remembered Lorna, standing distraught in the kitchen last Sunday evening after the funeral, surrounded by wailing women, while the men stood out on the porch and in the yard reckoning up the number gone. "...A burn that heal," she chanted, "A hand that wound, a death reveal, a Devil bound...!"

-- Later, she'd gone back to work in the fields. But she'd ground up ole Injin bone-dust from Mount Eden, with a pinch of crow-eye dust, wild mallow boiled up in hawthorn and nigguh-jelly, and every evening she'd go by the hanging tree and add a pinch of the scorched bark and a pinch of the scrap of rope left there on the branch, and she'd walk over to the churchyard and sprinkle the mixture over Dulorn's grave. Every evening without fail. Came April, the tree died. In May, Miss Alethea, Bowman's wife, died of the fever. Drought came and fungus killed off the cotton. Purdy fell into the manure pit in September, and old Bowman, trying to pull him out with a

rope, fell in, too, and suffocated along with him. The Bowman kinfolk came and all they could do, they couldn't get cotton, cowpeas or nothing else to grow on that land, not the next year, nor the next. Finally packed up and sold off the place to Thackery and never came back --

When they'd pulled Ben Rhoder out of the river, she hadn't thought to see about the money until it was too late. Lorna'd called Crouch to dress the body, that was when he'd told them. Said Ben Rhoder'd taken it out the bank the day he'd disappeared. But she didn't believe that! For a fact, she didn't believe Rhoder had taken it out at all! Crouch said he did. Crouch showed Lorna the account paper. Crouch, leaning over Lorna, there at the kitchen table with his arm round her shoulder and his two-tongued mouth at her ear....

A harsh cry like a warning made her look up from where she'd stooped to pluck the nightshade. A butcher bird on the willow across the road turned its black mask to scan the countryside. Basheeba tucked the plant into the pocket of her skirt and pushed herself to her feet. Her stomach rumbled, and she broke wind. It was Tuesday, she realized, his day, Eleggua's day. She could feel the hairs standing up on her limbs and at the back of her neck. Eshu-Eleggua, the Divine Trickster and Opener of the Path, she could sense him, he was out there! Swinging her hands before her as though warding off a siege of indigenous spirits, she lurched down the lurid wagontrack to meet him.

The road crossed a bald cypress slough that was as bleak and gloomy as Job's chapel, with trees shrouded in Spanish moss and their branches interlocked above the fuming water. She had to hold her skirt up over her face to keep from choking on the gnats, but they found their way through the gingham folds and clung to her eyes like malice. As she approached the old sawmill road at the end of the slough, she overheard voices.

"...Ledger don't belong to you! -- nor to him, neither!" a deep, unfamiliar voice was saying. "Yall stole it from the county clerk -- didn't they, Newk."

"God damn your soul --!" said the other voice, the two arguing without listening to one another.

"-- If I return it, I'd be doing a public --"

"Stop pushing that child in my face!"

"-- service. Newspaper's offering a nice--"

"Just gimme the goddamn ledger!"

"-- price for it, wanna expose the corruption goin' on here."

She could tell they were close by, their voices low and intense. She recognized one of them, it was Thomas Crouch, though his usual oily tone had clotted and turned fretful. The other, deep and resonant, she sensed belonged to the one she had conjured, Eleggua.

"...Man, you crazy!" she heard Crouch's voice saying. "You can't fuck with Clooder this way, believe me, I know him! You don't realize this thing is bigger than you imagine!"

"Aw, nigguh, just bag it! I've had nuffa your 'negotiating!' Yall want to dance with the Devil and don't want to pay the price. Fine, then you'll pay the consequences!"

"Wait! Wait! Awright...!"

"...That's better! Yeah, now you beginning to sound like a businessman," the deep voice said. "Sheeit, yall musta thought you was dealin' with another Delta nigguh, to spoze you coulda dumped that land on me, and then I'd just give it away when I was supposed to find out it was worthless!"

"But it is worthless! The land aint worth shit! -- I-mean-I-mean I didn't know that then, when we was cutting cards for it! See, they had me fooled, too, it was only later, when I found out --!"

"You a fool, awright, but you aint foolin' nobody but yourself! You fooled with the insurance on those other properties, though, it was doubled right before they started burning down."

"What you trying to pull --!"

"And some folks round here might be interested to know who been pocketing them hard-earned nickels they been puttin' in your *"Negro"* bank --!"

"Thassa goddamn lie! Nobody --!"

"-- I see Sheriff Clooder done bought himself a new Stetson today...."

"-- I run the --! You wouldn't appreciate it, but this is the first Negro-owned bank in the Delta, and it's an important step forward for the race, here! Naturally, I had to make certain arrangements -- Tsk, shit, what the hell difference that make to you? Will you give me the ledger and stop foolin' with that child!"

"Watch your tone, nigguh, you talking about my son!"

"Nevermind. Here's your money. Give me the ledger!"

There was a brief silence, then a car started up, and she heard Crouch say, "Hold on! I wanna examine the ledger before you --"

"Hush!"

"What...?"

"We got company!"

Basheeba heard footsteps running off. Another car door slammed and its engine started up. She stepped back into the cover of the bushes and the next minute a yellow Hudson accelerated passed her with its rear wheels spinning in the mud. Through the window she recognized Thomas Crouch hunched over the wheel. Watching him drive out of sight, she was thinking it strange to see the conservative undertaker in a bright yellow sports car.

She waited another moment, before stepping out of the bushes to see Crouch's Cadillac still parked there, with its convertible top creaking open like a trapdoor, and Eleggua, himself, perched like an insect on the hood. He was turned in profile, leaning forward on his elbows with his feet propped on the fender. Smoke was curling up out of his mouth and he was looking toward the old churchyard just beyond. He had something in his hand and his other hand moved rhythmically from side to side in a sewing motion. She heard a low rustling sound, like wind soughing through the trees, but there was no wind and so she thought she was hearing the wailing of lost souls as he sewed them into his nation sack.

She glanced toward the sunken graves and tumbled headstones overgrown with jimsonweed and morning-glory, then shifted her eyes to the charred ruins of the Spirit of the Redeemer Holy Sanctified Church, which lay sprawled next to the churchyard, a relic of the fires last time. She'd used to come down there to testify. The whitefolks had used to park outside in their wagons and cars, then, drawn by the shouting and singing and the righteous rhythm of the drum and the tambourine. Until the preacher had started talking about voting. Next thing they knew, the church had burned down and the preacher had disappeared. Before the fire, she reflected, the whitefolks used to see us all the time, without thinking much about watching us, but since then, they be watching us all the time but don't hardly seem to see us. She turned and looked again at the stranger, a dark figure against the dying crescent of the sun, cool as a Georgia Skin dealer in a chartreuse suit. The tops of his ears were hidden under a Panama now, but she'd seen their shadows plain enough as she'd turned the corner, shadows long and erect as pitchfork prongs cast across the road.

After a moment, he looked around, and she thought she glimpsed fresh blood at his throat.

"Well, lookahere," he said, showing no surprise at seeing her there. "The rain bringin' all kinda folks out this evenin'. What you doin' so far from home, Aunty?"

His voice was deep and rolling, and though he'd spoken softly, she felt a thrumming in the ground that stirred unspoken thoughts in her mind. She got a firmer grip on the bundle under her arm, and took a step forward.

"*Moyuba, Eshu-Elegba!*" she muttered.

"Say which?"

"I'm goin' bout my bidniz," she said curtly, raising her voice, and adding, "I see you goin' bout yours!"

"Oh?" He followed her glance, to what he held in his hands, which seemed to change before her eyes into a sheet of paper and an envelope. He calmly folded the paper, put it into the envelope, and then, running a finger along the edge, added, "What business you think I'm in, Aunty?"

Basheeba sucked her teeth, as though impatient at the obvious. It was then that she saw the baby. It was propped up in the passenger seat of the car, swaddled in a blanket. It was an ugly child, she thought, with a big head, out-sized hands and flattened features. It was toying with a pair of pliers, pulling the welting from the upholstered seat. That ripping sound had been the soughing she'd heard before, she realized. Her breath caught in her throat, and she swiveled her eyes toward the churchyard. "The spirit aint blind like the body," she said aloud. "The dead walk in wisdom!"

"Hmmn, like they say, a lil knowledge can be a dangerous thing...." The man had spoken with his eyes fixed on the envelope in his hand, as though he'd already forgotten her. But then he looked up and regarded her thoughtfully through the smoke of the cigarette that dangled in the corner of his mouth. His long, brown, horse-like face was crossed with thick bushy eyebrows that curled down over his drooping eyelids. "Yeah," he said, "you the mother o'the one they found in the river, aintcha."

"No, I aint!"

"Not the lil kid from up North, I mean. The other one."

"I got one daughter's living, and that's all I mind. But that aint nonna your --"

"Rhoder, yeah, that's his name. You was in the church, there, mournin' im, awright. With the widow and the little kids. Not a bad looking woman, the widow."

"She's nonna your bidniz! She's young and got a long life --!"

"Kinda skinny for my taste, but she got good le-egs."

"She got nothin' t'do with you, you --"

"Carries herself nice, got a lil class, that one. So, you *her* mamma, huh?"

"You just get your mind offa her! That's not what hit's about!"

"Not what what's about?"

Basheeba took out a small rag, a remnant of the shirt Rhoder'd had on when they'd pulled him out of the river, and which she'd soaked in an infusion of herbs and chicken blood. She waved it about in the air, chanting, *"Ago Ashe, omiero! Beni Geburah, donnay Netzach! Ago Ashe! Beni Geburah! Donnay Netzach!"*

The man rolled his eyes at this exhibition, "Jesuschrist! Now, I'm spoze to talk pig-Latin with a crazy woman! All that hoodoo bullshit couldn't cast a frog out a pond!" His hand traced an odd, quick figure in the air, "You Delta nigguhs is too much, all yall got flies buzzin' round ya head!"

He slipped into the driver's seat and started up the car. But he suddenly gave a yelp, as the baby struck his thigh with the pliers. "Boy, what's got into you!" He snatched the tool out of the child's hand and tossed it out of the car. Basheeba felt a chill go through her when she heard the iron ring against a stone. And all at once, the man looked uncomfortable. He twisted his neck around and took out a handkerchief, mopping the perspiration from his forehead, before letting the car roll to the edge of the road. He stopped when he came abreast of her. She saw, now, that what she'd thought at first was blood was a scarlet paisley tie that vibrated against the green of his suit. He wore a hatband of the same material as the tie, but they clashed with his black and tan leopard shirt, to which the tie was fixed with a cowry shell stickpin.

"Well, we can understand you being skittish and all," he said, idly tucking the ripped welting back into the seam of the seat between himself and the child. "I can see you a intelligent woman, but afterall, we aint had a chance to get acquainted yet...." As he spoke, the child was rummaging through a pile of papers in the glove compartment looking for something else to play with. "This here's Newk," he added, "My son. I named'm after my kid brother, Newton, but I call him Newk cause I think he kinda looks like Don Newcombe, don't you? And he's gonna be a great pitcher, too, one day, aint that right, Newk? Heh-heh, cute lil devil, aint he." Looking up, then, he said, "We know something about you, too, Aunty..."

His voice was round and seductive and he sought to catch her eye. But she made her eyes go flat and shifted them higher, so he'd have to scale the steep purpled wall of her forehead where the brows and lashes had been seared off years ago and probe the charred stubble of her hair, where the rheumy black beads would elude him. Dropping his gaze, finally, to the child, he removed his stickpin and, using it as a lock pick, reached over to close and secure the glove compartment.

"Trust me, Aunty," he said, then, "I can see we gonna get along just fine!"

"Bullshit!" She pulled away as he extended his arm over the door to pat her hand. "You don't see shit!" she said, provoked to anger by his patronizing tone. "Your tie don't even see what it's doin' on your shirt! What the fuck you know about anything!"

His jaw shot down and the tip of his long tongue curled up like a snake. He rocked his head back and forth, bugging his eyes at the baby. His shoulders jerked. He was laughing, a froth of spittle white and luminous in the corners of his mouth. He looked at her, then, and said, "You a real piss-cutter, aintcha! Yeah, I can see aint nobody gonna get away with messin' with you!" He drew the baby up close to him, revealing a large brown manila envelope it had been sitting on, which he put in his lap, and then he opened the passenger door beside her. "Come on, get in, we'll drop you off."

She muttered something he didn't catch, and took another step back. "I'll walk!"

"Humph. Now, that's too bad. Cause you lookin' a lil peaked, Aunty. And I believe we headin' the same way --"

"Yeah," she muttered, in pig-Latin under her breath, "but I know you don't never give nothin' away for free, and I aint about to trade my daughter --!"

"-- F'instance," he continued smoothly, ignoring her, "we both got us a problem bout Rhoder dying like he did. Boy had something for me, and somebody took it off him. On the other hand -- now, tell me if I'm wrong -- I'd guess Rhoder had something of yours, too. And *somebody*...done took that. You with me so far?"

"I donno whatcha talkin' bout."

"Uh-hunh." His eyes kept sliding away to the envelopes, the manila one in his lap and the white office envelope, whose contents he'd been reading before and which he held, now, upright in the fingers of his left hand, resting on the wheel, almost as though he wanted her to read what was on it. She saw that it bore the seal of the County Clerk of Dardan County, Alabama, and below, she read Crouch's name and address in Dividend.

He saw her staring at the envelope, "Can you read, Aunty?"

She took a step back and shook her head to deny it, "Huhn-uh."

He gave a wry smile, then looked at her shrewdly, "You know what, I think you're jealous!" Her mouth opened, but she didn't say anything, and he went on, "Yes you are, you're jealous! I bet you talked him into it, didn't you, you talked Rhoder into borrowing that money." She seemed to falter, and started muttering incomprehensibly again. "Yeah, sure!" he continued, gathering momentum, "Rhoder would've come to you, cause he'd of thought you was too *spiritual* to envy him. He didn't know your spirit was greed, and envy and resentment -- yes, and *lone-li-ness --!*"

"You fulla shit!" she blurted out. "I never wanted nothin'! I never axed him for nothin'! Or her, neither! I sent her to get educated, to think with her mind, not with her --!"

"*Lonely*, yeah! And why not. You ugly. You always been ugly. Born with that red stripe across your face, like a flag to draw a bull -- Look here!"

"Don't you look-here me! You look out, yown self! I aint no iggarent pickaninny --!"

"What you gonna do," he said, speaking over her, "when she git wise and throw you over! Leave you! She will, oh yes, your precious Lorna will! You know it, too! Soon as she quits grievin', she will!"

"I BEEN READIN' SIGN AND SPLITTIN' CHINE FOR FIFTY YEARS!" Basheeba continued, shouting now, as though to stanch the wound he'd opened with the force of her denial, "I CAN CUT QUICKER, CUSS BIGGER, AND MAKE A STRONG BULL SICKER THAN ANY CON-JUH WOMAN IN THE COUNTY! I AINT AFRAIDA NO-BODY! INCLUDING YOU, MISTER DEVIL! YOU CAN'T DO ME NO MORE HARM! I'M AWREADY BLACK AND LIVIN' IN THE DELTA! EVEN YOU CAN'T DO ME NO WORSER'N THAT!"

He looked at her a moment, watching her trying to catch her breath, as though she'd run clear across the county to tell him this, and his eyes changed, although Basheeba couldn't tell exactly what they'd changed from, or to. "Well," he said, "never mind, then. I just thought mebbe you and me could do a lil 'bidniz' of our own," he continued, mildly mocking her, "at somebody else's expense, for a change. For example, somebody might settle a few scores and even make herself some nice bread --"

"I...I aint goan put my daughter in danger --!"

"-- if she wanted to drop off these envelopes, here, to a couple people in town -- Your daughter? Lorna?" He looked at her curiously, then shrugged. "Aint nothin' good in this ole world come without a lil risk. But, if y'aint up to it...."

"Lorna got nothin' to do with this, y'hear me!"

"Uuh..." he paused, then nodded his head, as though with a new thought, "Crouch come round to see yall lately, Aunty?"

Basheeba turned her back on him, and touching her fingers to the stain across her eyes, murmured an invocation in her coded language. When she turned again, the sun had slipped beneath the horizon and the stranger's face had taken on a sulfurous glow, as though a nugget of brimstone burned in the back of his throat.

He worked his lips a moment, as though having trouble speaking. But when he did speak, his voice slipped about her like a coil of comfort, "We got somebody owe us a reckoning," he said. "Aint we."

10.
Gyves and the Mill

"Oh Lawdy La-awd, Oh Lawdy La-awd,
Ah wonder will Ah ever git home again!

"Ah traveled fah, an Ah traveled wide,
Lawd Ah bin hongry, an' Ah bin tired.
F'om Memphis City down ta Birmin'ham,
Da blues be walkin jus' like a man.

"Ah says Ah wonder, Oh Lawd Ah wonder,
Will Ah ever git back home ali-i-i-ve...!"

The Reverend Harold Sampson heard the words of the
song echoing again in his mind late that evening, as he left
Lorna Rhoder's house and headed toward town. He was angry and badly shaken. He feared for Lorna, and wondered if
he'd done right to leave his boys there, on top of all her other
troubles, now, but he didn't know what else to do. He could
only hope they'd all be safe there for the time being. Compli-

cating his feeling for Lorna was the fact that he now found himself missing Benjamin. He and Ben hadn't always seen eye-to-eye, he'd found the man too rough-and-ready, but Ben had been staunch, and he missed the deacon's sturdiness and support. The bastard! he said to himself, thinking of Brennan -- then almost smiled when he imagined what Ben's response would have been.

But on passing Julep Road, his expression grew dour again as he made a note to himself to drive over and confront Thomas Crouch first thing in the morning. He passed his hand over his face, as though to put back the tide of events pressing in on him. He'd been on the road since early that morning, when the traffic going the other way had been packed nose to tailgate with mule carts and wagons heaped with raw cotton headed for the gin. There'd been white croppers among them, but most had been Negroes, and the Negroes had been singing. At one place, their voices had been raised together for nearly a mile, the verses spontaneously sung out by individuals from different points along the caravan, and the rest joining in the chorus, with one singer, in his enthusiasm, leaning way over backward from his perch atop the high white cloud of cotton like a black apostrophe on the gloss of Heaven. Sampson didn't generally approve of the blues, he found them rowdy and irreligious. And yet, all that day, as he'd driven through the intermittent rain to go, again, from house to house gathering signatures for the school integration petition, urging his people to register to vote and coaching them in the answers to the absurd, obstructive questions they'd be challenged with at the courthouse, the song had haunted him, the voices taking on the faces he remembered from the old logging teams of his youth. But earlier that same evening, as he'd pushed his old Studebaker as fast as it would go along the roads that had been mostly deserted by then, with Joshua, frightened and wide awake beside him, petting the battered dog in his lap, and the two younger boys asleep in the back seat, the song had echoed back with a dread resonance....

He'd stopped off at the church to put the petitions in a box he'd hidden in the floor under the pulpit for safekeeping, and was just locking up, wanting to get home in time to cook supper for the boys and sit with them over their daily exercises in reading and arithmetic, when he saw the yellow Hudson, pulled up beside his own car in front of the door....

"Evening, Rev."

"Good evening. Robinson, isn't it?"

The man studied him a moment without answering, then said, "You got a little reputation around here."

"Meaning?"

"They say you're an *hon-est* man...."

Robinson had pronounced the word in such a way that he couldn't be sure the emphasis was meant ironically. When he didn't say anything, Robinson continued.

"Wanted to know whether you could help out a friend of mine."

"Why don't you help him yourself?"

"Well, see, that's the thing. I'd like to, but I expect to be movin' on, shortly, and he's not available just now...so, I was kinda hopin' maybe I could help him -- through you."

"Oh? Who is he?"

He made a vague gesture, "Chances are, you don't know him, but I think I can arrange for the two of you to get together." He reached into his glove compartment and took out a thick envelope and held it out to him. "I'd like you to just pass this on to him -- that is, if you don't mind."

"What is it," he said, looking at the envelope without touching it.

Robinson smiled, "Why don't you look inside?"

He took the envelope and opened it, and caught his breath. "Where did you get this."

"It's only three, four thousand dollars in there, that's all. Feel free to count it, when you get a chance." He made as if to drive off.

"Just a minute!" he said, tossing the envelope back into Robinson's lap. "I don't approve of gambling, and I won't have anything to do with its proceeds."

Robinson put the clutch into neutral again and sat back to look at him. He, meanwhile, feeling the heat radiating off the hood of the car, became aware of how quietly its engine was running.

"Fact of the matter, Reverend, I'm a businessman. I do a little gambling, now and then — aint none of us perfect — but this money is from my real estate business." He handed him a card, "And, of course, I would expect that the church, here," he nodded his head, indicating the still-unfinished section of roofing, "could certainly use a contribution, which you should feel free to take out of that."

He said, "I think you'd better find another messenger, Robinson," and turned to get into his own car.

But Robinson called him back, "Like I said, Reverend, I'm a businessman. I wouldn't want it to get around that I'm an easy touch. This here's something you could say I kinda owe a certain young feller. And if you'd be willing to do a kid a good turn, why, then, we can get it all squared up -- anonymously."

"I'm afraid --"

"I have a hunch, Reverend, he might be needing this real soon. It might save him from some serious trouble. He aint done nothin', you understand, but this *is* LeVane County."

"Listen, Robinson, if this 'kid,' as you call him, needs help, he should --"

"Now, maybe -- 'scuse me, Reverend -- maybe the N-Double-A-CP might want to help him, but seems their account here is overdrawn."

"What? What do you mean!"

"Oh. Oh, sorry, you didn't know about that. Well, let's see...do you have a minute...?"

He'd refused the envelope, but he'd been so troubled over what Robinson had told him that he'd driven over to the courthouse before heading home. And later, preparing supper, he'd still been turning it over in his mind, not wanting to believe it -- but seeing, on the other hand, how it might fit together with something Beevis, at the NAACP office down in Jackson, had mentioned the other day. And then, the moment they'd sat down to eat, they'd heard a car pull up in front of the house. He remembered noticing, as he'd started out of his chair to see who it was, that he hadn't heard Buttercups bark...

Before he reached the hall, he heard a window smash and something hit the floor in the front room. Instinctively, he turned back and told the boys to get down under the table, just as a blinding flash lit up the hall and an explosion shook the house. Pictures were knocked down, and glass and crockery crashed to the floor. He made a sign to the boys to keep silent, though it was hardly necessary, they were too frightened to make a sound, and got up and ran in a crouch toward the living room, snatching his shotgun from the sideboard as he passed. There was a large broken Coke bottle lying on the area rug with small flames licking up and the smell of kerosene. He crept over to peer out the broken window, but it was dark by then and all he saw was a car he didn't recognize driving off with the fading sound of men's voices whooping and laughing. Turning from the window, he saw that the house hadn't suffered much damage. He called to the boys to fetch buckets of water to wet down the floor, and hauled the rug outside into the yard to stomp the fire out. Then as he started to circle the house with the shotgun to make sure no one else was out there, he saw Buttercups. She was lying on her side on the ground near the road. He called to her, but she only whined and raised her paw. When he went over to look at the little brown and white feist, he saw she'd been clubbed, there was a livid bruise swelling up along the side of her head. He picked her up in his arms and stood out there staring after the car, with the echo of those raucous voices baying in his ears...

...Like mad dogs, he remembered thinking, their savagery only making him more determined. But what was unforgivable, when he thought of his boys, what went deeper and more harrowing than any feeling of fear, was the brutal reminder that the innocence of another generation should be violated yet again....

Preoccupied as he was, and checking his rearview mirror for suspicious headlights tailing him, he didn't see the other car speeding out of the side road until it was almost too late. He blew his horn and swerved onto the shoulder, as the other car skidded passed. The Studebaker had stalled out, and he sat there a moment, fumbling for his handkerchief to wipe his brow and trying to calm himself down. But as he restarted the car, he saw taillights backing toward him, and he cursed himself for having left his shotgun at home in his haste to get the boys out of the house. When the car slid alongside, however, it was the face of Thomas Crouch he saw scowling out at him through the driver's window.

"Nigger, why the hell don't you watch where you're going!"

"Thomas, dammit, you scared me half to death!"

"Oh...Sampson...sorry, I...."

"Thomas, pull over, please. I was going to stop by the house tomorrow to see you." As he got out of his own car and went over to where Crouch was pulling off the road, he admonished himself to keep his temper and to try and find out what was really going on -- and if worse came to worse, to bring Crouch around through moral suasion....

"...Don't you be tellin' me that!"

"It's the truth, aint nothin' you can do!"

"Ruwana, the eldest girl, showed me where he'd dropped his pilot's cap --!"

"Ruwana's a child, they aint gonna take her word."

"I saw it there myself! He dropped it when Basheeba fired at him. She drove him off before he could...have his way with Lorna, but the fact is --!"

"The fact is, aint nothin' really happened! Let it rest, aint no need for you to be --"

"The point is, the bastard wantonly attacked her in her own house! Those children already just lost their father, now, they're scared to go out in their own yard! Brennan threatened to come back and burn the place down!"

"Lorna told you that?"

"Well, no, not exactly. Her mother told me."

"Her mother?"

"Lorna didn't want to talk about it. When I asked her, she just said she didn't want any more trouble. Anyway, what difference does it make?"

Crouch looked at him as if he hadn't heard him right. "Basheeba? Basheeba told you? You want to bring a white man to court in this county on the word of a crazywoman?' Man, what's got into you!"

"The bastard left his pilot's cap there, you telling me that's not evidence?"

231

"Listen, you can see Lorna's got enough sense to keep her mouth shut. If Basheeba scared him off, then I think you'd best let it go at that."

"He's not going to get away with it, no-sir! Not this time! Goddammit, no! They been threatening us long enough! Jesus Christ, man, you know, yourself, those two hoodlums took that boy right from out of his uncle's house just the other day and -- No! We've got to put a stop to it! 'THE STONE SHALL CRY OUT OF THE WALL," Sampson shouted, forgetting himself for a moment, "AND THE BEAM OUT OF THE TIMBER SHALL ANSWER IT!'" He banged his fist down on the hood of the car Crouch had been driving in emphasis, and then stood staring at the yellow Hudson, puzzled.

"You really got it bad for that gal, aint you?"

"...What? How dare you!"

"Look-here, Reverend, I can understand you're upset, but you're axin' for tro --!"

"Oh, no! You're not gonna get away with that, Thomas! How dare you suggest --! In fact, I'd like to know where you were just rushing off to, this time of night!"

"I happen to be heading home! Not that it's any of your damn business --!"

"...Oh...ahem. Well, my feeling for Lorna Rhoder is above reproach! She is part of my congregation, and I'd fight for any one of them who'd been wronged -- even you! And so help me, God, this time, we gonna get justice!" And *you*, Thomas Crouch, are going to help me!"

"Me!"

"Negroes got just as much right to live unmolested as anyone else! Every ignorant white hillbilly and swamp rat in America got a claim to justice! Don't tell me you're gonna just stand there...!"

Crouch shook his head and smiled ironically.

232

"You don't believe me? You really don't believe in progress, do you. Goddammit, even the Supreme Court has finally taken a stand!"

"Man, progress got to do with things, not people! How you get to live this long without common sense? You suddenly forget that the white man owns the courts and makes the laws down here? And even if you could get the law changed, you actually think it's gonna make people behave any different? You want to make a difference here, you gonna have to change the people! But the white man aint gonna change! What for? He got everything he want right now! And as for the colored...huh! With all due respect, Negroes been prayin' for a change for a long time down here, but how many you seen made any attempt to change theirselves!"

"You're talking like whitefolks, now."

What? You got some nerve --!"

"Listen --!"

"-- You call yourself a man of the cloth, but you up here talkin' like you stepped offa Cloud Nine! You seen Negroes getting beat up and shot up and thrown in every river in the goddamn county -- and for what! Been any laws changed? Can you name five new Negroes registered to vote in five years? You seen any Negroes in white churches, or any whites in yours? I been burying bodies outta this same funeral parlor for over ten years, here, in Dividend, and half of'em so full of alcohol they're fire hazards! They got they hands press together and they mouth pout up like they prayin', and every second one got a hoodoo vine up his ass! -- pardon my country --"

"-- Thomas --"

"-- Talking about they want a education, and they want to vote! Negroes want education, they oughta get it! I got it! I'm doing fine, here! But I plow my rows, and let the white man plow his. And I'd advise you to do the same. Any Negro trying to cross over, just axin' for trouble!"

"Are you giving me a warning, Thomas?"

"Tsk! Man, how much more warning do you need? Look, as you come to me, I'm just trying to talk to ya like a friend, here, as one intelligent black man to another --"

"Um-hm. Well, actually, I was coming to --"

Crouch glanced over his shoulder and lowered his voice, "And talk about voting, who they gonna vote for? That racist sunovabitch, Jess Arnett? Hiram White? Branford "Big Bee" Clooder? Shoot, one redneck same as another! We been through all this before. You forget how all them young Negro soldiers came back in 'Forty-Five full of pride and hope, like they'd won the War single-handed? Laws was passed then, too. President Truman went to address the N-Double-A-CP and integrated the federal Civil Service and the military. Everybody went around talkin' bout the Negroes finally gonna have their day in the sun, yeah, everybody was singing Don't Fence Me In! But here we are, ten years later, we done fought another war, and aint nothin' changed! And I'll tell ya something else, too, if Negroes ever do get elected to office down here, it just gonna be a new hitch to the same ole wagon. Then, the black man will take all the blame, and the white man will still hold the rein --!"

"Awright, Thomas! I appreciate your thoughts. But that's not what I --"

"Don't mention it, Reverend, glad to be of help. People like you and me put our heads together, we can accomplish a lot here. You aint like the resta these Negroes. Most of 'em'd quicker burn the furniture than cut wood! The truth --"

"The truth is --"

"-- the truth is, your average Delta Negro aint got enough self-respect and ambition --"

"-- some of us are willing to conspire --"

"-- or enterprise, to drag his behind out the tonk --"

"-- with certain whitefolks in powerful positions --"

"-- and stay sober long enough to get a education --"

"-- to embezzle public funds, defraud social agencies and betray their own race!"

"-- and -- What? What?" Crouch looked both ways along the dark, empty road and stepped closer, "Wait a minute, what are you talking about!"

"I'm talking about why you broke ranks with the rest of us and voted to endorse Governor White's proposal for 'voluntary' segregation in the public schools --!"

The banker laughed, then, and opened his car door, as if to drive off, "Oh, Jesus! And I thought you was an intelligent man --!"

"-- I'm talking about defrauding the NAACP of funds that were supposed to --"

"Goddammit, I'm a lifetime member of the NAACP!"

"You became one only last week! You wouldn't have anything to do with them before! Why?"

"That's a lie! I always supported --!"

"Those funds are precious! They're supposed to provide support for court cases for LeVane Negroes bringing actions against the County Clerk and Registrar --"

"My bank and my funeral business sponsor the free-lunch programs in the Negro schools! I done raised funds --"

"-- for obstructing their Constitutional right to vote! But twenty thousand dollars is missing from that legal fund!"

"-- for the NAACP! -- What you mean, 'missing!'"

"The money was used to pay off gambling debts," Sampson said, pointing his finger at him, "and to cover up for funds missing from Dividend Associates and the Afro-American Savings Bank --!"

"'Gamb --!'" He turned his back, as Sampson continued, got into the Hudson and slammed the door.

"-- that you were afraid was going to be discovered by the real owners of those businesses!"

As he keyed the ignition, Crouch looked back through the driver's window, "Man, you done gone crazy! You headed for trouble!"

"The money's missing, Thomas, and you know it!"

"My reputation's unquestioned in this community! My businesses support the Afro-American Association Orphanage, provide loans to -- Eh, wait a minute, what was that you said about 'real owners?' What 'real owners?' I own --!"

"You can call yourself 'President,' 'Chairman,' or 'Chief Hog-Washer,' but fact is, Clooder and Thackery own those companies. You're just a front, a white man's token, and you know it!" Sampson paused, then added, meaningfully, "-- and I know it."

Crouch stepped out of the car again, his neck swelling in anger, "Just who the hell do you think you are, talking to me like that!"

But Sampson stood his ground, "I'm talking about bowing to pressure from the White Citizens Council to close out the bank accounts of Negroes that dare to stand up for their rights --!"

"Goddammit, nig -- listen, you runnin' fast 'n' loose offa the mouth --!"

"-- I'm talking about exactly what happens to money put in a bank that's supposed to be owned by Negroes -- but isn't!"

"That's enough! Goddammit, that's enough!" Crouch said, waving his finger threateningly in Sampson's face, "You best git your lyin' preacher ass back in your car and get on outta here, or I'll --!"

"AND... I'm talking about who just happens to make a profit now and then off of the insurance when the likes of

Brennan and his hoodlums try to intimidate the Negroes around town by burning down their homes! Shall I go on?"

Taken completely by surprise by the last accusation, Crouch glared at him long and hard, "What is it you want...!"

...Bald-faced, hypocritical motherfucker! Crouch was saying to himself, as he drove away, moments later. Who the hell he think he is, talking to me like that! He don't know who he's dealing with! I make one phone call down to the Baptist Synod, and his preachin' ass'll be hauled back to where he come from before the nickel drop. They don't go for agitators in their church, and I aint gonna put up with any two-faced monkey in a black robe pullin' no 'moral blackmail' bullshit on me -- and that fool probably won't know it, but I'll be doing him a favor, too, the way he's carrying on....!

But as he drove on, he began to wonder how Sampson had come up with all that information. All right, he thought, about his offer as bank president to take responsibility for the NAACP legal fund, maybe. He supposed he had been a little careless there. Sampson had his own contacts with the Jackson office, afterall. And Bidder-them must've run off at the mouth about the gambling. But how had he found out about the ownership of the bank? And even if he'd looked up the insurance on Ida Temple's place in the public records, why should he have? Why would he dare, dare to imply that he, Thomas Crouch, of all people, might've had something to do with burning down a whorehouse! It had occurred to him immediately, of course, that Robinson had put Sampson wise, and he would've demanded to know whether the two of them were in cahoots together -- but being seen, as he was, driving Robinson's car, he didn't think that was the right moment. Besides, he thought, it didn't make sense, anyhow. Sampson wasn't a schemer, and he wasn't the sort to have any truck with the likes of Robinson. And as for Robinson, he wasn't the type to do shit for nothing, so what could he possibly have to gain from a deal with the preacher? Anyway, he said to himself, patting the package on the seat beside him and settling back in the car, it was all just talk, bullshit. It'd cost him a lot, but he'd finally gotten the ledger back, nobody could prove anything.

Still, Sampson had his nerve, butting his head into his business like that and making demands: restitution of the NAACP legal fund; set up a trust fund for the Rhoder children; provide a lawyer for this boy and the cripple the police were looking for, supposed to have burned down Ida's place and killed that girl, Marvella -- That was a joke! Why was he supposed to give a shit about some niggers getting caught with their pants down in a whorehouse! The Dundees-them always been troublemakers, anyhow. Boy shoulda stayed put wherever he was, it was good riddance! He can't expect to be held responsible because the fools decided to turn up here on the wrong night! And as for Rhoder, Lorna'd had no business marrying him anyway! Ben Rhoder's another one been begging for trouble, going round like Sampson with school integration petitions and voter registration forms. Trust fund! Can you beat that? Damn, what's the matter with all these niggers, anyhow, they think he's a millionaire? He's got his own children to support! He's a businessman, that's all! But these Delta niggers see a black man with a dollar, they think...! He sucked his teeth, and thought, Rhoder should've looked out for his own children! And Sampson wasn't fooling nobody, neither, damn hypocrite! A preacher who coveted his own deacon's widow, trying to lay responsibility for the woman's children at his, Crouch's, door! Nerve of him, he said to himself, to ask me, Where I'm "rushing off to that time of night!" As though suggesting I was on my way to see the bitch! What the hell, I'm a married man with kids of my own, a respectable businessman and pillar of the goddamn community! Does he think I got nothing better to do than go around trying to sneak a piece offa every bereaved widow in the county? -- And if I did, I sure wouldn't need to be "rushing off" about it! Shit, he reflected, outside pussy aint no problem in this town. People think being a funeral director is strange, but they shoulda seen his daddy, back home, commiserating with all them widows hanging off his arms like bees on a honeycomb! And successful as he, himself, is now? Sheeet! Gotta scrape'em off with a butterknife! Plus, he got all the extra he wanted over at Ida's -- or had, until now. But whorehouses were a dime-a-dozen, and Ida was getting too uppity, anyhow.

Lorna was something else, though, he admitted to himself, a sexy little bitch without even trying. The woods were full of niggers bugging their eyes at that woman. And what if Brennan should get "his way with her," what difference would it make anyhow, he mused, cynically, that shit went on down here all the time. Besides which, Brennan was Clooder's boy, he's the one handle the sheriff's dirty-work. Clooder aint gonna come down on his own bozo for shit like that. Course, Sampson's still new here, he don't know about Brennan and Clooder, in fact, he don't know the half of what goes on in LeVane, he's too busy trying to change it. The man had more warmth than wit. He was hot-headed, arrogant, arbitrary and on the wrong side of his own fence half the time! A born fool, as only an educated simpleton could be. He'd seen all kinda fools come through LeVane, but Sampson's kind was the worst! They stirred up the most confusion and caused the greatest anguish! They got just enough brains to articulate problems nobody knows how to resolve! Waste of potential and a goddamn shame. He shook his head, picturing Sampson stamping up and down out there in the dark road like he thought he was St. George going to slay the dragon -- and thinking of the "souvenir" that the chief deputy had hanging in his car, and wondering how long it would be before another preacher talked himself into a lynching.

-- And fuck that new chief deputy, anyway! he said to himself, as his mind leaped back in agitation to recall the earlier encounter, just before meeting Sampson. Where he come off at, following him around, chasing him halfway back to Dividend in the dark of night, like he was some desperate criminal! Then again, it occurred to him, as he turned off the highway onto Julep Road, the deputy might actually have thought he was following Robinson, because he was driving Robinson's car. And when the deputy had finally caught up with him and realized who he was, he'd just stood there scratching his jaw looking surprised and mumbling something about a stolen car. But he, having been quick enough to stash the record book out of sight under the seat during the chase, had simply cut the boy off and dropped the hint that the high sheriff might be interested to know why his deputy had stopped him, Thomas Crouch, on the road for no good reason! And, sure enough, the cop had handed him back his license and let him go.

Except, as he was about to step on the gas, the cop had put that ugly steel claw of his on the door and started asking him some strange questions. He'd just told the boy he didn't know what he was talking about and driven off. But it occurred to him, now, as he pulled into his own driveway and shut the engine, that the deputy was old Sheriff Hope's son, and Clooder had better watch his back.

II.
Cat's Paw

"I used to live here, man!" Lot says in a hushed tone. "Aint that a bitch?" His face has suddenly grown childlike, bewildered. "See? That's our house, over there. And over there, where they got the cement mixer and shit, that used to be the chicken hutch...!"

It's all ashambles and rotting away, the toolshed and the chicken hutch and the house across the yard. Jones sees them through the barn door that's open and off its hinges and through the gaping holes in the walls. Sitting there and unable to turn his head, he nevertheless seems able to see the ruin all around him, see it with the unnatural clarity of a dream. He's delirious, he thinks, he must be. Faint, lightheaded and somehow removed from himself. Like an owl perched high in the rafters he looks down upon the house collapsed, the fields overgrown by weeds and brambles, and mysterious pieces of unfinished wooden framing suspended in loops of chain hanging from the beams of the barn. Assorted lengths of lumber are stacked neatly on racks running the length of one wall, a cultivator sits in a corner beside a decaying cotton wagon. And there on the floor, lying in the shadows at the back of the barn among the litter of old harness, farm implements and discarded shakes, is something he has no feeling for anymore, something he can barely recognize, himself, a ghost, aged, grimy and gaunt, sprawled like a scarecrow in a burst bale of hay. The boy, meanwhile, is walking around slowly with his own eyes squeezed shut, muttering to himself and running his hands along the stall posts and partitions. Blind, Jones thinks, like a man feeling his way among dreams lost to the light of day. Here and there a bend of bright wood, old leather or glittering iron is momentarily caught in the light and shines like a beacon through the years of accumulated dust. But the boy passes them by, unseeing.

"...What mirror?" the old woman, Basheeba, had said. "What you see is what you brung in here with you. I don't need no tricks, or no magic mirrors, neither. Yall tricky enough...!"

It was when they were still in the cemetery, where she'd first stumbled upon them. She'd come back with food and medicine, as she'd promised. His arm was swollen and discolored and he'd caught the stink of the wound where the hand had been burned as she'd removed the bandage.

"I was just wondering how you knew who I was," Lot had said, then, leaning back on his elbow and picking over the gnawed bones as he watched her cleaning out the wound by the light of a candle. She'd brought them fried chicken backs and fishheads wrapped in butcher paper.

"You the ram in the bramble," she'd said, enigmatically, "anywhich way you turn, little Isaac laugh to see you comin'!"

The boy hadn't known what she was talking about. He'd sighed and changed the subject, "Man, we was gettin' pretty hungry! Least, I was. I aint so sure about him, no more. He takes a little water, but I mean, like you just seen, when I try to feed him, he don't seem much interested. Don't seem to matter to him whether he eat or not. I imagine that arm must hurt him. I guess he's real sick, huh?"

The hoodoo woman hadn't answered, concentrating on packing the open wound with live maggots, pressing them into the gangrenous flesh. When she'd done, she'd covered the wound with a clay poultice of what she'd said was black hellebore, winter cress and ivy.

"Shit," the boy'd said, "I don't even know what the fuck I'm doin' here!"

"Your daddy called you here," the old woman had said, then, winding a long cotton rag round and round Jones's arm....

-- More than enough to hang a man, Jones had thought.... All the way back to Charlotte, he'd kept thinking about his mother's funeral and seeing the rope in his mind scrolling off the deck and snaking through his fingers as they'd lowered the coffin --

Lot, meanwhile, is still running his hands along the barn walls with his eyes shut, skirting a bucket of oakum kicked over on the floor, passed bits of waste wood, iron clamps and what looks like a broken mold, all strewn about among the rubbish, before he finally stops at a large tool chest, where he opens his eyes and looks inside...

"...Your daddy call you back here," the old woman had repeated, trying to get Lot to hear.

"Say what?"

"You got unfinished business here. He want you to --"

"You watch your mouth, old woman!" the boy'd snapped. "What you know about my daddy! Yall niggers don't know shit about my daddy! Yall just hating him cause you're jealous, cause he owned his own farm and tried to make something outta himself --!"

"Folks don't hate him," she'd said. "They scared of him --"

"-- Fuckin' pone-head uncle toms scared of they own shadow!" the boy'd railed on, not listening to what the woman had been trying to tell him, yelling as though the long days and nights of hunger, fear and frustration had finally boiled over, "'Scared of him!' Bullshit! He's dead, what they got to be scared of?"

"They scared because --"

"Shit, yall niggers make me sick!" he'd said, "All I want to do is get the fuck outta this fuckin' place! I'm sick of yall! Shit, I'm sick of the smell of my own clothes --!"

"-- They scared," she'd persisted, "cause Fontana bought this place from Thackery, the old Bowman place --"

"-- Every night we been out here shivering in the fuckin' swamps and sweltering in the heat all fuckin' day, and I'm carryin' this cripple all over the fuckin' place from West Hell to the highway --"

"-- Aint nothin' growed on it since Bowman died. Fontana --"

"-- I'm tired and I'm hungry and I'm thirsty and all I fuckin' want is a fuckin' ride outta here --"

"-- Fontana made it grow good cotton --"

"-- And steada helping, all I see is niggers talking trash about my daddy and running for cover --!"

"-- Fontana did things people said couldn't nobody do --" she'd continued, her voice remaining calm.

"-- Well, fuck yall! You and this whole fuckin' county can go fuck yourselves --!"

"-- folks said Fontana could make a desert bloom --"

"-- Aint nothing here but hate and heat and bugs and bullshit! If you can't fuckin' help get us outta here, then just shut the fuck up, that's all, just shut up...!"

The boy, looking into the tool chest now, sees it has been ransacked and is mostly empty. There are only a few rusted tools remaining, a saw blade, an auger, some caulking irons, and at the bottom a handful of treenails and pledgets gone dry and brittle. Lot stoops to run his hand over a wooden rudder leaning up against the chest, and says softly over his shoulder, as though speaking to himself, "My daddy built boats! Damn, I'd forgotten that! He was good with his hands, he could use either hand just the same, too, like me!"

-- It was all that mystery had pissed him off, Jones is suddenly thinking. Venus would never talk about herself, where she wanted to go, or what she wanted to do next, she'd just spring it on him. She'd never even talk about her past or her own family. All she'd say was, she didn't ever want to go back to North Carolina. Close as he was to his own family, that bothered him, but whenever he'd asked her about it, her mouth would curve down in bitterness and she'd change the subject... On the drive to Alabama, he'd kept thinking about her. He'd asked her to come with him. But instead of saying Okay, or even, It's about time! she'd got all hot and bothered. Right out of the blue. Said she wasn't ready yet to deal with family. Said she still wasn't sure how he really felt about her. Talked all out of her head. He'd got pissed off and they'd had their first bad fight. It was at the motel just before he'd taken off. They'd left the place a wreck, broken mirrors and perfume bottles and breakfast dishes all over the place. She'd clawed and bitten like a tiger and thrown whatever had come to hand. They'd always fought a lot. Gal'd blow her top quicker than any other woman he'd known, her slow, sweet half-smile changing into a Samurai mask at the least offense. She could punch like a man, too. Didn't hesitate, didn't pull back. All there, all the time, and he was crazy about her. Partly because the making-up was so good! But that last time, he'd gone overboard, knocked her down, blacked her eye, and by the time he'd reached the street and started the car, he couldn't remember, anymore, what it'd been about. Except he could hear again, in his mind, her saying he'd never told her he loved her! But, God damn, if he didn't love her, why else would he've gone through all that! What difference did it make whether he actually said the words! Words were just words, bullshit! Hating

to leave her, hating the whole situation, he'd floored the gas and -- Where had they been going, yelling at each other with the car racing over the blacktop as the rain struck --?

"...No two boats were the same," the boy is saying, "he'd make each one a little different. Folks used to come round all the time asking him to make'em one. One I remember was special ordered by the sheriff, old Sheriff Hope. It was a real beauty, carvel-built with the planks syphered, you know, so the edges lay over against one another, making a tight, smooth surface. That was the last one Daddy took me out in, before...."

-- It was on their way to Miami. It wasn't until then, when he and Venus were in the car, that he'd noticed, just since the last time he'd seen her, there was gray in her hair. But he'd make it up to her, he told himself, everything would be fine once they got to Cuba. Salazar wanted him to play ball again down there, offered three grand for the season, plus expenses. More than twice what he got in the States. And it was Easy Street down there. Pitched balls didn't jitter as much in the thin mountain air as they did at sea-level in the States. A hit ball sailed a mile. And the fishing was great --!

"...Each time he'd finish one, he'd take me out with him on the bogue to try it out. He never took Newton. Newton was scared of the water. But me and Daddy would go out, and after awhile, I'd say, 'What you think, Daddy?' And he'd wink and smile that crooked smile he had -- Damn! I can see him now plain as day!" He laughs, "He got to smiling crooked that way cause the second year after he had bought the farm he went over to Highville and had a gold tooth put in, over here, at the side," the boy pulled his own lip back and pointed to an upper canine, to demonstrate, "and he didn't want the whitefolks to know he could afford one...! Rico? You still with me, man? How you doin' over there...?"

But Jones is elsewhere, moving under a night sky purpled with thunder and lightning... and the sound of a car approaching in the distance.... He's in the car, behind the wheel, driving too fast and feeling the tires planing over the wet surface of the road.... Heading south on 21, they'd passed Ft. Lawn and were just approaching the Catawba River, when the storm hit. Out of what had seemed a clear, calm night the rain was suddenly falling in torrents with roadside trees whipping and cracking in the wind. The car, buffeted by gusts, began to skate in the curves. He and Venus had been arguing since they'd left the house and were now yelling at each other over the storm. In anger, he raised a hand off the wheel --!

"...I was standing right here, helping Daddy sand it down," Lot's saying, "when Sheriff Hope came by to see how it was coming." The boy's standing between a pair of sawhorses, talking over his shoulder and sniffing at a crescent of glue mired and hardened in the can. "And I remember he told my father, he said some of the whitefolks was upset about what he was doing, I mean my father, they thought he was getting out of line going round with them voter registration papers. But the sheriff was friendly, you know? I mean, my father and Sheriff Hope aint never had no trouble between'em. I don't think either one of them really expected anything to happen...!"

-- Coming back from Dardan after the funeral he, Jones, had sped passed the turnoff to the base at Cape Lookout and continued on toward Charlotte. He wasn't going to stop because he knew they'd only have put him in the stockade. He'd had to go AWOL to attend the funeral because the commander of the base wouldn't give colored soldiers emergency leave. But he didn't give a shit, anymore. He was going to get Venus, take her away, drive to Miami and catch a boat to Cuba. Three thousand plus expenses! Him and Venus could live like a natural-born man and woman, go where they pleased. Fuck the Army, he told himself, he was going to leave all that bogus, bigoted crap behind him. Cuba was a different story, Negroes were the cream in a colored country -- and he, Rico Jones, was a hero of his race, they'd told him so! It was late by the time he'd pulled up before the unpainted pineboard shack. Crossing the planked-over drainage ditch that passed for a sidewalk, he'd gone inside and woken Venus out of bed. But she hadn't want to go, and when he'd insisted, she'd wanted time to pack and prepare, to say good-byes.

He didn't have time for that shit, they had to get gone. She wanted to know why, but he wouldn't explain. She got stubborn and started in about the kid. She wanted to take the boy with them, he was his son, she said, he shouldn't leave him. And while they argued, the kid woke up and started screaming. But he'd just had his fill of family. And if the police caught up with him before he got on the boat, he wasn't planning to let them take him. He didn't want the extra baggage. He finally got her into the car, promising to send for the boy later. But they were still fighting when the storm hit --

-- Something's out there, Jones says to himself, now, drawn out of his reverie by something he's heard, or felt. But the boy doesn't seem to notice. He's wandered into the stall across the way and is trying to loosen the knot on a cord that ties down a dusty tarp. Lot finally cuts the cord with his knife and throws back the tarp, then stands gaping at what he's uncovered.

"Damn," the boys says, "this is it!"

But at the same moment, a train whistle blows in the near distance. The boy starts, and looks toward the small window high up on the back wall. He can't see much more than a patch of sky from where he stands, but he knows the tracks are out there, behind the farm. He turns toward Jones, then hesitates, and glances back toward the window. Jones can see he's trying to gauge his chances, calculating whether he can move fast enough burdened down with a cripple to catch that train. They both know he can't, but he has only a few seconds to decide. He swipes at the air before his face as though to clear his mind, then looks through the open doorway toward something outside. He glances back at Jones, but they've both heard it, the sound of a car door closing, and now the voices of men approaching. The boy wheels and makes a dash for the window. It's a couple of feet over his head and narrow, but he makes it in one leap, pulls himself up and swings a leg over the sill. Glancing back over his shoulder, he solemnly waves a hand then drops out of sight, as two shadows cross the doorway.

"...I'd just started to put my head in the barn, here, when I caught sight of him, pulled up over there, at the end of the gravel road. Even in the early light, that slick new Hudson convertible sticks out a mile round here. I'd sure like to know how he come by it!"

"No sign of the other two?"

"Only the mojo woman, rummaging around the graveyard collecting bone-dust. But I figured they'd turn up."

Cops, Jones says to himself. There's only two of them, one in khakis wearing a deputy's badge and the other, taller and heavier, in a pressed white linen suit that's nearly blinding in the sun. They don't see him yet, sitting amid the hay in the shadows at the back. They stand in the doorway talking and letting their eyes adjust to the dim light in the barn.

"Let's get on with it," the taller one says, then, stepping inside, "I got to get back to the courthouse."

"Right. Anyway, Robinson musta spotted me soon as I saw him, and by the time I got back to my car, he'd taken off. I followed him far as Augury, then lost him at the forks. That's where you saw me scratchin' my head this morning when you drove passed -- now you know why. Sumbitch was really moving, too --!"

"What makes you think they'll turn up here?"

"Well, one did, I figure it's more than likely the other one will, too. This used to be home."

"Home...?" The older man draws up and cocks his head, as though listening for something.

But the deputy moves on, walking carefully to one side and casting his eyes about, intent, Jones reckons, on looking for signs of himself and the boy, as he continues, talking over his shoulder, "Well, like I told you, I recognized Lotrelle, the young one that was driving with the cripple, back at Rue

River. And it turns out the other one, the one calling himself Robinson, is actually Newton, his older bro -- Yeah, somebody's been here, awright! You can tell this stuff's been moved around, fresh footprints all along here."

With a curse, the older man reaches up to slap himself on the back of his neck, then pauses to examine what he's pulled away in his fingers.

"Christ Almighty!" the deputy says, then, standing with his back to Jones in the stall across the way. "Sheriff, take a look at this, will ya!"

"It'll be good riddance," the sheriff mutters, "when they finally bulldoze this place!" He steps lightly passed the possible evidence on the floor, his badge barely visible under his jacket as he approaches. "What's the matter?"

"Look!"

"Yeah? What about it?"

"Don'tcha see? It's my daddy's boat!"

"Your daddy's.... Boy, what are you talking about!"

"This is his boat, I'd know it anywhere! This is his boat!" The deputy chucks the tarpaulin off to one side and stands back to reveal what Lot had discovered when the sound of the oncoming train had distracted him. It's a small, graceful boat, carvel-built with a tapered bow and narrow beam, sitting in the stall propped up on stanchions.

"Tsk, don't be foolish, you know it can't be!"

"It can't be, but it is! See here? That's the name I painted on it myself, 'Cat's Paw.'"

The sheriff steps forward for a closer look, and after a moment, he says, "Del, son, you're mistaken. You know, well as I do, your daddy's boat sunk. We dragged that bogue for days looking for it, but it had drifted in the currents and buried itself somewhere in the mud out there. Hell, you know what the rivers round here are like, the fish can't see to breed. Sides, that was a long time ago --"

"Seems like only yesterday to me.... I'm telling you, it's his boat! I couldn't be mistaken about that. I was there when he brought it home. There isn't another boat in the county like it. Sonovagun...! Aside from a little dried mud and natural aging, it looks good as new, too. In fact, you can see here, where the tarp didn't quite cover it," he adds, tracing a line on the gunwale with the steel tip of his claw, "the dust is thick as it is on everything else here, but inside, the boat's clean -- except for that hornets' nest up in the bow, there."

"Uhmn..." The sheriff offers him a stick of gum, and when the deputy waves it away, puts it into his own mouth and chews on it thoughtfully. "Well, awright," he says then, "Fine. Why don't you take it home. Keep it, aint no problem bout that --"

"What I don't understand..." the deputy continues, following his own thoughts, "I mean, like you said, it sank and it couldn't be found. Everybody knows that. So, what's it doing here...?"

The sheriff doesn't answer, he seems preoccupied toying with the gum wrapper, folding it meticulously into smaller and smaller squares.

Jones, meanwhile, becomes aware of a low, angry humming, as of insects seething around him.

"Mm, mm, mm," the sheriff says then, grunting to himself, and filliping the wrapper in the direction of the boat, he turns away. Then he pauses a moment, peers into the shadows, and gives a rasping laugh, "If that don't beat beacon!"

They're standing less than twenty feet away from Jones when the sheriff's glance meets his eyes.

"Find the other one!" the sheriff says over his shoulder, "He can't be far!"

The deputy, roused to action again, turns to check the stalls, while the sheriff heads toward Jones, demanding to know where "the other boy" is. When Jones doesn't answer, the cop begins cuffing him about the head, cursing and threatening him with jail and worse if he doesn't talk, then knocks him over, kneels on his chest and commences slapping him forehand and backhand. The blows fall heavy as bricks, but the hand swings loosely and without heat, as though the man is thinking of something else. Then a shape suddenly lunges out of the shadows, tackling the sheriff and bowling him over.

"Leave'im alone!" Jones hears the voice yell, muffled against the sheriff's chest as the two figures grapple on the ground beside him, "Damn you, leave'im alone, he aint done nothin'!"

It's the boy, Lot, who'd slipped back into the barn unnoticed. Fool, Jones wants to tell him, Fool, you should've run!

The deputy, who'd gone up to search the loft, charges back down the ladder to grab the boy, and after a struggle, manages to pull him away and hold him down trying to handcuff him.

"Bring the sonovabitch over here!" the sheriff says, reaching for his own handcuffs and rolling Jones face down in the dirt.

But as the sheriff yanks Jones's arms up behind him to slap the cuffs on, Jones realizes the cop has inadvertently bent within his reach, and with a glance at the boy to catch his eye, he drives his good arm around the sheriff's neck and pulls him down. There's a loud crack, the sheriff yells, and as the deputy looks up, the boy rolls free. The sheriff rears his heels in the air and flips over, landing on his back, punching and struggling unsuccessfully to free himself from Jones, who is now sprawled on top of him and holding him in a headlock. The deputy, caught off-guard, hesitates, trying to decide whether to go to the aid of the sheriff or to go after the boy who is now racing for the door. Then with a bellow, the sheriff lunges to his feet and staggers blindly forward carrying

Jones, who's blocking his view, swaying on his shoulders like a great black wing. Jones, meanwhile, increases the pressure and feels the shape of the man's skull beginning to change in the crook of his arm. They blunder into a stanchion, and the sheriff, backing a few paces, charges forward, purposely ramming Jones into the solid wooden pillar. The force shakes the framework of the barn and knocks the boat in the stall off its blocks, but Jones doesn't let go. The sheriff backs and drives Jones head-first into the pillar again, and then again, but still Jones holds on. The pounding shatters his vision, unhinges his jaw, turns the air in his lungs to sulfur and ignites the deadened nerve-ends of his body. But he holds on. Then, as if from a long way off, he hears a boy's voice shout through the screaming of hornets --

-- And with a roar, the viaduct gives way and they fall twenty feet into the raging river -- in the instant he'd let go the wheel the road had collapsed and his hand must have grazed her jaw when the car dropped he'd never intended to hurt her! -- he's struggling to get the car door open as they sink and roll over in the current but when he finally gets it open the water rushes in choking him and then he's spinning alone in the torrent with the car gone unable to see anything in the dark flood he reaches out blindly with hands and feet and somehow tumbles onto it again and manages to pull Venus free "Baby!" he cries when he brings her to the surface "Baby just hang on we'll get though this!" holding her close and keeping their heads above water while the rain beats down and the boiling current tosses them about like straws and then huge logs begin pounding passed and they're bruised and buffeted like wheat in a thresher until they finally drift into the branches of an overhanging tree where he clings fast till morning talking to her all through the night telling her not to give up not to be afraid telling her they'd make it and then day breaks and he's still talking to her though the rain has stopped and he sees her cheekbone catch the light and her gray eyes smile up at him with her lips parted above the dimple in her chin and her beautiful brown face turning pale under the diadem of tiny rainbows glittering in her hair and her head lolling back over his arm with her neck broken but not willing to accept that he's

lost her he keeps talking to her telling her all the things she's wanted to hear him say as if the words in her ear were the breath of life as if he could steal her back but when he looks up at the wreckage around him there are coffins floating passed dozens of wooden coffins that he'd thought during the night were logs but it's the dead only the dead nameless and mute plowing down the river like demon mules --!

12.
Wormwood

"...You got some nerve, butting into my business and making demands!"
he said. "What the hell's all this got to do with me!" he said. "My reputa-
tion's unquestioned in this community! I sponsor the free-lunch program in
the school!" he said. "My reputation's unquestioned! Unquestioned....!"

He woke to the telephone ringing downstairs. He lay in bed a moment, listening to his wife, Pattycake, snoring lightly beside him, then rose quietly and started down the hall in the dark to answer it. But he was still half-consciously trying to resolve the argument in the dream as he descended into the pale starlight filtering through the window curtain in the foyer.

Later, having washed and dressed, he stood outside the screen door cussing to himself and chewing on a piece of cold chicken. The heat was already oppressive and the air heavy and stale. As the rim of the sun showed over the trees, he rested his cup of instant, still half-full, on the gallery rail and started down the steps toward the mortuary, a square, whitewashed building without windows that stood facing the road behind the house. It was only a short walk down the path through the garden, but by the time he had reached the entrance, his shirt was sticking to his underarms and his tongue was dry as cotton in his mouth. He unlocked the door and pushed it open, feeling a teasing resistance, as though there were someone pushing back from the other side. His footsteps, echoing on the stone floor in the entryway, were greeted with a gentle susurration and a rush of cold air, like a welcoming balm against the heat. It was all merely the effects of the difference in temperature between the air outside and the cool, cavernous interior, but he found it invigorating, and as the heavy door swung closed behind him, the morning glories in the pot out front danced like signal fires.

Once inside, he synchronized his watch with the clock on the wall, then went over to the metal cabinet, where he took out a freshly starched white lab smock and put it on over his street clothes. He washed his hands, got a new pair of rubber gloves and his goggles and put them on, then set out fresh sponges and clean pans on the stainless steel counter. He filled one pan with a mixture of isopropanol, hydrogen peroxide and iodine, one with germicidal soap, and another with water, using feed and drainage tubes leading from and to the sink to keep the water at just above room temperature and running fresh. When he had everything prepared, he went into the refrigerator, opposite, for the body. He rolled the steel table into position, locked the wheels, and then, starting at the scalp, methodically began to wash it down.

Gradually, the familiar effluvium of chemical agents and the sense of solidity in the surrounding structure calmed him. He'd had the building completely rebuilt and air-conditioned to his own specifications shortly after they'd moved into the house. The concrete floor had been leveled and the plaster walls sealed airtight and immaculately tiled. He observed his hands now, as he worked, like a connoisseur observing the hands of an artist. Their strength and steadiness had always been his pride. He wouldn't let haste interfere with his artistry. And yet, at the back of his mind, he couldn't help wondering what Thackery wanted to see him about.

All these whitefolks be so high-on-the-hog, he said to himself, and can't wipe they own asses! No matter that between the two of'em, Thackery and Clooder, one practically owning the county and the other one running it for him, it was still him, Crouch, that they had to call out of bed in the dead of night to "straighten out" their mess! Shit, if he didn't have so much invested in this town, himself, it'd be almost worth it to just pull out and let Clooder-them fall to the dogs. Arrogant sonsabitches deserved it, to think they could get away with that shit anyway. Not only did Clooder and Thackery own the land Thackery's television company wanted to build on, but as all the permits had to go through the sheriff's office, naturally Clooder's earth-moving company had won the bid on the contract. Any fool looking at the records would see through that "Dividend Associates" bullshit in a trice! Even Clooder'd realized that eventually. When he'd heard the state auditors were coming up from Jackson, he'd had one of his redneck buddies "mislay" the Property Deeds and Taxes ledger out of the circuit clerk's office and bring it to him, Crouch, to doctor up, telling him, "Hurry up! Quick! Hide the land, sell it off, whatever -- but don't lose it!" Like the sheriff thought he was some kinda magician. And yet, damned if he hadn't come up with the solution after all -- or, rather, *thought* he had! As a nocount transient Negro, Robinson was a perfect middleman, a rambling gambler with plenty of loose cash...but the motherfucker had to go and act slick --!

-- The disinfectant shot from his hands. He made a grab for it, only to knock it out of reach, cursing as the enameled pan hit the floor and careened under the chemical cabinet against the wall. Goddamn that Robinson to Hell, anyway!

he muttered, trying to push the man to the back of his mind. But it seemed that in everything he had to deal with now, Robinson kept popping up. It put his teeth on edge! Rising, he struck his funny bone against the edge of the steel table. Trying to keep his rubber gloves unsoiled, he used his forearms to roll the cabinet aside on its castors, and stooped over, fumbling at the rim of the overturned pan. The isopropanol would evaporate and the hydrogen peroxide was water soluble, but the iodine would stain the white tiles, unless washed up immediately. He carried the pan over to the sink and got the mop. Despite the air conditioning, his goggles began to fog up, and he pushed them onto his forehead. He was careful to wash away the disinfectant from the baseboard to avoid corrosion and seepage.

He'd best get his ass moving, he said to himself, glancing at the clock, as he returned to the table and set about washing down the limbs and torso, and rinsing them with lukewarm water and the germicidal soap.

...But he cursed, in spite of himself, as he thought, it had all seemed so easy! He'd simply "lost" the property to Robinson in a hand of poker. But instead of accepting his generous offer to buy it back, the bastard had put him off, raising the price absurdly -- meanwhile, going behind his back to pose as an executive of Dividend Associates and selling the property to this goddamned Memphis canning company to develop a catfish farm! And as if that hadn't been balls enough, the nigger had turned around and stolen the clerk's property ledger from out of his private office at the Channel Cat, then put two and two together, and blackmailed him to get the ledger back!

But who the hell was Robinson, anyway? Shit, he'd really been sloppy about that, he admitted now, by letting himself be pressured into acting hastily, and being a little too cocksure of himself. He didn't even know where that long-tall ugly nigger had come from! Robinson had simply appeared in the crowded club one night with his gaudy mismatched clothes standing out like a caution sign -- and that's not even funny, he admonished himself, because he'd clearly mistaken the man for a fool. But Robinson had somehow talked Bidder into letting him run the trifling gambling concession there and suddenly, from that moment on, the Channel Cat had become the hottest juke joint in the Delta. Crouch shook his head, finding it incredible that he'd been so blind! He'd seen the money rolling in all summer long and hadn't given Robinson another thought...!

He found yellowish clusters of fly eggs in the corners of the corpse's eyes. Using kerosene swabs, he removed them, then he began the process of cleaning the remaining orifices thoroughly and packing them with cotton saturated with phenol solution. He'd been able to dispense with the pediculicide as there'd been no signs of scabies or infestation by body lice. Which was surprising, he thought, since the body had been found in the river. Or rather, on top of the river, he corrected himself, where it must have fallen from the levee, and where it might not have been found at all had it not been for the fish bearing it up. Ever since they'd switched on that new atomic generator at the electric plant up in Augury, the fish had been dying up there in droves. Their rotting carcasses could be seen floating thick as a blanket up and down the river for hundreds of yards, and the stench extended for miles. "Progress!" he said to himself, quoting Sampson, with a dry laugh, progress got a price just like everything else. He hesitated a moment, before deciding to go ahead with brushing the nails and shampooing the hair, and to skip shaving the body.

...It rankled him when he recalled how that sonuvabitch, Robinson, had pulled that cheap trick, making him drive all the way out to the swamp in the rain that evening for nothing! His blood boiled, just to think of it now! He'd paid Robinson the money and had barely got his hands on the ledger, when they'd spotted the police car pulling up under the tree at the crossroads. Alarmed at the thought of himself, a pillar of the Negro community, being caught in that compromising situation, huddling over a stolen county ledger out in the swamp at night with that tawdry gambler, he'd let Robinson talk him into switching cars -- which, of course, had served Robinson's purpose, and certainly not his own, since it turned out the deputy had been chasing Robinson, all along. He'd had to undergo the embarrassment of being chased over the highways and accosted by that chief deputy as though he were a common criminal – then had the additional aggravation of that roadside confrontation with Sampson – so that it wasn't until later, when he'd pulled into his own garage at home, that he'd had a chance to examine the ledger. Talk about gall! He'd been dumfounded, outraged! He'd felt like a god-damned clown, that night, sitting in Robinson's urine-yellow Hudson sports car and staring at a bundle of old cotton quotes! He couldn't believe it! The motherfucker had actually cut the leaves out of the ledger's covers and substituted a stack of old newspapers! Jesus, if Clooder ever found out...!

Having purged the mouth of moisture, he aligned the heavy jaws, pressed the lips back, and applied the injector needle, shooting a barb into the gums to clamp the mandible and maxilla.

Next morning, he recalled, he'd driven the Hudson back out to the Channel Cat and found his own Cadillac in the club's parking lot, but Robinson, himself, was gone. He'd raged and threatened Bidder with financial ruin, with imprisonment for running a drinking and gambling joint, with everything he could think of, but Bidder swore he didn't know where Robinson was. And over the following days he'd put pressure on all his old snitches, but nobody'd admitted to knowing where Robinson might've gone. Yet when he'd gone

back to the Channel Cat, the yellow Hudson had mysteriously disappeared, too!

Then, four-thirty this morning, he'd got that panicked
call from the sheriff. The man sounded strange on the phone,
talking low and slurring his words, like he'd been drinking.
But he'd been expecting as much, having seen the *Times* the
previous afternoon. "The first installment," it had said, of "an
exclusive, documented story of scandal at the highest county
level," which it promised to serialize over the following week.
Robinson had obviously sold the real county records to the
newspaper! And as he, Crouch, had sat at his desk at the bank
reading the story, the call had come from the lawyer representing the canning company demanding to see the deeds
on the Dividend property because they had "a suspicion of
fraud!" But where's he supposed to get the money to give them
back their down payment? he asked himself, when Robinson
done run off with everything! Nigger's probably in Chicago
by now. Meanwhile, Southern Aid's started making inquiries now, too, about the fires on the bank's other properties,
questioning *his* conflict of interest as the insurance company's
agent in the Delta. But to hell with them, anyway! he said to
himself. Bunch of dumb uppity Richmond niggers were in
over their heads in a business he knew more about than they
ever would! They may be working for the oldest black-owned
insurance company in the country, but he'd have'em eating
out of his hand before he got done...!

He checked the clock. He'd just make it, he thought. He'd
already planned to drive out to the Channel Cat when he'd
finished up here, to squeeze Bidder for advances on the rent,
usage and gambling fees -- and to lean on him some more
to see if he was holding back anything about where to find
Robinson. But now they tell him he has to go into the bank
vault and pour over land titles and faked record entries going
back seven years to recreate the missing Property volume, so

Clooder could sneak it into the circuit clerk's office for the state auditors who were coming tomorrow. It was only two weeks ago that he'd had to do the same thing for the County Business Records, when Calley Donaghue, the clerk, had told Clooder somebody -- it suddenly dawned on Crouch that it must've been Robinson, again! -- had cut sixty pages out of *that* book! The sonuvabitch...!

He paused to remove his goggles, wipe them clear with a sterile cloth, and replace them over his eyes. He had to make the body presentable. A lot of people were going to file past to scrutinize it. That guy, Beavis, from the NAACP, and the reporters had already come beating down the door. The FBI had called, too, but typically for them, hadn't bothered to show up.

...The long day ahead was beginning to wear on him already, just thinking about it. Because Clooder'd told him Thackery wanted to see him as soon as possible, after he'd finished recreating the property records. Except he anticipated fixing the books would take him the whole evening and a good part of the night. Which meant that, when he'd finally gotten done, he'd then have to drive back in the wee hours to meet Thackery out at the gin! He'd tried to explain the unreasonableness of the demand, given the time constraints, but Clooder'd insisted the meeting couldn't be put off. Shit, he said to himself, he wasn't all that fond of the fucking gin in the first place. Why the meetings always had to be out there he didn't know, but Thackery would never consider meeting him anywhere else. And as he went back to work on the corpse, he recalled his last regular business trip out there, Saturday passed, to collect the insurance premiums. He did that on Saturday afternoons before quitting time, making sure he got to the Negro laborers before they threw away their pay on corn liquor and craps. The temperature had been over a hundred for the tenth day running, but in the open shed behind the ginning machine it was always fifteen or twenty degrees hotter than outside. The high corrugated iron roof they had there to protect the workers from the sun only seemed to trap the air and press the heat down on you like an oven. He'd just started on his rounds when the last batch of ginned cotton was being baled. As the compression chamber opened, two men had climbed down inside to run a set of wire bands around the bale. He hadn't been watching them, he'd been tending to his own business, but he'd seen it countless times. They'd slip a width of burlap around the bale to cover the sample-hole and then pull the ends of the bands together to buckle them. Crouched on either side of the bale, and dwarfed by it, one man would push the bands over the top and the other one pull them down and return them from underneath. That's the way they'd always done it. But that afternoon, Thackery'd had a big open-house party there, celebrating his twentieth anniversary in business and the one millionth bale of cotton he'd produced at the gin, and that old reprobate, Jess Arnett, had come down to speak, because he was running for governor, and in all the confusion of music and guests and plates of hop-n-john and hot-dogs being passed around, something must've gone wrong. First, they'd heard the rush of steam over the hubbub, as the ram had started out of its housing again, then the screams, and when they'd looked, the jaws of the compressor were closing and the two Negroes were struggling to get out of the chamber, with the ram advancing on them. But the men were trapped, pinned between the five-hundred pound bale and the closing jaws of the compressor. The operator had apparently gone off and left the switchbox unattended. He and everybody ran to help, jumping up onto the press and trying to pull the men out. They got one out, but the other one was caught, stooped over with his hands bound by the metal band under the bale. Then somebody -- he seems to remember it was Brennan, because Brennan had used to work there and knew how to run the machines -- Brennan hit the switch, and the steam roared again and they all froze, watching the ram waver before it finally drew back. He could still remember how it had felt to have his own hands locked in the trapped man's armpits, with the poor fool crouched there jerking like a chicken with its head cut off and the vibrations of the ram shuddering through the compression chamber. It had been on his mind later that same night, when he'd gone out there again to meet Thackery....

As he started to suture the nostrils of the corpse, he saw that the packing had slipped, and he repacked them with fresh cotton.

But now, something else began to gnaw at him. No one else had been there, he thought to himself, just himself and Thackery. How could anybody else have found out what they'd talked about? It'd been eleven o'clock that night when he'd gone back, and pouring rain. The place had been deserted when he'd pulled around to the back yard. The only other car there had been Thackery's. And despite the rain and the late hour, it had still been hot as hell in the work area when he'd stepped under the corrugated iron roof behind the gin. And yet, as he'd stood for a moment, purposely facing in the wrong direction -- playing Thackery's game and letting his own eyes adjust to the dark -- he'd begun to feel uneasy. And although he'd been expecting it, in fact, waiting for it, when he'd finally heard the sound of the match striking, he'd almost jumped out of his skin. It had only been Thackery, of course, and when he'd turned and seen the old man standing there, leaning against the compressor and lighting a cigarette in the rain like some bayou Bogart, he'd laughed out loud in spite of himself. Thackery's childish charade had always privately amused him. The man had once hobnobbed with presidents, and he still bought and sold local politicians and owned the only cotton gin and the biggest lumber mill in the county, not to mention the two biggest plantations in the state and most everything else of consequence in Dividend. And yet, to Crouch's mind, the short, stoop-shouldered old man standing there in wet, rumpled clothes looked more like a janitor than a gin owner. But Thackery hadn't laughed, he'd just stood there staring back at him with the burning match reflected in his glasses, looking like he held three flames in his hand. And as they'd stood talking, with him telling Thackery that he thought Ida Temple had been using the whorehouse to harbor outside agitators, he'd found his eyes involuntarily straying back to the compressor, with the sound echoing in his ears of those two men screaming, earlier that afternoon....

A dull crash reverberated through the walls of the mortuary. His arms jerked reflexively and he cursed, feeling the nasal bridge crack under his hands. The sound was the familiar sonic boom from the Air Force jets flying overhead, but he'd never gotten used to it. Lifting his hands away from the face, he saw that the nose, which had previously been straight, was now bent unnaturally out of line with the lips. Shit, he thought, the simplest things were getting complicated! Adjustment of the features here should've been perfunctory. He looked at his hands, and the way they were trembling now frightened him almost more than anything else.

"Calm, Thomas, calm yourself!" He said aloud. "Now, you know you can deal with all this shit. You're smarter than all of'em, including the big bad sheriff! Aint you the most successful funeral director in the county? Aint you the only Negro bank director in the Delta? And you still holding a couple aces in this game." If those crackers wanted to get cute, he continued to himself, he had plenty on them, on Thackery and Big Bee Clooder, too. With all those fake corporations buying and selling back and forth to each other, the faked land titles and surveys, the television station, the realty and the bank -- shit, Thackery's hand could be traced everywhere! The *Times* didn't have half the story, either. The state auditors and the IRS would just love to get their hands on that second set of ledgers he, himself, had been keeping from the beginning -- just in case! And as for Clooder, the man'd had his hand in the county cash box from the start. He oughta know, because Clooder, knowing him from back home, in Alabama, had told him early on that he figured he could "trust" him -- by which he knew, of course, Clooder had only meant that he was just another nigger he thought he could manipulate! But these papers that he'd got hold of, now, could ruin Clooder for life, destroy the man's marriage to Thackery's daughter and get his ass thrown clean out the state. The po' buckra'd thought he was being slick when he'd left Alabama and run off to the Navy back in 'Forty-One, thinking he could leave all that shit behind him. But he aint reckoned on Thomas Crouch! In his capacities as funeral director and insurance representative, he'd arranged to have the Dardan County Clerk forward him copies of the marriage certificate, from when Clooder'd been shotgunned into hooking up with that fifteen-year-old girl he'd knocked up, and the baby's birth certificate, too, naming Clooder as the father. He'd requested them just as a precaution, when he'd found out Robinson had taken the ledger. And if Clooder tried to threaten him over the missing money or the stolen book, he'd just ask the motherfucker what he thought Thackery would say, when the old man found out his daughter had married a bigamist!

-- Which reminded him, he'd forgotten, in his preoccupation with everything else, to put the certificates in the vault. He'd left them in the glove compartment of his car. Well, he'd take care of that, too, this evening. Meanwhile, Clooder would understand that what he had in that envelope was just a small indication of what he *could* bring to light, if he should have a mind...!

All right, he said to himself, turning his attention back to the corpse, here's what it is: there'd be no additional discoloration, for blood no longer flowed in those veins. The skin was remarkably clear, in fact. The only repairs that had been required, until now, were at the areas of impact of what must've been a high-velocity projectile. Most probably a .30-caliber bullet from a deer rifle, he thought, a popular weapon in the Delta. It had entered the back of the skull, making a puncture the size of a dime through the occipital bone, and exited through the forehead, leaving a larger hole, like an elongated starburst, in the glabella. Both wounds were fairly clean, and could be reconstructed externally, with padding, wax, worm sutures and paint. A cotton compress of bleaching and preserving chemical would reduce the swelling and discoloration around the eyes. The fracture he'd just introduced in the nasal bone would be a simple matter to fix. He reached for the dividers.

...Back when Clooder was still only a chief deputy there in LeVane County, the old sheriff had found out about his stealing and had threatened to expose Clooder and put him in jail if he didn't put the money back. But then, one day the old sheriff fell out of his own boat and drowned. Nobody could prove how it had happened. Clooder had been the only one there with him at the time. Clooder'd said later that he and Sheriff Hope had gone out fishing early that morning, and at one point, when he, himself, sitting in the stern, had struck a bass and had turned to reel it in, he'd heard a bang and the boat lurched. Clooder said that when he'd turned to see what was the matter, the sheriff had disappeared overboard and the boat was sinking, taking in water through a big hole in the bow, where a floorboard had sprung loose. Clooder said he'd called out and jumped in after the sheriff to look for him, but by the time he'd found him in that murky water and pulled him to dry land, all he could do, he couldn't bring the old man around. And when he'd looked up again, the boat was gone, too, sunk out of sight....

Crouch drew a deep breath. The eyecaps were implanted and the temporary sutures completed. Working quickly, he began to apply a heavy layer of cream to the face, to prevent the skin drying out during embalming.

....Clooder had said somebody must've purposely tampered with the boat, because it was new. And he said it was pretty clear who'd done the tampering, because at the time, Sheriff Hope had been investigating Fontana Dundee for going around trying to get the other Negroes to vote, and Fontana had been doing some work on the boat just before the incident. He, himself, had started getting a little concerned then, too, because the whole affair had brought up a lot of bad feeling between the races, when things had been pretty quiet for awhile, and his own businesses began to suffer. Of course, he never believed for a minute that Fontana'd really messed with the boat, but on the other hand, he felt Fontana'd brought trouble down on all of them with his voter registration bullshit. But fate, he mused, had its own way of working things out. Less than a week after the old sheriff had drowned, Fontana'd been killed driving into a tree. One more "coincidence" that had worked out to Clooder's advantage....

He straightened up from the table, stretched his back and went over to the glass instrument case. But as he reached for the cannula and the arterial and drainage tubes, he realized this was the third time within two weeks that a tragic and violent event had given him cause to use these instruments. Before this, there was Rhoder and the Hill boy. And the chilling thought came to him that things seemed to be getting out of hand, that wreaking vengeance on grown men was bad enough, but...! He felt again an upsurge of the anger he'd experienced at the news, the previous day, that Minton and Borden had been acquitted. Acquitted! And with that bastard, Brennan, who they worked for, lying up there on the witness stand, claiming they were with him in Highville at the time -- despite the fact that the two peckerwoods had admitted earlier, before the television cameras of the national press, to abducting the boy! It was a shame and an outrage! The boy's mother had insisted the body be left in the condition in which it was found, so she could show the world what had been done to her child. He, Crouch, had therefore simply disinfected and embalmed the body and shipped it back north, bruised and battered as it was, though it had pained him to do it. Lord Almighty, he said to himself, have things got so bad that the admitted murderers of little children can walk amongst us unpunished...?

He caught himself on the verge of forcing the cannula clear through to the other side of the carotid artery. "Get ahold of yourself!" he muttered. He anchored the cannula, then stepped away from the table to clear his goggles again. He removed the rubber gloves and rinsed his face with cold water. Had he broken the artery, he would have lost precious time repairing it. Worse still, he might've had to use the slower-flowing radial arteries alone. He put the rubber gloves back on and went to make sure the stopcock was securely fastened on the hub of the cannula, that the drain tube in the jugular vein was inserted toward the heart, and then, considering his frame of mind, double-checked the settings on the pressure gauges of the embalming machine, before rolling it up to the table to connect the delivery and drainage tubes. The electric pump was old and cranky, and even when new, could easily raise the air pressure enough to explode the glass jar holding the arterial fluid. It was highly volatile and the fumes were poisonous, in addition to the fact that the liquid was very flammable and toxic to the skin. He'd been planning to invest in one of the newer centrifugal pumps this fall. Now, that would have to wait --

He checked the clock. He was running late, he'd better hump it.

"Concentrate," he murmured to himself. "It'll all work out. You know what you have to do. Just concentrate!"

He connected the tubes, rechecked the gauges and seals, and started the pump. He watched the pressure gauges for a moment, as the pump groaned to life and the embalming fluid entered the delivery tubes. Then he went over to the cosmetic shelf and ran his eyes along the jars, looking for the right wax. He found the color he wanted, opened the jar and tested the rich alluvial-brown wound filler with his fingertips. It was firmer than surface restorer or lip wax, both of which were too soft for use in the hot Southern climate. He scooped out a large handful, and began to knead it, gradually adding starch and petroleum jelly. The starch lent opacity, controlled texture and reduced tackiness so that it was more pliable and less likely to stick to the manipulator's fingers, while the petroleum jelly made it tacky enough to adhere to the cold flesh of the deceased. Kneading the mixture in his hands calmed him, now, bringing to mind the strength and presence of his father, a man with a naturally artistic bent. He remembered an afternoon back home when he was a child, sitting beside his father in the front seat of the hearse, his legs still too short to reach the floor. They were driving back from the cemetery after a funeral, and his father had pulled over beside a dam and pointed through the window, for him to look at the trees across the road. The play of sunlight off the water had looked like the spokes of a great wheel gliding along the underside of the leaves, and it was as if he had been given a peek at the engines of the Lord.

Adding a pinch of cold cream to soften the mixture in his hands, he turned back to the table and began to patch the hole in the forehead of the late Harold Sampson.

When he'd finished, he quickly washed up, sterilized the instruments and put them away. He went out through the covered way to the garage, checking to make sure he'd locked the door behind him, before starting the car and raising the convertible top. Then he unlocked the glove compartment and slid his hand back and forth through the thick stack of papers pertaining to bank, insurance and mortuary business, absently aware, as he searched vainly for his pliers, that the letter from the county clerk in Alabama, the one about Clooder's previous marriage and paternity, didn't seem to be on top where he thought he'd left it. "Shit," he said, as the car top touched down on the frame of the windshield. His boys were always borrowing his tools and not remembering to return them! The Caddy was hardly a year old, but the knobs used to fasten down the top were already stiff with rust. Fucking rust got into everything here! he said to himself impatiently, and reaching up to tighten the knobs with his fingers, split a nail. Sucking his teeth in annoyance, he fished an emery board out of the ashtray, and while waiting for the air conditioning to take effect, he sniffed the air. The odor of chemicals permeated his clothes, his breath, every aspect of his being. He could never be rid of it. It had always been the greatest cause of discord between himself and Pattycake. Commercial preparations of embalming fluid all contained formaldehyde, methyl alcohol and reodorants. Other constituents varied, but made little difference. It was the reodorants, the perfuming and masking agents, that mattered. Over the years, he'd experimented with different additives to dubious effect. Bergamot and lemongrass had a tendency to sour. Rose, gardenia and lilac were too evocative of the mortuary, and strawberry and peach had made him smell like a fruit pie. Today, he'd tried something the manufacturer called "Old Vineyard," essentially absinthium, extracted from wormwood. But he was beginning to have doubts already. He raised the garage doors and then, as he reached for the gear shift, he noticed a business card lying on the passenger seat beside him. It wasn't one of his, and he picked it up and read it:

Virgil Robinson Pope, III
Real Estate and Investigations
Southern Aid Insurance Company, Inc.
Richmond, Virginia

"You sonuvabitch!" he said, aloud. "You sly, thievish sonuvabitch! Well fuck you, then!" He flung the card angrily to the floor, and the car tires screamed as he roared out of the driveway. "You think you slick but, nigguh, you got another think coming! I got powerful friends in this county, you and your fucking little Richmond nigguhs can't do shit to me out here! Fucking sonuvabitch...!"

He gritted his teeth in an effort to restrain himself, for he knew he had more immediate things to attend to, and he resolved to put Robinson and Southern Aid out of his mind for the time being. As he swung around the corner at the end of the block, he saw the hoodoo woman, Basheeba, waddling along barefoot and grubby in the ditch at the side of the road. Like some ancestral Ethiopian nightmare, he thought to himself, almost grateful for the distraction and rolling his eyes at the climax basket overflowing with roots and yarrow stalks that she carried balanced on her head. It was true, he admitted now, that he'd been trying to get into Lorna's drawers, she'd made a good-looking widow, afterall. But the woman was always trying to be so prim and proper, and she'd been resisting him. Not to mention, he added to himself, this evil witch, Basheeba, who through some incomprehensible accident of nature had managed to be the mother of the lovely Lorna, and who had always been hanging around as though haunting the house whenever he'd gone to visit. The old woman turned to stare at him soberly now as he drove by, but when he glanced back at her in the rearview mirror, her mouth had split open like a gash.

"What the hell you got to grin about, Mis'ry?" he muttered to her reflection, and with a shiver, turned down the air conditioning. But he realized that, unconsciously, he'd still had Thackery on his mind. He forced himself to think of more pleasant things. Such as taking Pattycake over to Highville the following Sunday to see the Negro All-Star game. The glamour of the old Negro leagues was gone, now that the stars like Campanella, Willie Mays and Hank Aaron had moved on, but still, he did love that special, almost proprietary excitement of being out there in the stands and watching those colored boys striving to best one another! Now, in the last light of day, he was admiring the late summer wildflowers that were blooming in glorious profusion all along the roadside. He switched on the radio and began to nod his head to the rhythm of Ruth Brown singing *5-10-15 Hours*....

13.
The Raven's Fee

"...For a minute there, I thought you'd shuddenly got religion." They were in the sheriff's inner office, and Clooder, speaking with an unnatural lisp, had responded over his shoulder.

DelRay, his question unanswered and his mind racing, stood in the open doorway biting his lip, trying to contain the turmoil within him, as he waited for the sheriff to continue. He could hear the muffled strains of the brass band coming from the courthouse square outside, behind the jailhouse, where an election rally was in progress. They were playing *Harvest Moon*. The incumbent governor had come down for the occasion and Clooder was scheduled to address the crowd. Through the window, he could see to the end of the street, where a blue jay perched, flicking its tail on the bronze bayonet of the Confederate monument. It was still early. The heat had finally lifted. It was trying to be a perfect Indian summer day.

"You finished fingerprinting the prishoner?" Clooder said.

DelRay studied him a moment, as the sheriff remained with his back turned, cooling his neck in the breeze from the air conditioner. Having just come out of hospital, after suffering a concussion, a fractured collarbone and a broken jaw in that struggle in the barn with the Negro, Jones, Clooder, standing there now against the light from the window, enveloped in a plaster cast that reached from his midriff to his ears and that held his left elbow bent rigidly out to the side, looked even larger than life.

"Well?" the sheriff said, turning to face him.

"We won't be getting any prints off him, he's been stirring up a mash barrel. It doesn't matter, we know the gun's his, he hasn't been seen anywhere without it hanging off his arm in twenty years."

"You busht up the shtill?"

"He wouldn't tell me where it was. I'll look for it later. Sheriff --"

"Shonovabitch!" Clooder said, accidentally banging his elevated elbow against the filing cabinet as he started to sidle crabwise down the narrow space leading to his desk. "I wash telling Thackery jusht yeshterday, it might be gettin' time for me to retire. I almosht cut my own throat shaving thish morning, trying to work the razor around inshide-a thish damn plashter coffin. I feel like a ham hung up in a chimney. I told'm I wash thinkin' of letting you take over. You know, he sheemsh to cotton to you, Thackery doesh. By the way, did you ever get around to ashkin' that pretty little Farrah Leesh to the ball?" But when he looked up and caught the chief deputy's expression, he waved the question away, "Oop, shorry! You're right, nonna my bishnessh. Well, anyway, far ash I'm concherned, thish job jusht might get to be more trouble than it'sh worth now, the way theesh monkeysh are carryin' on down in Washington. Might be time to get shome young blood in here. How'd you like to have the run of the county, be your own bossh for a change?"

It was the second time that morning, DelRay thought to himself, that somebody'd tried to promote him. "Look, Bee," he said, "let's not get --"

"Yar, yar, I know. But you keep it in mind all the shame. Meantime," he added, lifting a haunch onto the desktop, after finding himself too encumbered by the cast to squeeze into his chair, "fill me in on thish bishnessh out at the gin." As he spoke, he absently swatted at a bluebottle fly that had grazed his face.

DelRay followed the fly with his eyes as it dodged away to light on a crack in the wall above the evidence locker, and his eye lingered for a moment on the two guns visible there, behind the black metal grate, a high-powered 30-06 Browning deer rifle with a telescopic sight, and an antiquated L.D. Smith 12-gauge shotgun. "Apparently," he began, "nobody saw it happen...." But he broke off, as the front door opened and Calley Donaghue stuck his head in.

"Special delivery for you, Dell." As DelRay went to take the envelope from him, Donaghue turned to the sheriff, "Oh, and the folks're waitin' for ya out there, Bee. Governor's ready to make his speech."

"Awright, Calley, I'll be along directly," Clooder said, as the circuit clerk withdrew.

DelRay slit open the envelope and glanced briefly at its contents. When he raised his eyes again, the sheriff was looking at him expectantly. "Ah, yeah...Lorette, the foreman, found the body when he opened up this morning," he said, resuming his previous report. "Thackery's under the impression Crouch must've gone there to meet a client coming off the second shift last night, and somehow crossed paths with Old Paully, who's been wandering around in a rage the past few days over the demolition of his house out on Mount Eden."

Clooder watched him toss the envelope, without comment, on his own desk. "Unfortunate," he said.

"Yeah...except there're some problems with it."

"That right?"

"For one thing, even if nobody'd heard the shot, the night men claim the last bale was removed and stacked for shipping, as usual, before they went home. Why was it still in the compression chamber this morning? And how could Crouch have ended up under it? The body was...well, it wasn't easy to identify, aside from the papers in his wallet and his usual pinstriped suit. More to the point, there's the question of how the two of them came together. If Crouch or Old Paully had been in the workshed while the crew was still on duty, somebody would've noticed them. But nobody did, I went round and checked." He nodded toward the shotgun in the evidence locker, "And that old scattergun couldn't fire accurately over that distance from outside the fence -- although that's where I found it -- the old man would've had to've been inside the compound. But if the crew had already gone, how did the two of them get in? The foreman said the gates were locked when he arrived this morning."

"What doesh the old geezher shay?"

"Paully? You know him, he wanders all over the yard. I'm not even sure he understands why I locked him up."

"Well, where wash he when you arreshted him?"

"Stomping around the ruins of his house, out at the cemetery."

"Doesh he admit to the killing?"

DelRay made a wry face, "...That's hard to say."

"Humph." Clooder turned to look thoughtfully in the direction of the cell block, behind the office, where the prisoner was being held.

"Say, Sheriff?" It was Donaghue again, sticking his head in the front door, breathless now, apparently having jogged back through the alley from the courthouse square. "They're gettin' impatient. The governor says --"

"Awright, Calley," Clooder said, rising and starting forward to meet him. "Del, you follow up on that."

"Hold up, Sheriff," DelRay said. "Calley, would you mind...?"

The clerk, taken aback, looked from one to the other, then stepped out and closed the door. Clooder turned and stood with an eyebrow raised, his hand on the doorknob.

"Sheriff, back on that first day I started, why did you tell me to lay off Crouch?"

Clooder glanced casually over the flyspecked fish and game notices pinned to the bulletin board on the wall beside him, as he said, "Boy'd come to me with shome private trouble, I wash tryin' to help him out. Don't know that it mattersh, now. You put a wire out on that other one give you the shlip out at the barn?"

"I'm taking care of that."

"Fine. Then let'sh not keep the shitizensh waiting."

Moments later, DelRay was in the big blue and white Merc heading out to the Brennan place. The one thing he did not have to worry about right now, he thought to himself, was finding Lotrelle Dundee. The boy had done more than his share, and proven to be more helpful than he, DelRay, could ever have hoped. The day of the incident at the barn, the boy had, as Clooder'd just reminded him, given him the slip while the sheriff had been grappling with Jones. But after establishing that Jones had been killed, and then driving the sheriff to the hospital, he'd returned to the barn that same evening to examine the boat he'd found there, checking every seam and nail hole, every scratch and stain, not to prove its identity, for he had no question that it had been his father's boat, but to confirm its condition. And just as a precaution, he'd arranged to have two witnesses present there in the barn with him, while he went over it. The first was his old friend Judge McCoomb, whom he'd picked up at the barbershop on the way back out to the old Fontana place. He trusted McCoomb, as his father had, and he felt the fact that the judge had retired from the bench should remove the old man from the pressures of politics, while making him the sort of witness a LeVane County jury would believe. Then, to cover all the bases, he'd also arranged for the reporter, Phil Kurf, to meet them at the barn. Kurf was a wild card. He'd been around a long time, and he, DelRay, personally disliked him. Kurf had always curried favor with those in power, including his father, Sheriff Hope, and now Clooder. But Kurf couldn't resist a scandal, either, and as a result, nobody trusted him. Kurf had made more enemies than friends over the years, and had ended up a cynical drudge in mid-career still waiting for his big breaking story. He, DelRay, had anticipated that when Kurf saw the boat, the reporter's first impulse would've been to go to Clooder for a reaction. On the other hand, the sheriff had stepped on Kurf's toes often enough to hurt his feelings, and the paper he worked for, *The Dividend Times*, had been publishing daily updates for the passed week on an exposé pointing to, and all but naming, the sheriff, himself, as the culprit responsible for an apparent misappropriation of county funds.

"Electioneering bullshit," Clooder had remarked, disdainfully, when he'd asked him about it. "Mud runs cheap in the Delta."

In the event, he'd figured it was pretty good odds that he could strike a bargain with Kurf out at the barn, offering an exclusive on the biggest story to hit LeVane since the end of the war, in exchange for Kurf keeping his counsel.

Having the witnesses present had turned out to be a good idea. Because when he'd returned the following morning to cordon off the barn, he'd arrived just in time to see it being demolished. The earth-moving gang that had been clearing the whole area around the Mount Eden Cemetery for the new TV station was at that moment in the process of bulldozing every structure remaining on the old Fontana place. He'd halted the operation around the barn and sifted through the wreckage looking for the boat, but hadn't been able to recover any trace of it. And then Brennan, who was bossing the wrecking crew, had sauntered over.

"Well, DelRay," he'd said, "what's the matter, anything important in there?"

"Tell your men," he'd told him, "not to touch that barn again till I say so. If I come back and find one splinter moved, you're going to jail for trespassing on the scene of a crime, destroying material evidence and obstructing justice. You understand me?"

"Scene of a crime! Well, in that case, sure, Dell, sure thing, no problem. Leave it to me, I'll take care of everything, I always do."

But walking back to the Merc, he'd gone to war with himself for having lost the boat again. Then, a tall Negro, who'd been directing the work of a black gang that was digging up the graves across the way and stacking the old coffins for transport to another cemetery, stepped away and approached him as he reached the cruiser.

"Say, boss? Mind if I say a word?"

He knew the fellow, generally an all right sort, a seasonal worker with an unlucky habit of petty theft who spent a lot of his off-seasons in jail. But at that moment, he'd been in no mood for idle chatter, and had started to brush him off, "Another time, Stitches."

"Sorry, boss, but I thought you might wanna know. It's about a boat."

At that, he'd turned around again so fast he'd almost tripped over his own bad hip. Glancing back to see that Brennan and the others had moved off out of sight, he'd looked the Negro in the eye and waited for him to continue.

"Well, boss, see, I got to work here a little early this morning, like I usually do. Aint nobody else had showed up yet...."

As he'd started to set up the work for his crew, Stitches had said, he'd noticed a young black boy sneaking into the barn. From the description, it had been Lotrelle Dundee. According to Stitches, when he'd caught the boy snooping around, Lotrelle had told him he'd come back to find out what had happened to his friend, Rico Jones, whose body, of course, had been removed to the morgue the previous evening. Stitches had gone on to say that since he, himself, had known the boy's father, Fontana, he'd listened sympathetically to the boy's story. And when Lot had shown him the boat, he'd recognized it and realized its significance.

"...And knowin' as how the place was likely to be demolish'," Stitches said, "-- although I *didn't* know it was goin' to happen *to-day*, until Mr. Brennan come this mornin' and tol' us -- I agreed to he'p him move it to a safer place...."

When he asked, Stitches told him where the boat was hidden.

"And what about the boy, Lotrelle."

Stitches pulled on the peak of his cap and glanced away, "He went off."

"Why are you telling me all this," he asked, then.

"Beggin' your pardon, boss," Stitches said, "but I knowed old Sheriff Hope, too. He was a fair man."

Reflecting on it later, DelRay, who'd been pretty sure Stitches had known where Lotrelle was holed up, but had let it go, thinking he could find the boy himself when the time came, figured it was probably just as well that the boy stay hidden for the time being, for his own protection. The sheriff still wanted him as a material witness in the Rhoder case and a suspect in the fire at Ida Temple's in which the girl, Marvella, had been killed. The chief deputy admitted to himself that he hadn't made much progress on the arson, but the fact was, fire-bombings were escalating all over the state, and seemed to be a community-wide problem. Meanwhile, in his own mind, Lotrelle wasn't a suspect in any crimes he knew about. He had made a point, however, of going and checking on the boat, and he'd found it right where Stitches had said it was. He'd had to laugh, then, because he couldn't have thought of a better place to hide it, himself.

Meanwhile, the long odds were paying off. He'd been aware that the state auditors were in town and conducting a hush-hush investigation into financial matters in the sheriff's office. But because he, DelRay, was an employee in that office, they wouldn't tell him anything. Kurf, however, had told him that Clooder's arrogance and rapid rise to power in LeVane had apparently offended some folks down in the state capital, and political jealousies had been aroused. Scenting blood, the reporter had used his own resources and had brought back information about evidence the auditors had uncovered, which seemed to confirm the chief deputy's own suspicion that the death of Thomas Crouch had not been a coincidence.

Thinking of Crouch's murder reminded him of Old Paully, the "suspect" he'd brought in that morning, and how frightened and confused the old man had been, raving on about the destruction of his property....

"...Goddam stupid sonsabitches! Nigguhs dyin' in droves, and you try and tell'em to stop -- Moldy bones overflowin' down that dang hill on top *of me like to boil up on my front porch! -- I aint even got a soul buried up in there! -- Look like a junkyard. They got graves up there covered with light bulbs and alarm clocks, like they expect the bodies to wake up and walk off. Aint hardly a half-dozen proper white crosses in the lot! Never seen such a race for dyin! -- And you tell these sonsabitches to come dig'em up, they wreck the house, try to drive me offa my own place! -- Think they slick, but you watch, they show their face again, I'ma blow'em to hell back where they come from...!"*

Driving on, DelRay recalled the grisly scene earlier, at the gin, where Crouch's body had been found, and then the ride out to Mount Eden, afterward, with Earl Thackery.

"...Tsk! Damn shame," Thackery had said, as he'd climbed into the police car beside him, "Damn shame...!" And then, after they'd turned onto the highway and driven a few miles, he heard Thackery reciting a verse, as though just thinking aloud, "'...Strange is the Lord of Division, who cleaveth the birthright in twain...!' You ever read the classics, Del?"

He shook his head, no, and Thackery turned back to look out the window, his face gray and drawn, apparently still registering the shock he must have experienced when he'd arrived that morning to have his foreman show him Crouch's body in the compressor.

"Hell of a way to wind up a good week!" Thackery said abruptly. "By the way, are you going to be starting against Creekdale on Sunday?"

"They've got me in the lineup, yes, sir -- unless some other nonsense interferes."

"You've been pretty hot with that spitter of yours."

"Like the Preacher said, 'it's my money pitch!' Frankly, I think I'd be in trouble if the league goes ahead and bans it, like they been talkin' about. The majors did, last year."

"Is that why Preacher Roe retired?"

"I think he even got quoted sayin' so, himself."

"Good ole boy, the Preacher. I believe he's from out by Viola."

"Yeah. But like me, not much of a hitter."

"Well, I seem to remember he hit a home run, once."

DelRay laughed, "He did -- once!"

They drove on, squinting their eyes against the glare as the sun climbed higher, turning the countryside into a vast blaze of bronze, where the fields stood bare, now, of cotton and the crows banked and swooped unmolested down the rows of dying stalks.

"It took a special race of men to tame this country," Thackery mused aloud. "They raised up a nation by their own bootstraps. It took a clear head, a strong heart and a steel hand. Not many of that kind left.... We had high hopes for Paully at one time. Paully was the one rode the fast horses, shot the straightest and had the high grades, right up through law school. Who knows, like they say, maybe too much sun stole his judgment. Broke his daddy's heart...." Thackery glanced over at him, then, and added, "I expect you'll be stepping into old Sheriff Hope's shoes, yourself, one of these days...."

But DelRay, preoccupied, was only half-listening and didn't respond. His own mind had been racing, going over the questions and answers at the murder scene back at the gin, and trying to fit the new development into the scheme of things he'd been investigating -- because, despite his own suspicions, there was no physical evidence connecting the sheriff to Crouch's murder. Given the presence of the shotgun at the scene, he had to arrest the old man, if only to protect him from himself. He didn't believe for a minute that the old codger had actually murdered Crouch -- or, at least, that he'd done so knowingly and intentionally. But Clooder hadn't gotten out of hospital until that morning -- and probably wouldn't have stooped to dirty his hands with Crouch, anyway, as long as he could get someone else to act on his behalf.

And in this case, someone who knew his way around the gin. But the more he thought about it, something else about the crime didn't make sense to him....

"...It'd be dishonest," Thackery was saying, "to deny the coloreds have been treated a little unfairly, from time to time -- not that they're all angels, either. But this poor fella -- Crouch, I mean -- always courteous and respectful. Did all anyone could expect for his own people. Don't think he had an enemy in the county. He clearly wasn't personally a target, just in the wrong place at the wrong time, a victim of the misdirected anger that's sweeping the country, now...."

What the chief deputy couldn't get a handle on was the fact that Crouch had been killed on Thackery's property. Clooder'd had a good thing going with Thackery, and the sheriff was too smart to have spoiled that....

"...No one's taken the time," Thackery continued, "to address the question of readiness. As somebody once said, a man's worst difficulties only begin when he's free to do as he likes. But this kind of thing turns my stomach! And I'm afraid it's just the beginning...."

Thackery, DelRay was thinking, had given Clooder shelter and support. How much Thackery knew about Clooder's shadier dealings, he, DelRay, didn't know, but Clooder had been touting the virtues of Earl G. Thackery as far back as he could remember. If the sheriff had wanted to get rid of Crouch, even if he'd felt suddenly pressured to do so by the arrival of the state auditors and had simply panicked, he could easily have arranged to have it done on a back road somewhere, and disposed of the body in a swamp or the bogue, where it might never have been discovered. Why do something like this -- it almost amounted to a public crucifixion -- on his patron's doorstep...?

"...What I wanted to talk to you about, Del," Thackery was saying, now, having shifted in his seat to look at him more directly, "a few of us here, in LeVane, the more *responsible* among us, you might say," he added with an ironic wink, "are forming a little committee to try and get a handle on this thing, in the hope of avoiding the worst. And I was hoping you'd be willing to join us."

He gave Thackery a sharp look, wondering what the man was getting at.

"We've made a proposal to the governor," Thackery continued, "who's promised to help, by the way, if he's reelected -- that the state provide matching funds, to put together with what we've already raised amongst ourselves, to build a new vocational school for the young colored here, in LeVane. We also plan to put up an orphanage. The state facility is decrepit and overcrowded. These things would provide work for the older folks, you see, and some guidance and hope for the youth. We admit it's a modest plan, but it's a start. In fact, I was thinking of letting Lorna Rhoder, Benjamin's widow, run the orphanage. I understand that poor woman's lost her job in the school, and now has that preacher, Sampson's, four small children to look out for as well as her own, so I thought this would suit her nicely, sort of kill two birds with one stone...."

DelRay didn't say anything. He'd just been struck by something Thackery had inadvertently reminded him of, earlier in the conversation. He had returned to the jailhouse late one night the previous week to retrieve the starting lineup for the game that weekend -- only because he'd jotted a note to himself on the same piece of paper to remember to call Farrah Lise, and he hadn't wanted to give anybody a chance to tease him about it, in case the sheriff or one of the other deputies had found it lying around. But he now recalled that when he hadn't found the paper on his desk, he'd had to search the office for it, and had finally fished it out of the evidence locker with the fly-swatter. It must have fallen out of his pocket earlier in the day, when he'd replaced a gun after test-firing it for ballistics -- but the gun itself wasn't there...!

"...You wouldn't be asked to contribute any money, of course," Thackery continued, that won't be necessary. But having you aboard would add a lot for us. You're well-liked here, and old Sheriff Hope's name still evokes feelings of loyalty among those of us who remember him. Not to mention, your participation would likely bring you some attention down in the capital. Think about it, and let me know."

As they rode on, DelRay became aware, in a way he hadn't before, of the vast emptiness of the landscape. It seemed as though it had been peeled bare of artifacts, or as if the land had simply swallowed up all trace of those who'd inhabited it. For a moment, he could almost feel its flatness pressing heavily in upon him, making him uneasy, as though he were treading over an ever narrowing strand where all the rivers flowed into one and all thoughts were bound by the same two dimensions. And then he caught his breath, in spite of himself, as he saw Mount Eden looming up in the distance. As if he'd never seen it before, he watched it rising alone out of the shimmering plain, its sphinx-like configuration suddenly astonishing and mysterious.

"D'you know the old Choctaw legend about the Indian mounds?" Thackery said casually, as though reading his mind.

Preoccupied, DelRay, shook his head vaguely without taking his eyes off the road.

"The Choctaw name for Mount Eden was '*Nanih Chah-ta*,'" Thackery said, shifting more comfortably in his seat. "It means 'Hill of Man.' It was sacred to them, they thought it was the place their people originated. The legend says the mound is made up of eight gates, one gate for each of the Seven First Men who issued from them, and one, they call 'The Gate of Return,' through which the Last Man will return to The Dream. Now, this Dream they're talkin' about, with a capital D, is sort of like the *con-cep-tu-al* realm of the Great Spirit, see, a sort of *par-al-lel* universe to the reality here, on Earth, ifya' follow. That's where all living things were first conceived, before they were made, and where they'll return -- I mean their *concepts* will -- after they become extinct." He winked again, and with a boyish laugh, waved it away.

But DelRay thought it was the first time he'd seen Thackery laugh, and it made the man seem more human. "Go on," he said.

"You're interested? Well, the legend says that the Seven First Men, who were mighty warriors, immediately became jealous of one another and fell into mortal battle, in which five of them were slain. The two warriors remaining -- one was called *Tannap Abi*, meaning 'Killer of Many', and the other, *Chula Waiya*, or what you might say, 'Subtle Fox' -- these two sons of the devil cut up each of their five dead brothers into two hundred pieces and scattered the pieces all over the continent, burying each piece in a different place. That done, they agreed to go their separate ways, and they each engendered a people, who became the Choctaws and the Chickasaws.

"You know, it's interesting," Thackery said interrupting his own narrative, "it wasn't until the early 'Twenties -- well, I guess it must've been the summer of 'Twenty-Two, when Charlie Lindberg and I went up in one of those old biplanes to take some of the first aerial photographs of the Lower Mississippi Basin -- it wasn't until then that we realized this homely ole Mount Eden of ours, *Nanih Chahta*, actually formed a geometrically perfect octagon. It seemed just a happy coincidence at the time, because the official view held that the early Indians had not been sophisticated enough to know geometry. Since then, of course, as you probably know, we've discovered that the great majority of the Indian mounds are clearly built in recognizable shapes, some being very accurate geometrical figures, others graphical forms, effigies, representing birds, animals, fish and so on.

"Anyway," he continued, "the legend goes on to say that the one thousand burial sites of the five slain First Warriors are the one thousand Indian mounds in America -- there are really more than that, of course -- and that each is made in a certain shape that forms a character, and that these characters, all together, form a riddle. And when, in the end, one comes along who will be able to decipher these characters and solve the riddle, then *Tannap Abi* and *Chula Waiya* will come together again in the Last Battle, which was foreordained to take place between them at the end of the world, and the winner will come back to Nanih Chahta and reenter the Gate of Return, going back to The Dream...."

DelRay, meanwhile, had turned off the highway onto the old cemetery road, and now both men sat forward, as he slowed the car, with their eyes scouring the area around the excavation, looking for signs of Old Paully. They found the wreckage of the wooden house before the cemetery gate, but didn't see the old man himself. The work crew had apparently arrived only moments earlier, and as they caught sight of Brennan in the distance, directing a couple of mechanics to get the huge earth-moving machines fired up for the start of the workday, the thought crossed DelRay's mind that maybe Clooder and Thackery had come to a parting of the ways. He stopped the car and started to get out, but paused when he saw Thackery still sitting there, staring fixedly out at Brennan over the open passenger door.

"Oh, about the committee, I mentioned," Thackery said, feeling the chief deputy's eyes upon him, "it's only a small group of private citizens. We haven't invited some others, as we wanted to keep it small. You need not mention it to the sheriff."

Thackery turned away, as if to forestall any questions, but then turned back to rest his eye on the curious item hanging from the cruiser's rearview mirror. It was the dried human ear cut off the victim of an old lynching that Bee-Line had got from his father and had hung there as a crude joke when he'd owned the car.

Thackery calmly studied the souvenir hanging on the mirror between them now and said, "That fellow, Brennan, is a troublemaker. I had to fire him when he worked for me, years ago. Couldn't keep his temper on the job. I was wondering whether you-all had found any connection between him and that ugly business in Augury with the colored preacher. I thought I heard the sheriff say he'd been seen up around there that night...."

They eventually found Old Pauly hiding behind a pile of disinterred coffins. He refused to come out, cursing at them and yelling that he wanted his shotgun back, and then leading them on a hot chase through the wreckage of headstones and upturned heaps of earth, meanwhile dodging dangerously among the earth-moving machines that were now in motion around them. Fearing for the old man's safety, DelRay agreed to let Thackery approach him alone and appear to offer to return the gun -- empty -- in order to lure the old man back toward the cruiser, while he stood by, waiting to put the cuffs on him as soon as he came within reach. Thackery went ahead and spoke gently to the old man, trying to calm him down and gradually lead him away from where the machines were working, meanwhile holding the gun out to draw him on. They progressed that way for a few steps until, with a clever feint, Old Pauly snatched the shotgun from Thackery's hands and, turning it on him, threatened him with it. DelRay started forward to help, but Thackery waved him off, and just kept talking to the old man, cajoling him, speaking in a soft, reassuring voice as he backed away, keeping his own hands visible and empty, unintimidating, and leading his demented brother steadily toward the cruiser. Like trying to tame a wild animal, DelRay thought to himself, sadly. And then, when Thackery had him almost within their grasp, Old Paully suddenly dodged away, evading their outstretched hands, and ran screaming up onto the ruins of his wooden house, where he began charging back and forth with one hand up shading his eyes and peering out into the rind of daylight, as if seeking a haven from the arms of destruction that were tugging at him like a tide. Thackery gestured for DelRay to be patient, until finally, Paully stopped screaming and settled down, quietly reeling about on the pitching roof, plying his shotgun like an oar.

As DelRay, alone now, drove on toward Brennan's plantation, it came to him again how so many apparently disparate things were suddenly falling together. And it occurred to him that he'd better start looking over his own shoulder, because if he didn't watch his step, the trap he was setting might spring before he was ready. Killing was in the air and he could be next. Almost anything he touched, from here on, was going to tighten the noose at the other end, and he was going up alone against a sly, calculating, murderous sonuvabitch...!

He became aware of the smell of burning wood as he pulled into the driveway of Brennan's plantation.

"Damn, you just don't never give up, do you!" Minton said, flinging down his axe. "What're you harassin' me for, now?"

"The word is 'arresting.' I'm arresting you for murder. Turn around and put your hands behind your back."

"You can't do this!" Minton said, "I'm innocent! The jury said so! Hey, Borden! C'mere, tell'im!"

"Stay right where you are, Borden!" DelRay said, glancing over his shoulder to warn off the second man, who'd put down his saw and started forward. "I'll let you know when it's your turn!"

He'd found the two men out in Brennan's back field cutting logs off a dead tree chained to a tractor. They were splitting and stacking the wood in small bundles for a handful of Negro workers who were binding some in rags to use as torches and setting out the rest as kindling at marked positions across the field. The rows of dead cotton stalks stretching away on either side were picked clean, bone-bare of leaves, and in the far reaches of the field, already ablaze in the seasonal burning.

DelRay led Minton over to the police cruiser and handcuffed him to the front bumper.

"Go get Brennan!," Minton called out to Borden, " Tell'm to come down here and git me outta this!"

But when Borden made as if to climb aboard the tractor, DelRay calmly raised his steel claw, as though offering it for his inspection, while advancing toward him. Borden stayed put, until the chief deputy handcuffed both his wrists, looping the chain through the hole in the towbar of the tractor.

"Whaddya doin'," he said, then. "I didn't do nothin'! Well, at least wait a minute, willya, I gotta -- Hey, wait --!"

DelRay turned without a word and walked back toward his cruiser, leaving Borden hunched over the towbar and twisting about in the branches of the dead tree like a bear in a thicket. The Negroes had quietly dispersed. He was alone with the two men in the empty field, with the farm buildings off in the distance. Knowing that Brennan was working with the demolition crew up at Mount Eden, he was satisfied they wouldn't be disturbed for a time. He got into the car, with Minton still handcuffed to the front bumper, and started backing up, dragging the man behind him, kicking and howling, until they were out of earshot of Borden.

"God damn!" Minton said, with his eyes rolling, as DelRay stopped the car and got out, "You're crazy as a coot! You're a goddamn crazy cop! You can't do this to me, I --!"

"Just relax," DelRay said, approaching him, "You and I are gonna have a little chat."

"Don't you touch me!" Minton said, backing against the car and eyeing the chief deputy's steel claw. "I'm gonna report you! The jury --!"

"You aint been tried for this one yet, bo."

"Huh? What're you talkin' about?"

"I'll ask the questions. Let's start with an easy one: Who was with you the day you shot Benjamin Rhoder?"

"Wha...?"

Minton immediately began to protest his innocence and ignorance of the entire matter, but his face had blanched at the question, and DelRay continued to press him, because he had the evidence he needed. The special delivery envelope Donaghue had handed him that morning contained, among other things, confirmation from the state police in the capital that the bullets found in Rhoder's body had been fired from the deer rifle in the evidence locker at the office. The rifle belonged to Minton, who, as he'd claimed, had been acquitted, along with his sidekick, Borden, of the murder of the Hill boy. The rifle hadn't really figured as evidence in that case, for the Hill boy had been bludgeoned to death. But just on a hunch, while Minton was being held, DelRay had test-fired the rifle and sent the bullets, together with those taken from Rhoder's body, to the ballistics lab. The report verified the fact that Rhoder had been shot with Minton's rifle. And though that didn't prove Minton did the shooting, DelRay thought it likely Minton had been present at the time. Rhoder had been beaten up pretty badly before he was killed, and even if he'd been caught by surprise, it would've taken two or more strong men to handle him. Having lost the Hill case, it was going to give him a certain grim satisfaction, DelRay admitted to himself, to put Minton behind bars again. But he expected the man would only turn out to have been an accomplice, because he knew there'd been trouble between Rhoder and Minton's boss, Brennan.

"...Well then, if you didn't shoot him yourself, who did? Who'd you give the rifle to?"

"I didn't give it to nobody!"

"So, you shot Rhoder yourself, then."

"I didn't shoot nobody! I wasn't even there, I was...I was out huntin' that day with-with-with Brennan -- yeah, me and Borden, both!" He glanced anxiously down the field toward the other man, who was still chafing against the towbar. "You kin ax'em! We was all out huntin' a painter been causin' some trouble round here. Go on, ax'em!"

"Uh-huh." DelRay nodded patiently. Since Brennan had been willing to perjure himself to give Minton and Borden their alibi the last time, he'd expected them to try for the same tactic again. "So how do you explain the fact that your rifle was used to kill Rhoder?"

"How do I know! Somebody musta stole it!"

"Somebody stole your rifle to shoot Rhoder? You didn't report the rifle stolen. You were in possession of it when I saw you again afterward, when did you notice it was missing?"

"When...? Well, I mean, I didn't...."

"Uhm. That's a brand new gun, isn't it?"

"Y-ye-ah...?"

"How long've you had it?"

"Four-five weeks, mebbe -- I didn't steal it, I bought it, I showed you the receipt when-when --!"

"Oh, yeah, I remember, now...."

"Well, so....?"

"New model, nice feel to it. I always did like Brownings. Good balance. Have you tried it out?"

"Well, I -- I didn't kill nobody with it, if that's --!"

"I mean, have you used it at all, maybe taken it out hunting or target shooting or something."

"I only took it out once! -- before you arrested me the last time!"

"Uhm. When was that."

"You mean, when did I take it out? Well, I guess, like I said, when I went huntin' with Brennan and B --"

"Did you get him?"

"Who?"

"The panther."

"The...? Oh...ye --" he glanced back toward the tractor, but Borden was preoccupied in a curious dance between the towbar and the dead tree, trying to keep his pants dry as he peed into the branches. "...Uh, nah, nah, he got away."

"Too bad. By the way, what day was that...?"

"...?" Minton jerked himself back against the car, until he remembered which hand was free, then used it to scratch the far side of his cheek.

"And while we're on the subject of your new rifle," Del-Ray said, "how do you explain the fact that it was also used to kill that Negro preacher, Sampson?"

"Shit-on-a-fuckin'-brick! I didn't have nothin' to do with that, I was in jail...!"

DelRay could hardly have been surprised at the man's indignation, being well aware that Minton had still been securely under lock and key, awaiting the jury's verdict on the Hill murder, when Sampson had been shot. But the question he'd asked was real and still puzzled him. He'd proceeded to interrogate first one man, then the other, alternately, that afternoon, grilling them about the Rhoder killing, until the two had gotten so tangled up in their own lies that they'd finally admitted to being present at the scene and participating in the beating of Rhoder, while claiming that it had been Brennan who'd done the actual shooting. At the same time, he'd kept coming back to the matter of Sampson, until he'd convinced himself that neither of the men knew anything about the preacher's murder, because certain things about that case didn't seem to make sense. Matters got even more complicated later, when he left Minton and Borden in the hands of junior deputies to be taken and locked up separately in jail, and went back out to Mount Eden to deal with the sheriff's odd-job man.

"...I don't believe it!" Brennan said. "I don't believe they said any such thing!"

"They said it -- and they'll stick to it, or they know it'll be their own necks in the noose."

"Bull shit! And even so, I guess that just makes it my word against theirs!"

"That's one," DelRay said, enigmatically. "Then there's the question of how you'd explain how your fingerprints came to be on the rifle."

"Bull shit! I never touched it...! I mean, Minton was showing the gun off to every damn body when he first got it, I maybe just laid a finger on it, for a minute, then, but he wouldn't let anybody touch it! Ask his old pal, Borden, *he* wanted to try it out, but Minton wouldn't let it out of his hands!"

"That's two," DelRay said, nodding again. But he gave himself extra points for that, because in fact, the only clear print found on the rifle had been Minton's, too many other people had handled it. "And you can't deny," he went on, "there'd been trouble about money between you and Rhoder --"

"Bull shit! He was the one causin' trouble! I got witnesses to that! If I told that nigguh once, I told'm a dozen times, he better --!"

"That's three. So, unless you come up with a good alibi, it looks like you're out."

"Bull shit! Bull shit!" Brennan stood up from where he'd been sitting, on an overturned headstone, and stomped off toward the steam-shovel, still idling where DelRay had found him on his arrival, excavating the fifty-foot wall of the Indian mound. The big-toothed dipper of the machine remained suspended in the air, vibrating high over their heads. But as Brennan raised his foot for the first metal rung of the steps, he hesitated, as though daunted by the prospect of trying to climb back into cab with his hands cuffed behind him. Then he turned abruptly and yelled back over the noise of the machine, "You're bluffin'! You aint got nothin' on me! And besides that, I wasn't anywhere near there, when Rhoder got killed, and I can get witnesses to prove it...!"

But DelRay, who'd turned to follow him, wasn't listening. He was looking passed Brennan's shoulder at the wrecked wooden house that had stood alone by the side of the cemetery gate. "Where were you last night?" he said, turning back, to see Brennan grinning at him.

"Last night...?"

What Brennan had said, a moment ago, about Minton's not letting his new rifle out of his hands, had struck a bell with the chief deputy. The old man and his shotgun had been inseparable. Even if he had shot Crouch, in an excess of rage, provoked by the excavation crew's having demolished his house, and associating the undertaker with the graves that he'd been complaining were overrunning his property for years, the old codger would never have gone off and left his gun like that. But someone could have taken it from him, shot Crouch, and left the gun there to frame the old man, who'd been notorious for brandishing it at every funeral party that had carried a body passed his house on the way to the cemetery. And as Thackery had reminded him, earlier that morning, Brennan would have known his way around the ginning machines because he'd worked at the gin for years, before he'd gone to work for Clooder.

Brennan, meanwhile, caught by surprise, was unable to come up with a verifiable alibi for the previous night. And though there'd been no prints on the gun, for it had been wiped clean, as DelRay proceeded to press Brennan about various other details regarding the Rhoder and Crouch killings, Brennan began to buckle, and the cases seemed to becoming together in the chief deputy's mind. But the biggest piece was still missing. DelRay wanted the man who had ordered Brennan to kill Crouch, but Brennan was still hedging, apparently too afraid of Clooder to go any further.

Changing the subject abruptly, DelRay said, "Why did you kill Sampson."

Brennan looked at him, puzzled, "Who?"

"Harold Sampson, the Negro preacher."

"Sampson! What the fuck...? He the one got shot up by Augury?"

"You should know."

"How the hell should I know, I wasn't nowhere near Augury that night! What the fuck you tryin' to do, blame me for every god-damn nigger-killin' in the state!"

"Don't fight it, Brennan, you were seen up in Augury that night, just prior to the killing --"

"Bull shit! Bull shit! Aint nobody saw me there, cause I wasn't there! I was --!"

"I've got it on good authority."

"I was in Highville! In Highville! I wasn't anywhere near Augury, and I can prove it! Boy, you must be crazy! Whoever the fuck told you I was in Augury is a fuckin' liar! Oh, boy, you just wait'll I tell Clooder about this, he's gonna fix your wagon!"

"You might have to call him a liar to his face, then."

"...What?"

"You heard me."

"...Are you sayin' Clooder...? Clooder told you I was in Augury?"

"I said I had it on good authority."

"...You're bullshittin' me, aint you," Brennan said, attempting a smile. But he was visibly shaken, and when the chief deputy didn't say anything, he continued, "I swear, I was at the Air Force Base in Highville! I went to deliver a truckload of lumber, and I was supposed to pick up a check for it, but the quartermaster wasn't there to write it, and I had to stay with the truck overnight, and go back to the office and get it the next morning...." Seeing the skeptical look on DelRay's face, he added, "I slept in the goddamn barracks that night! -- that's the night you're talkin' about -- you can ask them at the base! And I was back in the quartermaster's office seven o'clock the next mornin', when it opened, and got the check, cause Mr. Thackery told me not to unload the truck without gettin' the check first, cause they owed him a lot of money. God damn, I was on a job for Thackery! Ask'im! Ask Thackery, he'll tell ya! I was in Highville!"

It was DelRay's turn to be shaken. He tried not to show it, but when Brennan saw him hesitate, the man laughed in his face. "Kiss my ass!" Brennan said. "You really had me goin' there, for a minute! Boy, you're one sorry-assed cop! What's the matter, you still mad about the boat?"

"What boat," DelRay said, piercing him with a look.

Brennan turned pale. He looked first one way, then the other, and then seemed to deflate as he slid down against the side of the steam-shovel to sit with his legs sprawled on the ground....

"...You see, I was really only feelin' my way along," Del-Ray was saying, late the following day, "hoping that I could pressure one of them into divulging something they might know that might lead me somewhere, because I had so little to go on. For example, I don't know if I mentioned it at the time, but just for the hell of it, I'd also forwarded a spent 30-06 cartridge I'd found in the bushes near where Sampson had been killed to the ballistics lab for testing. As you know, the bullet had passed right through his head and we never found that, but the lab report said the shell had definitely been fired from Minton's rifle. The problem is, as you and I both know, the rifle was also secured. We had it locked up in the evidence locker, back in the office, where it should have been the morning Sampson was killed. I considered the possibility that the shell could have been ejected and left there when the gun had been used on some earlier occasion, but it seemed unlikely. That whole area around the new atomic reactor, up there at Augury, is patrolled and off-limits for gun use. Now, we know Rhoder was shot at point-blank range, probably in the reeds over there," he gestured toward a dense growth of cattails and arrowwood, a few yards away along the bank, "where, according to Brennan and the others, they beat him, and then dragged his body over here, where they dumped it in the bogue. But I figure whoever shot Sampson must've been an expert marksman, because that's a wide-open field, up there. The only fresh tire tracks that morning were Sampson's, and the nearest cover is a stand of sycamore, over two-hundred and fifty yards from the levee. The shooter made a clean kill with one shot over a considerable distance, in light no better than this...."

Made curious, when he'd spotted a fox rummaging in the bushes, while he'd been up in Augury investigating the shooting, DelRay had gone over to examine the area, which edged an access road, and found a cardboard pizza box torn open with only the crumbs remaining, a couple of crushed beer cans, a neatly folded gum wrapper, and the embers of a small campfire. Looking further, he'd found the ejected cartridge. It all suggested that somebody had been waiting there, in ambush, for an hour or more, in a direct line-of-sight from where the preacher had often been known to say his morning prayers, and where his old Studebaker had been found, abandoned on the levee, a few steps from where Sampson himself must've been standing when the bullet had struck him down in the false light before dawn.

"...I think I know who the crack shots are around here," he continued, "and Minton is only fair. But him and Borden aren't in the picture, anyway. I hadn't thought of Brennan in connection with Sampson, until I was told he'd been seen up around Augury that night, just before the preacher was killed."

Clooder, still lodged in his body cast, pushed his hat back on his head and shifted his gunbelt to rest his foot up on a stump. "Sheemsh to me your barkin' up the wrong tree. Who told you that."

"I found out it wasn't true," DelRay said. "Brennan wasn't anywhere near Augury that night. He was at the Air Force Base in Highville."

"You checked that?"

"I did."

"Well, there you are."

"He was on a job for Thackery."

"...For Thackery," Clooder repeated, dryly, but DelRay thought he'd caught a flicker of interest in the sheriff's eyes.

As they spoke, the light was beginning to fade. There was an acrid smell of smoke, and a fine ash hung in the air from the dead cotton stalks burning in the surrounding fields. He and the sheriff were standing alone on the bank of the river, and as he watched the sun going down over the Rue, DelRay had the taste of ashes, bitter and salt, on his tongue.

"Sho, you're back where you shtarted," Clooder said.

"Not exactly. One night last week I had to go back to the office to get something I'd forgotten, and I happened to notice Minton's rifle was missing from the evidence locker. But it was there again when I got in the following morning, so I'd just assumed you'd removed it temporarily for some official purpose, since you had the only key, and I didn't think to mention it at the time. Except it turns out that was the night Sampson was killed. And then I remembered that you were there."

Clooder shifted his feet impatiently, "...There, *where!*"

"In Augury." When Clooder looked at him without saying anything, DelRay added, "So was I."

"What're you talkin' about!"

It had taken him longer than it should have, DelRay thought to himself, to figure out what Thackery had been up to, when he'd told him the sheriff had said Brennan had been seen in Augury. Whatever petty grudge Earl Thackery had against Brennan -- even if he'd thought, as DelRay himself had suspected, that Brennan had killed Crouch and made it look as if it had been his, Thackery's, brother, Old Paully -- it hadn't made sense to him that a man like Thackery would tell a blatant lie that could so easily be disproved. He'd kept going round and round it fruitlessly, until it had finally dawned on him -- earlier this afternoon, when he'd met the clerk, Calley Donaghue, at the courthouse -- that the point of the lie hadn't been to deceive him about Brennan, but to *un*deceive him about the sheriff!

"We were both there," he said. You were heading back to Dividend -- remember? -- when you drove passed me that morning and saw me sitting there at the forks, scratching my head, because I'd just lost that fellow, Robinson, I'd been chasing."

Clooder flexed his lips, as though to smile, "Yar?"

"It took me awhile to come up with a motive that would make sense, though. Any of a dozen dimwitted bozos we have around here might've wanted to kill Sampson, his outspokenness and uppity ways set a lot of folks' teeth on edge. But, again, it was the timing. Then, earlier this afternoon, I ran into Donaghue at the courthouse, and he told me Sampson had spent an afternoon there, recently, pouring over the county business and property ledgers, asking questions about the missing pages -- and taking notes. He only mentioned it in the course of conversation, as an example of how Negroes like Sampson tend to bring trouble on themselves by, as he put it, 'sticking their nose in where it don't belong.'"

"Yar?"

"And he told me -- Calley did -- that he'd mentioned it to you -- on what turned out to be the day before Sampson was killed...when, as you knew, Brennan was out of town and his two stand-ins were in jail -- and this was only a few days before the state auditors were due to arrive."

"Boy, what're you tryin' to shay!"

But DelRay hesitated, his voice caught in his throat. For as he opened his mouth to speak, it occurred to him that he had missed the significance of something else Thackery had been saying. The point of all that quoting of scripture, or whatever it was, and the long, rambling gobbledygook about the Indian mounds seemed obvious to him now: the man had been talking about himself and his brother, Paully. Although he couldn't prove it in court, he now realized Thackery must have known all along that Paully was innocent, because he, himself, had been a party to the set-up, it'd been a very simple way of evicting Paully from the land he needed for his TV station, without opening himself to being blamed for the poor old codger's being locked away in the asylum for the rest of his life. But he probably hadn't anticipated having anything as dramatic as Crouch's murder take place at his doorstep. That must've been a warning from Clooder, DelRay thought, or maybe even a threat. Meanwhile, Thackery was in a position to be able to put the finger on Clooder for being involved in Sampson's murder, because Thackery was the sort of person who would make it his business to know everything that went on in LeVane County that might affect his own interests. And he'd clearly understood that Clooder's usefulness to him had run its course, once all the investigations had begun. He might never know, DelRay reflected, whether Thackery had condoned the murder of his father, Sheriff Hope, but it wasn't much of a stretch to suppose that what Thackery had really been trying to tell him, after all, was that the time had come for him, DelRay, to take up his father's unfinished business. And so, now here he was, he thought, confronting this man, who'd been like a father to him, nurtured him when his own father had died, and had almost single-handedly resurrected him when he'd been sinking into self-oblivion in the VA hospital so recently. He was seeing, now, vividly in his mind's eye, the moment on the previous day when he'd followed the sheriff out the door of the jailhouse and had stood watching, as Clooder, shuffling awkwardly in his cast, had sidled down the alley toward the courthouse square and the cheering election crowd that had parted before him like a bow wave before a battleship....

His voice was husky with emotion, as he said, "Remember yesterday, when you said you thought I'd suddenly got religion? Well, the idols I meant were only human, I wasn't...I wanted to know...!" He stopped again, unable to continue for a moment.

Clooder instinctively reached out to him, a compassionate gesture, his hand hovering in midair, as he said, "What ish it, shon. Go on, it'sh awright. What're you tryin' to tell me?"

"Well," DelRay said, finally, "I know you killed Sampson."

"Wha...?" Clooder reared back and studied him, incredulous, his hand retracting to trace the ridge of plaster that encased his own jaw.

"I may not be able to prove it," DelRay added, "I have only circumstantial evidence, but I know you did it. But I can prove that you ordered Brennan to kill Crouch -- I have Brennan's signed confession to that effect -- wait! There's more. He also admitted in his statement that he served as your accomplice in another murder -- here! -- in this bogue, ten years ago. He said he helped you to sink the boat and hide the evidence, when you drowned my --!"

"DelRAY! SHTOP IT!" Clooder bellowed, cutting him off, "I SHAID SHTOP it, now! Get ahold of yourshelf, boy, you're making no shensh!" Then he narrowed his eyes shrewdly, and as though deciding that his chief deputy had lost his grip on himself and was attempting to make some sort of deranged joke, he gave a dry rasp through his clenched teeth, "Haar! Lishen shon, lishen, take it eashy. I know all thish shit goin' on here, lately...well, it'd be enough to make even a shound man half-crazy. But pleash, don't let me think you dragged me out here tonight to be eaten alive by moshquitoesh, jusht to tell me you're shome kinda damned fool!"

"No," DelRay said, "I brought you here to settle an old debt." Turning, he signaled toward the tall reeds.

Two armed deputies suddenly appeared stepping out of the reeds. They came forward and relieved Clooder of his gun and handcuffed him, as the sheriff stood staring at his chief deputy in amazement.

"Branford Clooder," DelRay continued, evenly, "I'm arresting you for the murder of Sheriff Vance Hope."

14.
A Hand So Various

"...Newton? Newton, my brother? Newton's alive?"

"That's what he said to tell you. Said to tell you Newton's alive, and he work for a 'surance company down in Richmond, Southern Aid. Said that's his card, there, in the paper."

Lot looked at the card again, trying to make sense of it. The name on it was "Virgil Robinson Pope, III." "But how's he know it's him?" he said. "Why's he callin' himself 'Virgil Pope'?"

"I don't know. The man didn't say. But when he come by with the trumpet this mornin', he said to tell you that's your brother, Newton. And the chief deputy, he's a man like his father was, he don't mess with folks, so if he say it's him, it's him, awright."

"But, I mean, how does the man know that's Newton? He seen him? Has Newton been back here?"

"Well," Stitches said, pulling on the peak of his cap, "I b'lieve so!" He got up and walked around the wooden chair he'd been sitting on, then bent over to lean his long elbows on the chair back and added, "Lotrelle, you wanna know somethin' funny? Cause, now, I'm rememberin' Newton myself, though I aint seen'im since he was a boy, well, I guess since Fontana -- your daddy -- died. And this guy, here, I seen him a coupla times, over at the Cat. He was runnin' the gamblin' there. Folks at the Channel Cat, they called'im Robbie. But the thing is, he really look like Newton, too, with that long jaw and the big ears. But in my mind, I remember Newton kinda real country, you know, rough edges-like stickin' out all around. And this guy, Robbie, he was so sophisticate, I honestly never thought to put the two together. Huh, I mean, that nigger was *smooth!* Didn't nobody else reckonize him, neither, I don't believe.... Well, now I think back, it could be maybe Jim Bidder did. But if'n he did, he didn't let on. But maybe that's why he was so quick to let Robbie -- I mean, Newton -- take that action over, in the first place, cause Bidder don't trust nobody just like that, he aint no fool. He was real good, too, Robbie was, made a whole lotta dough. I know he got some of mine...!'"

Lot picked up the trumpet and examined it carefully, noticing as he did so that his hands were trembling. One pearl keypad was missing. The bell was tarnished and distorted by heat, but the metal didn't seem cracked. And the valves, when he tried them, hadn't seized up, they'd be fine again with use. It was his Selma, all right, the same fine E-flat horn he'd lost in the fire at Ida Temple's. The same, and not the same, he thought, correcting himself. Like the horn, he felt that he, too, had been tricked into an evil mould and twisted in some way...

...So much seemed to be happening all at once, and at the same time somehow eluding him, as if he were stuck on a merry-go-round and everything else was going on around him, just out of reach, but his timing was off and he was afraid to jump. He didn't understand his own feelings. He'd just been told -- told again, really, because Basheeba had come running to tell him last night, although he'd been glad to have had Stitches confirm it this morning, as he'd had misgivings about the old woman's sanity -- and, no question, there it was, headlined in today's newspaper, the one the chief deputy had wrapped the trumpet in when he'd given it to Stitches to return to him:

"Sheriff Clooder Convicted of Murder!!!"

And then he's told that Newton's alive! He should be jumping for joy, like Basheeba last night, when she'd brought back the news from town. She'd rushed in clapping her hands and chanting, over and over again,

> *"Crouch an' Clooder gone to pe'dition,*
> *An' thirty-nine mo' done signed the petition!*
> *Crouch an' Clooder gone to pe'dition,*
> *An' thirty-nine mo' done signed the petition!*
> *Glory, halleloo...!"*

"What?" he'd said, not understanding, "What? Basheeba, what're you talking about?"

But she'd just laughed and grabbed his hands and danced him around the tiny shack,

"...Glory, halleloo...!"

When she'd calmed down enough to try and talk, she was able to make him understand that the "petition" she'd been carrying on about was the school integration petition that the Negroes in the county had been too afraid to put their names to -- until the news of Clooder's conviction had brought them out of their houses to come lining up at her daughter's door to sign the paper. But for the rest, she hadn't made much sense. She'd claimed credit for bringing both Crouch and the sheriff to judgment by having folded some mysterious letter she'd received "from the devil's own hand!" in with Mrs. Thackery's laundry! -- then she'd turned and dashed back out the door and disappeared into the dark woods. She hadn't returned by the time he'd awakened this morning, and he hadn't seen her since.

But he remembered having dreamt last night about that old oak boat and his father sitting in it, drifting slowly around on the water and smiling up at the fresh snow falling on the branches and the feeling of wings circling above him in the winter light. He'd awoken early and feeling pretty good after that, until he'd stepped out the front door to see a big owl staring him in the face. It sat there, perched in the black willow in the yard, eyeing him malevolently and making its strange call over and over,

"Who cooks for yo-o-u-u?"

until he'd finally given a yell and thrown a stick at it to frighten it off. Afterward, all that had remained with him of the dream was the lingering feeling of the chill of winter and of the shadow of those wings circling overhead, as if something was telling him that even when he did get out of this place, wherever he went it would always be there, circling and circling, ready to pounce the moment he'd dropped his guard...!

This damn place was twisting his mind, he said to himself, he never used to think like that! What he should be doing, what he wanted to do most of all, right now, was to go and find Newton! But instead, he was still just sitting there, only thinking about it, talking to himself like he'd gone and lost his mind, unable to move, planted, like a stone on the plain dirt floor. He felt numb, exhausted and bewildered. The sheriff was in jail, but as far as he knew, he, himself, was still a fugitive, nobody'd told him he wasn't -- although he still didn't know why, because he was innocent! Then he finds out that Newton had been there and gone, while he'd been dragging himself and Rico Jones up and down the length of the county hiding from the cops, and never having a clue that his own big brother was right there at the same time and could've helped them escape! The only thing he felt he *had* been a part of was what had happened to Rico. He held himself responsible for that, for Rico's death -- and so, he wasn't really so innocent, after all. But ever since Rico got killed, he'd been wanting to leave, but for some reason he hadn't been able to. He'd been holed up there, in the old conjure woman's tarpaper shack, eating her crackling and chickenbacks until they were coming out of his ears, when he should have been halfway to Chicago by now! With Rico dead, there'd been nothing to hold him there. He'd walked down to the IC tracks three or four times and stood, stiff as a tree, watching the scurf of dead fish scrolling passed the levee wall at his feet and feeling the smoke from the fields burning in his throat and making his eyes water, just stood there, daydreaming about his father -- and about his mother, too, who'd died when he was so young that he didn't really know or remember much about her -- and daydreaming about Newton and his baby brother, Robbie, too, imagining them all together, riding around in that pretty oak boat, just laughing and having a good ole time...! Until the trains came. And then he'd stood there watching the boxcars rolling by as if they weren't real, as if they were just a trick of daylight, part of the weirdness of that whole country that was continually throwing up one thing after another to fool you, to make you think you understood what was going on and how things stood, when in fact you didn't at all! And then, when the last train had left, and he'd realized he hadn't made a move to try and get on one -- as if thinking that a train he couldn't believe in couldn't take him anywhere that made any sense! -- he'd just turned around and come back, just like that, day after day, wandering back and forth feeling lost, feeling as though he were tilted off-balance and looking for something to replace the weight of Jones that he wasn't carrying anymore...!

313

"Was that you? Playing, I mean?"

He glanced up, to see a woman standing in the open doorway, through which he'd thought Stitches had gone off only a moment before. A woman with the hem of her dress stirring softly in the breeze. He dropped his eyes to the trumpet in his hand, staring at it as though seeing it for the first time. Playing...?...he'd only been thinking.... He put the trumpet down, carefully, a strange, fragile object out of some longforgotten dream.

"Where's Basheeba?"

At the sound of the crisp, no-nonsense tone, he looked up again, astonished to see her still there, a tall, slender woman, standing in the light of the little wooden doorway, and cradling a large covered pot wrapped in towels against her hip. He'd half expected her to vanish, like one of the phantoms that had just been revolving in his mind's eye. She was studying him curiously out of large, dark brown eyes that seemed almost too prominent in her face, eyes that seemed oddly familiar, although he couldn't recall where he might have seen anything like them before.

"You must be the one I heard they were looking for," the woman said, stepping in passed him. "Basheeba's always pickin' up strays."

He watched her cross the room, nimbly avoiding the litter of crude clay and wooden effigies, hand drums, rattles and bundles of dried yarrow stalks and whatnot that lay about on the floor, and decided she wasn't really that tall, after all. But she moved with a sort of long-limbed grace.

"I brought you-all some real food," she said, setting the heavy pot down on the table next to an iron washtub and a pile of dirty dishes that were there. Then, turning to face him, she added, with a laugh, "I know you must be tired of my mother's chickenbacks!" It was an unexpected, open, girlish laugh, it showed a bit of her gums and the small space between her two front teeth.

"You play that trumpet pretty nice. Is that blues, or jazz, or what?"

He nodded his head vaguely, as if to say it lay somewhere in the in-betweens.

"It doesn't sound like any of the music that I know -- but then, I don't really get a chance to hear that much. But I'm surprised Basheeba lets you play that stuff in her house, jazz music's the only thing I know of that scares her."

"Ah."

Folding her arms, she leaned back and stood regarding him for a moment. Not really pretty, he thought to himself, but not a bad-looking woman, either, and younger than she'd seemed, at first. He wanted to dwell on that smile and the way she tilted her head and the soft bulge of her hip against the table edge. But the forcefulness of her gaze made him uneasy. There was almost too much feeling in it. And yet, apart from the deep shadows under her eyes that suggested a long bout of sleeplessness, her eyes gave him no hint of what she might have been thinking. They seemed to envelope him and at the same time to be trying to see right into him. They had the unabashed intensity of a child seeing something for the first time, he thought -- but a knowing child, who was studying this new thing for what it -- or, in this case, he -- might signify. Had it been anyone else staring at him like that, he'd have resented it. But because of that odd and vulnerable childlike quality she had, he somehow didn't. On the other hand, he didn't know how to respond to it, either, and so he let his own glance slip away, as though to elude her scrutiny amid the dust and clutter of the room, where the rough wooden table, one rickety straight-backed chair, and a wood stove were the only pieces of furniture. There was only one room in the shack, and no bed. He had no idea where Basheeba slept, or for that matter, whether she slept at all. The old woman had simply let him clear a corner for himself to sleep on a blanket. But often, when he'd wake up in the middle of the night disturbed by a noise or a bad dream, he'd see Basheeba, if she was there at all, still dressed as she had been all day, sitting at the table and muttering to herself, and maybe winding threads about some clay or wooden doll, or boiling and binding up potent-smelling herbs by the light of a candle or of the moon coming through the open door. Or if he got up to walk off the dream, he might spot her tending her garden out there in the moonlight, or he might come upon her unexpectedly, dancing, or frozen in some grotesque ritual posture, way out in the dark woods, when the sight of her would frighten him out of his wits....

"You all right?" the woman before him said. "You look like you've seen a ghost."

"...You must be Lorna."

She nodded, but the smile was gone, and with it, that childlike quality was hidden again beneath the guise of the woman.

"Yeah...!" he said, and dropped his eyes to the newspaper, where the white hat in the photograph of Sheriff Clooder on the courthouse steps was visible, like a blind eye, through the brass loop of the trumpet. "...Yeah, I'm awright, I was just... thinkin'...."

"So, how come you're still here?" Lorna said, with a sudden edge to her voice. "Or did my mother put a spell on you."

Her voice was like a silk thread, he thought, it came softly to your ear, but could snap it off if you weren't paying attention. But when he looked up, her expression hadn't really changed, except now he thought he saw mischief in her eyes. "Aint nobody put a spell on me...!" he said, thinking to himself that he was going to have to do or say something to gain back the advantage, here. And the fact that this woman was a little older -- he couldn't guess her age exactly, for her appearance seemed to change so much with her expressions, or even with just a flick of her eyes -- but the fact that she was older made no difference, because by his own lights -- and except for a man's own mother -- a man naturally had the advantage, or should have it, coming in the door, and it was up to the man to keep it or lose it, and if he lost it, he might as well keep on walkin', because a woman, don't matter how "nice" she be, he said to himself, a woman's like a bulldog, and once she git ahold of a piece of you, she won't let go, she'll worry it right off your bones, if you let her.

"Look...," he began, composing his own face into a mask of sophistication --

But she'd already turned her back, as though she'd forgotten him, and was unwinding the towels and taking the cover off the pot. She rinsed off a dish in the tub of water, dried it with a cloth and ladled out some food. "Here," she said, handing him a steaming plate of hop-n-john and greens, and adding in an ironic tone, "hungry as you look, it's just a-maze and a wonder you find strength to blow your horn!"

The phrase caught him off-guard, he hadn't heard it since he was a child, himself, and it made him laugh.

"Go on, eat it before it gets cold."

"...Yes, ma'am," he said, then, putting the first forkfull obediently into his mouth.

"You're Lotrelle, aren't you, Fontana's boy."

"...Umm...um-hmn...."

"I remember him. I remember your mother, too," Lorna continued, seeming to get some pleasure out of watching him eat. "She had a beautiful voice, I used to love to hear her singing in church. She sang *Precious Lord* in a way I will never forget. You look like your father, but you have her mouth. I remember you, too. You were a real quiet little boy. You used to carry around a beat-up old tin horn with you all the time then, too, but you never played it. Sometimes, you'd put it up to your mouth, like you were going to play it, but nothing ever came out. Folks didn't think you had much of a future. Well, but I guess you've figured it out by now, huh? -- the horn, I mean...."

He was only half-listening. For the moment, he'd lost interest in talking as he savored the taste of the peas and rice. The rice was light and grainy, the way his mother used to make it, not clumped and soggy, the way most other people made it, and spicy as hell, the chili and pepper catching him at the back of his throat after he swallowed -- and up in his nostrils, too, until he remembered to exhale through his mouth -- but the stronger scents were of pork and curry and cumin and basil and garlic and thyme and other spices he couldn't identify. It was delicious -- better, he decided, even than his mother's. But he could feel the heat of the peppers raising the sweat on his scalp, and finally, he gasped.

"Food's kinda hot, huh?" she said.

He looked up, nodding his head in agreement, to see her holding out an opened bottle of Coke. It was warm, but welcome.

"I guess I have a heavy hand with pepper. Ben always used to complain about it. But I suppose if you're hungry enough you'll eat it." Her voice had taken on that bitter edge again, and she turned away.

But he cleared his throat to get her attention, and when she looked back, he poked his tongue in his cheek and held up his fork for her to see what he'd fished out of the plate.

She laughed, "I guess you just can't avoid chickenbones in this house, huh? But, hey, now that's a wishbone, that's a good sign!"

When she bent to reach for it, he held it away, "It's a very good sign," he said, "but that's the wrong hand, you don't want to be bringin' any more bad luck here, I been havin' enough of that already."

"No, uh-uh, I'm left-handed."

"Are you? Gee, that must be tough!" he said, ironically.

"That's no foolin'! When I was a child in school, the teachers would tie it behind my back to make me use my right hand to write with, or they'd put a glove on it and punish me when I took it off and used my left hand anyway -- because, really, it was just easier, you know...? Anyway, it's a silly story!"

"Actually, it's kinda nice."

"What's nice about havin' your hand tied behind your back?"

"No, I mean it's nice your tellin' me somethin' about yourself."

"...Oh, uh-huh." She was being ironic, now.

"Here." He took one leg of the wishbone in his hand and held it out for her to take the other, "Make a wish!"

But she didn't. She stared at the wishbone for a moment as though she'd forgotten what it was, then turning, she took up the ladle and began chopping at the food in the pot with a sudden, almost savage purpose, as though whatever was in it had been killed only moments before. "You had an older brother, Newton, I think," she said, abruptly, reaching down without looking at him to take away his plate and then hand it back to him refilled.

"You don't want to make a wish?"

"Newton was fresh and kinda mean, I remember," she continued, ignoring his question to busy herself with the dishes. "He did some nasty things to the girls...!" She was making more noise than necessary, rattling the dishes in the tub as she washed them. "And didn't you-all have a baby brother, I don't remember his name...?"

"...Robbie...!"

"Robbie, yeah...." Her voice trailed off and a stunned look crept into her eyes. She stood still, then, with a couple of wet dishes in her hands and the soapy water dripping down, staring out at the woods beyond the open door. After a while, she closed her eyes, and for a moment, it was as if a light had gone out in the room.

In his own mind, Lot saw, again, Benjamin Rhoder's body being pulled out of the water and carried over in blankets and set at her feet. Except he saw it, now, as he imagined Lorna must have seen it, her husband's body, bloated and disfigured, with a gaping eel's nest at the groin, where it had been mutilated. He gave an involuntary shudder and looked away, trying to put the horror behind him. But as he ran his eyes over the circles and strange symbols drawn in charcoal and chalk that covered the newsprint papering the walls, and the little sacks of grave-dust, anklebones and cock feathers hanging from the rafters, he was unable to put aside the stirring vision that had overlain that horror in his mind, for he'd imagined, in the same moment, Lorna, herself, bathing nude in the waters....

A crash startled them both, and he jumped to his feet. "Hey, you awright?" he said, going to help her pick up the broken dishes that had slipped from her hands.

"I'm sorry," she said, "I wasn't thinking for a moment. Don't you bother, I'll do it."

"No problem," he said, happy for the excuse to be moving close to her. "By the way, do you dig all this hoodoo stuff, too?"

She laughed, "No, I surely don't! I know I'm a conjure's child, but I never got involved with it. Basheeba's always telling me I'm naturally born to it -- I mean, shoot, its' bad enough I'm a Wednesday child, but like I told you, I am left-handed, and that's supposed to be a sign, too -- but I never wanted any part of hoodoo. And I don't believe in it, either! -- most of the time, anyway. Though sometimes, I do honestly wonder.... 'Don't play loose with the Powers, chile!'" she said, in a good imitation of the old woman's gruff tone. "'Once they choose you, you can't escape'em, an' if you don't learn how to deal with'em, they'll come round to dealin' with *you*!' -- Huh. Well, but I guess maybe that's the part that I --!"

She broke off as they stood up, close together in the cramped corner of the shack between the table and the stove, with him feeling her breath on his face and their fingers inadvertently interlaced, holding the broken crockery, and he became aware of her sweet, fresh scent which was not cologne but reminded him of wild sage, and he saw that she really was nearly as tall as he was. As he stood looking at her, she tried to turn away, but there was hardly room, without her brushing up against him, and then there was the problem of the crockery.

"You asked me -- before, I mean -- why I was still here...."

She gave him an embarrassed smile, "Well, I guess I should be asking myself the same question. Would you mind just...?"

She was gesturing for him to help her to put the broken dishes down on the table, but he made as if he didn't understand. "What do you mean, are you thinking of leaving?"

"What? Oh, I was just talkin'. Help me put this stuff down --?"

"No, really, why *are* you here?"

"What do you mean, why am I here, I live here, this is my home!"

"What I mean to say is...I mean, sure, I was born here, so somebody could say it's sort of my home, too -- except it really isn't. Not anymore. Not for a while. And so, I was thinkin', maybe you --"

"Oh?" she said, interrupting him. "Then, where *is* your home?"

"...Uh-well, I guess -- up until now -- you could say it's been in my music. But I was thinkin' --"

"In your music. Ah. And now?"

"...Now...?" He hesitated, his flood of confidence ebbing. He began to feel he couldn't put this woman on, he didn't even want to try. Her gaze held him, and for a moment, he felt she saw more clearly than he, himself, did, who he was. At the same time, she had seemed to let her own guard down a little, so that he saw, now, the hurt in her eyes, but also pride and a reserve of strength...and a deep seeking. He saw that Lorna must have really loved her husband, that with his death her world had been violently torn apart, and that she was searching for some truth, now, as one who'd been shipwrecked might search for a sail. And this deep seeking unnerved him, made him feel that his own needs were small and self-serving by comparison, that whatever truth he'd been looking for most of his life was more shallow than any truth this woman who stood before him might actually find.

"...Now," he heard himself saying, and as he said it, it was as if someone had pulled off the bedclothes and found him naked, "now, I don't know. Music is all I really know...I mean, I guess, all I really know is just music...!"

She studied him for a long moment without speaking, searching his eyes. And strangely, he found his embarrassment diminishing, as though he'd been pared down to the bone only to find that what remained wasn't a weakness, after all, but a strength of a sort he hadn't imagined -- and still really didn't understand, though it seemed to him that just having that, having discovered that strength within himself, was enough, for now....

They talked together, then, for a while. She asked about his life on the road, and seemed to understand when he told her how difficult it was to get people to be willing to listen to new music. And she told him something of what it was like to grow up a conjure woman's child. She'd put away the broken dishes and led him outside, pointing out the parsley, garlic, thyme, St. Johnswort, John-the-Conqueror, winter cress, nightshade, snakeroot and other herbs growing in her mother's strange but well-tended gardens that grew all around the shack. Then he followed her a little way through the woods and down to what she called her "secret place," a pond he hadn't seen before, hidden in a grove of trees. He walked along the narrow path behind this unpredictable girl-woman, enjoying her easy, swinging gate and unselfconscious sensuality. It was an "innocent," unaffected sensuality that seemed to spring from the air she breathed and partook more of an innate, feminine grace than of sex alone. He saw that Lorna was not trying to be attractive, and she wasn't coy at all, but she had this attractive manner about her that only a few women, once grown, still had, that so-called "pretty" women in his experience almost never had, and that women who were trying to be attractive might imitate, only to look cheap or silly.

Lorna led him along the edge of the pond to a huge red maple that towered above the neighboring trees, then plumped herself down on an exposed root and sat quietly, gazing up at a branch that extended far out over the water. When he followed her eyes, he saw an iridescent blue-green dragonfly there, hovering by the branch, then it darted off.

After a moment, she said, "When I was little, kids in school used to tease me all the time, saying I was a hoodoo woman's child and making up nasty rhymes about her and all. It used to bother me a lot, and I'd run home crying and tell Basheeba, and she'd get real angry and start to cussin'em and makin' potions to bring'em bad luck and stuff...!" She had an odd but engaging rhythm to her speech, he noticed, with shifting emphases and pauses where you wouldn't expect them, but that kept you hanging onto her words, and as she went on about her childhood -- and her affection for her mother was clear -- she gestured freely with her hands and her voice became more musical, with highs and lows that added color and a gentle irony to what she was saying. "...Course, Basheeba'd kinda brought all that on herself, cause she'd always be tellin' people, 'You know, Mrs. So-and-So, I had a dream about you last night, and I saw you in your grave!' or 'I saw you drinkin' poison!' or 'I saw your husband with another woman and they drove right off a cliff!' or something. And I'd tell her, 'Mama, you shouldn't go tellin' people how you dreamt about them dyin' and all that stuff! You know, people don't wanna be hearin' that all the time!' -- Besides the fact there aren't any cliffs around here, anyway. But she'd keep right on tellin'em, anybody she'd meet! Shoot!" She laughed.

"But anyway, whenever the kids teased me -- or Basheeba balled me out for doin' something wrong -- she never hit me, or hardly ever, but I wouldn't have minded that nearly as much, because Basheeba can ball you out for true! Lord, don't ever let her get mad at you, your ears'll burn for days! So anyway, then, I'd come down here, see. I'd come in the evening, mostly, cause whatever had happened during the day, I'd try and hold it in, so nobody'd know I was hurting, but then afterward, I'd come down here. I'd be feeling all blue, and I'd be crying and miserable and everything, and I'd just come down here and watch the dragonflies circling round and round the pond, and I'd take a comfort in them. I guess I thought -- you're gonna laugh at me, I know!"

"No, no!" He crossed his heart, "Tell me!"

"Well, I guess I thought they were the Powers that Basheeba was always talking about, and that they lived right here, at the pond, and they'd protect me from harm. And I'd talk to them -- well, I did! -- I'd just plop down here under this big ole maple tree and talk to them for hours...! See, you are laughing! Now, that's not fair, you said you wouldn't laugh!"

"Well, no, I just --"

"Well, it's silly. But you know, even now that I'm a grown-up and everything -- or at least, I'm supposed to be a grown-up! -- still, whenever I see dragonflies flyin' around, I feel that somehow things are going to be all right...!"

"Lorna...! Come with me! Lorna...?"

He was resting on his heels beside her, and for a moment, he thought she hadn't heard him. Then she reached out and took his hand in hers, "Baby..." she said, but it was in the patient tone you'd use for an impetuous child.

He tried to brush it away, "Really, Lorna, come up North with me! It'll be fine, you'll see, it'll be great --!"

"Baby --"

"I just have to make one quick trip to Virginia to find Newton. Then, in a week or so, I'll come back for you and we'll head up to Chicago, and I'll play my music, and you and me, we'll --!"

"Lotrelle, baby, listen. Try and understand me, now, okay? You're a beautiful man, I mean it, you're strong, and you have all your future ahead of you -- and I believe in you, and I know you're gonna make it! -- No, I'm not just saying that, I mean it! You carry some kind of good force with you! -- I mean, maybe you don't have any idea how much your coming back here has meant to people. Because of you, a lot has changed, here! People seem to have hope, now, and they didn't before. I can't...I don't know much about music, but I believe you have it in you to be great, really and truly great! What I heard you playing, today, when I was coming up the path to the house, it was...I don't know how to say it, it was powerful, it really got to me! It was different from anything I'd ever heard, but in a way, it almost kind of gave me the feeling of something I'd been wanting to hear!-- Does that sound crazy? And then...I can't tell you why, exactly, but it was a little frightening, too. It kind of went right through me, right through to places I've been trying to -- trying not to think about...! But look, you have to do this, you have to play your music! It probably won't be easy, because it's new and it's different, and like you said before, people tend to distrust what they don't understand --" she gave an embarrassed smile, "-- especially if it starts telling them things about themselves they may not want to hear! But it's important! And meanwhile, I have work to do here.... And I suppose I could say, now," she poked his shoulder, "that's partly your fault, because now, with Sheriff Clooder gone, it suddenly seems like what I've been trying to do might really be possible, after all! It won't be all that easy, either, and that scares me, too. Not just for myself, but I'm scared for my children, for all of us, really. Folks don't change all that easy, and no one knows what's really going to happen. But at least, now, it seems like we all have a better chance! And then...you know...maybe, someday...! Lotrelle... Lotrelle, do you understand what I'm trying to say...?"

He had understood. All too well. He had, although he'd resisted it and had argued with her, there, under the maple tree, and all the way back along the path, reasoned with her, even pleaded, trying to get her to change her mind, knowing he couldn't, and still trying, right up until finally watching her walking away, walking away from him through the trees until she was out of sight, until she was gone, gone mysteriously, like a lark in the morning when no one's seen it.

It was early on the following day, when he found the man he'd been looking for. He found him at the old fairground, out by the edge of Rue River, only a stone's throw from where he'd pulled Ben Rhoder's body out of the water, weeks earlier. The grass, which then had stood tall and lush all around, was now yellow and encrusted with fallen leaves, and as he approached, he could hear the cattails and arrowwood, turned brittle and metallic, rattling faintly in the breeze. He'd come looking for this man because he wanted to know, at first hand, the difference his own journey back to LeVane County might really have made. The impulse was only that, nothing he'd planned, he hadn't really thought about it consciously at all, and in fact, up until yesterday, it would have been something he'd have gone as far as possible out of his way to avoid. But as he'd started out this morning, he'd found himself asking people he'd met along the way to tell him about this man, and asking them where he could find him, because he, himself had seen him only once, that first time, before all that happened had happened, and all he remembered was a long-tall cop with a hook for a hand. But on this particular morning, he'd found himself growing powerfully curious.

The chief deputy was there alone, when Lot found him. He had the boat that his father, Fontana, had made for the old sheriff, ten years before, propped up on wooden blocks and was scrunched down inside it, with a lit cigarette hanging in the corner of his mouth, scraping off the old mud stains with a trowel and rubbing the wood down with fine-grade sandpaper.

The chief deputy glanced up, but didn't seem surprised when he saw him standing there, a short distance away, studying him. "Just taking it down to the finish," he said. "She'll be back in the water in a couple days."

Lot didn't say anything, but he saw that the clean grain of the wood was coming up again nicely. The hickory oarlocks were already gleaming and the ashwood framing and keel looked good as new. Poised there, with its sleek lines and the sun glancing off the gunwales, the boat looked as if it would take wing and soar right off the blocks at the first touch of a wind.

Laying his tools aside, the chief deputy stepped out of the boat and stood looking back at him. Lot met his gaze evenly, but neither spoke for a moment. Then the cop turned and reached a cold Budweiser out of the bucket of ice on the ground beside him. With a flick of his wrist he punched a keyhole into the top with his claw and offered the beer to Lot. Lot nodded, and the chief deputy tossed it over.

Lot caught it on the arc and stepped back smartly, dodging the spill, then looked sharply at the cop, wondering whether the man had intended to get him wet.

But the chief deputy had already raised another can to his own lips and was absorbed in drinking it down in one long swallow. Lot sipped his with more deliberation, glancing around warily. He saw the chief deputy's Mercury cruiser parked under a tree nearby with the boat trailer still attached and the trunk and car doors left ajar to air out. There was a bucket of water on the ground beside the car, next to a heap of wet rags and a burlap sack filled to overflowing with old magazines, a crab cage and other junk. The car itself was gleaming, it had been cleaned up, inside and out, washed and simonized. And that nasty souvenir that had been hanging from the rearview mirror was gone, too, Lot noted. He turned back to see the chief deputy, who, meanwhile, had downed his second beer, tossing the empty back into the bucket, then turning to look at him again through the smoke of his cigarette.

"So, how'ya doin'?"

Lot eyed him shrewdly, "You tell me...uh, sir."

"Seems to me you're doin' awright. Your daddy's name is cleared, thanks to you...and I got my daddy's boat back."

Lot suppressed a smile. He and Stitches had hidden the boat in a shed -- it would be too generous to call it a barn, it was barely big enough for two mules and a hammer -- that was situated on a small farm Stitches rented from Clooder, and that stood bang up against the sheriff's own back fence.

He shifted the trumpet self-consciously under his arm, and said, "What about the charges?"

"What charges."

"I don't know *what* charges, but yall been chasin' me all over the dang county for *some* reason!"

"That's over and done," the chief deputy said, dropping his cigarette butt into the ice bucket. "There's no charges filed against you -- and if there were, you can consider them dropped."

"So, you sayin' I'm free to go?"

The chief deputy turned and stepped back into the boat, replying over his shoulder, "That aint for me to say."

"Well, who then...!"

But the cop didn't answer. He simply tapped another cigarette out of the pack in his shirt pocket, lit it with his Zippo, and gave him a long, sober look. Then he picked up the sanding block and went back to work on the inside planking.

Lot stood watching the cop for a moment, with an unaccustomed feeling of elation welling up inside him, and wondered to himself what had happened to make this one so different. After a while, he turned and walked off, leaving the man sitting there, running his fingers over the sanded planks as if all that mattered to him was the oak's straight grain under his hand.

Later, riding between the moving cars with the fresh breeze blowing against his face, he saw images of Lorna, Rico Jones and his father flashing passed in his mind's eye. He tried to keep them fixed there, before him, but they were snatched away again and again, like memories of daylight glimpsed through the trees. He felt the rhythm of the bogies picking up the pace as the train raced onward, then he heard the train whistle blow, and it seemed to be saying that it was time to go, the sound rising with the bright gray smoke from the engine and rolling away behind him. He turned his face into the wind, toward the cities lying to the east, where the rivers branched out over the plain and the coppery burnish of the countryside came rushing toward him. The air felt warm and fine. He reached out and cupped it in his hand, testing its weight and consistency, as though he had dominion over it.

The End

4861401R0

Made in the USA
Charleston, SC
27 March 2010